T0248194

the
SUMMER
BETWEEN

— a novel —

the
SUMMER
BETWEEN

— a novel —

ROBERT RAASCH

GREENLEAF
BOOK GROUP PRESS

Published by Greenleaf Book Group Press
Austin, Texas
www.gbgpress.com

Distributed by Greenleaf Book Group

For ordering information or special discounts for bulk purchases, please contact Greenleaf Book Group at PO Box 91869, Austin, TX 78709, 512.891.6100.

Design and composition by Greenleaf Book Group and Mimi Bark
Cover design by Greenleaf Book Group and Mimi Bark
Cover image used under license from ©Shutterstock.com/Juan Diego Ospina

Publisher's Cataloging-in-Publication data is available.

Print ISBN: 979-8-88645-220-4

eBook ISBN: 979-8-88645-221-1

To offset the number of trees consumed in the printing of our books, Greenleaf donates a portion of the proceeds from each printing to the Arbor Day Foundation. Greenleaf Book Group has replaced over 50,000 trees since 2007.

Printed in the United States of America on acid-free paper

24 25 26 27 28 29 30 31   10 9 8 7 6 5 4 3 2 1

First Edition

For my mother

They always say that time changes things,
but you actually have to change them yourself.

—ANDY WARHOL, *The Philosophy of Andy Warhol*

Chapter 1

There are days you don't think you'll survive, and then—without warning—you do. With a translucent orange windbreaker tied around my waist on the sort of early summer evening when the warm sun stood in battle with an incoming chill, I jogged the dirt path skirting the riverbank. Marked by a "Carter/Mondale '76" decal and a graffiti tag professing "Good Vibes," there stood the park's one operable drinking fountain. As I pressed the button, an arc of water sent the wad of chewing gum cupped within the drain plate spinning like a roulette ball. I leaned in for a sip. A sulfurous stream carrying the stink of rotting eggs shot through the seam of my lips. Prepared to spew, I swallowed. Out of the corner of my eye, I spotted the willowy contour of Elena dressed in a red jumpsuit, paisley headscarf, and aviator shades, skipping toward the children's playground.

"Nutball! Don't drink that shit! It's polluted," she yelled.

"Yo, Freakazoid," I replied. "I just jogged two fast miles. I'm thirsty."

"My knees are cracking. I skipped dance class today and need to stretchhh," she sang, hopping up on a weathered bench. Elena placed her hands on the bench's seat and kicked up her left foot, announcing, "Three-legged dog. I'm into yoga now. Andy, let's swing!"

Like five-year-olds on sugar highs, we raced past the monkey bars and the jungle gym. "Wheee!" Elena said, revving the swing to maximum speed. We swung like a pendulum until my sneakers skidded us to a stop.

"Oh my God, that was . . . cathartic! Andy, why did you summon me? Do you have something scandalous to tell?"

"Can you believe graduation is in three days? Maple Ridge High can kiss my ass."

Elena gazed at me as if suddenly I'd grown two heads.

"I do have something to tell you." Like Moses on the mountaintop, I raised my arms and spoke: "I'm gay, bisexual, or whatever you want to call it."

Then, to diffuse my panic, I nose-dived my face within an inch of hers. "Well, say something!" I pleaded, making googly eyes.

Elena stuttered and backed up, "Wha? Andy . . . but you don't act gay." Her eyelids fluttered as the data registered in her brain. "Are you bi? Or gay?" she asked, enunciating the words as if speaking to a toddler.

"I'm not really sure." I shrugged and yanked up my shorts.

"I feel like I'm not supposed to be pissed off, but wow. Damn. I mean, did you know this when we dated?"

"Nope. Honest. It wasn't confirmed," I said, regretting my use of the word *confirmed*. Elena looked shocked and annoyed all at once. A tear trickled down my cheek.

"Don't cry," she said, coming toward me for a hug. We roosted with my head on the cusp of her shoulder, and I was bathed in the floral citrus of Charlie perfume.

"Well, I guess I'm a little relieved," Elena said. "It wasn't what we expected it to be—making love. I mean, Andy, it was nice, but hey . . . was I an experiment? Your lab rat?"

"No."

"I feel a little stupid, like I should have known. Or you should have told me."

"I'm sorry."

"Frankly, I'm pissed." She scowled and then softened. "Are you happy? I want you to be happy."

"Pending," I said, shrugging.

Elena reassured me I had her support. But her quietness on the drive home meant I'd tossed a grenade. Rarely mute, Elena tended to turn down her volume when the wheels inside her head kicked into overdrive. I had candy-coated my confession and made it shorter for convenience. I didn't share with her that there were endless moments when I was terrified, unsure if I'd survive the life of an outcast. A sinner. A faggot.

I pulled up to Elena's house just before sunset, eager to end the night. With the engine running, I shifted the gear to park and corrected my hangdog slouch while staring out the windshield. We sat in awkward silence. In slow motion, Elena unlocked her seatbelt, causing the buckle to snap toward the passenger door with rapid speed. Laughing soundlessly, I twisted my body toward hers. Elena leaned over for a kiss but abruptly backpedaled into a fumbled hug before making a theatrically soft exit.

When I arrived home minutes later, I retreated to my room, stacked four Elton John albums on the turntable, lowered the volume to a hum, and poured myself a drink. Wasted after four fingers of scotch, I passed out in the middle of "Someone Saved My Life Tonight" and woke to the refrain of "All the Girls Love Alice."

I got up to turn off the record player and the floorboards creaked, alerting my mom, Lia, who yodeled up the stairwell, "Andy, honey, everything okay?"

"Insomnia, Mom," I fired back.

I peered blearily at the clock radio. It was six a.m. Shit.

I lay in bed for another hour with the covers over my head, until I heard the front door close and the rev of Lia's car. In the clear, I crawled out of bed, poured a cup of coffee, and retreated to the den to watch TV. The moment a fly ball hit Wally in the eye on a rerun of *Leave It to Beaver*, Elena phoned.

"Meet me at Dunkin' Donuts for coffee."

My stomach was in knots, but I cold-rinsed my face and tossed a light sweatshirt over wrinkled denim shorts. The curled soles of the flip-flops

I slipped into (worn holdovers from the previous summer) forced me to walk like a duck.

When I entered the donut shop ten minutes later, a ricochet of sunlight blinded my vision, causing me to drive the gap between my big and second toe into the metal post of the "Please Seat Yourself" sign. I bowed in pain until I saw Elena waving from the corner booth, her face all smiles. Was her call to action nothing more than a peace offering?

The purple headscarf she sported was a cascade of chevrons. In the center of the table sat three jelly donuts on a paper plate and two cups of coffee. My former girlfriend cleared her throat and then fired a volley of questions.

"Did you pretend I was a boy when we made out?"

"No."

"Have you had sex with a man?"

"Once."

"Really? Don't tell me. No, tell me. I need to know."

"Um . . ."

"Did you fool around with any guys in our class?"

"No."

"Which guys in our class do you think are hot?"

I winced, not sure she needed to know. "Adam."

"Adam *is* pretty hot. When will you tell your mom?"

"I will never tell Lia."

And just like that, the pressure I had frantically taken on since my playground confession vanished. Elena's anger had passed.

In May of junior year, our transition from dating to friends had been equally nondramatic. I had taken the lead on ending our flailing romance but ended up stammering through a tortured alibi that ended with, "It's me, not you."

Mid-apology, Elena cut me off. "Andy, at our age this was inevitable. Better it happens now than later. Let's give it a go as *meilleurs amis.*"

"I have no clue what that means."

"*Meilleurs amis*? Best friends, you dork."

Today in the donut shop, Elena continued her interrogation with a piece of jammy blueberry donut pasted to her lower lip. "Ex-girlfriends get special privileges. It's an unwritten rule. I need to know. Do I know the guy you boned?"

"Boned? Oh, boy."

"Sorry. Is boned not an acceptable word? Is shagged better? And did you shag just one?"

"Are you sure you want to hear the gory details? And it was only one person, smart-ass," I said, sticking out my tongue. "It's weird telling you. It's been a roller-coaster of . . . emotion since last night."

"Spill. I'm a big girl."

"Swear on your life not to tell anyone? No joke. This is a big secret, Elena."

"Jesus Christ, Andy, you weren't molested as a child, were you?"

"Hell, no. I'm just saying you're the only person who will ever know."

"Can't you tell Ollie?" she asked. "That you're gay, I mean. Aren't you and Ollie bosom buddies? He's outrageously liberal. He could handle you being a homo."

"Could you say bi, please?" I said, whispering the words. "Ollie already knows. Elena, this is only half of it. There's a second part. Ollie is the first guy I slept with."

"Wait, what? Ollie Stork is gay? Andy, he's our fucking high school teacher."

"Bi, he's bi, whatever—who cares what he calls himself. Elena, you can't say anything to anyone. Now, never. Ever," I added, tangling my words.

"Wow, Andy. I mean, for shit's sake, wasn't Ollie married, getting a divorce? You slept with him?"

"It just kind of happened."

"Who came on to whom?"

"When he took me to that play, *Gemini*, as a birthday gift—"

"Hell, that was only two weeks ago."

"Afterward, we were driving home and talked about the main character who *was* gay. Ollie asked if I could relate in any way. That's when I told him I thought I was bi. Then he said he was too. Elena, it shocked the shit out of me. Long story short, a few nights later, I spent the night."

"No offense, but Ollie? Fucking weird. Ollie's old. Andy, he's like thirty. You're eighteen. Isn't that creepy?"

"I mean, I guess. Okay, it was a mistake . . . I think."

"I mean, I adore Ollie, but . . . did he prey on you?" She wiped crumbs from her mouth as she stared me down, awaiting an answer.

"No. I was flattered. Elena, he genuinely likes me."

"Andy," she sighed, rolling her eyes. "Many people like you. But they don't have sex with you."

Chapter 2

Elena Dolores Plesko was ethereal. When she spoke, her hands swirled through the air as if she held a magic wand that punctuated each meaningful word with a gesture.

Elena stood apart from the more popular schoolgirl kittens who wandered the halls of Maple Ridge High, flaunting feathered hair streaked with every shade of blond. Her brown hair was softly curled into a precise, sensible bob. She wore eyeglasses when pretty girls didn't. Not just glasses, but oversized orange-brown circles that rested on the bridge of her nose. The first thing anyone noticed about Elena was the vividly patterned scarves she wrapped around her forehead. If biblical Samson gained power from his hair, then Elena's swaths of shimmering fabric did the same trick. Blessed with the carriage of a dancer, chest out, arms lowered and convex, she appeared to glide rather than walk. Each cascading tailpiece flowed down the center of her back, evoking a budding Martha Graham. In our relationship, Elena was a peacock and I the placid owl.

Sophomore year, just as Elena had begun to style herself a punk rocker wrapped in safety pins and black tights, the death of Baba Plesko reversed the trend. Melancholic over the loss of her paternal grandmother, Elena treasured the vast collection of colorful scarves Baba had left behind. Embracing the peculiarity of the inheritance, Elena felt compelled to wear each of the two hundred and fourteen scarves in rotation. Believing their spirits were intertwined, Elena felt that wearing Baba's scarves on her head kept her grandmother close.

If Baba Plesko was the force behind Elena's eccentricity, Luba Plesko was the champion of her daughter's strength. Orphaned as a teenager, Elena's mother Luba emigrated from one of the Eastern European countries—Czechoslovakia, Latvia, Yugoslavia—I forget. She moved in with her father's cousin, a young widow who had inherited a modest house in Boonton, New Jersey. Four and a half years later, in 1958, academically gifted Luba earned her bachelor's degree from Caswell College for Women. One short week after graduation, Luba secured a position as a junior teller at a local bank several years before women won the right to open a checking account in their own name.

Many late afternoons, Luba walked in the door to find Elena and me doing homework on their kitchen table. She'd set down a bag or two of groceries and then reach inside to pull out a snack—a handful of raw almonds and two ripe peaches—placing them between us on a folded cloth napkin. Elena admired Luba for shopping daily at the A&P, deciding each night's meal based on the freshness of the produce. "This is how women in Europe shop," she'd boast.

Luba would tie a frilly apron over her pantsuit before methodically arranging the dinner ingredients on the kitchen's pearly-green Formica countertop. Though her stylishly frosted shag hairdo rode her head like a football helmet, a mod flash of tangerine polished her lips. As with Baba, you could easily spot traces of Luba in Elena, each carrying a bohemian sturdiness foreign to Maple Ridge.

The Plesko residence reeked of exotic cooking spices that clung to the wallpaper and dusted the carpet. A plethora of plants decorated each room: pots of greenery in every size, ferns suspended in macramé harnesses, prickly cacti within glass terrariums layered with earth-toned sand. While Elena and I studied, Luba would busily chop peppers or yellow onions, being careful not to disturb us. Before whacking cloves of garlic with the side of a knife, she'd say, "Children, cover your ears. Big apology." Luba often invited me to stay for dinner, particularly on goulash days, the darling of her culinary canon.

Luba had met Ham, short for something, at a birthday party organized by Baba Plesko twenty-three years earlier at a Hoboken tavern memorably named The Rose and the Thorn. With a stooped posture, Ham wore his prematurely grey locks side-parted, radically grazing his shoulders. The hip, shaggy math professor sported a bushy mustache and lambchop sideburns. Ham's pale-yellow teeth were evidence of being raised in a country without fluoride, but he made up for it with the biggest smile you'd ever seen. Within a year, Luba and Ham had married. Within two, Luba had given birth to Dora, a tomboy from the start who later went on to study lepidopterology at the University of Plattsburgh. Elena had arrived three years after Dora. Luba and Ham parented with a style that was relaxed, even for the unhinged '70s. Reluctant capitalists, at heart they were Euro-hippies who left decisions about curfew, alcohol—even weed—to the discretion of their daughters.

Chapter 3

On a spring afternoon, when the outside temperature spiked to eighty-one degrees, I sat in my flimsy black polyester graduation gown until the vice principal droned, "Andrew Jackson Pollock" into the microphone. I strutted across the stage to shake his hand and then grabbed my diploma and boogied limbo-style under the arch of blue and gold helium balloons created by the events committee. On the side stage, under a banner declaring "Class of '78," I joined Elena, who had received her diploma before me alphabetically. Chin raised, stomach bowed in ballet third position, she whispered, "We did it. We're blowing out of this shithole."

When the final name, Paul Michael Zelinski, was announced, Elena and I turned on our heels and paraded out of the stinking hot auditorium. As we left, I spotted my mother.

"Lia!" I yelled, seeing her wave from the second row.

Because of a neck longer than you'd wish on a female, she towered above her contemporaries. Above Lia's swan neck was an arrangement that served notice: green eyes beneath manicured brows, a disproportionately petite nose, and cheeks that bobbed like two rosy apples when she smiled. Her hair was the hue of warm honey. Lia's most startling feature was her laugh, a shrill cackle that stripped the reserve she otherwise feigned.

Fanning herself like an irate geisha with the mimeographed graduation program, she scuttled toward me. "Andy, I asked you not to call me Lia in public. It's disrespectful. I'm your mother." Resuming normal tenor, she added, "Elena, you were so poised, just radiant delivering the commencement speech. Grace under pressure in this humidity. Look at the two of you, such a beautiful couple."

"Mom, please stop. Elena and I are friends now."

"Andy, it's a simple compliment."

Suddenly, we were caught in the thick of three hundred guests and one hundred and seven graduates swarming out of the auditorium as quickly as if someone had yelled "fire." When we reached the front lobby, there was nowhere to turn. The flash thunderstorm drenching the schoolyard made the air as humid as a Mississippi swamp. Arms locked, Maria Santor, otherwise known as Gram—our doting family matriarch—and Lia wove through the crowd toward the far hallway with me and my Aunt Louisa in tow. When we reached a spot with room to breathe, we stopped and found my English lit teacher standing in front of a pedestal fan.

"I'm schvitzing like Shelley Winters trapped in *The Poseidon Adventure*," he said loudly. "Hi, I'm Mr. Beardsley. Andy, can I take a photo of your lovely family—before we all succumb to this unbearable mugginess?"

"There's a colored teacher in Maple Ridge?" Gram asked Lia under her breath. "Not only that, he talks like a Jew."

"Mom, we say Black and Jewish now. You know that."

"That one's an Oreo cookie. He's got some white in him, that's for sure," Gram whispered before calling out, "What a nice man you are."

Lia's tailored green pantsuit coordinated beautifully with Gram's coffee-colored version. At five-foot-eleven and long in the legs, Aunt Louisa stood one inch taller than her sister Lia. A flight attendant for Eastern Airlines, Louisa had arranged a stopover at LaGuardia so she could attend the ceremony. With her golden hair, saffron-colored jumpsuit, and matching platforms, she was an oversized Cheez Doodle hovering above Gram.

"One, two, three . . . Pepsi," Mr. Beardsley prompted as he snapped the shot. "You're a lucky man, Andy, surrounded by three gorgeous women."

These were the women who raised me. Not communally in one

household, but as a family held together with love. Since age seven, when Pop-pop died, I had been the lone male. If the four of us could be compared to a scrambled eggs breakfast, Gram was the butter gently coating the pan; Lia, three farm-fresh eggs perfectly cracked, gently stirred until congealed; Aunt Louisa, a grind of pepper and dash of salt. I was the slice of dry toast to mop up the yolk.

It had been forever since I'd seen the three women together. If I squinted, Gram could pass for the plump older sister. But up close, I could see the pupils of her eyes had flattened and dimmed in the ten years since Pop-pop's passing. She wore heartbreak like a tattered cardigan. Aunt Louisa, perpetually on the prowl, longed to be rescued from whatever drama was plaguing her life. Scanning the room left to right was Lia, whose eyes flashed bright as a lighthouse.

Elena rushed toward us with a plate of chocolate cupcakes. Aunt Louisa snatched one and walked across the hallway toward Ollie Stork, dressed in an off-season blue velvet blazer. Nervously, I watched her giggle and flirt with our shrimp-sized Spanish teacher. When Ollie caught my glare, I approached to ask, "You two have met before, correct?"

"No, just now," Aunt Louisa said. "Ollie and I are fast becoming friends. I'm so proud of you, little man. Don't you love Andy's hair cut short? Andy, it matures you. Andy gets his healthy head of hair from his mother, the Cavallo side of our family," she told Ollie. "But, those wooly eyebrows, one hundred percent Pollock, his father's side. Oh shit. Fellas, it's time for this stewardess to jet to the airport. Next time I'm in New York, let's do a bar hop to celebrate. Ollie, you're included," she said with a wink before breaking away for a round of goodbyes.

"Doing okay?" Ollie offered. The intensity of his patchouli was off-putting.

"Yeah, totally! I'm psyched for the party."

"Afterwards, let's sneak over to my place for an hour," Ollie said, offering a cheesy wink.

"Definitely," I lied.

Chapter 4

In the middle of March of senior year, on a night when the rain turned into hail, the divine women orchestrating my life cajoled me to dinner at Emilio's, our local haunt. The restaurant, dimly lit to conceal culinary mediocrity, was inviting. Walls were lined with red velvet damask, and a back wall banquette was capped by two corner booths upholstered in leather the color of cognac. It was time to finalize my choice for college, and the trio came to say their piece, with Elena serving as my inside operative.

Torn between two financially practical and one exceptional-but-expensive school, I eliminated one and then stalled.

Goldie, our regular waitress, flashed her eponymous gilded front tooth as she set the final cocktail on the table.

Lia started in: "Andy, it's time to choose. You need to understand the meaning of a deadline. I know you're leaning toward New York University . . . but living in New York? The city has never been as crime-infested as now. NYU is offering a student aid package, but Montclair State would still be the least expensive. Ultimately, it's your decision."

"Montclair—excellent college. Are you having the lasagna, Andrew?" Goldie asked, refilling our water glasses.

Gram, regal in her beehive hairdo, sipped her whiskey sour and then added, "Goldie and your mother are right. Montclair is a good school, and definitely cheaper. Closer to home. And you and Elena will be in school together. Move in with me and commute to Montclair."

"The way I see it, both schools are reasonable options," Elena added, splaying her hands. "If you can solve the financial aspect, with grants and scholarships, NYU seems like the better long-term investment. Of course, I'd love . . ." she said, tapping her brightly striped sweater atop her heart, "for Andy to go to Montclair State, but New York City is critical for an artist. Vital to Andy's soul."

"Slam dunk, Elena." I nodded.

"New York? Too dangerous," Goldie said, snatching our breadbasket. "Son of Sam, muggings, and that loser mayor, Abe Beame. Salads are coming," she said, waddling toward the kitchen.

"Elena, if you threw your pixie dust on a toad, it would turn into a prince," Lia said. "Andy, it's clear how much you want this. My dream has been for you to go to whatever college you wanted. Congratulations, it's NYU," she added, raising her wine glass.

Lia Cavello-Pollock was the first to admit that her tough childhood had molded her into the sort of mother who made sure her son wouldn't suffer as she did. For a strong-willed young woman, growing up in the postwar 1940s and conservative 1950s was suffocating. Behavior deemed naughty or illicit was kept secret. People got away with things, especially the men. Particularly her father, Pasquale. Like countless men of his generation, he was abusive to his wife and strict with both daughters, periodically doling out a smack across the cheek or an aggressive jostle. Aunt Louisa remembered clear as day the time her father decided his dinner was not piping hot, so he threw a heaping platter of pork chops and sauerkraut against the dining room wall and demanded that his wife cook him spaghetti with clam sauce.

Among Pasquale's peers, immigrant Italian men wore the pants: *Sei la mia famiglia!* You're *my* family, he'd boast, claiming ownership. So long as his generation provided their wives with beautiful homes and luxury goods, it entitled them to a double life of gambling, booze, and mistresses. That he owned three well-regarded hotels and a supper club named La Dolce Vita made matters easier.

In the wake of a salacious binge, Pasquale would waltz into the house, arms piled high with apologies disguised as ornately wrapped boxes. Inside were gold bracelets, jeweled earrings, and stylish dresses for the three females, each gift a mark of his naughtiness. Another time, returning from a "business trip," he walked in the door carrying a fox stole, the dead mammal's head serving as the clasp. Seeing the shawl, Gram threw her arms around Pasquale and squealed in delight, a signal that, like magic, the gift had erased his sexual infidelity. Pretending forgiveness was her means of survival. But behind his back, she deplored his wandering ways and nicknamed him "Pasquale the Bastard."

Days before her eleventh birthday, when Lia's menstrual cycle started, Pasquale was beside himself. "Boys will follow her scent," he screamed in Italian. He canceled her birthday party and forbade her to leave the house without a chaperone.

"If one of my daughters ever gets pregnant before marriage, I'll hang the *canaglia* by his balls."

Two years later, during a blizzard, while digging his Buick Roadmaster out from a snowdrift in the driveway, Pasquale dropped dead of a heart attack. It was a life shortened by heavy food and excess boozing. Widowed at age thirty, Gram only feigned mourning. Pasquale's passing brought peace. She boldly rejected the Roman Catholic practice of mourning, refusing to drape herself head-to-toe in black clothing.

Since the three females were liberated, Gram refused to exercise her late husband's strictness over the girls. Two years after Pasquale's death, Gram married Oscar Santor, my Pop-pop, a congenial fellow who merrily let his wife rule the household.

On June 14, 1959, days after her nineteenth birthday, a well-meaning cousin introduced Lia to the fellow who would become my father: U.S. Marine Staff Sergeant Andrew Michael Pollock. The story goes that the pair ignited quickly—like firecrackers and cherry bombs, Aunt Louisa recalled. Within days, they were dancing cheek-to-cheek to the song "Lipstick on Your Collar" at the Copacabana supper club in New

York City. The romance deepened so quickly that Lia and Andy marched down the aisle well before her twentieth birthday. Keeping pace with their accelerated love story, I, Andrew Jackson Pollock, arrived less than a year later.

It was Lia who concocted my clever birth name. She linked the names of the seventh president of the United States, Andrew Jackson, with abstract painter Jackson Pollock, whom she had read an article about in *Life* magazine, and declared, "Andrew Jackson Pollock, destined to be famous straight from the womb."

One month before the happy couple wed, Gram and Pop-pop insisted they move into the modest cottage behind their contemporary split-level in Maple Ridge. Magically, or by a wrench of Maria's arm, the cottage's tenants vacated the property, making it impossible for Lia and Andrew to reject the offer. Even though its bedroom window was within spitting distance of Gram's kitchen sink, Lia adored the house. Its screened porch overlooked a skirt of purple rhododendrons that Lia promptly pruned with hand clippers before planting a row of tulip bulbs to mask the roots of the bushes.

The morning before move-in day, Andrew arose to slap a fresh coat of paint on the cottage walls. Around lunchtime, Gram waltzed in, carrying a six-pack of 7 Up and roast beef and provolone on a Kaiser roll. "You don't mind if I sit, do you?" she said as Andrew lowered the volume on the transistor radio. She then plopped down cross-legged onto the new tweed carpet and began a rant about the difficulties of early marriage.

"Especially the first year, Andrew. You must have patience," she warned her future son-in-law. "Lia's naïveté combined with her ambition, well, that's going to be a ball-buster. If you don't mind me saying, don't be a pushover. Be the man and set the rules early. If you don't, my willful daughter will walk all over you just like she does me."

Silently furious, Andrew began wheeling the paint roller so rapidly that he lost his footing, knocking the aluminum paint tray heavy with beige latex off the ladder right onto Gram's lap. She sprang up, tipping a full can of paint onto the section of carpet uncovered by the drop cloth. Rushing to help, Andrew slipped on the puddle of paint and fell on top of Gram, triggering an audible crack.

Three weeks later, the mother of the bride walked down the aisle in a beaded aquamarine gown. Underneath was a wrap of bandages bracing three fractured ribs. "I was so hopped up on painkillers," Gram would tell anyone who would listen. "The only thing about the wedding I remember is the overpriced bill the banquet hall sent me a week later."

In the wake of the painting fiasco, nothing sat right between Gram and my father.

Habitually, Gram made it clear to Andrew that she had expected Lia to marry a prosperous man, not a military hack. She flat-out said to her son-in-law, "If you weren't so damn good-looking, Lia might have held off, gone to college, and married a doctor."

Lia demanded that Gram mind her business. Andrew and Lia argued.

Adding to the tension, Andrew had a jagged transition from the military to civilian life. He considered his position as the director of safety at a pharmaceutical company a downgrade from the extensive training of two years of military surveillance. "Corporate life is for pansies," he insisted.

After a while, my father showed signs that he was about to crack like an egg. In December 1964, Gram recalled, he unleashed his final maniacal outburst. I was blown away Lia hadn't told me the full story. Gram and I, cozy in her kitchen one wintery afternoon when I was fifteen, ate flourless chocolate cake warm from the oven as she spilled the beans. Apparently, my father was adamant about going on a deer hunting trip in eastern Pennsylvania with three buddies from the Marine Corps. The two fought the entire week before the event. Andrew argued that hunting deer was a difficult challenge. "They're fast, so actually nabbing one is exhilarating, and of course, we'll cut it up and eat the venison. Hunting is a man's sport—this is not something you need to understand," he reasoned.

"We can go to the A&P and buy all the groceries we want. Why in God's name do you want to shoot harmless deer, rabbit, pheasant, or anything else?" Lia had a difficult time accepting that the man she married enjoyed slaughtering beautiful creatures. The morning he left, the tension between them reached a boiling point, each holding their ground.

That afternoon, Lia received a phone call from one of the men in the hunting party. Andrew had accidentally shot Jimmy, the younger of the group, in the arm at fairly close range with Jimmy's own rifle, missing his chest by an inch or two. They had applied a tourniquet and rushed him to Lancaster General Hospital, where he was in critical but stable condition with a shattered humerus. Andrew was a wreck and wouldn't come to the phone. Jimmy was the father of recently born twins. No charges were made. Allegedly they were horsing around, and Andrew had no idea Jimmy hadn't restored the rifle's safety catch before stopping for lunch. Later it came out that, of course, beer drinking was involved. Jimmy took the blame, and so did Andrew. For Lia, the incident was the final nail in the coffin. Aside from tolerating his erratic moods, she reasoned he wasn't mature enough to be a husband and father. Gram reported they had an all-out rage when he returned. Lia, crying and in fear, called Gram and Oscar to the cottage to stop Andrew before he became violent. Humiliated, Andrew packed a bag, got into his car, and never returned.

One month to the day after Andrew abandoned Lia and me, a loosely bolted shaft in the assembly pit at the Ford auto plant in St. Paul crushed Andrew's own father to death. Awarded an exceptionally fat settlement, he and his Norwegian mother fled to her homeland faster than a wink of the eye and permanently vanished from our lives.

Eighteen months old and fatherless, you'd think I'd be unaware, but I sensed his absence. He lived in my mind as an abstraction, his image reduced to color-muted Polaroids tucked into a shoebox. There was one snapshot that I kept under a stack of comic books in my top dresser drawer. Dressed in a starched Marine uniform, he offered a crooked grin while butt-leaning against the panel of a butter-colored station wagon. *Easter 1961* was scribbled in pencil on the back of the glossy photograph, its border scalloped like ravioli. Aside from his squinty brown eyes below two fleecy brows, I failed to see a resemblance.

It was during the years of puberty that not having a father hit hard. Lia had already explained the clinical details of sex, but figuring out how to behave around girls remained a mystery.

One day, as the bell rang at the start of biology, Sara Loughrey flickered her tongue toward me like a lizard catching a fly. I laughed and then lapped my tongue right back at her. Sara and her girlfriends then cackled like wild hyenas, pointing at me as if I were a halfwit. I was mortified. It played over and over in my mind until a week later, when I was in the car with my best bud Tommy and his dad. Pals since fourth grade, Tommy and I first bonded over *The Hardy Boys* series of books and then later *To Kill a Mockingbird* and *Fahrenheit 451*.

I asked Tommy and his dad the significance of Sara's gesture. His dad flatly replied, "Blow job. The girl wants to suck your dick. Go for it, but don't tell your mom."

I may have been too chickenshit to follow up on Sara's prank, but I was grateful I had the balls to ask Tommy's father.

More than once, I asked Lia why my father remained out of touch. "Didn't he love us?"

"Andrew, in his own way—your father loves you. You're not old enough to understand, but he suffers from clinical depression. It's not ordinary sadness, like we all felt when Bobby Kennedy and Martin Luther King Jr. were assassinated. Your father's depression is deep and psychological; coupled with violent outbursts. Just because people saw him as the easy-going life of the party, that doesn't mean that's who he was behind closed doors."

Each time my father shifted into a rage, Lia had panicky flashbacks of her father, Pasquale the Bastard.

"Whenever Andrew cracked, your mother unraveled. It was a mess. The next day he'd sulk, and Lia looked like hell. Rinse, spin, repeat," Gram told me. "With those two, every day was World War II all over again."

Curiously, following Andrew's departure, Lia made frantic efforts to reconcile despite her dissatisfaction with their marriage. Letters, phone calls, appealing to his mother—nothing worked. Ultimately, citing abandonment, she had the marriage annulled. My father surrendered all parental rights.

Legally, he was finally erased. Our familial scale now tilted heavily maternal. Yearly, as far back as I could remember, I received a birthday card from Andrew's sister, June, who lived on the outskirts of St. Paul. Apparently, my father and June maintained a love-hate relationship. A witness to Andrew's manic bouts, she generally adored her brother who was five years her senior. June breathed the air of a different universe, surrounding herself with elephantine plushies, life-like dolls, and an army of dwarfish creatures. Though not slow of mind, she preferred the world of inanimate objects; my dad was perhaps her only friend.

Lia once said: "June never married, likely because she's so damn peculiar. Stepping into her apartment was like being whipped into a spin of cotton candy. Pinstriped pale blue wallpaper, a ceiling she hand-painted with feathery clouds, glass shelves lined with hundreds of bulging doll eyes just staring at you. I was waiting for Bette Davis, you know, in the movie *Whatever Happened to Baby Jane*, to burst into the room. Couldn't wait to get out of there."

At Lia and Andrew's wedding, June walked into the reception carrying a huge stuffed penguin. Gram shrieked because June's face was covered with makeup thick as a clown's. "Crazy June!" she declared.

My father was very succinct about his sister's eccentricity, explaining, "June is June. Let her be."

At Christmastime, when I was six, I received a parcel wrapped in brown Kraft paper addressed in ballpoint. Scrawled in the upper left was the name Pollock and a St. Paul address. I was convinced the package was from my father, believing he'd moved back from Norway, belatedly declaring his love.

Tearing through the paper and lifting the lid of the box, I discovered a reddish-brown pair of cowboy boots two sizes too large. Did cowboys even exist in Norway? Buried inside was a photograph of my father wearing a swollen parka, seated on the hood of a compact car the color of green sea glass. A jagged row of snow-covered mountains rose behind him. With brown hair, hard-parted to the right, he was clean-shaven and orderly. Tied to a bootstrap was a Christmas tag decorated with a pair of Santa's elves juggling pine cones. It was signed: *Love, Aunt June.* The shoebox was stamped: *Wiggin's Western Wear, St. Paul, Minnesota.*

Later, I sketched a thank you card for Aunt June, using the crayons Gram planted in my Christmas stocking. Lia remarked, "Andy, maybe one day we'll take a trip to visit your Aunt June. She's a bit bonkers, but in a charming way. Your father loved—loves his sister as much as he loves you." With that, Lia cried into her hands and ran from the room. Minutes later, she reappeared with false cheer written all over her face. She pointed to the drawing on the card and said, "That's the two of us standing in front of a Christmas tree. It's beautiful. Is that an elf next to you?"

"Yes, a big stuffed elf. Gram told me Crazy June loves dolls and fluffy animals." Clutching my shoulder, Lia whispered, "Don't call her Crazy June. She's your aunt. Be respectful. But how clever you are."

For unexplained reasons, the boots were the last gift Aunt June sent. Years later, while spring cleaning, I found the box at the bottom of my dusty closet.

I grew used to the idea of not knowing my father. Instead, we made it work, Lia and me. There weren't many one-parent households among my classmates, but I could relate to the fresh crop of single-parent sitcoms on the airwaves: *Julia, The Courtship of Eddie's Father,* and *Family Affair.* Like those fictional characters, Lia and I learned as we went. The most peculiar part of a one-parent family was the cloud of sympathy from family and friends—handling me as if I were the victim of something far worse than an absent father. The sorriest part was competing against other boys— specifically in sports. There was no one to stand behind and correct my posture at bat on home plate or to toss a football with on cold autumn days. In his absence, I took to solo activities like running and swimming laps in the town pool.

Pop-pop Oscar came closest to bridging the father chasm. Many nights after dinner during the summer after I turned six, we'd walk hand-in-hand to Eddy's, the local ice cream parlor. One evening, Pop-pop prompted, "Go ahead, ask the nice girl," hoisting me up to the counter by my waist.

"May I have five pretzel logs, please?" I chirped to the pretty soda jerk.

Her glossy pink lipstick outlined a mouthful of braces. "You may," she responded, placing the salty sticks in a brown paper bag. "You come here a lot, little man. What's your name?"

"Andy Pollock," I mumbled.

"Pleasure to meet you, Andy. I'm Dot."

"Hello, Dot," I replied, fidgeting.

Pop-pop teased, "Andy, I think Dot has a crush on you."

With that, I scuttled out the door, raced down the block, and hid behind a bamboo fence, fearful of her alleged flirtation.

We celebrated my seventh birthday one day early on April 30, 1967. It was a Sunday morning, and I watched as Gram prepared parsley ricotta to stuff four dozen ravioli. My spirits were so high, the pounding rain failed to dampen them. Lia was home making cupcakes to bring to my third-grade classmates the following day, a tradition. At two o'clock, I stood inside the bay window of Gram's sunporch, waiting for Pop-pop to return from an overnight fishing trip. The moment his Ford Fairlane pulled into view, I burst into the pelting rain. He opened the car door and cradled me in his arms.

"I sure missed you, birthday boy. Hurry, race to the porch. We're getting soaked," he said. Safely inside, I watched a puddle encircle my feet as Pop-pop fumbled out of his yellow slicker. He then dipped his hand into a pocket and twirled something behind his back, asking, "Ready?" Before I could respond, he revealed a gigantic wishbone.

"Andy, do you know what this is? It's a slingshot, hand-carved by Indians native to Pennsylvania," he said. "I didn't have any paper to wrap it."

"Wow, Pop-pop!" I cried. "Genuine Indians. Did you meet them?"

Scanning the hangtag fastened with red twine, he recited, "Lenape Native American Tribe. Delaware River Region. Andy, this slingshot was carved by a boy about your age from the branch of a tree, probably hard maple. Looks like nature's pitchfork!"

The slingshot looked hand-carved, but I quickly theorized Pop-pop purchased it at a roadside stand.

"See this rawhide?" he said, pointing to a red rubber band. "This rawhide was wrapped, then knotted around grooves on each side of the Y." Stretching the bands wide, he added, "This center leather pouch is where you put the rock. The stem's carved so that you can get a good grip. I bet this slingshot is as much as a hundred fifty years old," he fibbed.

"No way," I returned, determining it was brand new.

"It's meant as a hunting weapon, but you can shoot cans off the back fence. That's what the Indians did. Every time they knocked off a can, they'd pray to God."

"Pop-pop, there were tin cans a hundred-fifty years ago?"

"Well, for certain," he replied.

As the myth gained speed, I caught a pungent whiff of Michelob riding his breath.

The following night, the moon was as colorless as I'd ever seen. Around nine p.m., Lia rushed me into her car for the short drive to Gram's house.

"Pop-pop isn't feeling well," she explained.

When we arrived, we found Gram crying, flanked by two neighbors, another speaking to emergency dispatch.

"Honey, why don't you go and watch TV? You shouldn't be in here. Everything will be okay," Lia insisted.

I turned the television on to muffle the commotion when the siren of an ambulance grew close. Just tall enough to see above the bay window's ledge, I stood frozen, mesmerized by the flashing red light and the jerky moves of men in blue uniforms drawing the gurney from the vehicle. I watched, consumed by panic. During the opening theme song to *The Lucy Show*, Lia came into the living room and said, "Pop-pop took a heart attack. Let's pray."

I knew the situation was serious because we rarely prayed. I waited for someone to come running into the room yelling, "False alarm. Oscar is going to be fine." But by the end of *The Andy Griffith Show*, we could hear Gram screaming, "Please God, no, no, no. He wasn't ready." Pop-pop's heart had stopped beating.

The loss of my surrogate father crushed me. Instead of seeing him during visiting hours lying in the coffin or attending his funeral, I was kept away, watched over by a tenderhearted friend of Gram's who lived up the street. The fatality tore up Gram, Lia, and Aunt Louisa so much that I'm not sure anyone understood the impact Pop-pop's death had on me.

There was no one to sneak me sips of beer at Yankees games or to cuddle as we giggled through reruns of *McHale's Navy*. Pop-pop was gone. We never got to knock tin cans off the backyard fence, but I kept the slingshot under my pillow for a long time.

Over the years, other part-time dads attempted to fill the void. They included a distant uncle and the family butcher, but I had little interest in playing along. A neighboring father and his twin boys picked me up before dawn one morning to fish a smelly lake an hour north of Maple Ridge. Worms as bait, tangled lines, ham sandwiches squished between plastic wrap—I hated the entire nonsense. When I finally did hook a sunfish, watching it flap to a slow death in a wicker basket seemed criminal.

"This is torture," I announced as the father looked puzzled and his twins rolled their eyes. Pop-pop would have laughed at my comment and patted me on the back, accepting that I favored pursuits that didn't involve murder.

The unorthodox arrangement of our family created more stumbling blocks for Lia than for me. Switching between the roles of nurturing mother, dutiful father, and rambunctious sibling, her hands were full.

To counter the responsibilities that bogged her down, she employed silly humor. Saturday mornings, typically reserved for house cleaning, became an opportunity to shock each other with bizarre costumes. I'd enter the kitchen to find Lia mopping the floor in fluffy slippers, a chenille robe, pink curlers, and a cigarette dangling from her lips. Another time, I borrowed Gram's purple housecoat, put on garish sunglasses I bought at the drugstore, and mimicked Elton John.

Not only did we dress up, but we also sang whatever music was spinning on the record player at the top of our lungs. We'd typically begin with the song "Aquarius" from the Broadway musical *Hair*. I can't imagine a father would tolerate such antics.

As a single mother who didn't answer to a husband, Lia eyed success as a career woman. With subscriptions to *Ms.* and *Playgirl*, Lia saw herself in the style of Mary Tyler Moore's character Mary Richards. She aimed to be the liberated archetype Helen Reddy sang about in "I Am Woman." Trailblazers.

As a parent, Lia erred toward leniency: If anything I asked made a lick of sense, she'd approve. I guess she wanted to share the liberation she enjoyed. As director of marketing for Procter Life Insurance, she joined the fraction of women able to inch their way up in the male-dominated culture. As needed, she'd detonate her secret weapon: skirts at just the right length to accentuate her endless gams. As a boy, I cringed at the catcalls hollered when she walked past less-mannered dudes.

"Why can't Lia find a husband?" Gram's girlfriends would gripe over penny poker.

During the winter of 1968, when I attended third grade at John F. Kennedy Elementary School, Lia discovered a hard lump in her left breast. After a biopsy of the cyst, her oncologist advised removing the entire breast to prevent the cancer from spreading. As she prepared to go to the hospital, she told friends and neighbors that she was undergoing the removal of her appendix. People accepted the white lie. Only Gram and Aunt Louisa knew the truth.

Days later, when she entered the hospital, I was by her bedside. Lia confided in me that the doctors would have to remove "the slightest bit of cancer." I was aware that cancer signified something dreadful and bawled at the news.

The day after surgery, I brought a giant metal canister of Tootsie Roll candies to the hospital. When I opened her door, Lia was flat in the bed, weak and attached to beeping doodads. I began to cry all over again.

"Don't cry, honey," she soothed me. "All gone."

During recovery, Lia's fiery disposition was downright troubling. Whenever the pain medication wore off, she'd moan until a fresh dose brought relief, setting her to sleep for hours. Lia frittered wearily around the house most days as she recuperated away from work for the entire month of March and a good chunk of April. When she needed supervision, Gram took the day shift while watching *Days of Our Lives* followed by *General Hospital*—all the while making unsuccessful attempts to cheer up her daughter. Some days they'd bicker like two cats in a clothes basket before resolving with hugs and then dishing over whichever soap character was in crisis.

Every other day or two, Aunt Louisa would return from whichever layover city she was in to relieve Gram. Goldie once asked Lia if Louisa was two tacos short of a combo platter, and we burst into laughter. Louisa's freewheeling lifestyle often caused friction between the sisters, but during the cancer, they got on like peas and carrots.

Six months later, follow-up tests concluded that the ductal carcinoma was undetectable. Sweeping the good news aside, Lia clamored, "Andy, they butchered me."

Without pause, I responded, "Cancer lost, we won."

Time after time, over the years, I'd clumsily assure her that no one would ever know they erased her breast. To combat her sadness, I concocted an artillery of distractions: (1) Without warning, I'd spin the album *She's a Lady* by her favorite heartthrob, Tom Jones, at deafening volume. (2) I'd plop into her lap a towering stack of get-well cards I made from construction paper and Elmer's glue. (3) I'd beg her to play board games, like Trouble, Scrabble, and Monopoly. Although the ploys worked for a while, later I'd find Lia on the sofa, curled into a ball under her favorite purple patchwork blanket, with blankness in her eyes.

I wasn't aware at the time that Lia's mastectomy strained her romantic life. Lia pushed away men because she feared their reaction to her scar. When she was dressed, no one knew her left breast had been removed. But in private, even with the lights out, she didn't want her secret known.

Once in a blue moon, she'd accept an invitation to dinner by Tom, Dick, or Harry. At the end of each date, when I asked how the evening went, she'd cough up a barrage of excuses: "Andy, his teeth were yellow, wretched," or "That one, nothing but a low-class playboy!" or "Can you believe he asked me to split the check?"

Over time, her reviews seemed little more than excuses. But one night I overheard her say to her friend Ruth, "Another wasted night! They all expect to fuck me on the first date."

By that point, I was a teenager. Hearing Lia utter the curse wasn't upsetting, seeing as she was a liberated woman, but I wondered: Why wouldn't a single female with a subscription to *Ms.* and *Playgirl* want to fuck?

In traditional families, nudity was taboo and carried shame. In our laid-back household, seeing each other au naturel induced nothing worse than a good laugh. If by chance we saw each other naked, one of us would screech something comical before running in the opposite direction. Only once did I see Lia's bush. She was hoisting up a pair of pantyhose, spread-eagle on the edge of her bed, when I strolled in. Catching a panoramic view of her snatch, I squealed in mock-horror. Lia calmly stood, turned around, and finished dressing.

"Coast is clear," she said, resuming conversation, confident that this chance viewing wouldn't require a lifetime of therapy.

One evening later that same summer, the bathroom door was cracked an inch to allow the shower steam to escape. In passing, I saw Lia, dressed only in an aqua towel wrapped around her head. She stood blankly before the sink. In the mirror, I saw the reflection of her concave scar. Sensing my presence, she flinched, using the tail of the towel to cover her surviving breast. Breaking the silence, Lia whispered flatly, "It's okay, honey. You can look." So I poked my head in further.

"Lousy, isn't it? They cut the whole thing out."

Mesmerized, I saw that the void's contour took on a lopsided geometry directly above her heart. She strummed her fingertips over the incision's seam, a full shade lighter than her olive skin. Grinning, she muttered, "Now you've seen it—no more mystery."

The delicacy of the moment made my mother the most beautiful woman I'd ever seen.

Chapter 5

In Maple Ridge, we called New York City "the city." Occasionally we called it New York. Even Manhattan. Greenwich Village was always "the Village." Less than twenty miles from Manhattan, there were three options for travel to and from the city—car, train, or commuter bus. Sometime during the autumn of my senior year, I started cutting classes a few days a month. I reasoned that I'd discover more trekking into the city than suffering through humanities, French lit, or God forbid, rhythmic gymnastics.

There was something naughty about riding to the Port Authority Bus Terminal on 42nd Street and Eighth Avenue, an intersection of marquees that garishly promoted—day or night—one skanky porn flick after the other. Hookers and their tricks were darting in and out of dark alleys. Jacked cars blasted ghetto music. Smokers and winos stood propped against anything steady.

The frenetic scene captured my curiosity. Although I'd moved beyond my childhood obsession with cowboys, watching the movie *Butch Cassidy and the Sundance Kid* further uncorked my attraction to rugged outcasts. The week *Midnight Cowboy* screened at the retro cinema one town over from Maple, I brought Elena. The moment Joe Buck, the brawny hustler from Texas appeared on screen, my dick got hard.

"What's wrong with you tonight?" Elena scolded in the darkness. "Stop twitching!"

The following week, like Joe Buck, I took the bus back to the real Times Square. I slinked along the pavement on Eighth Avenue past a dimly lit marquee advertising ALL MALE ACTION. I didn't have the balls, age, or courage to step into the porn theater, only going so far as eyeballing the trade outside, who I assumed were just like Joe Buck.

I determined up close that it was a scuzzier scene than I cared for, so the following week, I traded my fleeting intrigue with bad boys for a more sophisticated lot—the elegant Upper East Side. Dressed in a blazer and tie, I wove my way through Rockefeller Center, past well-heeled NBC executives and their coiffed assistants, past Radio City Music Hall, before scooting up to Fifth Avenue facing Central Park and its row of stately door-man buildings. I fantasized that passersby would mistake me for a private prep-school student returning to my family duplex, where our housekeeper would prepare rare roast beef on toasted rye as a snack. I'd roam the halls of the Metropolitan Museum of Art, wishful that a sophisticated rich hunk would cut me a smile then swoop in and carry me off to his penthouse to engage in salacious acts I could barely comprehend.

If the Upper East Side was the neighborhood where I'd be spoiled, and Times Square the district where I'd be paid for sex, downtown was where I could be myself. Greenwich Village was the epicenter of 1960s countercul-ture and swarming with gays.

Gay/gā/: lighthearted and carefree: MERRY: exuberant

Lighthearted and carefree—seriously? How about scorned, persecuted, and sinful?

Sexually, my limited experience with Elena and the other girls was sat-isfying, but—like grabbing the wrong coat from the pile on the bed at a party—heterosexuality didn't fit; the shoulders sat too tight and the arms too short.

It was in Manhattan, particularly the Village, where I knew I'd find my people. Artists, struggling musicians, intellectuals, and homosexuals. My age. As I came to grips with my sexuality over many months, the fact I was raised by women and about to enter a culture of men was not lost on me. I was half-titillated, half-freaked. I was aching to kiss, to cuddle, to make love to a man, and the wait was torture. While I was agonizing how others would judge me, I knew my hankering for guys was as natural as wildflowers in the spring. Although the trendy and cool people supported the Gay Power Movement, conservatives scorned those who were bi, gay, and anything in between like buzzards circling a dead rabbit.

Despite all the hoopla, I saw myself as a red-blooded ordinary American boy—nothing short of normal. I dared anyone to just try calling me a faggot or fag or sissy or pansy or queer or Nellie or fudge-packer or homo or poof or queen or swish or Nancy, or queer as a three-dollar bill. Just try.

Chapter 6

At the end of summer, I was bound for a kick-ass fine arts program at NYU. But first, I started an obligatory summer job inconsistent with anything I cared about: twelve weeks as a hardhat on the Public General Electric college work crew.

To relatives in our Italian American family, the stint signified a rite of passage, a ticket to manhood, particularly for a rascal without a father. The position was arranged as a favor by a church-going suitor of Gram's, a bald, working-class hero who barely knew my name. He was just another hard-pressed crusader aching to win favor with the women in my family by positioning himself as a life preserver for the fatherless boy. Rejecting the offer would have designated me a snob—or worse, a mama's boy.

Public General Electric, known as PGE, was situated in the middle of nowhere New Jersey. It was an imposing compound of skeletal towers, boxy sheds, and electrical fields tucked under twisting highways and overpasses. Lining the perimeter was a toxic swampland marketed misleadingly as the Meadowlands.

My daily routine: wake at six, on-site before eight, and then shuffle into what was dubbed the barracks to stash my lunch box and thermos into a locker. On day one, the supervisor handed me a DYMO label maker to punch out my name—*Andy Pollock*. I unpeeled the tape and placed the glossy black strip of raised white letters vertically on the locker, defiant of my coworkers' horizontally arranged names. The gesture, a brazen break with conformity, was meant to send the message that I wasn't one of them.

While I was still a rookie, one meatball from the macho stew baptized me "bush brows," thanks to the unibrow above my eyelids.

"Hey, bush brows, you related to Eddie Munster?" the rogue buzzed, followed by, "Or maybe you're John Belushi's little brother? I'm just playing with you, kid."

Too intimidated to respond, I offered a half-smile, pretending to surrender to his pranks. Unpracticed in sophomoric hazing, I felt the coming three months would be pretty bleak. Not since gym class in junior high, where mockery was mandatory, had I been subject to nicknames. *Bush brows?*

To celebrate the start of my summer job, Lia suggested dinner. Emilio's was crowded, noisy, smoky—delightful for a Thursday night. After climbing inside the corner booth under a reproduction of Caravaggio's agitated *The Supper at Emmaus*, Lia began to unwind. Fatigued by four days of work and two nights of exams at Fairleigh Dickinson University, her weariness was offset by the soft sweep of chestnut hair cupping her face. An added touch of lipstick might have rekindled her natural beauty.

"Finally, just the two of us," Lia said. "Let's order some wine. Tell me, how's your first week at PGE?"

"It sucks. I hate waking up so early. The guys are alright, some of them are jerks. There's one I get along with. Sam. He's going to Carnegie Mellon in September for engineering. He always looks like he just rolled out of bed, messed-up hair, oh, and he smells like Cheerios. Look at my fingernails, Mom. I was spray-painting a loading dock, and the black enamel crap seeped right through the gloves. But first paycheck tomorrow."

"You can always quit if you're that miserable, but the money is fantastic. Where is Goldie?"

Seconds later, Goldie dropped a small antipasto platter and two leather-bound menus on the table. "Crazy night, kids," she said, racing off.

As I pierced a curl of prosciutto, Lia expressed anxiety about her coming weekend demonstration in Washington, D.C.

"Andy, organizing a protest with hundreds of women sits with me like a bad oyster. Why did I say yes?"

Ruth, Lia's closest friend and women's lib guru, had coaxed her into a planning event in D.C. for a protest formally called March for the Equal Rights Amendment. The rally, set for some time in July, was to support ratification of the amendment guaranteeing equal legal rights for all American citizens, regardless of sex. "Ruth can be persuasive," I said.

Years earlier, Lia and Ruth had bonded at a women-in-business seminar. Both single, their differences were Ruth's lack of children—and cigarettes, Virginia Slims, to be exact. At thirty-four, petite, and exquisitely pulled together, Ruth still wasn't a threat. To most folks, she was animated to the point of annoying. She ended most sentences in a rapid tone with her elbows pinned to her waist, forearms upright, hands wide open—as if she bore feathers but couldn't fly—like an emu. In doses, Ruth's playful attention-getting manner was amusing and her enthusiasm for women's liberation endearing.

Goldie broke in with two glasses of Chianti. "On the house."

While she and Mom babbled, my mind wandered back to my secret plan: a solo excursion into New York while Lia was away. It was decided. I'd change clothes, which first required showering in the locker room, and then drive to the city while still daylight. Given PGE's proximity to the Holland Tunnel, I would arrive early. I'd have some cheap dinner in the West Village and then explore two gay bars I had researched. The thought of entering a gay bar still terrified me.

I only half-listened as Lia resumed lamenting about her trip to D.C. until Goldie returned with the main course and Lia's second glass of Chianti. I nodded mechanically and reassured her of the day's success so she wouldn't cancel the trip and sabotage my mission. Given that D.C. was a stone's throw from Proctor Life corporate headquarters in Fairfax, Virginia, I knew my gay immersion weekend would be uninterrupted. Lia had no valid excuse to disappoint Ruth, a tightly wound woman who wouldn't take a late cancellation easily.

After a bite of osso buco, Lia suggested that Ruth was substituting fem-inist activism for the husband she claimed was impossible to land.

"Is Ruth maybe a lesbian?"

"I doubt it, although the thought has crossed my mind. Andy, being a feminist does not imply you're a lesbian. For Chrissakes, it's 1978."

"I know that. I can't believe women don't have equal rights. Listen, I've got a busy weekend planned while you're away; I'm driving into the city after work tomorrow."

"Alone? Why don't you ask one of your friends? I'd feel much more comfortable," Lia said, twirling her fork into my bowl of spaghetti with clam sauce. "I'd feel better if Elena or even Ollie went with you."

"Ollie's left for Spain. Mom, I'm an adult. I can make my own decisions."

"Yes, I know Ollie's in Spain," she snapped. "What play are you seeing?"

"*Deathtrap*," I fibbed on the spot.

"But you saw it last month. Said you loved it."

"Yes, that's why I want to see it again. Ollie's friends, the married English couple who live in the city, picked up four cheap tickets through the teachers union."

Lying to Lia didn't come naturally. But there was no alternative. I didn't want to go into the city without her knowing, just in case something hap-pened. Visitors, even residents, were mugged and stabbed daily. If he hadn't left for Madrid, Ollie would have been a good foil.

Scanning the check, Lia continued, "Okay, here is twenty dollars. I know you hate taking money. But please park in a lot. They cost five dol-lars. Use the rest for whatever," she said, giggling as she drained the Chianti. "Where's Goldie? Let's get out of here, Ruth is picking me up at nine a.m."

At 4:40 p.m. on Friday afternoon, about the same time Lia was check-ing into her D.C. hotel, the shift whistle blew, ending the second week of my tedious job on the site maintenance crew. At 4:41, the day crew of Utility Workers Union Local A601 transformed the locker room into a testoster-one-fueled cellblock. Incoming rowdies waved their paychecks into the air, eager to rinse off the day's soot.

The onslaught of men, all shapes and sizes, put me on edge. To my left, a hulking brute snapped his wet towel across the ass of a fleshy younger blond. The kid jumped a foot into the air, only to return the gesture. I averted my eyes to untie my construction boots, hoping no one could see the lust in my eyes. Like most locker rooms, the smell was distinctive: sour notes of perspiration, musty shower steam, and the stink of unwashed socks. Clouds of aerosolized Gillette, Brut, and Hai Karate collided midair, molesting my nostrils. Ear-splitting howls clamored for rank, one tribe whooping for the Mets, the other the Yankees, both in play that night.

I decided the jerk who baptized me bush brows was harmless enough. He looked like a low-rent Burt Reynolds with his handlebar mustache and chest fuzz as black as shoe polish. He wore his foreman's uniform so snug that his shapely caboose looked like a bubble ready to pop. Sam, my lone buddy at PGE, dubbed this cheesy fellow "Smokey" after Burt's character in *Smokey and the Bandit*. The chump, blind to the reference, seemed to enjoy the moniker. Smokey stopped the teasing—mostly—and soon warmed up to Sam and me.

That Friday afternoon, as I was dressing for my trek into the city, Smokey barked, "Getting yourself all pretty. What you doing tonight, College? Taking your girl to the junior prom?"

I shot back, "Funny guy. No, Smokey, I'm gonna screw your girl all weekend." I pointed to the fading mermaid tattoo on his bicep.

"Cheeky," he replied, drumming his index finger down the crook of my spine before he trotted to the exit.

In one shot I discovered how to hold my own in the locker room. Lia had taught me masculinity wasn't acting like a bully. Yet, when in the trenches, I needed street smarts to establish my dominance. Chivalry, wisdom, and integrity were all valid traits, but this was the macho era of *Rocky* and *The Godfather*.

The split-personality approach I developed in high school spilled over to the summer. Weekdays, I did my best to play the brawny brute at PGE. On Saturday afternoons, I'd escape the suburbs to walk the cobbled streets of the West Village to study men. I learned that gay men who dressed like action figures were called "clones." Just like the band the Village People, who were iconic homoerotic characters. The occasional excursions to the city were look, don't touch.

NYU student housing was located smack in the middle of Union Square, north of the Lower East Side. This would serve as my base for my official transformation into a gay man. Every autumn, students from all over the world swarmed to the Village to attend the university.

I cringed at the idea of being a bridge-and-tunnel dude, able to go home to Jersey for dinner and be back before lights out. With classes starting in September, there was little time to fabricate a compelling narrative, a character who could thrive among the artists, struggling musicians, and introspective writers I admired. I rejected the idea of becoming a clone. The plan was to quickly befriend a quirky troupe of iconoclasts, those lingering about Village coffee shops drumming their pencils to Joan Armatrading's contralto while immersed in Beckett or Salinger. Gorgeous creatures of every sort: black, white, brown, purple, pink, and green. Women, men, and anything in between. But especially men.

Burning time until the last PGE worker left the locker room, I had no option but to brave the showers before heading into the city. Aside from one chubby fellow in the far corner, the vaulted chamber of the group showers was unoccupied. Green-tiled from floor to ceiling, the place flat-out stunk. But it also offered the temptation of seeing hunky guys with soap running down their ripples.

I feared I'd spring a boner seeing one particular redhead lathered up and naked. I didn't know his name, but whenever I spotted him lumbering down the hallway, swinging his thick freckled forearms, my fluttering heart sent an urgent message to my dick. I would imagine him on the sofa, spread-eagle in his underwear, watching a Mets game. Bursts of bright red hair would be sprouting from his milky skin. His name would be Bud or Buck. I'd walk toward him, kick off my sneakers, and burrow myself into his forearms and finally deep into his armpits.

In 1978, aside from the gay clones, two styles were popular—cowboy and disco. Given my childhood bent for the actor who portrayed Little Joe on *Bonanza*, cowboy seemed the logical pick. I removed a pair of carefully folded jeans and a blue and brown western shirt from my duffel bag. I vetoed going commando, pulled the jeans over my briefs, and then leaned against the lockers on my tippy-toes to yank on white tube socks. Moving quickly to avoid the grimy concrete, I donned each honey-colored Frye boot.

Aside from my genetic unibrow, everything about me was ordinary. Brown hair, brown eyes, average height, average weight, medium shirt size, medium Jockey briefs, medium, medium, medium. I worked a palmful of mousse through my hair, pumped a squirt of Aramis onto the whiskers sprouting on my chest, and clicked each pearly shirt snap closed save the top two. I stepped before the full-length mirror and didn't hate the person I saw.

I marched across the parking lot, kicking up gravel in bug-infested air with every step to reach my escape vehicle. My '65 Ford Galaxy was repainted aquamarine with flecks of glitter, and my pal Tommy baptized it "the Blue Whale." Eight months later, she still looked sleek but was a disaster under the hood. Every turn of the ignition was a roll of the dice. With fingers crossed, I drove past the oppressive PGE gatehouse and turned up the volume on ABBA's "Take a Chance on Me."

Within miles, as the birds fly, the city's magnificent skyline pumped my body with adrenaline. I was among hundreds of cars, rounding the spiraling ramp, a sea of steel glistening under the sun, each pointed to the Holland Tunnel's entrance. It was Friday night rush hour. Slow dancing through serpentine lanes of traffic, my thoughts drifted to Ollie. Without fail, whenever we had driven to the city in the final months of senior year to see a concert at Madison Square Garden or a play off-off-Broadway, we had mock-argued over who was paying the toll: "Andy, stop. You're a student. Keep your money," Ollie would say, pushing my handful of coins away.

"Thank you, sugar daddy," I'd joke. It had been a month since driving through the Holland Tunnel that Ollie dropped the bisexual bombshell that blew my mind. Elena's reaction to my confession had me thinking. She only focused on Ollie being our teacher, and older. I recall Ollie insisting, "I don't want you to have a bad first experience with a stranger." Was he offering affection or just a lesson in practicality?

As I idled toward the tollbooth, a new round of fear struck. *Are you sure you're ready to venture into the Village alone at night, hotshot?* I noticed a final off-ramp, my last opportunity to abort the mission before entering the tunnel. With a determined foot, I raced ahead, dropped three quarters into the toll basket, and floored the gas pedal toward the mouth of the tunnel.

I scrapped Lia's idea of parking in a lot and kept the twenty for my fact-finding mission instead. As a result of eighteenth-century urban planning, each side street in the West Village resembled the next. Lines of dented garbage cans accompanied densely packed cars. Scoring a street spot took patience. I finished the fifth loop before catching a decade-old Rambler with Connecticut plates wiggling onto the one-way street. I pulled forward, trailed by honking taxis, and slid in. I key-locked the door and walked toward Washington Square Park. The stench of Hudson River silt, street cart sausage, and centuries of decay pickled the air. At the corner of Greenwich and Sixth Avenue, the low sun ricocheted off a skyscraper's glass façade, directing me south. Looking left, I saw West Fourth's sheltering elms form a parasol of filtered light. Reggae mingled with the ripple of sweet-smelling herb. Puerto Ricans danced salsa beside Irish lads chancing poker on a makeshift table. One strained chess match ended with a cheer in Russian. Gawkers shuffled through an area lined by watercolor paintings. The park was alive.

Stomach grumbling, I ordered a large Coke and three slices of pizza from a perspiring counter girl. Her frizzy hair bounced like a cone of cotton candy. Catching my eye, she asked, "NYU?"

"September," I replied. "Just scoping things out."

"Gotcha. I'm Carla," she sang.

"I'm Carla, make Ray's your pizza par-la," I improvised.

She laughed, revealing a wad of pink gum stuck to her upper braces. I plopped onto a wobbly wooden stool beside the bay window. Carla delivered a fan of paper plates one draped over the next, saying, "Italian, right? From Jersey? It's the haircut."

"Bingo. Thank you, Carla pizza par-la," I said.

Showering each slice with red pepper flakes, I folded the crispiest piece first to drain its oil. Outside, two punks spiked the air with matching mohawks. A frumpier version of Woody Allen read a fully unfolded *New York Times* as he walked. A trio of matrons waddled by with grocery bags. Five greasy napkins later, I ripped a carbonated burp on my way to the exit.

"Classy, Jersey!" Carla yelled. "See ya 'round."

Meandering along Greenwich Avenue, I scanned passing faces for some encouragement as I wandered onto Christopher—"the street crawling with queers," as Maple Ridge neighbors described it. Raising my hand, I looked again at the word "courage" I had scrawled in black ballpoint below my knuckles.

The temporary tattoo egged me on.

Courage, I recited to my inner warrior. Energized, I fished out of my pocket a scrap of paper bearing the addresses of two watering holes. I'd found them in *The Gay Man's Guide to NYC*.

Tucked within a ramshackle row of brownstones, illuminated behind a small square pane of glass was "Spurs n' Saddles" in red neon. The pub looked dead as a doorknob. I cupped my hands around my eyes to look inside and saw nothing but black behind the dust-coated window. Deep breath. I cracked open the door and saw a long, dimly lit bar dotted with stools. Yeast seeping through a century of beer kegs pounded my nostrils like ammonia. It was a tavern no different from the one Pop-pop frequented in Maple most Fridays. Seeing the door open, a trio who looked straight out of the cantina scene in *Star Wars* broke their conversation and stared. They were two shirtless men wearing fringe vests, cowboy chaps, and what looked like vinyl policemen caps, beside a person in a billowy white frock, cat-eye glasses, and roller skates. I shut the door, pivoted quick as a squirrel, and ran. On a side street a full block south, I doubled over to catch my breath.

Fuck. Why was I so scared if I had already waltzed through the Village on previous weekends?

I thought of Ollie and his forceful orientation process. If he hadn't been such an eager coach, my curiosity would have deferred until college. Instead of creeping around in the dark tonight, I'd be watching some action movie at the mall in Jersey. I was hellbent on bagging the entire experiment, but my fidgety, skanky Jersey Boy libido took over, convincing me to cancel a cowardly retreat back to Maple.

Not that I was in search of a sexual encounter with a stranger, the thought of which freaked me out. I preferred the torturous mix of utter horniness and undeniable fear. *Courage*, I told myself. No one knows who you are. To walk off the panic, I ambled down Christopher Street toward the Hudson River, only to stumble upon a coffee-colored sign dangling: "Tug's." Bar number two.

Patches of sweat patterned my shirt, one drop trickling down the center of my spine, stopping at my waistband. A welcome breeze caught a branch of leaves, and I enjoyed the chill that dried my sweat. From behind a tree, I spied a trio of ordinary-looking guys walking toward Tug's. A scatter of men began to form along the sidewalk, dragging on cigarettes and shooting the bull. They were the sturdy sort straight out of the PGE locker room, salty with muscle.

Once the sun sank behind the Hudson, Christopher Street transformed into a block party. Bodies glided along the narrow sidewalk like night owls foraging for prey. I noticed the same people pass by on their third or fourth loop and knew I had to make a decisive move. Confusing courage with velocity, I sprinted like a cheetah into the pack crowding the doorway.

"What's your problem?" one fellow snapped.

"Somebody is thirsty, and not for alcohol," another snarked.

I pulled back, embarrassed. Once they herded the pack through the door, I entered slowly. Politely. Elbowing toward the bar, I slipped in between two indifferent strangers. The bartender, with a blanket of fuzzy grey peeking from his open shirt, called out, "How old are you, kid?"

"Eighteen. Last month," I said, louder then intended and offered my driver's license. Waving it off, he laughed. "Just kidding. This is New York—we don't give a fuck. Whattaya having, kid?"

"A Bud, thanks." As I chugged the can, my eyes fixed on the soundless Mets-Philly game on TV above the bar.

Courage.

Tracking sawdust under my boots, I slithered to the back wall, camou-flaged against the dark paneling. I listened as Linda Ronstadt softened the edges of my anxiety with "Blue Bayou."

Despite my deer-in-the-headlights glare, eyes began connecting with mine—only to dart away and then return seconds later. This ritual, I'd read, was known as "cruising." I rotated my head to see my fellow drinkers mostly in fringed denim cut-offs, pastel tank tops, plaid shirts perfectly frayed, and tube socks stretched over work boots. Most in the boxy room were chatting, telling stories.

Around one a.m., desperation began seeping in. Men started leaving, making the room less packed. A ripped, Hispanic man in blue plaid flatly offered a bold, extended stare. In the seconds it took me the guts to return a smile, another guy sporting a mustache gripped my admirer's forearm and whispered into his ear. Suddenly they marched toward the exit.

I needed lots more beer.

"I'll take another Bud."

I dodged and darted back to my spot to find it occupied by a streaked blond on rollerblades. Eager to reclaim my roost, I blocked his view. He huffed and wobbled across the room.

I was sucking the last drops of my fifth Budweiser when a remarkably short frat guy crowded me and released a string of garbled words. Before I could decode his message, he took off. En route to catch a piss, I saw the frat boy draping the jukebox. When I offered a smile, he turned his back.

Defiantly, I fixed my eyes on him like a hawk to a mouse. But he weaved toward me, shook his head, and bolted toward the exit. Abandoned, I raced toward the back of the bar to the john.

After emptying my bladder, I confronted the mirror at the sink.

I saw ugly.

My face looked nothing like the Tug's crowd. There was no escaping my baby face bursting with freckles. The bushy stripe of brow above my eyes appeared grotesque, no substitute for a cool handlebar mustache or tightly cropped beard.

I suddenly recalled how Carla from the pizza par-la said she could tell I was from Jersey by my haircut.

Someone barked, "Hurry in there."

I stuffed my Jersey talismans—a class ring and the gold neck chain Gram gave me on my seventeenth birthday—into the pocket of my jeans. Then I applied tap water to flatten my hair, unsnapped the third shirt button, and headed back to the war zone. I approached the older, whiskered bartender, now wearing a buckskin vest and black jeans, to place my order. He set up a Bud with a Red-Hot sidecar—on the house. As I guzzled the combo for courage, our grins caught.

When the burn faded, I felt good. Determined. But the crowd had thinned to a dozen. Two bald chaps smiled and beckoned. One handed me what looked like a bullet, gesturing to inhale. I hesitated, but they stared me down, so I lifted the bottle to my nostril to suck in its vapor. Instantly, antifreeze firebombed my trachea. My pulse rocketed. The room careened out of focus. As the honeyed waves of Styx's "Come Sail Away" bounced off the tin ceiling, I felt a ridiculous grin hijack my face. I teetered on the edge of a barstool, shamelessly hammered.

Chapter 7

A garbage truck churned in the street below, rousing me. The only thing I knew was that I was face down and naked on a futon somewhere in Lower Manhattan. I felt an acidic gurgle in my stomach. A rub of my temples only worsened the pain. I felt the weight of a body next to mine—but whose?

I imagined Elena whispering in my ear, "Andy, get out."

Opening my eyes was a struggle. Slivers of light through the plastic blinds told me it was morning. An electric fan gently rolled the thin sheet over me. I stretched to look at a plastic digital alarm clock: 7:05. The glass ashtray next to it overflowed with cigarette stubs. Next to that sat a yellowed half-doobie and two brown bottles of pills. A framed Bob Dylan poster with rings of hippie color swirling from his head hung on the wall.

June—it was June. Saturday. Progress.

I had to pee in the worst way. I sat upright and looked over at the lanky body under the sheet. A Jesus beard scraped the pillow, framed by long Jesus hair. He looked older than I expected, confirming I had been beyond wasted last night.

Careful not to make noise, I stood up and walked toward the hallway where a primitive wall-hanging nearly spooked the crap out of me. On top was a headdress composed of spiky reeds with a blast of colorfully dyed feathers at the center. A pair of curved white bones forming a circle dangled from the brow. Underneath was a spear, its point tipped with red paint.

I regained my footing and located his bathroom next to the tiny galley kitchen, feeling pebbles adhere to my feet with each step. The phone-booth-sized toilet was disturbingly tidy. Geometric wallpaper danced up the wall. With one sticky foot, I quietly pressed the door shut. A loud, gassy round of farts began, so I aimed a torrent of piss into the bowl water to muffle the sound. I exhaled, feeling relief. I lifted my head and spotted a bottle of Excedrin in a wicker basket. I dry-swallowed three aspirin and then checked the mirror. If I didn't like myself last night in the bar, I hated myself now. Turning to leave, I jostled a plastic litter box, explaining the pebbles underfoot.

I returned to the bedroom and saw that the body under the sheet hadn't budged. As I quietly untangled my socks, I spotted a tabby roosting on my jeans, its green cat eyes fixed on me. She appeared well cared for, fat, and groomed. The moment she scatted, I wobbled into a leg of my smoky jeans and hoisted the pants to my waist. As I did, a pain rippled from my butt down my leg. I squelched a yelp, afraid I would awaken my so-called host.

Hazy details flashed through my brain like images in a View-Master: rocker guy handing me a shot, his ear pierced with gold, telling me his name was—something. Genesis's "Follow You Follow Me" was diddling in the background. Then blank, a gap. Lights on, last call. We scattered like cockroaches into the night. He and I sat on a smelly stoop and talked. Then I guess I was steered back to his place.

Rocker guy's stringy hair brushed my lips. Stairs. Several flights of stairs. I drank something from a purple tin cup—the same sort Lia used for serving iced tea at family barbecues. He led me onto a too-low mattress. I hard-kissed his cigarette mouth. Hated it. The cheek of my face was scratched by the wiry fiber carpeting his chest. I recalled a burst of pain. It must have been my ass, pierced by his hard penis.

I shuddered at the flashback and felt my ass twinge again. Was I bleeding? I felt myself collapsing inside. But there was no time for that. I glared at rocker guy, disgusted by his angelic expression, his head resting calmly on the pillow—oblivious to my panic.

Fiddling with the snaps of my shirt, I tried to lean into the memory. Eighteen years old, my first gay bar. Is this what happens?

Elena's voice returned: "Get out—now."

Fearful he'd wake, I lifted my boots, and carried them to the door, watching the soles shed cat litter and barroom sawdust. Pulling them on, I noticed a pad and pencil.

I imagined the note I would write if I had bigger balls: *Sorry I didn't wait to say goodbye, dude. Thanks for letting me crash even though you fucked me while I was dead to the world. You suck.*

On a ledge beside the desk were two tickets. I shoved them into my back pocket—payback for shredding my ass. Something needed to be taken from this fucking fucker. That was his name, I decided: Fucking-fuck.

I turned the deadbolt, careful not to let the door slam.

Slinking down the narrow stairwell, I shuffled out to the stoop, pausing as a sweeper glided down the street leaving a slippery trail. Oranges and piss. I was on Barrow Street, but I had no idea where I had parked the car. I anxiously zigzagged the maze of Village streets, finally tripping upon Christopher Street. Passing the blue façade of the police station, I turned at the corner where, like a behemoth rising from the mist, sat the Blue Whale. Climbing inside, I locked the door and sat, feeling my anus pulsate as rapidly as the bass in a Led Zeppelin song.

Minutes passed before I could find the strength to drive.

As the engine rattled, I skated my palm down the silky strands of the blue and gold graduation tassel dangling from the rearview mirror—a reminder of who I was. Reaching for the lemon-lime Gatorade, I again thought of Elena. It was only weeks ago, on the drive home after *Jaws 2*, when she spit a mouthful of Gatorade all over the closed window and herself, thinking the window was rolled down.

As I drove, I swore to myself that Elena would never know about this trouble I got myself into. No one would.

Wrapping my fingers over the steering wheel, I noticed smudges the color of charcoal peeking from under my sleeve, bruises soured to a mottled shade of red. It looked like the faint imprint of braided rope on my wrists. Confirmation that the Fucking-fuck had bound and restrained me before slipping it in.

Violated. I felt puke well up in my throat.

My body shook, releasing a spate of shivers and a torrent of tears. Snot clogged my nostrils. My body reminded me of what my brain refused to accept. Was going home with someone the universal approval for anything goes?

I had been raped. Men don't get raped. Maybe in prison, but this was in a stranger's bed. With that, I stopped at a street corner, flung the car door open and heaved a bucketload of vomit onto the asphalt.

I wiped my mouth with a Dairy Queen napkin from the glove compartment and resumed driving. I made my way along the West Side Highway toward the entrance to the Holland Tunnel. Staring blankly at its green ceramic walls, I felt the return of the gurgle in my stomach. Exiting the tunnel, I pictured being home in the comfort of my childhood bed, hearing the hum of lawnmowers crisscrossing neighbors' lawns.

Luckily, it was a deserted Saturday morning, and the roads were kind. A right at the turnpike's third stoplight led to the spacious freeway. The Maple Ridge exit soon gave way to the rolling, tree-lined streets, signaling I'd be home in minutes. We lived on the greener side of town, dotted with parks along the river. The white-shingled Cape Cod rested on a crest with thick shrubs on either side. The stairs to the second floor opened to a study with a wall of bookshelves. Between a matched set of aqua and orange director's chairs stood my bedroom, equipped with an 8-track stereo, a television set within a mod cube resembling a marshmallow, and a Princess telephone mounted to the wall. The perks of being a fatherless child.

I stripped my clothes in the first-floor bathroom. In an act of contrition, I showered under an icy-cold stream of water for as long as I could bear. I was surprised that I didn't see pools of blood cascading from my ravaged butt. Rather than wallow like a martyr, I cut the penalty short. Folded into the navy-blue terry cloth robe Aunt Louisa had given me for Christmas, I retreated to my room and turned the air conditioner on high, drowning the silence. Then, I remembered the pair of tickets I snagged from Fucking-fuck's apartment. I sprang back downstairs and unraveled my jeans from the heap. Scrunched into the back pocket were the two tickets.

Rolling Stones. The Palladium, 126 East 14th Street. Box 2.

Monday, June 19, 1978. Special Access.

I decided that Elena, a Stones zealot, would benefit from my fuckup. I just had to make up a story of how I got them—and not by getting anally penetrated.

A feat as monumental as seeing the band perform live, with Elena in tow, would almost be payback for my loss. But then I realized: When that asshole discovered the tickets missing, he'd know who took them.

Tough shit. I didn't leave a forwarding address. I was home free.

I crawled back into bed, grateful that my ass was not aching as much after the shower. Curling my body knees-up, I tucked a pillow into my fold, willing myself to sleep for the remainder of the day.

Chapter 8

The day after the assault was shit. My brain wouldn't quit; sleep came by default. Could I get away with hiding my bruises, now purpler than they were earlier that morning? The answer seemed to be no.

In one night, I had changed forever: from naïve suburban Andy into a rapist's plaything, which made me an embarrassing, colossal fuckup. Another handful of Excedrin and a swig of grape juice barely relieved my sick stomach, even though I knew my mind was making me feel rotten.

I dragged myself to the kitchen to toast an English muffin, hoping bland food would offset the nausea in my body. I kept it down. Good sign. Then I crawled back to bed.

No way that Elena would get the truth. She would be really, really pissed if she knew. After she'd overreact—first anger then pity—she'd find a way to tell me this never would have happened if I had stayed with her. She'd laugh about it, but I would know she meant what she said.

Who would hear my truth? Who could I confide in? With Ollie on another continent, there was no one to turn to without deploying a bomb. This is what Ollie meant by saying, "I don't want you to have a bad first experience with a stranger." But Ollie being my first didn't prevent me from having a second bad experience. Fuck.

Run, Andy, run. Disappear.

It worked for my father when things got tough.

Empty my savings account of close to eight thousand dollars. Head to California, Canada, far. Running away seemed a better option than suicide.

Maybe Montreal? It was cool when Lia took me to Man and his World, Expo '67.

Disappear? That would freak out the central person in my life. My champion. Mother of the Century. Running off would devastate Lia.

I pulled the bedspread over my head and burrowed the side of my cheek against the pillow. I closed my eyes and counted backward but couldn't fall asleep. The feeling of being raped clung like dirt.

Before I understood anything about the act of sex, there was infatuation. I had developed crushes on celebrities during elementary school. There was perky Karen Valentine on the high school sitcom *Room 222*, and Shelley Fabares playing a teen queen on reruns of *The Donna Reed Show*. David and little Shaun Cassidy, Robby Benson, and Bobby Sherman also ranked, but none came close to the rugged men riding across the western plains: cowboys. Squirrelly Little Joe on *Bonanza*, Trampas always quick to flash a smile on *The Virginian*, but best of all was Christopher Jones, the lead on the ABC-TV series *The Legend of Jesse James*. Chiseled, with a Southern twang, Jones was a weird hybrid of the boy-next-door and a bucking bad-ass. When *Jesse James* was canceled after one season, I wrote a letter of protest to the president of ABC Networks.

In the months that followed, while expecting a reply from ABC, my fickle devotion turned from cowboys to astronauts. Intelligent young scientists locked inside a spacecraft proved far more captivating than dusty, slow-poke cowboys. Astronauts signified the future, cowboys the past. Rather than hitch my rocket to Neil Armstrong, the first man to walk on the moon, I fixated on his shipmate Edwin "Buzz" Aldrin. Buzz's baby blues, jumbo ears, and wide smile made him boyish, approachable. One day, I piped up to Lia, "Mom, why don't you marry Buzz? Wouldn't he make the coolest husband ever?"

When I was ten years old, Lia introduced me to *Where Did I Come From?*, a children's book illustrating the how of male and female reproduction. The lesson initiated my first conversation about sex. Side-by-side on the sofa one evening after chicken pot pies, Lia traced her finger across each drawing as we read the descriptions in unison. Then she'd recap: "An orgasm is like a sneeze, but instead of coming out of your nose, the seminal fluid, similar to the consistency of mucus, ejects from the tip of the penis."

"From the same hole as pee? How does it switch from pee to semen?"

"Yes, the same hole, different tubes. Andy, don't jump ahead. We're getting to the part about the vagina."

I'll never forget the date, April 20, 1971, when I woke to a glorious twitch. Just like Lia had explained through *Where Did I Come From?*, my penis sneezed.

I was eleven.

Ignorant to the phenomenon but aware of the mechanics of reproduction, my first thought was, *Holy shit, I'm a man, capable of fathering a child.*

I peered at the pool of semen dripping from my belly to the bedsheet and remembered that it carried up to a hundred million sperm, swimming circles in search of a truant egg. For a solid year, once a week, I'd wake to an erection, wiggling in dry surprise—until my brain finally caught up with my body.

From then on, my boner intervened at the most inconvenient times in life. The smallest thing would trigger it. Like our substitute algebra teacher, Mr. Stelling, a hunk rocking tight polyester slacks. As he diagrammed the cubic polynomial on the chalkboard, my boner stood at attention in admiration. I was left to figure out how to conceal my condition when the end-of-class bell rang and we all filed out.

Unlike other boys my age, I felt my libidinous thoughts about guys seemed natural. Thank liberal Lia for that. But spontaneous boners invoked panic. For months, I listened to my buddies brag about jerking off to *Penthouse* and *Playboy* centerfolds. It wasn't until I pulled Tommy aside and asked, "When you tell me you jerked off, how is that different than calling the school janitor a jerk-off? Is a jerk-off something good or bad?"

"Andy, Andy, Andy," Tommy moaned, shaking his head. "A jerk-off is a putz. Jerking off is playing with yourself. Masturbation. Here's a tip. If you roll a sock over your dick, it catches the jizz. Then throw the sock in the laundry bin. The custard washes right out. Your mother will never know."

The next time I went to his house, Tommy handed me a stack of his father's dirty magazines to practice. That night, while Lia was at class, I fanned open a *Hustler* dated April 1970, featuring a freckled nurse wearing nothing but a stethoscope. In an October 1972 issue of *Juggs*, I stopped on page thirty-three, spotting a dewy-eyed cowboy encircled by twelve knockers the size of cantaloupes. In a rumpled *Playboy*, I discovered a nude blond woman holding a sexy brown-haired fireman by the hose. My dick was not responding as it should have. Finally, I uncreased the double-page spread of a *Sears Catalog* loaded with photos of men with Ken doll crotches, modeling underwear. The dudes brought me to completion. In no time.

The trajectory of sexual experience moved forward quickly. In a few months, I went from wet dreams to jerking off to photos to fantasizing scenarios with real people. I'd imagine coming around algebra class after school to ask the substitute for extra help with an equation. I imagined Mr. Stelling, tight pants stuffed nicely, closing the door, turning to me, and purring, "You can call me Matt." The study session would reach a peak when the teacher would insistently rub his leg against mine. That was as far as my imagination went and all I needed to attain my quest.

Then there was the lanky redhead in the tight blue Speedo practicing dives at the town pool. I'd imagine sitting on a bench in the men's changing room once the swim team had gone. Discreetly, I'd eyeball the bulge inside his wet swimsuit. Slowly he'd roll the suit down his creamy white thighs as his blushing penis swelled. That's where the illusion ended because, at that age, I had no knowledge of how two guys went about horsing around naked.

The summer of '74, between eighth and ninth grade, a new kid moved to the neighborhood. Joey moved in a few doors down from Tommy. He tried everything to work his way into our crew. Joey, with his spiky dark hair, was a space cadet who always had a pack of Kool menthols poking out of the rear pocket of his jeans. Archie, a classmate and occasional third wheel to Tommy and me, found Joey crude and not up to our standards. I took pity on Joey, who knew no one. One scorching weekday, we were walking to an air-conditioned matinee of *The Towering Inferno* and passed Joey on his porch.

"Can I come too?" he yelled. The ballsy squirt joined us before anyone could answer. Archie bullied Joey into sitting one row behind us. During the opening credits, little Joey loudly cracked, "These seats smell like ass."

Archie forced me and Tommy to follow him three rows down, leaving Joey stranded during the film. On the walk home, when Joey would not stop ranting about how much better his old town of Red Bank was than Maple Ridge, Archie yelled, "Then move back. Shut the fuck up, Joey. You're so annoying."

Joey got the message and made himself scarce for a few weeks.

It was in the dog days of August when Joey tempted Tommy, Archie, and me to his attic with an offer we couldn't refuse. We sat in silence as Joey loaded the film spool onto the projector, explaining that we were about to see a Portuguese movie called *Television Repairman*.

We watched in silence as a naked housewife, weighed down by huge knockers, answered the door. In walks a TV repairman, scrawny except carrying what looks like a baseball bat down one leg of his trousers. He puts down his toolbox, unzips his fly, and she drops to her knees and sucks his cock.

Joey knew he had us, and he squealed, "Tell me, fellas, is that not the biggest dick you've ever seen?" Tommy, Archie, and I watched in silence.

Not only was it the biggest dick I'd ever seen, but it was also the only erect dick I'd seen other than my own. I felt my own boner swell inside my cut-offs and contorted my body to hide it. When the repairman shot his load on the housewife's massive tits, Tommy sputtered, "Yessss," as if watching the Allies blow up the Nazis in *The Dirty Dozen*. Everyone else was hard too, based on how they carefully got up when the film ended.

"Thank you, Joseph," Archie called up from the stairwell, a silent indication that the ballsy squirt had been officially accepted into our group.

I doubt anyone else had been turned on by the repairman like me, but I realized that Joey had shaken my earth off of its axis. I wondered if he was on to me. But we never discussed the private screening again.

During my freshman year of high school, I was able to explore my secret orientation by following the gender-bending performers from British rock and punk. David Bowie, Gary Glitter, even tame Elton John . . . spoonfuls of sugar for the medicine I'd later swallow. This radical kink did more than designate me as cool; it pushed the notion of acceptance. Art class, a place where perverse outcasts could hide, proved to be a fertile testing ground. Behind the studio's swinging doors, you'd find Alice Brokowski sculpting wet clay in a black Ramones tee, torn then reattached with safety pins. She had a flair for applying punk rock makeup more skillfully than the art she crafted, earning Alice great respect. Another person who thrived in art was James, an effeminate, pencil-thin senior who excelled in the painting room. I feared guilt by association, so I'd ignore James in the hallway, but inside the art studio, we'd stand side by side, replicating Bowie's *Diamond Dogs* album cover in vibrant gouache.

But outside of that art haven, it was dicier to take a stand. Shooting hoops with the guys one night, I decided to defend Lou Reed's provocative hit song about hustlers and drag queens, "Walk on the Wild Side."

"The song is fucking brilliant," I shouted to Archie.

"The guy's perverted," Archie spat out.

"The guy's name is Lou Reed. He's a big-name rocker, for Chrissakes. He's like Jagger, and you love Jagger."

"Jagger isn't a fag."

I chanted the lyrics about Holly Woodlawn who dressed as a woman all the time, to test my friend.

"Andy, don't tell me you're a freaking fruitcake!"

"Fuck you," I yelled, laughing it off. "You're a *doofus extremis*, Archie."

But time went by, and I grew more careless, unwilling to repress myself twenty-four hours a day. So clues started to leak out.

"Do you know that dude?" Tommy once asked, catching me staring at a sales clerk rocking a handlebar mustache at Herman's World of Sporting Goods.

"Yeah. He's a friend of Lia's. He doesn't remember me," I lied.

To avoid being busted, I learned to refine my method. Exiting a hockey game with my buddies, I catcalled, "Nine o'clock, smoking chick in the red halter top under the Rangers sign." The tactic allowed me to rubberneck her hot 'n' spicy boyfriend while Tommy and Archie ogled the girl.

Crushing on any of my male friends was too close for comfort. Instead, I shadowed unattainable figures like sandy-haired Skip from Dairy Queen. I'd imagine us sharing a large bucket of popcorn in the balcony of the multiplex as Barbra Streisand sang "How Lucky Can You Get" in *Funny Lady*. In my fantasy, I would reach into the bucket of popcorn, only to have Skip grab my hand and deliver a tight squeeze.

Skip became my main inspiration, my leading man when jerking off in my bedroom with the door locked. My fantasies of Skip became more elaborate, the most common being a friendly day hike along the trails of Ramapo Mountain that would lead to heart-stopping dick-play in a remote cave. At that point of the fantasy, I'd ejaculate into my sock, sigh, and go downstairs for a handful of Oreos.

Early in sophomore year, I decided my obsessions were getting out of hand. My fixation on Skip abruptly ended when I spotted him fondling the ponytail of a chick from Catholic school at Arby's. And Tommy and Archie called me out more than once for ogling dudes.

I had no choice but to split my personality into two. Private Andy would beat off thinking of guys. Public Andy would play high school stud, talking smack and dating girls.

The strategy paid off. Within a week, prompted by cheap vodka, Public Andy had his first make-out session with a girl in full view of everyone at Archie's party. Wendy Fenstermacher, a bouncy cheerleader of midlevel popularity, was determined to have me on her arm. To secure this position, she increased her campaign. The following afternoon, Wendy gave me a toe-curling blow job against a mausoleum in the town cemetery. In the ensuing months, whenever Wendy had the urge, she'd drag me to a musky loveseat in a corner of her basement and blow my pipe. There was something thrilling, even kinky, about satisfying her desire—with the possibility of her hunky older brother walking in. A college freshman, Dan had jet-black hair flawlessly parted at the side and draped over his right eye. Whenever he greeted me—"Howdy, Andy"—his stare lingered a second or two more than was right.

To be fair, I wasn't faking things with Wendy. She loved sucking dick, and I loved getting my dick sucked—even by a girl. It just required closing my eyes and thinking about a guy, often Dan.

Luckily, she didn't need more than fellatio. Only once did my fingertips roam the whiskers of her pussycat before she snatched my hand away and said, "Enough!"

Oral sex between us worked. Apart from that, we barely liked each other.

But sex only takes you so far. One night, following a late screening of *The Other Side of the Mountain*, I yelled at her in the parking lot, "Wendy, you're only in this for the blow jobs." Two days later, she dumped me, trading up for a varsity baseball player, telling me, "Troy and I have been in love since Christmas."

Elena and I became close friends in junior year when the principal put us in charge of sourcing artists for an event to benefit the new pediatric wing of a local hospital. We put two finalists up for popular vote. Three to one, the student body voted for The Harlem Globetrotters over a folk singer Mr. Beasley nominated, Tom Rush, certain to draw parents to the event.

During the process of learning to book acts, Elena and I realized we were compatible. We shared affinities for cheese pizza, Jackson Browne, and the need to get the hell out of Maple. One frigid winter afternoon, Elena convinced me to cut advanced typing class to pick up McDonald's hot apple pie and two hot chocolates. Elena parked her Vega, raced inside, and returned with a crumpled white bag.

"These are fucking heaven," she said, nibbling the gummy center of the pie.

"Do you think these are real apples?"

"Duh. What's a fake apple?" As she continued nibbling, Elena reached into her hideous brocade satchel and pulled out a paperback.

"*The Front Runner*, Patricia Nell Warren. Oh, this book is so good. It's making the rounds in the girls' volleyball squad."

"Never heard of it."

"Scandalous. It's about a runner, like you. This older college track coach falls in love with his star athlete. I'm not sure why . . . but the story is really kind of hot, Andy. Guy-on-guy sex."

"Gross," I said, too loudly. Seeing her face cringe like a dry sponge, I added diplomatically, "But cool. To each his own. Good for them."

"It's a love story, kind of. I'm two-thirds through. If you're really going to apply to colleges in the city, better keep an open mind, Andy Pollock."

The following afternoon, I drove twenty miles through light snow to B. Dalton's at Paramus Park Mall to find the book Elena had pushed on me. The only thing I remembered was its light blue cover, the word *Runner* in the title, and the author's surname started with *Wa*. Purchasing a book about homosexuals freaked me out, but I needed to read about how two men love. I fast-walked the bookstore aisles, making certain no one shopping was familiar to me. I found the fiction section, awkwardly close to the front window, and located the book. With trembling fingers, I inched out a copy and hastily covered the gap with a misfiled volume of Doris Kearns Goodwin's *Lyndon Johnson and the American Dream*. The distracted cashier paid no attention to my purchase.

On Friday night, I locked my bedroom door and ripped into *The Front Runner*, reading fifty pages until my eyes blurred. The next morning, I turned off the digital alarm and reached for the paperback again. I read as the closeted, conservative coach Harlan Brown was taking star runner Billy Sive to New York for a track event and hopefully intimacy. Fifty more pages later, I wandered downstairs as Lia said, "Andy, it's Saturday. Cleaning day."

"I need an hour, Mom."

"What are you doing up there, honey? It's nine thirty."

"Reading a great book, Mom. *Lyndon Johnson and the American Dream*."

"An interesting choice. Can you start the dusting? I left the Pledge and a few Handi Wipes on top of the stereo. Please use Old English on the coffee table—it's looking a bit drab. What should we listen to today? How about the soundtrack to *The Wiz*?"

Ten minutes later, while reluctantly swiping clockwise as Stephanie Mills belted out the song "Home," it dawned on me. The pages I'd read left me hopeful. Guys could fall in love with other guys. *The Front Runner* left me feeling less alone.

By Valentine's Day '76, Elena and I were locked into dating mode. She was the only person I wanted to spend time with. By George Washington's birthday, I asked her to go steady. Given that I worshiped her kooky, capricious behavior, I thought maybe this could work. After all, my sexual hunger for guys was still untested.

Lo and behold, at a Saturday night drinking party, Elena and I made out like mad on Tommy's parents' bed. My aroused penis slipped inside the soft burrow of Elena's vagina for a few seconds before I recalled I wasn't wearing a condom. We stopped cold.

A few days later, in the Arby's parking lot, Elena asked, "Andy, are we going to do this the correct way? I mean, all the way. I want to. I think I'm in love with you."

Once I said yes, she confessed, "Andy, this won't be my first time."

Stuffed with french fries, my jaw dropped. "Who?" I asked.

"That doesn't matter. No one you know."

"Maybe we should wait, E. I want to make love if we're each other's first, but on second thought—I don't think I'm ready."

Elena burst into tears, threw her roast beef sandwich on the car floor, and unleashed a heartfelt monologue about wanting a real relationship. Her previous guy was a douchebag.

"Andy, I want to erase that shitty memory and replace it with you."

"Yes," I responded clinically, making her eyes light up.

Watching Elena skip out of the car to hurl our trash in the bin, I recognized she was more magnificent than any of the nameless guys flirt-ing with my consciousness. Elena popped Vicki Sue Robinson's "Turn the Beat Around" into the 8-track as I fired the engine. We drove in silence, stopping for the drawbridge to lower over the river. As we sat, I thought about how she offered a deep confession. Should I offer my own?

No, the moment was Elena's.

We planned the exact night to lose my virginity. *An Evening of Romance and Intercourse* was the dreadful title Elena wrote on a handwritten invita-tion to dispel our anxiety. The scheduled event would take place at Elena's house on the weekend Luba and Ham were scheduled to visit her sister Dora while she competed in a College Democrats of America debate at SUNY Plattsburgh. I almost considered drumming up an excuse to get out of this before reminding myself this was not only for Elena. It was also for me. Instead of faking a romantic dinner, we decided to advance the action by beginning with cocktails at eight o'clock. We poured tall glasses of imported whiskey from Ham's stash and bounced up to her bedroom.

"What happened to your kazillion stuffed animals?" I asked.

"Boxed," she replied. "Time to grow up."

The room showcased three New York City Ballet posters on the wall opposite her shrine to the Rolling Stones. Elena turned down the pink bedspread on her twin bed. A purple headscarf lazed over her bedside lamp, muting its luster.

"Foreplay," Elena announced, "occurs before intercourse," as the Runaways' "Cherry Bomb" began. Clumsily, I stripped down and crawled under the sheets as Elena lit the peach-scented Pier One candle I had bought for her birthday. She slipped out of a velour jumpsuit and joined me under the covers.

We were fully naked together for the first time, and the sensation of skin on skin was a revelation. Elena's dancer's body was limber and, in repose, more muscular than anticipated. Lying on our sides, face to face, we put our lips to work—more than pecks, less than sucking face. It was a premeditated plan, being that I'd seen the technique displayed in countless romantic scenes in PG-rated movies, and as such, it bought me time to calm my jitters.

I cleared the first bar rather quickly: In no time, I had an erection. I rolled my body on top of hers, excited not only by the warmness of her legs but by the hardness of my dick pressing against my abs, as if I was with another guy. With Elena on the pill, I was spared the obligation of a condom.

Elena squirmed. I nibbled the stretch of her neck, nursed on the lobe of her ear, and tongued the hole she had pierced for the pair of gold hoops her parents had given her for Christmas. When I lifted her arm and licked her tender, sweaty pit, Elena wrapped her legs around my waist and squeezed. The wooliness of her bush was a pleasant surprise. Despite Elena researching numerous positions, we settled on basic missionary. My slender dick slipped into her vagina with such ease that I suddenly remembered this wasn't her first time. I opened my eyes to see hers rolling back, cooing with pleasure. The wetness and warmth, the swell of her clitoris around my shaft, felt so good that I quivered and jizzed after my second thrust. I withdrew sheepishly and rolled flat to her side. That was it. Pleasure came naturally and quickly. Curled against my chest, Elena assumed the fetal position, and we slept.

The following morning, hearing the shower water running in the bathroom, I sat alone in bed. I was relieved I hadn't failed to perform. I was confident I had erased Elena's experience of bonking some unknown jerk.

The night had an unexpected result—the rest of that weekend, we retreated. In the pit of my stomach, I had the feeling that a follow-up was doubtful, like finishing your first marathon with no desire to run another. As satisfying as our lovemaking was, curiosity was noticeably absent. In truth, although being inside Elena felt damn good, marginally better than a blow job, I didn't have a longing desire to repeat it. Something was off, but more so, it became crystal clear that us having sex was like lying to Elena. Given how much I loved her, the deceit made me feel lousy. On the flip side, I was so horned up simply from having sex that when I returned home, I beat off while fantasizing about the buff red-haired swimmer at the town pool.

Elena and I bubbled on the phone that afternoon over how amazing it was, but neither of us suggested hanging out that night. We took a breather, and the following week we returned to our standard beat as if making love had never happened.

We carried on as boyfriend and girlfriend into spring of junior year, although making out seemed to only happen when we were in front of friends at parties or in the hallway at school.

When Elena and I had time alone, we studied, watched movies, and shared meals.

But we never seemed to get around to sex like before. Our repeat sessions of undercover blow jobs suddenly evaporated.

We casually discussed fucking again, but it didn't happen. I told myself that there never seemed to be a private place available that fit into our busy schedules. Of course, this was just an excuse. I wasn't into a repeat performance and Elena wasn't pushing it either.

We maintained all the outward signs of a romantic couple; not one person at school knew we'd split. But both of us seemed fearful of speaking about the obvious. Then one night, while sharing a banana split at the Dairy Queen, Elena finally brought up the issue.

"Eat the maraschino cherry," I joked. "I know you want it."

"You're too good to me, mister," Elena said. "First a brazier burger and fries, now the cherry!"

"I'm a generous guy." I shrugged, laughing.

"What a lucky chick I am. You know, it's true . . . you're the best friend, boyfriend, and brother I never had—all wrapped into one."

"That's how you see me? Seriously? Sounds a little schizo."

Elena thought for a second and then added, "Yeah, best friend first. Boyfriend only kinda, because at seventeen we're like an old married couple. And yeah, maybe you're more like a brother now . . . because it's been weeks since our fuck, remember?"

"Yeah, your special instructional class." I looked down and paused before I could go on. "Hey, are you pissed we don't screw all the time?"

"No, not really. I'm content with what we have. I just finished reading something that really changed the way I think about life."

"Sounds heavy."

"For that final psych paper, I'm reporting on the book *I'm OK— You're OK*."

"Shit, that's due next week," I said.

"Yeah, you procrastinator. Anyway, this book's from 1967. It talks about how every person is made up of three alter ego states—Parent, Adult, Child—and—"

"I think I want a Dilly Bar," I said.

"Andy! Could you listen for a minute? You might learn something!"

"Sorry," I said sheepishly, getting myself psyched for an Elena lecture when I really wanted ice cream.

"So the book says you need to go through a process to finally arrive at 'I'm okay.'"

"So how long does that process take? A lifetime?"

"No! You first have to recognize your emotional patterns, then change them. Sounds complex, but it's doable. Reading the book made me think of us. We're okay."

"I thought we were," I said defensively.

"I mean, we value each other as we are, without exception—I think. That's Thomas Harris's entire premise. To be healthy. Empowered."

"Empowered? I think I'll need to read the book to understand what the hell you're saying. But okay! Good. I'm glad we're okay!"

"Andy, you can be my best friend. I mean, you already are. And in some ways, you're also a boyfriend and a brother. I value all of those traits in you."

"So you're okay if we don't fuck . . . make love. We can stay as we are?" I asked desperately.

"Yes, if you are," she replied.

"If we do screw, we do," I said, wanting to keep the door open.

"Yeah, I think that ship's sailed, Andy."

"But, hey, please don't use us as an example in your final report."

"You are such a dork. Still worrying about what others think?"

"I don't—I mean, not always."

"Don't worry, hot shot. And yeah, you can borrow the book—if you really plan to read it. But you should work on your psych paper first, or you're gonna be sorry."

"Where's Skip?" I said, eager to change the subject and talk about the DQ hunk who seemed to dominate my thoughts lately. "He usually comes in at about six o'clock on Thursdays."

"Andy, I think Skipper might be gay."

"You're crazy!" I said, trying to hide the fact that my heart almost stopped when she said that.

"Sure, he gives us refills, doubles up on the fries. But when he does it, it seems he's always looking at you."

"Ridiculous," I said. "I barely know the guy; he doesn't live in Maple. And, if he is gay, who cares? We get free food."

Was Elena baiting me to test my reaction or—was it possible that my fantasy sofa jerk was the same as me? It was a mind-blowing notion.

Every day after classes for the rest of that week, I stopped by the DQ to see if Skip was behind the window. I had no intention of doing anything aside from testing Elena's theory. I would do that, I decided, with my own lingering stare accompanied by a winning smile. Maybe a compliment like: "Skip, where do you get your hair buzzed? It always looks solid."

Elena's comment, "It seems he's always looking at you," played over and over in my head for the next week or so. If there was even a remote possibility of a life with Skip, then I'd quickly demote Elena to loving friend.

As I struggled to study for final exams, I took repeated breaks, daydreaming about "accidentally" touching Skip's milky skin as he handed me a Buster Bar through the window. Or I'd envision the two of us rolling around naked in my bedroom on rainy afternoons. My mind raced into the future. We'd fall in love, me and the ice cream guy, and grow old together. That would fix everything.

But after five days of cruising by the DQ with no sight of Skip, I finally got the nerve up and approached Debbie, the bubbly, middle-aged mom manning the window.

"Hi. Good afternoon. Hey, where's Skip been all week?" I hoped my question seemed casual. I had practiced it enough in my head.

Debbie was cleaning congealed ice cream off the counter with a wet rag as she explained that Skip had to quit. He'd won a gymnastics scholarship to the University of Maryland.

"Oh, good for him," I shrugged, eager to leave so I could tend to my heartbreak alone. But Debbie wasn't finished.

She told me that Skip moved to Baltimore so he could live with his sister and her boyfriend for the summer before college.

"Yeah, okay. Well, thanks," I said, moving away from the window because I didn't want her to see the hurt in my face.

"Skip was a good worker," she called out as I headed to my car. "Maybe he'll find work at a DQ in Maryland."

Me and Elena didn't know Skip outside of the DQ. He wasn't a friend. But I started to feel hurt that he didn't tell us his plans. I mean, after giving us all that free food? He could have at least said goodbye, I pouted to myself. It was obvious to me that his departure would mean the end of my sofa jerks. I started to get desperate inside. How far was Baltimore? No more than a few hours' drive. I almost went back to the window to ask Debbie if Skip had left a forwarding address. But if I asked that, I would have exposed my stupid little crush. That night, studying for finals was pretty near impossible. I kept thinking about Skip. But my thoughts were sad, joyless. Debbie's news had shattered a dream.

The next day, totally unprepared, I took my chemistry exam. I scored a lousy 2.5. Thanks, Skip.

The August before the start of senior year, Elena and I began working on the yearbook. That meant we became entangled with teachers who served as yearbook advisers and a quintet of exceptional mentors. While most instructors were asleep at the wheel, these educators opened our eyes to the world beyond our unimaginative hamlet. Joshua MacMillan was a forty-ish, hippie-dippie art teacher who lived with his mother. A towering person, Mr. Mac wore a natty suede vest and dark-rimmed Malcolm X frames. Our French teacher, Dolores Stein, was often at his side. Mrs. Stein was on the sexy side of middle age, bolstered by bright red lips and a teased pouf of auburn hair. Regularly, she'd drop stories of her year in Saint-Tropez, sipping Pernod with Brigitte Bardot, which few of us believed.

Joan Didion's essays and the novels of James Baldwin were introduced by Vin Beardsley. He was the only Black person at our school. Beardsley took no crap, spurring conversations on apartheid or the Black Liberation Army. He made the rounds with Kay Kyle, a plump, short, boyish woman whose bowl haircut magnified her roundness. A ballbreaker in the classroom, Ms. Kyle would mellow after several glasses of Chardonnay on ice.

Completing this group was Ollie Stork. He was twenty-nine, short and compact, with a bushy copper mustache likely meant to detract from the pockmarks nestling his cheeks. Shaggy flaxen tresses and a pair of wire-rimmed glasses set him apart from the square teachers stuck in another era. Born and raised in Southern California, Ollie projected the vibe of a mellow surfer, the kind silhouetted against an orange sunset. Spanish levels one, two, and three were his domain, as well as a sparsely attended welding elective. Ollie kept two cabinets in his Español classroom filled with props from Mexico, Argentina, and Spain. Among them, a dozen sombreros, castanets, and foreign-language films, including *The Art of Flamenco*. He'd sprinkle his laid-back California vernacular with Spanish.

As co-editors of the Class of '78 Yearbook, Elena oversaw content, leaving design and layout to me. Toiling in the school basement, we counted on lead adviser Ollie, especially during yearbook deadlines. It was during those production marathons that our alliance blossomed. Although cultured more than most, Ollie was a dude—more freewheeler than authoritarian. Every Friday, he wore a strand of pearly white pukka beads and an untucked Hawaiian shirt. Ollie reminded me of David Soul from the *Starsky and Hutch* TV series.

Early in the school year, Ollie took me under his wing, elevating my coolness factor among classmates. His attention boosted my self-esteem. We seemed to share a bent for off-beat humor and pop culture, so our bond swiftly advanced beyond student and teacher to budding amigos. The friendship reassured Lia because she was traveling more often for work and leaving me solo. A couple of times, Lia joined us, most notably for the awesome Rod Stewart Foot Loose and Fancy Free concert at Madison Square Garden. Ollie was the first adult male who expressed interest in me since Pop-pop died.

Chapter 9

"Andy, is everything okay?" Gram called up in a panic. The matriarch had a pesky habit of tracking the whereabouts of her flock, day or night.

"I'm sleeping in, Gram. I was up late reading."

"When your mother's away, you always call me. Let me know if you're coming over for supper? Nothing fancy. Go back to sleep."

Fifteen minutes later, Lia called. "Andy, everything okay?"

"Mom, yes. Sleeping late. How's D.C.?"

"We're staying in Fairfax. It's a jam-packed schedule. We're playing tennis in a few minutes, and the ERA conference in D.C. is tomorrow. Tonight is the Sixties dinner dance. Ruth is my date, isn't that a riot?"

I grunted in response until she finally ran out of things to say and hung up.

I squatted on the toilet, thumbing through the latest *Reader's Digest*. A round of gas fired out of my ass, followed by spots of blood as bright as a valentine. I freaked out. What if it got worse? If I had to go to the emergency room, what would I say? I broke into a sweat, stood up, and realized I was overreacting. The drops of blood were minuscule. Taking my second shower, I held my wrists up to the window. The asshole's rope marks had darkened, the skin circling the bruises was mottled. For no logical reason, I pressed my index finger deep into the bruises, prompting a ripple of pain to my shoulder. Touching the rim of my anus sparked slight throbbing.

I called Gram to tell her I'd be skipping supper, claiming a stomach bug. "Oh. Really?" She could tell that I was lying. But she let it go with a slight grumble.

Pulling on a pair of sweats, I stared blankly at the wall for what seemed like an eternity, pondering my defiled butt, until the phone rattled.

"Andy, what's up? I'm in Montclair until tomorrow. It's rad! What are you doing?"

"I have a surprise for you, Elena!"

"Uh-oh, what now?"

"This isn't another Andy crisis. It's good news."

"I'm listening," she said, skepticism undisguised.

"I have two tickets for us to see the Stones. Monday night—in the city."

"Andy, I don't believe you. I didn't hear anything about them playing in New York. Where?"

"Special concert at the Palladium, on Fourteenth Street. I bought the tickets from . . . a guy. At work. His wife is about to have a baby. He can't go."

"Holy shit, Andy, I can't believe this! Mick in the flesh? Yes, yes, yes. I have to work Monday, but I'll definitely leave early."

"Sick day for me. I'll pick you up at five. We'll take the train in."

"Ummm, I'll tell Luba we're going with Beardsley, coz she'd be fine with that. Andy, hanging out with Maya in Montclair is a blast. We're going to see some experimental play, then disco dancing. Maya has a friend, Rocco—he might be gay."

"Really?" Suddenly I was interested.

"Yeah, he's in the theater department. We all have to go out sometime."

"Let's do it."

"Andy, are you okay? It's Saturday and you're home. Are you down?"

"I'm fine. Just woke from a nap. I'm hanging here tonight. Lia's away. Stoked about seeing the Stones. Love you."

"Love you, Andy Pollock!"

By Sunday morning, all alone, I was utterly depressed. Taking my third shower in twenty-four hours, I scoured my skin until it was raw. I looked at my body in the mirror. My body. A pasty roll of baby fat hung at my mid-section while hair sprouted across my chest, forearms, and legs. My body. The body I proudly tended. Height and weight—in proportion. Broad shoulders by way of a million laps in the town pool. My dick, respectable. Sizable thighs supporting runner's calves.

My body, wronged by a stranger.

My mind recalled the evening when Fucking-fuck violated my body. I suddenly belched up undigested pizza into the toilet bowl. The air stank. I picked up a can of Glade and spritzed the bathroom. The stench prompted another round of barfing.

I stomped up the stairwell to put on a pair of shorts. I tripped over the top step and my waist towel flew, causing my left knee to scrape across the coarse carpet. A bright circle of red dots rose to the surface.

As I reached for the white towel, my body spasmed in fury.

Fuck you. Fuck you. Fuck you. Fuck you. FUCK YOU. You fucking ass-hole. FUCK YOU. Fuck you. Fuck you. Fuck you. FUCK YOU.

I grabbed an *Encyclopedia Britannica* and hurled it against the drywall. I belly-flopped onto the bed, motionless, and watched another gout of blood trickle along my calf.

FUCKKKKKKKKKKKKKK YOUUUUUUU.

Tugging on a pair of gym shorts commando, I applied a wad of Kleenex to the wound and bounded downstairs for a Band-Aid. Rummaging past Lia's basket of brushes and creams, I found a jar of flesh-colored blush. Cover-up. I slathered two fingers of the wet powder onto the underside of my wrists to hide the rope burns.

Restless, needing to prove something to myself, I tossed on a light-weight flannel and drove into town to pick up the *New York Times* Sunday edition.

Hours later, I drove six blocks to Gram's for lunch. The moment I reached the Dutch door to the kitchen, the aroma of meatballs simmer-ing in tomato sauce erased all that had gone wrong. Gram and I hugged. I poured seltzer into squat glasses on the table she set with flowers from the side garden. The meatballs were paired with rigatoni and a romaine salad showered with shaved carrot and oregano.

"Andy! Tell me, how's your job at PGE? It's good money," she said, grating a mountain of Parmesan onto the rigatoni.

"The money is great, Gram, but I'm glad it's not forever."

"People would kill for that job. You could move up in the company after college."

"Ummmm—"

"Your mother will be home Tuesday?" she added, changing the subject. "Why is she protesting? I never know if she's telling me the whole story."

"She's not protesting. It's a planning meeting, and Monday she's working at the Fairfax headquarters. Tuesday she and Ruth drive home."

"Ruth, I don't know about her. She's a bit horsey," Gram croaked. "How is your mother going to get along once you go to college? You'll come home on weekends, won't you?" She pouted.

"Whenever I can. But I will have tons of homework."

"Guess who called? Crazy June."

"Why do you call her Crazy June, Gram?"

"Crazy because she's a kook. A lonely kook. You wouldn't remember this, but her left eyeball rolls to one side. You never can tell if she's looking right at you. Like that comedian with the bulging eyes—Marty something."

"Marty Feldman. From *Young Frankenstein*."

"Anyway, all she talks about are her damn cats. She never married."

"Never married? Is she a lesbian?" I said, testing the word on Gram.

"Lesbian? No, I don't think. She's very religious. Oh, and those damn stuffed animals and dolls everywhere. Who could live with that?"

"Did she say anything about her family?" I asked.

"About your father? No, Andy. Not really."

I could feel my eyes start to mist up.

"Okay, don't tell Lia—she'll get upset I said anything—but I do know Andrew still lives in Norway with your grandmother. He was dating a Norwegian girl, but it didn't work out."

The mention of my invisible father's name was a punch to the gut.

We ended the meal with strong black coffee and fresh-baked sweet cream puffs. Gram arranged the remaining pastries on a chipped antique plate, covering them with aluminum foil.

"Andy, want to come back tonight? We can watch TV and eat leftovers. Or order a pizza from Lou's Tavern, your favorite? I'm here all alone." She paused expertly to let the guilt sink in.

"I'd love to, but I have things to do tonight. I'll take a few meatballs home if you have enough?"

She sighed and shrugged, spooning six on top of pasta inside a Tupperware container. "You know how to heat this, right? In a small pot with a little water, burner on low, so it doesn't scorch."

"Gram, your meatballs are the most delicious I've ever had."

I lunged for a tender hug as she kissed my nape, her garlicky breath comforting. I suddenly realized she was embracing the same body that had been violated only a day earlier and felt ashamed.

I went home and refrigerated the leftovers and then changed into a swimsuit. I headed to the patio to wilt under the afternoon sun. Splayed on my back across a lounge chair, the light played tricks with my eyes. Patterns, twirling red spirals, and flecks of monochromatic sparkle danced erratically. Suddenly, I cracked. Not delicate tears—chest-rolling swells. A sour mix of saline and tanning oil ran down my cheeks, seeping into my mouth. Out of nowhere sprang a guttural wail. Concerned I'd scare the neighbors, I fled to the kitchen. Catching my breath at the sink, I vowed to the chintzy curtains that I would never go out alone again and get wasted.

I heard a noise at the screen door and yelped in panic.

"Unlock the door, you loser," Elena snapped, waving a paper bag.

Throwing on the oversized flannel, I scolded, "You freak! It's unlocked."

"Andy, are you okay? You look like shit. Were you crying?"

"I was laying out in the sun. Lotion got into my eyes," I said, dramatically rubbing both sockets.

"Yeah, okay," she said skeptically. "I thought someone died. Look at these beauties," she said, shaking out a pair of identical black Stones T-shirts, emblazoned with the bright red tongue. "We're wearing these tomorrow night. We're going to look so hot, my man. Speaking of which—aren't you a little sweaty in that flannel?"

"Uh, yeah, I guess—"

"Andy, the dance party last night was bananas. Can't wait for you to meet Maya and Rocco!"

Elena was no fool; she knew something was off. Grabbing me, she offered a merciful hug, adding, "Gotta run, it's goulash night."

Chapter 10

Like the first frame in *The Texas Chainsaw Massacre*, when Leatherface dominates the screen, blurry flashes of Fucking-fuck whizzed before my eyes between hours of restless sleep. As I tossed and turned, the memory haunted me until the alarm buzzed at 6:45 a.m.

"Sick as a dog," I informed my supervisor. "No way I'll make it in today."

I brewed a pot of Maxwell House to break out of my stupor. Setting a mug on the counter, I noticed that the color of my wrists was fading but my skin was still bruised.

After a day of lying in bed watching TV, it was soon time to pick up Elena. I decided my old Timex with a double-wide leather strap, despite it being out of fashion, would hide the bruise. I layered the black Stones tee Elena gave me over a long-sleeved one, and covered the layers with a green plaid shirt, unbuttoned and loose. Before leaving, I gave myself a quick pat-down: tickets, car keys, wallet, license. Check.

As I pulled the Blue Whale in front of Elena's house, she jumped up from the stoop, feverishly. Mick's graphic tongue bounced about her chest.

"Whaaa, no headscarf?" I called.

"Smart-ass! Baba didn't seem appropriate for the occasion," Elena barked.

Wearing a bright yellow apron, Luba appeared in the screen door waving both hands as we hustled to catch the train.

Forty-five minutes later, we arrived at West Fourteenth Street, six trashy avenues west of the theater.

"Andy, all this garbage and graffiti! You sure you can handle living in the city? The Village is sleazy, but at least it's—quaint. This area is disgusting."

"The city is a pit. That's part of the charm," I said, trying to sound like a regular. "The dorm is a few blocks that way, so it's a little bit safer," I said, pointing to Union Square. "The trick when walking in fishy areas is to never look anyone in the eye."

"Well, you better be careful, mister. Don't go walking alone at night. I'm not sure I could live here."

"Nonsense," I said. "You love the city as much as I do."

We arrived at the Palladium way too early. The doors were bolted with thick chains, the marquee coyly announcing, CONCERT June 19.

A sporadic breeze carried the pungent smell of rotting waste down Fourteenth Street. As a dozen or so Stones zealots hovered near the entrance, Elena asked one whether the concert was for real.

"Yes, yes, yes," he responded. "Peter Tosh is opening."

"Thank God!" Elena screamed, hopping in a circle like a kangaroo. "Andy, it's happening. We're gonna see Mick in the flesh!"

Elena continued gabbing with other equally rabid groupies. It was an hour before the doors opened. Flashing the stolen tickets, I asked a hump-backed doorman if "Special Access" permitted us to enter first. He scanned the tickets, unimpressed.

"Special Access doesn't mean zilch. You've got box seats. When you get inside, make a left up the stairs."

By now a crowd had gathered, and we shuffled like sheep among the crush. I suddenly panicked, thinking the cops would know these were stolen tickets. Maybe the asshole called ahead and they were looking for me?

I solicited the gods: Please, please, don't let us get caught. Afraid I'd black out, I grabbed Elena's shoulders. A stubby Slavic woman placed the tickets under a black light to make sure they weren't counterfeit and then barked instructions for finding our seats upstairs.

We were in. I could breathe again.

The theater, far smaller than Madison Square Garden, was swathed in passé decor. We climbed the curved stairs to the balcony, spotting our section. The box contained two petite rows of six seats. With the spot hovering over stage-right, Elena began to cry, overwhelmed. She'd soon have an unobstructed view, no more than ten feet away, of Jagger.

Just then another wave of panic arose. What if Fucking-fuck suddenly appeared? I might not recognize him before he saw me. He might vault into the box and shout out, "Him! That's the thief, arrest him."

A group of four college-aged kids filed toward the seats to my left. I scrutinized their faces. Not one looked like they'd associate with a molester. The fellow to my left pitched a cooler-than-thou chin-nod as he settled in beside me. On the aisle was a chubby Hispanic guy with a toothy smile. Next to him sat a possibly albino lad with a flap of white hair over his left eye. Alongside him was a posh chick in a bleached bob, clad in a black jumper, black leotards, and black Doc Martens boots.

Soon the air was stewed in the sweet smell of wood. As the lights flicked off, a round of cheers erupted. I squeezed Elena's hand to temper her nerves. Then a rally of boos as the lights went on again.

Hunching over, the guy with denim knees leaned into me.

"Hey, I'm Ben," he said in a polished monotone. "How's it going? You're not who I thought you'd be. Are you pumped for the concert?"

Not who he thought I'd be? I felt ill again. But I pushed through it, saying, "Hey, Ben. Andy. This is Elena. She's a Jagger junky."

His greenish-grey eyes were angelic. His cheeks were bright and rosy. A curl of coffee-colored hair waved about his forehead as he shifted.

"Andy. Elena. Got it. Excellent seats, right?"

"Unbelievable. I'm stoked."

Ben introduced us to his friends, Lula, Mikel, and Roberto.

"Andy, your matching T-shirts are rad. You gotta be the coolest boyfriend in the world for taking your girl to see the Stones."

"Thanks," I said, laughing. "Elena's not my girlfriend. Anymore. We're best friends."

"Apologies. You got a job for the summer?"

"A summer construction gig at Public General Electric."

"Not sure what that is, but excellent," Ben shrugged. "Construction is hard, man. Do you guys live in the city?"

"I start school here in September."

"Where you going?"

"NYU."

"No fucking way! That's where I finished up. You must be stoked."

"You have no idea! Of course, my neighbors think the city is a joke," I exaggerated.

"I went to NYU for communications. Advertising mainly."

"I'm going into fine arts."

"The burbs . . . so, Bronx? the Island?"

"Jersey," I said, making a thumbs-down signal, knowing New Yorkers looked down on the Garden State. "So, Ben, you're out of college? I figured you were a student."

"No, I graduated two years ago. Jersey's cool—I mean, you live there, so it must be, right?"

The theater blacked out, and Peter Tosh and his band appeared.

"He's awesome, wait until he plays 'Get Up, Stand Up,'" Ben whispered close enough that I could smell the weed on his breath. On her feet, Elena danced, hands waving in choreographed circles.

Ben explained that Tosh was a member of Bob Marley and the Wailers. We sat in idle silence through his brief set. Tosh got booed as he exited. The four ducklings to my left scurried to the lobby, leaving us to prattle with an intoxicated woman in the row behind us. Every few minutes, the spotlights flashed but never went out. Elena was losing patience. Soon, the lights went out for good, and the crowd erupted.

We saw microphone stands and exposed instruments sitting naked under a trio of rotating spots. Soon, strokes of white light eddied around Keith Richards as he came out and screamed, "Crank it up, motherfuckers."

Ben and his pals returned as the hi-hat and kick drum reverberated. Then, like an acrobat, Mick leaped into the glow, making mincemeat of Chuck Berry's "Let It Rock." As Keith strummed the first chords of "Honky Tonk Women," the theater burst like thunder. Elena pulled me up to dance beside her. The row behind us jumped up and down so heavily that I feared our decrepit box would collapse. By the end of "When the Whip Comes Down," Jagger was a sweaty mess. Swooning like a drugged hobo, he then warbled the lyrics of "Miss You."

"My favorite," I yelled out loud to no one.

"Me too," Ben screamed in my ear. I smelled the weed mixed with his sweat. I inhaled again, a little deeper. This straight guy was sexy.

Mouthing the lyrics, Elena screamed as a drenched Mick mock-collapsed center stage, and the last chords of "Beast of Burden" led into intermission.

"Beer! Tequila! Shots!" crowed Lula with British girly cheer.

"Andy, Elena—want anything?" Ben's boyish grin was as wide as Wyoming. "Are you guys legal? It doesn't matter, but are you?"

"Yes," I yelled, "over eighteen."

"Come with Lula and me—both of you."

The six of us sliced a path through the chaos to the lounge. Ben pulled a fat joint from his shirt pocket.

"You guys in?"

"Totally, where can we smoke?" I said, speaking for Elena.

Ben led us to a column that was supposed to provide concealment from ushers who didn't really seem to care.

"Let's smoke this, then grab beers and shots," Ben pressed. He fired the joint with his orange BIC before passing it to Elena.

I finally got a chance to assess Ben for the first time. He was a dude, like countless other straight, college-aged guys. My hunch was he was from the Midwest. Someplace with dairy farms. His skin was as creamy as a baby's butt. Whatever they fed him as a child had worked. Peeking from under a plaid button-down was the *Ha* of a Hall and Oates black tee sloppily tucked beneath a thick leather belt. His Wrangler jeans, neither tight nor loose, reached a pair of worn chukka boots I instantly wanted.

Ben's girlfriend, Lula, was the type of girl you wanted to be seen with.

She sparkled. If Ben was a milk-fed Butch Cassidy, Lula was a combo of Twiggy and Goldie Hawn. Under heavy makeup, her face was beautiful. I wanted Elena and me to grow up to be Ben and Lula.

"Mick's bladdered. Positively off his game," Lula bellowed in a Manhattan-edged Cockney. "I read he was unwell in Philly, but he seems *bloody fucked-up* if you ask me."

"He's Mick Jagger," said Elena. "Who cares? He's gorgeous, a beast. We expect him to be fucked up!"

"Ladies, let's grab shots," Ben interrupted.

The house lights flashed as he ordered four tequilas and four beers, springing for the tab.

"I'll get next round," I insisted.

"Yay to our new friends," Lula toasted. "And to Mick, fucked-up or *whateva*."

"Where are Roberto and Mikel from?" I asked Ben.

"Mikel's from Holland, Roberto lives in the Bronx. Da Bronx," Ben mocked. "We all work in the same department at MSP, an advertising firm, except for Lula. She and I met at a typography class at NYU."

"Andy, do you work in the city?" Lula asked, pronouncing my name *On-day*, blowing the smoke from a clove cigarette away from our faces.

"No, no. I'm a hardhat at a utility plant in Jersey. It's just for the summer. NYU in September, fine arts."

"Hard hat. That all sounds very blue-collar. Whatever it takes, I suppose," Lula said.

We got back to our seats and downed our beers.

Leaning in, Ben asked, "Andy, how did you score your tickets? The VP of my firm generously gave us six. Your seats were given to Damon. Damon Piccard, you must know him? He's a freelance art director at the firm."

I stopped breathing. Fucking-fuck has a name. And this dude knows my seats were pinched.

"Weird. No—a work buddy gave them to me. His wife is having a baby this weekend," I said, recycling the lie I had told Elena.

"Maybe your coworker knows Damon. He thinks I'm a junior-ranking putz. So I'm glad I didn't have to sit next to him tonight."

I was relieved that I wasn't a suspect. And it made me feel better that this Ben dude didn't like Fucking-fuck either.

I wiped my sweaty palms across my pants and asked, "What do you do at the ad agency?"

"Junior art director, primarily working on advertising campaigns. I started right after NYU." He smiled, blitzed from the joint, tequila, and beer.

Also glowing from the booze, I added, "Where are you from?" I got to look at his boyish face boldly at this point.

"Columbus. I moved to Manhattan for school. I love New York," he said. "What are your goals after college?"

"Maybe advertising. Possibly architecture, or commercial art and painting." I shrugged, rummaging through options.

"The world's your oyster since you're going to NYU, dude!"

As the chords to "Far Away Eyes" ignited, Ben called out, "Seat swap. I am *roasted, toasted, and burnt*" and then plopped down next to me. His woodsy scent nearly sent me over the guardrail into the orchestra pit. "Mick's fucking destroyed. He can barely stand up," Ben roared in my ear.

The crowd roared to "Brown Sugar" before the band launched into "Jumpin' Jack Flash."

"Fuck, I can't take it!" Elena cried.

Then, like a Buick crashing into a concrete wall, the concert ended abruptly. Bright lights revealed a gauzy curtain of weed vapor. Ben leaned in, wobbly, and I almost had a heart attack when his lips accidentally grazed my ear.

"If I give you my number, will you call?"

"Yeah, of course," I said, wondering if I was just reading him wrong.

"Lula, Lula, got a pen?" Ben yelled, getting a ballpoint as we funneled into the exit traffic. As we hit gridlock, Ben asked me to turn around so he could scribble his info against my back. Each stroke was like a come-on. Ben stuffed the paper into my hand, holding it in place a few seconds longer than expected. Ben's greenish-grey eyes radiated, and I felt shivers to the tips of my toes.

"We're headed to the right, so we may lose you guys. Night, Andy! Night, Elena!"

"Call *me*," Elena told Lula while giving Ben a generous hug—a hug I would have liked to give. Mikel waved. Roberto vanished.

As the concertgoers trekked along Fourteenth Street, Elena danced in the breeze.

"Thank you, Andy Pollock! That was the most incredible night of my life. Let's move to New York—now. I love our new friends."

"They left pretty quickly," I replied with a pout.

"It's a Monday night, Andy. They have to work tomorrow. We'll call Lula and Ben this week, don't worry."

"I'm still buzzed. Let's bolt to the train. This street is fucking shady."

I clasped Elena's hand and we sprinted to the station. Piss and vomit painted the stairwell. When we heard the screech of the oncoming train, we raced through the turnstile. We plopped into two seats closest to the door of the nearly empty car.

"Should I get contact lenses? Would I look sexier? Lula has a beautiful face, doesn't she?" Elena rambled.

"Hey, you think Lula and Ben are a couple? Wasn't it weird, they didn't sit together the second half?"

"Noooooo. He and Lula are friends. Ben's bi or into guys. He's not sure. He seemed into you, Andy."

"Ben's gay? Are you sure? He did give me his number, but—"

"Duh. Yes, Andy—I'm sure. Girls talk. Plus, he's cute, in a Luke Skywalker way. I'd date him in a minute."

As the train rounded a curve, Elena dropped her head against my shoulder. I was buzzing, processing the news. Ben was a mix of hot 'n hunky, crossed with wholesome, funny, and nice. So nice. And smart, the way his eyes flickered as he spoke, as if his mind was three steps ahead of his words. And soft, like a warm flannel blanket I wanted to curl into. Ben was beautiful.

Ben is gay. Ben is gay. Ben is gay. Ben is gay.

The muscles in my face were hijacked by a gaping, wicked smile that would not quit. And I had that Fucking-fuck to thank for it all. Damn it.

Chapter 11

I decided to call in sick the next day, obsessed with planning my next steps with Ben.

How long do I wait before calling?

What do I say? "Hey Ben, is it true you're a homo? If so, are you into me?"

I planned to call him that night. As I counted down the hours like a psycho, I riffled through Monday's mail and found a glossy postcard with crimson edges. It had a photograph of a matador dressed in an ornate gold jacket defying a charging bull. On the back was:

> Olé Andy!
>
> Saludos de la corazón del magnífico *Madrid*. Eating count-less tapas and drinking way too much vino. My summer flat is muy pequinito but close to the university. Wish you were here! Hugs to Lia.
>
> Hasta luego—Ollie XO!

He was having a good time. Good to know.

But I was still upset by Elena's accusation. Did Ollie take advantage of me? Did it matter? Instead of cheering me up, Ollie's postcard crystallized a new round of anxiety. His introducing me to gay sex only to abandon me for the remainder of the summer had left me swimming in a confusion so dark and perilous it threatened to consume me.

I thought of the depression I slogged through in puberty when my attraction to guys took the form of lust—a twisted version of the emotional longing I harbored. The experience of being discovered, cast off, and unloved repeatedly was crippling.

Why was I heading to a dark place? I had been dancing on air after the high of meeting dream boy Ben. It was fucked up letting my mood torpedo so damned fast. The only thing to do was sleep it off. Escaping into an afternoon nap was a good move considering the overcast afternoon sky.

A sharp slap of thunder suddenly bolted me up from the couch. With a lazy hand, I cranked the living room window. The dewy air from low-hanging clouds sprayed my cheeks, nose, and forehead. Mildly refreshed, I removed the grey smoked-plastic stereo lid to spin the LP *Running on Empty*. Basking in Jackson Browne's husky sound, I jerked a fresh bottle of Dewar's out of the booze cabinet. I stacked three ice cubes from the freezer tray into a fancy, cut-crystal tumbler typically reserved for company. Deciding the first pour was skimpy, I multiplied it by three and plopped onto the crushed velvet sofa.

Liquid medicine was a surefire way out of the swamp.

The first sip of scotch pricked my gums. The second pull, once the backwash calmed, arrived with toasted caramel and gratitude—my blues would soon be gone. I was impatient, but it was too early in the evening to call Ben, so I lingered on foolish, needy thoughts of Ollie. I tried to dismiss Elena's accusation of his motives but wondered if she was really right.

Three weeks before Ollie and I shagged, Elena had organized an outing to celebrate sending the Class of '78 Yearbook off to the printer. Ten months of creating copy, organizing photoshoots, and designing layouts were finally finished. Mrs. Stein, who oversaw photography, suggested we attend a preview of *The Threepenny Opera* in Central Park. Loaded down with nibbles and libations, five of us piled into Ollie's Honda early one Saturday afternoon. Ollie directed me to the front passenger seat, appointing me his copilot. The girls and Mr. Beardsley sat in the rear. Mr. Mac, after spraining his foot line-dancing, had bowed out.

Driving to the city in a car of teachers who were usually tyrants in the classroom was dizzying. It was as if Elena and I had been inducted into their forbidden guild, where they dropped their grumpy masks.

Ollie parked on a tree-lined street next to the Museum of Natural History. With armfuls of blankets and totes, we made our way to the Delacorte Theater lawn. Lia had made a cold macaroni salad with sliced green olives. Ollie brought two thermoses of sangria. Elena brought walnut brownies in a Tupperware. Mrs. Stein, wearing a flowing maxi dress, brought five roast beef sandwiches with Dijon on baguettes. Wearing a Grateful Dead T-shirt, Mr. Beardsley carried two bottles of Chablis, black cherries, and a Calabrian pepperoni in a cooler decorated with ERA stickers.

By the time the opera began, we were toast—me being seventeen and underage was ignored. Pouring the fruity wine into paper cups, Ollie smirked. "It's only sangria, and your eighteenth birthday is weeks away. You'll be sober by the time we leave." As I was stooped between the two, Elena and Ollie poked and ribbed me from both sides as Bertolt Brecht's drama unfolded on stage.

At the end of the show, as we leaped to our feet in applause, I knew something had changed. I was aware that Ollie adored Elena, but that night under the twinkling stars, I realized that cooler-than-cool Ollie saw me not as a student but as an equal.

The following Wednesday night, our group had dinner at Ming Dynasty, treated by the teachers. With the end of school near, we were all giddy. Over tasty Chinese, Ollie and I chatted each other up like peers. Elena noticed.

"Whoever thought I'd be replaced by Stork as your best bud. Is he taking you to a titty bar later, now that you're practically a man?" Elena snapped when we went to the bathroom together.

"Please don't tell me that you're jealous of Ollie. Elena, that's psycho. You'll always be my girl."

As the week closed, my interaction with Ollie buzzed into overdrive. Without final exams, seniors were now sloppy about attending class. I found excuses for hanging out with Ollie, be it lunchtime runs to McDonald's or goofing around the Spanish lab after his classes. We were wedged somewhere in age between father and big brother, and Ollie instilled confidence. When I'd stumbled about—wavering over saying yes to the summer job at PGE or having conflict with Lia over my independence—Ollie doled out level-headed advice.

After graduation ceremony practice one evening, Ollie and I saw a rerelease of *American Graffiti* at a cinema in Paramus. We shared a large bucket of popcorn, no butter, and two medium Tabs. At first, sitting beside Ollie in the dark, uncrowded theater made me uneasy. Since going to the movie had been my idea, I grew worried he'd misread the invitation as a date and had begun to suspect I was gay. Then Olivia Newton-John appeared on screen as the hot version of her character Sandy in a preview for the musical *Grease.* We stomped our feet and catcalled like two horny frat bros, thereby reassuring me that Ollie was clueless to my bent.

Afterward, at Beefsteak Charlie's, he gossiped about Mr. Bard, our aging gym teacher, and his affair with the school nurse. Ollie trusted me. When our top-heavy waitress delivered the menus, Ollie read her name badge and quipped, "Management must know I have a thing for big boobs, Dolores."

She laughed and I was bolstered enough to add, "I prefer knockers the size of cupcakes." She laughed even harder.

On his third mug of beer, as we dredged the final french fries through a heap of ketchup, Ollie turned serious.

"Don't get married until you're much older, Andy. My ex-wife and I were twenty-two. Just kids at the time. Clueless. Divorce sucks. I feel like a raft floating aimlessly downriver."

Ollie's confessions drew me in like no other.

As a gift for my eighteenth birthday a few weeks later, Ollie surprised me with tickets to *Gemini*, an off-Broadway play I'd never heard of. That Saturday, we drove into the city to meet his friends Ted and Isabel for cocktails and nachos at a downtown bar. The chatty, middle-aged couple were

dressed in diaphanous fabrics, seemingly left over from the flower-power
'60s. Isabel, with purple and aqua beads braided into her frizzy grey hair,
had a pretty face with glowing skin. Ted had black pearls wrapped around
a ponytail that flowed down his spine. Neither of them seemed to find it
peculiar that Ollie was out on a Friday night with a pupil.

"Do you know Ollie from Southern California?" I asked, trying to
sound grown-up.

"Ted and I grew up on Staten Island," Isabel laughed. "We all taught at
P.S. 35 in Hell's Kitchen—with Ollie's wife. That is, his ex-wife."

We took seats in the fifth row. From the moment the play started, I was
mesmerized. *Gemini*'s lead character, Francis Geminiani, was a precocious
college student attempting to come out of the closet to his dysfunctional
Italian family. When two male characters kissed, I squirmed—with pleasure.

"That was spectacular," I said, as we left the theater. "How could anyone
not sympathize with Francis's pain? And Bunny? Hilarious!" We all babbled
on until we hugged goodbye at the Sheridan Square subway station. As we
rambled toward the Westside Highway to get Ollie's car, I checked out the
parade of gay men passing us along the sidewalk. I fell silent.

Ollie asked, "Cat got your tongue? Why so quiet?"

"No reason," I said. "Ted and Isabel are outstanding!"

We drove north as Ollie prattled on about plans for Madrid. But I was
still bulldozed by the play and being in the thick of men attracted to other
men—hundreds of them—at night in the Village.

"Halloo, are you listening? Would you want to come to Spain next
summer?"

"Definitely," I said, shaken from my trance. "Art school in Spain, I'm
in. But Ollie, can I talk to you about something?"

"Is it about Lia? I know you guys are struggling with you leaving for
college."

"It's more serious. It's about *Gemini*," I said, sputtering. "I could
relate to Francis. This isn't easy to say . . . so here goes. I think I might
be bisexual."

As I watched his face for a reaction, Ollie's eyes briefly popped, but he kept his eyes on the road.

"Whoa, Andy. Holy shit, I never suspected. I'm not sure what to say."

My frame withered low in my seat.

"No, it's okay," he reassured me. "It's good you told me."

I wasn't sure how to respond, so I kept quiet.

"This is crazy, Andy," he added. "And I've never said this to anyone before, but . . . so am I. Bisexual. I think."

I made a large gulping noise that I couldn't hide.

Ollie screamed, "Aaaaaaaaah!"

And I echoed him, "Aaaaaaaaah."

Then we both laughed, and I felt a part of the world again—even better.

As we exited the Holland Tunnel, Ollie pulled into a Burger King lot, parked the car, and looked closely at me. I smiled back, but warily.

"Let's sleep together? Just an idea. No pressure. We'll make it romantic."

Sex and Ollie were two things that didn't add up. I looked into his face, my thrill tangled with panic. Pockmarks dotted his face, scars offset by a scattering of blond curls. He didn't look like David Soul at that moment. No effin' way.

"Friday night at my place—but only if you're certain. I've only been with one dude before, but I could teach you things, Andy. I don't want your first time to be with a stranger."

Huh? We should sleep together so my first guy wouldn't be a stranger? But . . . I had no intention of ever having sex with someone I didn't know. I had no response and just looked at him.

"Andy, this will be our secret. You can't tell a soul. I could lose my teaching position."

"Yes," I mumbled.

I didn't say yes because I was keen to get naked with Ollie. But I needed to be with another guy to be sure I was really like Francis. Kissing Ollie wasn't my first choice, not the way I wanted to ease into this world, but it would prove things. I hoped. And the fatherless kid in me felt grateful for the offer, no matter how fucked up that sounds.

"I'll make dinner. You can spend the night. Andy . . . it's also okay if you change your mind. I'm serious."

I nodded and tried not to gulp loudly again, betraying my horror, my disgust, or my curiosity.

I told myself that Ollie knew best. Okay, maybe he was taking the hands-on mentor thing a little too far. But the idea that a man wanted to look after me like that was touching. I guess that damned Andy Sr. had really done a number on me when he abandoned us.

So I said yeah to Ollie. Maybe I said it too fast. But I sure as hell couldn't take it back now. Rejecting him was out of the question at this point. We were helping each other out; that's what buddies do, right? He had helped me grow up this semester. This was one more lesson. I just didn't see this one coming.

Buckets of rain dropped all Saturday, giving me time to reflect. It was a good weekend for feeling mellow and introspective. I needed a break from the nonstop chaos of this final month of senior year.

Lia experimented with a recipe for vegetarian lasagna that slow-baked at 325 degrees. While she did, we played multiple rounds of Scrabble. She won all but one game. That's because I was distracted, my thoughts consumed by Ollie's insane proposal. As I read a novel, my eyes stayed locked on the same lines and couldn't move forward. This Ollie thing again.

I liked him. Like a friend and surrogate dad. My affection for Ollie was genuine, but I liked a lot of people—and I wasn't screwing them.

I could ask Lia her advice on almost anything. That's how close we were. But not this time. No way. If Lia had any indication of what mess I had agreed to, she surely would have blown a gasket, called the cops on Ollie, and then grounded me for the summer. Maybe she'd reserve me a room in a loony bin, straitjacket and everything.

I told myself that she'd never know. It would kill her.

But that meant that I was alone in this crisis. No one to confide in. No one to ask if this was the right thing to do.

It was a gloomy Sunday. And that was perfect because it reflected my own inner blues. By late afternoon, the sun suddenly cracked through. I drove to the aquatic center, knowing the pool was usually uncrowded at that time. I had to work out my anxiety, and swimming seemed a good use of my energies.

As predicted, it was quiet. Two older men with moles on their arms and chests waded in the shallow area. One of them looked like he could have been handsome when he was younger. A girl lifeguard, little more than five feet tall, sat dangling her calves in the water beside a meek, skinny fellow with long legs and big feet. I assumed it was her boyfriend.

Big feet. Lucky her, I thought.

I stripped out of my cover-up sweats to the aqua Speedo I had recently purchased. I plunged into the nearest speed lane.

As I propelled through the overly chlorinated water, I tried to empty my head of the stress of the Ollie situation. No luck. Before I knew it, as I kicked through my lane, I imagined Ollie Stork standing in front of the classroom lecturing with that clever look on his face, like always. But this time, he was naked. None of the other classmates seemed to realize he was naked. Only me. So I could look at him without anyone thinking I was a fag.

I looked him up and down so I could have a sneak preview of our night together. His body was a mix of several things. He had firm shoulders and arms with medium-sized muscles from his surfing days. But because he was a shameless glutton at meals, he had a bit of a spare tire around his middle. Not gross but it interrupted the firmness everywhere else.

I looked at the light scattering of chest hair that led downward to his belly flab and then down farther to his pubic area. Looking around to make sure my classmates were still seeing Ollie clothed, I took time to look closely at his penis.

It was soft. But as I stared, Ollie smiled at me. He knew where I was looking, even if nobody else did. In response to my staring, his dick began to slowly swell and thicken. I stared a bit longer, and it began to rise until it was standing up flat against his stomach. It looked a lot like mine but maybe a couple of inches longer.

"Andy," Ollie said loudly from the front of the classroom, "I need your help. Come up here, please."

I shook my head side to side in the water, and the daydream—Ollie, the class, the whole room—quickly evaporated.

But that crazy fantasy told me one thing: Ollie may not be much to look at—certainly not "sex on a stick," as one of my gay magazines had described someone—but fuck it, he was my only sexual option right now. And I was horny. I would take it. I would make it work. And then I would think about the consequences later.

On Monday morning, I was walking the hallways of Maple High again, surrounded by scores of classmates and faculty. Suddenly I panicked. How could I have sex with my teacher? Someone was bound to find out. A neighbor. A passerby. A classmate who by chance followed me in their car and saw me park outside of Ollie's home. Anything was possible. If word got out that I was preparing to shag Mr. Stork, it would be a scandal of epic proportions.

Over the subsequent days, my stomach stayed knotted and my mind did flip-flops. My position wavered between proceeding full steam ahead to faking a last-minute stomach flu.

But alone at night, feeling horny and unable to scratch my itch sufficiently by jerking off, I went back to my original position. Your first didn't have to be your best; it only had to be your first. You had to start somewhere. Even with someone like Ollie. Fuck it. Get the sex out of the way. Then move on.

I came up with an excuse to give Lia for the Ollie sleepover. I hope it was convincing. We were catching an eleven p.m. showing of *La Semana del Asesino*, *The Cannibal Man*, a Spanish thriller, at the Eighth Street Playhouse. She agreed to the sudden plans with a catch, but a small one: I had to promise to call her from Ollie's, regardless of what time we got back from the city.

When the day finally arrived, I receded with a serious case of the jitters—but differently from the day Elena and I decided to have sex. I knew if I had bowed out with Elena, she'd get over it. But Ollie? What if my dick didn't get hard? He'd be insulted. He had a thin skin. Liquor was going to be necessary. Maybe weed. Both.

Just after lunch period, I passed Ollie in the second-floor hallway. Grinning like a Cheshire cat, Ollie pantomimed zipping his lips and throwing away the key. "Looking forward to a *magnifico* film," he called out.

The scheme was a rush, yet something about it also felt creepy, as if I were hooking up with Elena's dad or Lia's hunky boss. I started to feel like a high school girl when an aggressive guy sees her as a piece of meat. Not a person. I started to feel suspicious of Ollie's ulterior motives. But it was too late to back out.

Too anxious about running into Ollie again before the evening, I decided to go home to paint for a few hours. Inspired by the Andy Warhol *Campbell's Soup Can* prints I'd seen at the Museum of Modern Art, I started my own series of jumbo-sized food paintings: two fried eggs, a carton of milk, and peas and carrots in a blue ceramic bowl. Artists steal from each other all the time, right?

While mixing a palette for the colors of fried bacon, I allowed Ollie's narrative to creep back into my head: "I don't want your first time to be with a stranger." I told myself this was a paternal type of protection. This was just a trial run. Nothing serious. My fantasy plan was to find a guy closer to my age who I'd get to know, and then we'd experiment. A male Elena.

Distracted by the jumble of my thoughts, I fucked up the painting. The three slices of bacon looked like a soggy river raft made of logs. I quit.

I scanned the closet for threads. As I did, I realized something weird: I was dressing for another dude for the first time. What might Ollie find sexy? And did I really want to look sexy for him? I mean, he was gonna do me no matter how I looked, I figured. Did guys like the same things chicks liked? Starching a button-down for dinner at Ollie's house seemed forced. I cut the tags off a new pair of dark Sasson jeans that fit tight to the crotch and threw on a rust-colored pullover. White Stan Smiths, no socks. It was kind of a date, after all. Dinner and a guaranteed sleepover. And a guaranteed whatever sex-wise. What would he do to me? Would I be able to handle it? Would he do that thing up my butt? Did I even want him to?

We agreed to seven o'clock. Leaving my house by six thirty would guarantee I avoided seeing Lia and rehashing the late film lie. Instead, I scribbled a short note and left it atop the day's mail: *See you in the morning. Love, A.* I clipped three pink roses from the garden and arranged them in an Archie and Veronica jelly glass to accent the note.

It was the sort of late spring evening when the yellowy light and mint-tinged air united to elevate all five senses. As I locked the side door, the abundant stillness of the yard amplified the shakes in my hands and legs, like I was somehow moving quickly and slowly at the same time. I sat inside the Blue Whale and took a minute. Ollie will be a skillful pilot, I told myself. He'll be easy on me. If he isn't, I'll let him know so loudly that the neighbors will hear me. That idea calmed me down a bit.

With the windows closed, it quickly became apparent I'd overdosed on Aramis spray; the scent was so strong I gagged. "Fuck," I yelled. I rolled down all four windows and set sail.

The just-released Hall and Oates album with live versions of "Rich Girl" and "Sara Smile" sat on the passenger seat, a gift for Ollie. Twelve miles later, I pulled into the spot in front of his fairytale cottage, the dark shingles trimmed in white, paned windows bracketed with steely blue shutters. Bordering the picket fence was a line of pale blue Virginia day-flowers and a goldenrod or two. I heard Neil Young warbling as I walked toward the side patio.

I'd been to Ollie's house a handful of times—with Elena one evening for a yearbook meeting and to pick up cassettes for the homecoming dance, but never for dinner. Ollie existed in a tequila sunrise world; everything was brown, orange, and blue. His carroty Honda, pukka beads, and billowy linen V-neck shirts reflected his Laguna Beach upbringing. I remember being dazzled by the decor of the house: a group of brightly painted ukuleles centered on a wall the color of the ocean. Down the hallway were two surfboards and a collage of stolen road signs from Malibu,

Pacific Coast Highway, and Veracruz. Flowing from the fieldstone patio into the living room was a seamless cascade of flowering bushes and plants in Mexican pots. I imagined Ollie's cottage was a blueprint for the apartment I'd have in the city one day, but mine would have stacks of books, a library of music, and walls covered with drawings and paintings.

"Halloo," Ollie said, waving me in while rubbing spices into a bloody slab of meat on the kitchen counter. He was dressed in a nut-brown V-neck and drawstring pants. His center-parted hair and his thick 'stache were still wet. He was one part *Jesus Christ Superstar*, two parts *Godspell*. His wireframes, dotted with cooking oil, needed a wipe.

"I thought we'd grill steaks," he said, and I almost grinned to see he was exhibiting a case of jitters comparable to my own. "Make yourself at home. You know where everything is."

As I entered, Ollie sniffed the air. "Let me guess, Aramis?" he teased. Too jumpy to respond, I just nodded.

"Drinks," Ollie said. "You're in charge of beverages. And we're having grilled steaks. Oh, I already told you that. That comes with asparagus and salad . . . and wine, lots of wine," he said, rinsing his fingers of a soy sauce marinade.

So this is my date, I thought, *my maturity lesson*. The idea of the sexual side of Ollie still terrified me.

I extended the Hall and Oates album, which I had jokingly covered in Christmas wrapping. He tore it open, laughed, almost kissed me but decided against it, and then he pointed to the stereo. The oak dining table was set with orange woven mats, taupe and white checkered napkins, and chunky wine goblets. Spicy candles of clove, persimmon, and bamboo sat on the coffee table.

Prepping the grill, Ollie quizzed, "Feeling good? Remember—there's no pressure tonight."

I nodded excessively, trying too hard to please my seducer.

"How was your day?" he asked as if this were an ordinary visit. It was anything but.

"It flew," I said, lying. "I left school early—the best part of graduating is there's not much to do. Rehearsal, graduation, party!"

He gave me a grin that caused his pitted, crepe-paper skin to wrinkle up. He looked less foxy every time I saw him. I shuddered within. Would this even work? I wasn't sure anymore. But I also knew there was no backing out.

Shifting gears, I asked, "Are you stoked for Madrid? Duh, of course. You leave in what . . . less than three weeks?"

"Yes. So much crap to do before I go."

Guzzling cold white burgundy to calm my nerves, we gossiped about my classmates (who happened to be his students) and about the latest controversy: parents flipping out over the yearbook's Bowiesque cover depicting a strung-out alien tripping the universe.

By the time we plated dinner, my inner butterflies were shitfaced. I asked nervously, "Are we on a date? You're putting out, so it must be a date, correct?"

Shaking his head, Ollie chuckled. "Yeah, I guess it is."

The charred fat of the steak hung over the edge of my plate. Ollie told me they were medium-rare, but as I cut into the T-bone, a stream of bloody juice oozed out.

"The iron in medium-rare steak increases the oxygen in your blood," Ollie said. "Good for stamina and strength," he added, reaching over and squeezing my hand.

I laughed, uncertain if the comment was a preview for what was to come later.

He made me feel special, serving a dessert of vanilla ice cream with blackberries. When we finished, we cleared the table, loading each rinsed plate into the dishwasher. The stereo abruptly shifted to Parliament's "Flash Light."

In a boozy gesture, still feeling nervous but also playful, I shot Ollie a hip bump. He shimmied in place and hit me back with one, then another. Like two white boys pathetically miscast on *Soul Train*, we danced until I was laughing so hard I couldn't breathe. Then Ollie fell to the floor, holding his stomach, and I expected chunks of raw steak to come flying from his mouth. Ollie got up and excused himself to the bathroom for a good five minutes before returning with a flaming matchstick.

"Setting the mood," he cracked.

We were both smiling sheepishly, aware of the sweet absurdity of what was about to happen. Ollie inhaled the scent of each candle he lit. I loaded six albums onto the turntable for extended play.

"Aja," Ollie whispered, "Good choice. I love Steely Dan." He stepped behind me, twisted me around to face him, and then planted a gentle, short kiss on my lips.

"Icebreaker," he said, smiling.

I suppressed a giggle because it didn't seem romantic. But was this supposed to be romantic? Or just one item being checked off a list?

It was my first kiss not only with a male but with one who was also my teacher. The simple gesture stunned me. It was pleasantly warm, not bad actually, but I pulled away. The odor from Ollie's short, stocky body was robust. The patchouli stung my nostrils. The texture of his cheek was rough, his whiskers coarse.

"Come with me," Ollie whispered, leading me down the hall into a room dominated by the largest bed I'd ever seen. On the nearest wall was a circle of five carved masks Ollie had brought back from a trip to the Amazon. On the table beneath the display sat five flickering candles. Beige sheets turned down to a perfect fold were accented by a tropical print comforter, reminding me of a Venus flytrap.

Ollie, buzzed by wine, stepped clumsily out of his flip-flops. I kicked off my sneakers, equally clumsily. Ollie moved closer to peel off my jersey and then slithered out of his shirt. He removed his wireframes and then his watch. I trembled, not sure if I was supposed to take off my pants and crawl into bed, so I waited for direction. His pale torso, with a smattering of light hair, was smooth in contrast to the gravelly texture of his face.

I watched Ollie drop his boxers. Under a bush of yellow pubic hair rose his pink dick, stubby even at full attention. Like a good student, I followed his lead and tugged at the elastic waistband of my underwear, dropping them to my ankles. Naked and an arm's length away, I stood, ridiculous with panic.

"Smile," Ollie urged me. "This is supposed to be fun."

He drew me toward his paunch, holding steady for a second, before pulling me onto the bed.

We rolled, writhed, licked, sucked, nibbled, and fumbled for an incalculable amount of time. It wasn't magical. At least, not for me. Ollie oohed, aahed, and moaned. I pretended to do the same so he wouldn't feel abandoned. At times, I felt as if we were two frogs hopping about the mattress. Distracted in thought, I had to repeatedly convince myself to enjoy the orientation lesson.

I must have peeled my mind away from my body for a time because I came to just as Diana Ross cooed the words to "Touch Me in the Morning" from the third album I had stacked on the turntable. I calculated that two hours had passed. I felt like a balloon purged of a lifetime buildup of helium. At long last, affirmation—my inclination toward men was undeniable. The shock of another man's body was electrifying—even this one. Foreign yet familiar. Touching an erection that was not my own ranked beyond everything I'd ever known. Sniffing this, licking that, fondling there . . . When Ollie paused occasionally to administer instruction, I laughed nervously and then momentarily softened before I had to will my boner back to life. We nuzzled and sucked, poking and prodding mutually before jerking off onto our bellies.

This was my virgin jamboree. I expected classical music to play to drive home the major moment. But I heard no orchestra. Just Ollie breathing heavily from the effort. As we prepared for sleep, I asked, "Was it okay?"

Ollie nodded. "Indeed. A-plus, Andy," he answered as if we were in the classroom.

"Mom!" I blurted.

He looked around in shock, as if Lia had just entered the room.

"I promised to call Lia," I reminded him. "Be right back," I said, scuttling for my briefs as I hopped toward the wall phone in Ollie's kitchen. I didn't feel right calling her naked.

"Mom. We're back at Ollie's. The movie was intense. See you in the a.m. Love you."

Happy, she still couldn't resist one final scold: "Finally! It's one thirty. Now I gotta sleep, honey."

I returned to Ollie's bedroom, wondering whether there would be a rematch. I hoped not. I had had enough lessons for one evening. Lucky for me, he switched off the light as I climbed into bed. We settled into a snuggle. But I wriggled loose the moment Ollie drifted to sleep.

What was accomplished by sleeping with Ollie? Did it change who we were to each other?

Were we a couple now bound by sexuality? Lovers automatically?

Ollie was still—Ollie. I lay there for hours, wide-eyed, trying to define what I had just experienced—still in a haze. I was taken aback when the window shade revealed a slice of dawn.

Later, Ollie stirred and slowly but insistently initiated a new session. I wasn't interested but went along. I felt like I was giving a major performance.

I insisted that I take a shower alone, even though he was feeling frisky again. After I washed off the patchouli and cum, we met in the kitchen. Dressed in the previous night's clothes, I sat at the table and sipped coffee poured through a filter and picked at thick slices of buttered toast.

Ollie stood there grinning as if he had given me the gift of life, like he deserved the Teacher of the Year award. It made him look pathetic.

I thanked him for the initiation. He beamed from ear to ear. But I did not oversell my praise and prayed that Ollie realized I would not need a refresher course in the future.

Buttering his toast a second time, Ollie cautioned me, "Remember, Andy, this is our secret."

I nodded. I had decided the previous night that I would die of shame if anyone else ever knew about this soggy little adventure.

The following week, it was clear that I had not extinguished Ollie's flame.

He ticked up the courtship a notch. I went along with it, not wanting to disappoint him. He'd plant salty, unsigned notes in clandestine nooks, through the air vents in my locker door, or under my windshield wiper. In the hallway, there'd be a cryptic high-five or a whack across the butt if no one was looking. Spending the final weeks of school flirting with danger seemed arousing.

At his insistence, we got frisky in Ollie's Honda following a Saturday hike in the Delaware River Gorge. He gave me a blow job and then jerked himself off.

I was more confused about our relationship. Sex and affection were bound together in a bizarre package as if we were dating. I gave in, hoping my feelings would eventually match his. For the time being, even an imperfect bond met my immature emotional needs.

As Ollie's departure for Madrid grew close, my anxiety unjustifiably intensified. The dread of him being gone for the entire summer freaked me. Not only would I have to fend for myself as a new gay, but I was also afraid of feeling a new surge of abandonment first planted by my father. I'd miss Ollie badly even though I knew he and I should not be having sex.

The day before Ollie's flight, I drove to his cottage. I stretched across his bed as he manically packed. "Don't stress! They have stores in Madrid," I joked.

No response, and that unnerved me. I felt like Daddy was abandoning me again.

"Ollie? Hello? Did you already leave?" I spoke to him as a lover might, and not as a student. That evening, we shared a goodbye dinner at a French bistro within walking distance of his place. Over steak frites and a bottle of cheap burgundy, we chatted about the approaching summer. After the second pour of wine, for reasons that did not involve feeling drunk, I told Ollie I loved him. Unable to squelch my pathetic neediness, I asked, "Do you love me?"

As the words passed through my lips, I shook inside. What the fuck was I asking? And why?

"Whoa, Andy, I'm flattered. I love you too. I'm just not sure in what form."

I felt like I was about to cry. Maybe it was just the wine, I told myself.

"You're talking as if we've been seeing each other for a long time. I appreciate the magic we found. But let's enjoy our summer apart. It will be a time of growth for us both."

I wanted to punch him in the mouth. Rejecting me? Sounds like he was preparing for extra dick in Spain.

Is this how all gays treat newcomers? Fuck this gay thing!

I thought I was feeling tears of hurt welling up, but they were now tears of anger. I still kept them from flowing.

"In September, we can share our stories over bottles of wine. By then, Andy, we both might be different people!"

"Oh, you mean that I might be known as Andrew then?" It was the best I could do for a comeback. And it was lame. I had watched films with Lià where a rejected lady threw a glass of wine in her lover's face. Could I do that here?

Instead, I whimpered. He pacified me in a low voice. Unsuccessfully. By the time the soppy crème brûlée arrived, we had both slumped into silence.

"You have the whole world ahead of you, Andy," he said, trying again to wriggle out of what I thought were Ollie's clear responsibilities. "NYU, the city. You're going to make new friends—and one day be famous."

I sulked, silently. Out in the parking lot, I capped our goodbye with a lingering hug and a fleeting peck in the shadows. He pulled back from the kiss, I noticed.

The tears finally flowed once he got into his car, and I hated myself. Through the blur, I watched as Ollie floated away as if the force of gravity carried no weight.

Chapter 12

U nfolding the paper containing Ben's phone number, I studied his handwriting for clues:

BEN 212-664-7665

Block print, no last name. I copied the number onto a back page of the *TV Guide*, tore it off, and stashed it in my sock drawer.

Possibility revived my spirit, so I drove to the A&P to pick up a two-pound London broil, two large spuds, a head of garlic, sour cream, and a bunch of spinach for Lia's welcome home dinner. Gram had left three ripe Jersey tomatoes and a cucumber from her neighbor's garden on the back porch. I was eager to see Lia, but fearful I'd trip over my lies about roaming the city alone Friday night, getting shitfaced and, in short, raped. Jesus Christ, now I knew what Vietnam vets meant by a clusterfuck. Was I stumbling into chaos?

Roaming the supermarket aisles, I mulled over the appropriate time to call Ben. Before six, when Lia was expected home, would be the safest, but would a New York City dude be home at five thirty on a Tuesday? Unlikely.

When I walked in the door, I dropped the groceries and dialed 212-664-7665.

"Hello, you've reached the home of Ben and Neal. Leave a message after the tone."

I hung up in a panic. Who the fuck was Neal? Roommate? Brother? Lover? I needed to know. Seconds later, I redialed. Clearing my throat, I doubled down after the three beeps:

"Uh, hey. This message is for Ben. It's Andy from the Stones concert. Hey, great to meet you. Elena says hi. Guess I'll try you later . . . Uhm, bye."

Lame, lame, lame, but—off my plate.

I decided that calling back at nine o'clock wasn't too early or too late. But leaving my home number wasn't feasible. I didn't want an interrogation from Lia when Ben called asking for me. There was one thing in his favor: Ben's voice didn't sound bi, gay, or whatever.

Given the chaotic weekend, I was delighted by the simple comfort of preparing dinner for Lia. The rope bruises on my wrists now looked like a slight case of dermatitis. What still remained damaged was my psyche.

Rather than dwell, I did a load of laundry, whisked the grill clean, and marinated the beef in garlic and soy sauce before crashing on the sofa. Halfway through the article "The Reality of the Imposter Syndrome" in the June issue of *Psychology Today*, I heard Lia's car pull into the drive. Flinging the screen door open, I rushed out.

"Andy! You're already home? I'm so happy. I had no quarters to call, so I decided to just drive home."

"I figured you'd be stuck on the tarmac. I'm making dinner. I didn't go to work. Elena and I got home late."

"How were the Stones? Were you and Elena careful getting home?"

"We had a blast. No, we are not dating again," I said.

I made a chopped salad of tomatoes with scallions, cucumbers, and black olives while Lia unpacked. I'd already set the kitchen table with our yellow and white everyday plates and hastily folded napkins. The handful of daisies I had brought in from the side yard had concealed an army of black ants. They were now marching single file down the vase and across a placemat. Hastily, I crushed the insects and tossed the arrangement.

Lia came back down and fixed her signature dressing of red wine vinegar, olive oil, and oregano as she recounted her trip.

"The symposium was chaos but a lot of fun," she chattered. "Half the women were fanatics, the other half were intelligent, driven. You should come to the march if Ruth and I go. They expect seventy-five thousand people. Ratification is so important. Many lesbians, but who cares. I made so many new friends. I brought you a button: ERA YES."

Nibbling a charred end slice of the London broil, Lia said, "Andy, this is delicious. The steak is perfect. Medium-rare. And baked potatoes with sour cream, wow."

"Glad you like it, Lia. Welcome home."

"Andy, I have news."

"Are you pregnant?"

"Wise-ass. Yesterday the CEO offered me a big promotion. The official title is VP of U.S. Marketing. But it means relocating to headquarters in Fairfax. I'd make a lot more money, but how can I relocate with you starting college?"

"Uh—" I stammered.

"On the other hand, we could afford your tuition *and* room and board. I have no idea what to do."

"Mom, I'm so proud of you. You earned this."

"Really, you're not upset? I would be appointed the company's first woman executive. We have weeks to think about it," she said, sounding both giddy and guilt-ridden.

I decided I wouldn't prevent her from accepting the transfer. Over slivers of peach pie, we were discussing the promotion when her bosom buddy Ruth phoned.

Hanging up after forty-five minutes, Lia announced, "Ruth did some digging. The offer is twelve thousand dollars a year less than what men in the same position earn. She thinks I should ask for more money. I'm going to speak up tomorrow."

"Why don't you treat yourself to a hot bubble bath and relax to prep yourself for the battle tomorrow? While you're soaking, I'll call Tommy in Boston, okay?"

I pulled the phone into my room, lowered the stereo volume, and rehearsed three variations.

"Hello Ben, Andy Pollock here."

"Yo, Ben. Andy!"

"Hey, Ben, this is Andrew."

After two short rings, he picked up. I gulped and said, "Ben? It's Andy."

"Andy! Hey, how's it going? Hoping you'd call."

He was hoping.

"Wasn't the concert great?" I said, trying hard to sound casual. "I stayed home today so my hearing could come back."

"I got to the studio around ten. I'm wiped out, but it was worth it. Lucky you, playing hooky. So you missed a day as a construction worker? You wimp," he joked.

I decided not to correct him about my job. "How was your day?"

"Long. We started a storyboard for a new campaign, but it wasn't flowing, so we gave up after a few hours. We'll try again tomorrow. I'm determined."

"So, um . . . I was glad to hear that Lula isn't your . . . girlfriend." Lowering my voice, I added, "Lula told Elena you were bi or something. Is that true?"

"Uhhhhh . . . yeah, I guess you could say that."

"You don't sound too sure."

"I'm pretty certain, I think. Andy, what's your story?"

Belly down on the carpet, I whispered, "It's not easy to talk about right now. No, I mean it's all kind of new. Plus, I'm living at home."

"Been there. I get it." Ben chuckled. "Your secret is safe with me. Hey, Neal has to use the phone."

"Sure. Hey, who's Neal—your roommate?"

"Yes. Neal's great, from New Orleans. Runs a gallery below Houston Street. A good egg. You'd like him. Everybody likes Neal. Want to get together next weekend?"

Unfamiliar with the term "good egg," I rolled with it, responding, "How about Saturday? I'll come to the city."

"Saturday it is! I'm downtown—oh, I told you that. South of the Palladium. Let me plan something. I'll call in a day or two with details. What's good for you on Saturday—daytime? Nighttime? Both?" Ben giggled.

"Daytime is good, but I'd have to be back at night. Ben, I feel weird giving you my home number, nothing personal—"

"Oh right, no sweat. Hey, call me on Thursday night around nine and we'll confirm. We'll go to a movie—let's see *Pretty Baby* . . . and get food. You have nothing to worry about. I'm a nice guy from Ohio."

"Great. So I'll call you Thursday at nine. Night, Ben."

"Goodnight, Andy-boy, sweet dreams," he said, sending shivers down my spine.

What seemed a far-flung dream suddenly looked like a reality. A date with Ben, a good-looking regular dude whose voice triggered a boner. Andy Pollock has a date with a guy! I wanted to tell the world my news.

Chapter 13

Hunched over like Quasimodo, I jerked the string attached to the bare hanging lightbulb under the attic's eave. I decided to dig into the hidden archives to prepare for my date with Ben. Under a loose floorboard, I had stashed three brown paper bags. Whenever the *New York Times* or the *Village Voice* reviewed a book with a homosexual theme, I'd log its title in a purple journal. Over the months, this formed a syllabus, divided between fiction and nonfiction. Beside the journal were books, magazines, and articles I'd gathered from various sources.

Back in March, I noticed an ad in the *Voice* for a bookstore with the slogan, "Think Straight, Be Gay." The following Tuesday, I cut school and took the train into the city to The Oscar Wilde Memorial Bookstore, located on the same street as Tug's. It was raining, so I covered my head with my raincoat hood for anonymity and sprinted to the address on Christopher Street.

It was located up a short flight of stairs in a brownstone close to Sheridan Square. Stepping into the exquisitely paneled parlor room, my eyes were drawn to a rack of magazines opposite the front door. *Blueboy* was a homo version of *Playboy* and *Penthouse*. Petrified by the explicit images on the cover, I did an about-face and raced toward more academic publications displayed on a mahogany bookshelf. Although I had come for a copy of *The Best Little Boy in the World*, a novel well-reviewed in the *Voice*, I added a few issues of journals to my stash. More than anything, I wanted two or three copies of *Blueboy*, but I feared that lightning would strike the second I left the store. With the memoir and publications in hand, I approached the bespectacled clerk behind the desk.

"I wager you're a high school student. True?" he asked.

"I'm seventeen, eighteen in May. Am I allowed to buy these?"

"Oh, yes, for certain," he responded. "There are no restrictions. If you have questions or need recommendations, let me know."

This exchange was casual, and that made it all the more remarkable—my first dialogue with an openly gay man.

While my fear of being inside the shop did not evaporate, I revisited the Oscar Wilde Memorial Bookstore a few times that spring to add to the library stockpiled beneath the attic planks.

I slid aside the doormat and lifted the floorboard to uncover my stash. I was looking for the book titled *Men Loving Men*. Maybe it might have a few tips on dating etiquette. Under a tattered copy of *The Front Runner* sat a cheesy novel titled *Mountain Stud*. I had picked it out of the free bin in a used bookstore on Bleecker Street. On the cover was an illustration of a straggly-haired bad boy.

The illustration gave me an immediate gut punch—the grungy dude reminded me of Fucking-fuck. My body shuddered as I recalled that Ben worked with Damon whoeverthefuck his name was. Ben didn't seem to like the guy—and had told me so. Questioning Ben about Damon would generate suspicion. Even worse, what if Ben asked Damon, "Do you know Andy, the kid with the unibrow sitting in your seats?" Would Damon tell Ben about the night we spent together and describe me as a drunk, a cocktease, and a thief? All three labels, I guess, would have been accurate that night.

The ringing of the telephone distracted me from my pity party. It was Elena.

"We're going to see Maya's friend Rocco in summer theater in Montclair Saturday night. *Carousel*, *Gigi*, or maybe it's *Showboat* . . . one of those ridiculously upbeat old-fashioned musicals. Maya said it was *campy*—what's that mean?"

"E, campy means tacky-kitschy-silly. It's kind of a gay word, I think," I said, trying to sound unsure. "I want to meet Maya and Rocco, but I have plans Saturday. I'm going to a movie with Ben—and Lula," I added defensively.

"You are? Come to Montclair. I mean, hanging out with Ben and Lula sounds fun, but you can do that anytime. And you hardly know them. These are important friends I want you to meet," she prodded.

"Yeah, but—"

"Plus, Rocco will be there. You have to meet him. He's gay. He's cute!"

"How about next weekend? I'm already committed. I also need to spend more time in the city since I'm going to be living there in a couple of months."

"I get it, cutie-pie Ben is way cool. Hey, Andy—it's really only Ben, isn't it?"

"Yes." I gulped.

"Be careful. There's a lot of bad shit going down in the city, especially at night."

"What are you talking about? We just defied death by walking Fourteenth Street after the concert."

"I can't believe I haven't seen you since Monday."

"It's only Wednesday. By the way, Lia is seriously considering the transfer."

"Good for Lia. Good for you too. What movie are you and Ben seeing?"

"*Pretty Baby*. It's that art film with Brooke Shields. We're seeing a Saturday matinee."

"So why can't you come that night to Montclair? Hey, we should go see *Thank God It's Friday*. Maya said it was hilarious. *Grease* opened last week. Let's go see that Sunday."

"*Grease* on Sunday. It's a date."

"I'm dying to hear how it goes with Ben, 'cause it sounds like a date. Wait—you can't join me because you're spending the night with Ben. Oh my God—"

"Nah, it's just a movie. Tell Maya and Rocco I'll meet them soon. Love ya."

"Oh my God, an honest-to-goodness sleepover with Ben. Good luck."

Ben and I spoke Thursday night. This time I wasn't as neurotic. Praying for a lengthy chat, I poured a cranberry juice on the rocks, propped myself on the bed, and closed the door. Ben told me he and Neal were heading out for Indian food on East Sixth Street. I didn't admit that Indian cuisine had never grazed my lips, but did assert I knew the difference between South Asian Indians and Native American Indians. Saturday's plan: we'd meet on Sixth Avenue at two o'clock in front of the Waverly Theater. Ben would buy the tickets.

Ben informed me that the director, Louis Malle, was a master of essential cinema, and it was controversial because of twelve-year-old Brooke Shields simulating sex with a bordello john. I didn't tell him I'd already read the *Times* review. I understood I needed to step up my game around Ben.

Saturday morning I woke with one feverish thought: Kissing Ben on our date was a priority. Also a pressing concern: What do I wear? The outfit I wore to Ollie's was too casual, and daytime would be warmer. Cut-offs? Baggy denim overalls? I fumbled through my closet and found a tan pullover with red stripes. Bingo. I added faded Levi's and royal blue Tigers, the same trainers Billy Sive sported in *The Front Runner.* I didn't want to show up in the Stan Smiths I wore to the Stones.

Then a thought seized me: Damon. What if I ran into that fuck while walking with Ben? It would be curtains for us.

I found Lia scrubbing the floor in her dingiest clothes and sidestepped her for a splash of java.

"I can't believe how dirty this floor gets with just the two of us. Morning, honey. You sure slept in!"

"Morning, Mom. What can I do to help?"

"Please stay off the wet spots. Vacuum the carpet when you're awake? What are your plans today?"

"I'm taking the train into the city around lunchtime."

"Want me to come with you?"

"I'm meeting Ben and Lula for a movie, the couple Elena and I met at the Stones concert. He's at NYU, so I'm learning about school from him." A modest fib. "Mom, I need to meet people in the city. I'm going to be living in the dorm in two months."

"Don't you think I know that? The day is circled on my calendar in black marker. Please be careful—there are too many crazy people these days. What time will you be home?"

"I have no idea . . . home before ten, okay?"

"That's too late. Be home by nine, before it gets dark."

"You've got to be kidding—"

"Okay, okay, you're a man now—ten at the latest. Now help me move the chairs. I have to scrub under the table."

Chapter 14

Coming out onto Sixth Avenue, I saw *Pretty Baby* in jumbo black letters on the Waverly Theater's marquee. My Timex put me seven minutes late, yet there was no line, only Ben, cross-legged on the concrete, reading a paperback under the ticket window. His cheeks were shiny pink sponges absorbing the sunlight, topped by a fluffy mop of brown hair and offset by the gold rims of his aviator sunglasses. He stretched his forearms as he saw me approach. His black tee had Lou Reed's face silk-screened across the front in white ink.

"I got tickets. Look, no line. I guess because the movie opened a couple of weeks ago. Want to walk around before showtime?"

Eager to offer a cool-dude attitude, I responded, "Sounds like a plan. How much do I owe you for the tix?"

"Tickets are on me. You can pick up the popcorn. How was your trip in? You said it's a short train ride, right?"

"On Saturdays, the trains run slow," I said, brushing perspiration from my forehead.

"In New York, being tardy is expected," he grinned. We ducked onto quiet Cornelia Street, which was lined with maple saplings. "Watch out! Dog shit," I cried, swerving Ben from the curb, my valor forcing me to grab his arm.

"Close one. Thanks. Do you know where your dorm is?" Ben asked.

"At the end of University Place on Union Square West," I said. "My adviser told me I'll only have one roommate. One day, I want to live in one of these classic brownstones. Cast-iron fencing is so beautiful. I'd love to know who lives in these buildings."

"My Uncle Jack lives in a brownstone like this, over on Ninth. It's a great street with a triangle of greenery in the center. He lives with Perry. They're a couple, usually."

"Whoa, you have a gay uncle here in the city. That's wild. Is he queeny?" Immediately I wanted to withdraw the stupid question.

"No," Ben said, laughing, "Not at all. Who cares if he was though. Andy, do you have issues about being gay?"

I winced and pasted an apologetic smile on my face. I was going to mess this date up. Stupid Jersey kid with macho hang-ups. Fuck!

"People are people. Uncle Jack is great. He helped me get settled in the city. He jokes that he knew I was gay before I did, something I'm still trying to figure out."

"You don't look gay. How would your uncle know?"

"There you go again with the judgment," Ben said, his upper lip tightening. "There are all kinds of gays. You have a lot to learn: butch, femme. Your radar will get better once you start living here."

Scared he was going to get pissed off and leave me, I changed the subject.

"So, remind me, you went to Ohio University and then NYU. How long have you been in the city?"

"A little over two years. I transferred junior year. My photography prof used to live here. He's gay and knows my uncle. They plotted together to get me to New York."

I forced a laugh in hopes of getting back on Ben's good side.

"They both suspected I was gay. They wanted me to have a better shot at being myself. Anyway, given my interest in photography, film, and communications, they helped me to transfer to NYU."

"Having family here, you're lucky, Ben."

"How did you decide on NYU?" he asked.

"Good question. I didn't even know they had a fine arts department. Two of my art teachers helped me build a portfolio. They advised me on applying to places like Carnegie Mellon, Montclair State, Tyler in Philly. Oh, and Cooper Union. After the interview at NYU, I was sold."

"I'll take you on a tour of the campus," Ben offered.

I avoided asking Ben about his agency job, scared it would lead to Damon and the tickets.

"Hey, it's two-forty," he said. "I'm totally craving popcorn, so let's head over."

"Sure," I said, wondering if he would hold my hand in the movie.

"Hey, did you know that tomorrow is the Gay and Lesbian Pride March?"

"Yeah, I read about it in the *Voice*. Did you plan on going?"

Judging thousands of gay men as my competition, I hoped Ben would say no. I added, "I'm not ready for that scene yet. I saw TV coverage of last year's parade. I saw a lot of freaks: guys in leather, drag queens. It makes the parade look like a joke."

Scrunching his face, Ben countered, "There you go again with your prejudice. This community is made up of a lot of people. They're all trying to be who they are. Just because they aren't like you, that doesn't make them wrong."

Shit! I did it again. Opened my idiot Jersey mouth. Strike two.

"Well, I'm going—as a spectator. I might take my Nikon to snap photos. A good vantage point is Washington Square Park. Uncle Jack asked me to march, but I'm not sure I'm ready to jump in. Still, I don't bad-mouth other people."

I gave Ben a sad look that I hoped would serve as an apology. I was really sticking my foot in it.

After we got inside, I took a long-delayed piss in the men's room, as Ben ordered popcorn, no butter, and two Cokes. As he brushed away my fistful of dollars, I wondered if sharing one large bucket was frugality or confirmation we were on a date.

As the film unspooled, we learned that Susan Sarandon's character, a prostitute named Hattie, was raising her beautiful young daughter, Violet, in a New Orleans cathouse at the turn of the twentieth century. During the languid first scene, I began to feel aroused beside Ben.

My mind drifted. I imagined Ben and me as a couple, holed up in a cozy Village apartment on a rainy day with a crock of beef stewing in the oven. On the sofa in sweatpants and thick wooly socks, we'd huddle as a Hitchcock film flickered on the TV. Just as the scenario lulled me into a catnap, one of the bordello johns fired a gun, and Ben dropped the popcorn bucket on the floor with a clunk.

Tittering with embarrassment, we rocked in our seats. That's when I caught the first whiff of Ben's underarms. Warm shivers tickled my spine. I leaned back to peer at Ben out of the corner of my eye. He sat still, arms crossed, as if hypnotized by the screen.

When Brooke Shields reentered the frame, Ben pitched forward, elbows to his knees to absorb her exquisiteness. I considered leaning my leg toward Ben's, curious how he'd react when they touched. I fantasized that he'd return the gesture and then rest his stout fingers on top of mine and squeeze. As my leg drifted toward Ben's, the scene on the screen involved a dinner party where Violet was perched erotically on a silver tray, the table of ravenous men hungry for her youth. Ben lurched forward at the incredible visual, away from my yearning knee.

I never got another chance to flirt. The final credits began rolling.

"Well, that was disturbing," I whispered.

"Tremendous," Ben countered.

I stood up, preparing to exit. Just then, I felt Ben's meaty hand on my arm, and I swooned.

"Hold on," Ben whispered. "Wait until the credits are over, out of respect to the filmmakers," he said, suddenly removing his hand from my forearm. I froze, disappointed, and then plunged back into the seat.

Later, as we walked east toward Washington Square Park, Ben was bubbling over.

"Malle is definitely one of the most poetic directors working today. The close-ups of Brooke's face—portraits of a woman ripening inside the body of a child."

"I found it creepy. Did you see the way the men licked their chops like popping a young girl's virginity was a prize? Men can be pigs."

"That's the whole point . . . to make the audience uncomfortable. That's what true art does! Malle is saying that in 1917, this was the way of life for some. It may seem revolting, and reviews have been mixed, I'll give you that."

"Have you seen a lot of Malle's movies?"

"Yep, but this is his first film in English. We should go see *Murmur of the Heart*. It's impressive. He paints a portrait of intimacy between a mother and her son."

The only word I heard was "we."

"Have you been to Europe, Ben?"

"Not yet. Uncle Jack and Perry want to take me to Spain and France next summer. They go all the time. Have you?"

"No, but I went to Bermuda last spring break with Mom."

"Hey, let's go to Kiev!"

"That's a long way from here. Russia?"

"Not the city." Ben chuckled, lightly punching my shoulder and making me start to harden. "It's a diner in my neighborhood on Second Avenue— Ukrainian Village. They have superb pierogis. Delicious and cheap."

"I've never eaten Ukrainian food."

"Andy, what time do you have to head back?"

"It sucks, but I have to be home by ten. I kind of have a curfew."

"We'll make sure you're home by ten," Ben assured. "September will be here before you know it."

I took in the cluttered fuss of the Kiev Diner. The place was only half-full, but the diners were a mix of Ukrainians, punk rockers, and artists. We snagged a booth by the window, sliding in over the worn red vinyl.

Face-to-face, Ben asked, "What's your family like? Brothers? Sisters?"

"Nope, just Lia and me. My parents separated after I was born. Actually, my father up and left."

"Andy, that's intense. You don't see him at all?"

"Nope," I said, trying to sound casual but wondering how much to reveal on a first date.

"Where does he live?"

"Norway. He's an ex-Marine. He had mental health issues. The responsibility was too much for him," I explained, adopting Lia's words. "Lia raised me alone. She's fucking awesome."

"Wait—you call your mom Lia?"

"I call her Lia because we have a unique relationship. Many kids call their parents by their first name these days. It's progressive."

"If I called my mom Ellen, she'd send me to a shrink. Does Lia have a career?" Ben asked.

"Yep, an ambitious career woman in marketing," I said. "Honestly, she's Wonder Woman."

"Your mom is Lynda Carter? Hot!" Ben said, laughing. "Sounds like you absolutely adore her. That's radical, Andy."

A pudgy waitress approached, her grey bun capped by black netting. The tag on her uniform identified her as Zlata. She placed two plastic menus and amber-toned tumblers of water on the table without a word.

"What about you . . . parents, brothers, sisters?"

"I'm the second youngest of five boys, and the rest of the litter live in Ohio."

"Damn," I mouthed.

"Yep, we have a big old farmhouse outside of Columbus in New Albany, but we're not farmers. Dad has a pipe-fitting business—about a hundred employees. Mom's a housewife. Church, committees, all that. They're okay. I mean, I love them. A little small-minded occasionally. Three of my brothers work for my dad. Josh, the youngest, will be a freshman at Ohio State. He's a total zipperhead. He's your age."

"Zipperhead?" I puzzled.

"Buzzcut. He might break away from the pack to do pre-med next year. I escaped for good, but it's nice to go home for a few days now and then. Eat Buckeye pie, play with the dogs. Four, all golden retrievers. Andy, how did you get to be so mature for your age? Eighteen-year-olds back home are randy punks. Josh spends half his time playing baseball. You're like an adult packaged into a teenager."

"I'm flattered, dude," I said, fighting a blush. "I'm big and hairy for my age, so don't let this baby face fool you."

I sounded fucking ridiculous, but Ben grinned anyway.

"Would you like to order?" said Zlata, emerging out of nowhere.

"Ben? You first," I insisted, deciding I'd just repeat his order because every damned thing on the menu was foreign.

"Chicken Kiev. And a Coke, please. Pickled cabbage on the side," Ben said.

"Same for me, thanks," I said, trying to sound confident.

Zlata headed to the kitchen.

I asked Ben, "Okay, what did I order? What's Chicken Kiev?"

"Oh, right, Chicken Kiev . . . It's chicken stuffed with butter and more butter. It arrives on a platter, looking like an albino football. When you cut into the center, the butter squirts, coating the rice. It's kind of neat."

"Uh, okay. I'm game," I lied, wanting to impress my date.

"It must be amazing, growing up just outside New York," Ben added. "Better than the Ohio boonies like me."

"It is. Anyway, Maple is quirky."

"Maple? That's the name of your town?"

"Sorry, Maple Ridge. We all call it Maple. Anyway, it's a suburb—and very lily-white. Mr. Beardsley, the English teacher, is the lone Black person, and behind his back . . . well, people suck. Not one Japanese, no Asians at all. I can't wait to be in the city and make friends from all over the world. You have no idea how many of my neighbors wouldn't step a foot inside New York. Scared they'd get mugged or shot."

"Andy, to be honest, New York isn't safe these days, but it's worth it to be around so many creative deviants. You just have to be careful. Stay out of Central Park at night. South Bronx. And the Westside Piers. Oh, and the alphabet streets A, B, C, D. They're packed with burnt-out tenements, drug dens."

"That doesn't leave many safe spaces," I grinned. "Thanks for the pep talk. Jeez."

Zlata returned with two steaming platters containing glistening mounds covered with bright orange seasoning. As Ben expertly stabbed the center of his chicken, a burst of oily lava secreted onto the plate. I did likewise. As the knife pierced the fowl, its sauce squirted halfway across the laminate tabletop. We giggled like five-year-olds.

Ben declared the first bite "scrumptious" before resuming his tutorial. "The best music clubs? All downtown. The most excellent ethnic food—Chinese, Mexican, Italian, and Indian—is on Sixth Street. All downtown."

Before long, we were chewing the final bites of our dinner. Ben leaned across the table, his blue-grey eyes piercing me.

"It's only seven thirty. Want to see my place? Just two blocks away. I'll get you in a cab to the train before ten? My treat."

"Sure," I smiled. This was sounding more like a date every moment.

Ben grabbed the check Zlata had placed face down on the table. "This one's on me, sport."

"Then I'm leaving a tip," I said, tucking four crisp dollars under my plate.

Five minutes later, walking south under sprinkling rain, we turned into the vestibule of Ben's sturdy red-limestone building.

"The owners live on the top floor," Ben explained, wiping rain from my forehead and making me swoon. "They're two Irish ladies who know Uncle Jack. They keep an eye on me by delivering scones, fresh vegetables, oxtail stew. Neal suspects they're a lesbian couple. Once in a blue moon, they invite me to sit in the garden and sip sweet wine as they talk about growing up outside Dublin. Come on in, sport. This is my place."

The main room had a lived-in hippie vibe. There were pieces of worn furniture. Oriental rugs on the floor, old-world wood-framed prints, and photos hanging on walls that were painted forest green.

"The best part is the washer and dryer. They're old, but they work. In New York, washers and dryers are like gold."

"I love the beaded curtain," I lied.

The kitchen consisted of an abrupt counter, a thinner-than-standard fridge, and an enormous white porcelain stove that housed six gas burners.

Cookware dangled from a hammered metal rack, and on the window ledge hung little pots of herbs. Beyond the garden door was a rain-soaked garden containing wrought-iron chairs and a wooden bench, all needing fresh paint. A crooked assembly of plant beds lined the stone wall. One tree had branches touching all three buildings in its perimeter.

"We have tomatoes growing over there. They ripen by mid-July. Forgive my manners, I should be playing host, not tour guide. Do you favor beer, red wine, orange soda, or cold tap water?"

"Beer," I said, wanting to appear as regular as Ben. He headed for the fridge.

"Heineken," he announced, springing the caps midair.

I fit my lips around the bottle top when I really wanted to plant a wet one on Ben's lips. But I wasn't convinced this would happen. My childish ego was afraid that the romance I'd built up was simply an illusion. But then Ben tilted his head and grinned at me, holding the stare a few dreamy seconds longer than expected. If Ben's invitation took a strange turn into butt sex—I might have to race out the door. But I was still up for some high school smooching.

"Do you know the Patti Smith album—*Horses*? It's incredible."

"I know Patti Smith. She's from New Jersey, like Bruce."

"I haven't heard her perform live yet, but she's played CGBG a handful of times."

I presumed that CBGB was a club. I didn't ask because I didn't want to look uncool.

"So you're into Patti, Bruce, the Stones," I said. "Do you listen to Elton John? *Goodbye Yellow Brick Road* is my all-time favorite. Do you think Elton's gay? What about Bowie?"

"Elton John? Brilliant. *Madman across the Water, Caribou, Tumbleweed Connection*, freaking *Captain Fantastic*. And yes, I'm a hundred and ten percent sure Elton is gay. Bowie claims he's bi. Both are radical. I've been getting more into punk. The Clash, the Ramones, Sex Pistols. Blondie is pretty hot. Heard about the Dead Kennedys?"

I could only nod yes, overwhelmed.

Placing the needle on vinyl, Ben liberated Patti's gruff sound while lighting a yellow candle on the shorter of two walnut bookcases. As he stepped into the kitchen, I scanned his library containing textbooks on cinema, photography, and a short stack that looked unread, *The Basketball Diaries, Eye of the Needle*, and *Metropolitan Life*.

I picked up a gadget. "Is this a slingshot?" I asked, remembering my own sweet past with this weapon and my grandfather.

"Good call, sport," Ben said when he returned.

Did I suddenly have a nickname?

"My brothers and I carved and sold slingshots as kids. We named it Hoppe Shots because that's my last name. Sadly, slingshots were never a hot commodity in New Albany. This one is from Chinatown. Uncle Jack bought it for me as a childhood reminder. He said if thieves break into the apartment, I can shoot them with Raisinets."

"My Pop-pop gave me a slingshot for my eighth birthday. He said it was hand-carved by an Indian tribe in Pennsylvania."

My mind wandered. As Patti barked the last notes of "Redondo Beach," Ben lunged his face into mine, and our mouths locked.

"Helloooo, anybody home?"

"Hey, Neal," Ben said, disengaging quickly and trying to sound casual. "Hi . . . you're home early."

"They closed the gallery for the night, so here I am. Sorry, am I interrupting y'all? I can leave."

"This is Andy, and we just got back from Kiev."

"Hey, Andy," he said, placing two bags of groceries on the counter. "Welcome to our paradise. I'm going to make andouille with dirty rice. Should be ready by ten."

"Neal's from Louisiana. He's the best cook I know," Ben said.

"Hi, Neal, excellent to meet you," I said, smothering my annoyance that he had interrupted the kiss I had been waiting for all night.

Neal was as bony as a skeleton. But a dollop of chestnut hair swooped over his right eye, making him more alluring. His face was offset by sky-blue eyes that were bugged-out and weird. He had a fluffy handlebar mustache. Although a Southern transplant, Neal's style screamed avant-garde New Yorker. A bold, brown-striped blouse fused into a pair of beige flares that were offset by a suede shoulder bag. I put out my hand. Neal limply returned the shake.

"Darling, you're pretty," he drawled. "How old are you?"

"Eighteen."

"Eighteen? Chicken! Well, good for you. Don't let me get in the way, boys," he grinned.

"Neal, I'm going to get Andy a cab. He has to head home—back in ten."

"Well, Andy darlin', I hope to see more of you."

Ben was resolved to keep me on schedule. We walked with a fast clip along the sidewalk, Ben's hands buried deep into his pockets and eyes suddenly downcast, so I worried that I had made him mad.

"Andy . . . this was so . . . cool," he said, whisking away my fear. "Can we do something next weekend? Come on Saturday and stay over? I'll plan something outstanding."

"Totally," I blurted out before he had finished. "I'll call you—tomorrow? I'm definitely coming back next weekend."

He found me a cab just as the rain resumed.

"Take him to the Christopher Street station, please."

As I was climbing into the back seat, Ben ducked his head in the cab for a goodbye kiss. I was uptight in front of the taxi driver, and I flinched so that Ben's lips landed on my cheek.

"He doesn't care," Ben whispered, stretching in to land another one on my lips. It was short but intense.

Chapter 15

As the cab raced across East Seventh Street, I felt giddy. All day I had agonized over Ben's intentions. Being an insecure moron in times of doubt, I wasn't able to distinguish between his cryptic cues and my hopeful delusions.

When like a puma in the thicket he pounced, I was fervent prey. I suspected that we could have played in Ben's sandbox for hours if his roommate hadn't shown up.

Lame-O Neal!

Lia was reclining across the sofa in a light summer robe, *Gather Together in My Name* against her bosom when I trickled through the front door minutes after ten.

"Andy. I must have dozed off. I'm glad you're home."

"Enjoying Angelou's memoir, Mom?" I said evenly, hiding my lasting excitement over the kiss.

"Yes, every bit as good as *Caged Bird*," she answered, shaking off the sleep. "Also the mother of a young son, so I can relate. How was the city?"

"*Pretty Baby* was interesting. You should see it. We went for Ukrainian food and walked around Washington Square. Tons of people were out, until it rained."

"Your friends—they are in college, correct?"

"Lula's in her third year at NYU, in something to do with fashion. She's from London."

"Lula . . . will Elena be jealous?"

"Mom, I've told you a million times, Elena and I are now friends. Nothing romantic. Lula, Ben, and I are all friends. Remember we met them at the Stones concert? City friends—which I need!"

"I'm sleepy, so I think I'll read in bed. Night, honey."

There were limits to our unconventional relationship as cool mother and son. For one, I wasn't ready to report on my first date with a dude. *Mom—guess what? There's this awesome guy I have a crush on.*

It was no secret Lia regarded me as the ideal son who would one day marry and produce plenty of grandchildren for her to spoil. Back when I first reported that Elena and I had split, she looked upset and asked me in confusion, "Andy, what type of girls do you like?"

I replied, "All depends on the girl, but I wouldn't exclude Black, Hispanic, Asian, whoever."

"As long as you love her, nationality, religion, or skin color doesn't matter."

It was a very generous point of view, but I knew her permissiveness had limits. Any type of girl was fine—as long as she was a biological female.

Sunday morning, my Charlie Brown mug sat on the kitchen table next to a box of Entenmann's Coffee Cake and a note: *Playing tennis with Ruth, be home after lunch, love you.* As I poured coffee, the phone rang.

"Andy, what are you doing today?" Elena asked. "No—forget that and just tell me, how was your date with Mr. Perfect?"

"Hold your horses. I'll tell you everything later. Let's go to the park around noon and lay out. It's a gorgeous day. Tonight, we can see *Grease*."

"Sounds fabulous! I'll make sandwiches if you bring soda. I'll pick you up. So . . . no preview, Mr. Secretive?"

"*Pretty Baby* was exceptional."

"You are sooo impossible. Okay, later."

"Okay. One word: It was outstanding!"

"You big dope, that's three words." She laughed. "Okay, I expect every detail later. See you at twelve," Elena said, hanging up before I could reply.

Later at the park, Elena lifted a wicker basket from her trunk. "Here comes Little Red Riding Hood," I teased.

"That's me!" she said, swishing the tail of one of her Baba's floral scarves off her shoulder. "Mystery-meat sandwiches, two peaches Luba picked up at a roadside stand, one gigantic box of raisins." Clad in fringed Daisy Dukes, a knotted white T-shirt, and the vintage headgear, Elena was a vision of eccentricity.

"Let's go where there are no people. I'm tired of idiots," she said, pointing the painted nail of her index finger. "Over there, close to the spooky trees."

"Okay, but let's sit in the sun since I'm here to get some color. Hunt down a dry spot," I said, "'coz it rained last night."

As soon as the blanket skimmed the grass, Elena blurted, "Tell me everything. Don't worry, I'm comfortable with all that gay stuff now."

"You never said you were uncomfortable," I said, unpacking the basket as she popped the pull tabs on two cans of 7 Up.

"Well, it's a process. Gimme some time. I love you, and now I have to share you with someone else. A boy. Don't worry, I don't *love* love you. But I adore you," Elena conceded.

"I love you too. It's a little weird. I feel like I'm cheating on you."

"Andy, if he were a girl, I'd be pissed. Not really. Well, maybe. What's Ben like outside of stoner-concert-dude mode?"

"Rad. After *Pretty Baby*, we got food in the East Village, walked around. Oh, I met his roommate. Neal."

"Hot movie followed by dinner—definitely a date. Did you have sex?"

"Nooo. The Ukrainian restaurant was near Ben's apartment, so after dinner, he invited me over. He's from a town called New Albany in Ohio. Has four brothers, an uncle in the city. A gay uncle."

"A gay uncle?" She giggled.

"Hey, I'm starving," I said, chomping into what tasted like salami and provolone on rye, allowing spicy mustard to ooze down my chin.

"Wait . . . Yugoslavian? I'll have to take Luba and Ham—"

"Ukrainian, not Yugoslavian. Ben's apartment is a legit grown-up pad. Furniture, tons of books, curtains, everything. And a garden. In the city— a garden."

"He must be rich. Andy has a rich boyfriend," she chanted three times, interrupted by bites of sandwich.

"Stop. He only rents. As for my boyfriend, can you say that about two guys?"

"Jesus, grow up, Andy. What else would he be?"

"People say 'lover.' I've read that a lot. Like—*Armando's Latin lover, Carlos.*"

"'Lover' sounds far too dramatic. I hate that shit. Stick with 'boyfriend.' Or call him your friend. Who gives a fuck?"

"Ben's so normal. Once we got to his apartment, we mashed—just a little, until his roommate Neal barged in. Anyway, Neal is a stellar guy, totally New York fa-fa-fa. I had to leave at that point anyway—Lia's curfew. Ben put me in a cab, and we had one last kiss. End of story."

"Andy, this is huge. Did you tell Lia?" she asked, before exploding into laughs. "I'm kidding! So now what?"

"I'm supposed to call him today. I'm nervous, but I've decided I'm going to give him my phone number. Plus, his voice doesn't sound gay. I told Lia that you joined us at the movie."

"Oh, now I'm implicated? Use me, Andy. Use me!" she said, removing her jumbo eyeglasses and stretching her swan's neck toward the sun.

"How can I go on dates and be home at ten? This sucks. I need to stay in the city overnight . . . at least on weekends," I said, tossing a ball of wax paper into the trash can, disturbing a hovering swarm of bees.

"Andy, careful . . . pickle juice, Jesus. Rocco said there's a loft party downtown next Saturday night. This might be the solution to your dilemma. You invite Ben, Lula. We'll figure out something to tell Lia so you can stay overnight."

She was thinking like the Elena I loved.

"That could work. Can we stop talking about Ben now, please? I don't wanna jinx it. What did you do last night?"

"Oh, I was with people from the office—my boss, some architect friends. We went to a fancy bar in Sparta, had a couple of cocktails. Home by nine."

"Sounds grown up."

"Yes, people in their thirties. No big deal. Hey, mind if we postpone *Grease* tonight? I want to lie low," Elena asked. "The warm sunshine feels soooo good," she continued, screening her eyes with the palm of her hand. "Have you heard from Tommy? I miss him."

"We talked last week. Tommy's happy at MIT. He shares a tiny room with a geek from Connecticut who snores. He's already got a crop of buddies, but he's studying nonstop. Can't figure out why he didn't take the summer off. He'll be back in late August, but I'll be on the Vineyard."

Surrendering to the heat, I slipped into a hazy snooze when Elena ripped a burp. "It's that damn 7 Up," she screamed, giggling so hard that I gave in. We couldn't stop laughing.

———

"Hey, Mom . . . I'm calling Elena upstairs," I announced after drying the dinner dishes. "Please stay off the phone, okay?"

First, I phoned Elena to ask if Maya had details for the weekend. Saturday's loft party in the city was for Rocco's birthday. We were invited to crash at his friend's apartment on Mott Street, which provided an alibi to sleep over at Ben's. Now I could invite Ben.

"Hey Andy, I was sitting here, strumming the guitar, thinking about you."

He was thinking about me.

"You play the guitar?"

"I'm a rookie on a folk guitar. Did you get home okay last night? Your mom wasn't worried?"

"Getting back was easy. Thanks again for planning the day," I said, almost saying *the date.* "I had a fantastic time. Do you still want to get together Saturday?"

"Yeah, that was the plan. What should we do, sport?"

"Elena's friends invited us to a party downtown. Lula too. The hosts are in the theater program at Montclair State. It's Rocco's birthday. How does that sound?"

"Look at you, Jersey boy, inviting me to a snazzy city party. Is it casual?"

"Totally. Dancing, music, and booze. It's in a loft warehouse. We could meet you at Corner Bistro at nine."

"Sounds like a plan. I'll ask Lula—and roll a few joints. Hey, Andy, if you want to sleep over here, you can, you're welcome to. Neal's in Baton Rouge next weekend."

"Sure!" My heart jumped. "I should bring a change of clothes?"

"I have stuff you can borrow. You don't need anything. Sunday we can go to the park, hang out."

"I'm stoked. Ben, I wish it were already Saturday."

"Yeah, the workweek better fly. All will be easier once you live in the city."

Struck by Ben's reassurance, "All will be easier once you live in the city," I pounded the floor with excitement.

"Oh, did you go to the Gay and Lesbian Pride March today?" I asked.

"I chickened out. Maybe next year."

"Cool. Can I call you later this week to firm up plans?"

"Yes, Andy-boy—anytime. Have a solid Monday, sport. Goodnight."

Hankering to rip a smooch sound, I resisted. Once the phone snapped to its cradle, I frog-hopped about the room until I fell starry-eyed into the shag carpet.

Chapter 16

Elena answered the door wearing a hot pink, navy, and crème geometric-patterned headscarf. Oversized gold hoops and magenta lipstick complemented her midnight-blue midriff and denim bell bottoms. She'd lined her eyes with black mascara.

"Too much?" she asked, reading my expression.

"A little too *Valley of the Dolls*," I said.

"I'll ditch Baba's scarf," Elena said. My plaid shirt was demure alongside Elena's ensemble. I was dressing for Ben, still thinking I needed to be butch because anything else was faggy. Since our last date, I had picked up camel leather desert boots at Buster Brown's, identical to Ben's.

Elena bubbled about my finally meeting Maya and Rocco. I didn't tell her the party was unimportant, just foreplay for a sleepover at Ben's.

Minutes later, Rocco's gleaming Chevy Malibu came to a halt in front of Elena's split-level. Elena raced from the porch for a hug, singing "Happy Birthday!" I cowered as Elena made introductions, sounding like the emcee on *The Dating Game*.

"Andy!" Maya called, leaping out of the car.

"Can I have your eyebrows like now, please? Andy, promise me you'll never do drag," said Rocco, leaning in for a friendly hug. Rocco Pulia was no dark, brooding Italian. A burst of rusty orange hair topped his generous forehead. The length of his protruding ears matched that of his schnoz. He had pointed boots, a black western shirt with pearly white snaps, designer jeans with a gaudy buckle, and an authentic cowboy hat.

Maya labeled herself a Black Korean. Her greenish-brown eyes were the size of saucers, resembling Margaret Keane's pixie paintings of the '60s. Maya's mocha complexion was showered with freckles.

Gunning toward the train station, we harmonized to the *Saturday Night Fever* disco hit "If I Can't Have You" Rocco played. He parked in a loading zone in the full lot, just as we heard the train coming.

"It's Saturday, so we'll be fine," he said. We raced toward the platform like a pack of crazies before the door closed. I plopped next to Maya.

"I can't believe we're finally meeting, Andy," Maya said. "Elena talks about you nonstop."

Maya and I discussed being only children. She had a Caribbean mother who was a singer and a Korean father who played electric guitar in a band.

Twenty minutes later, strutting through the West Village, I noticed that we were close to asshole rapist Damon's apartment. I had a flashback of agony and had to shake my head to disperse the nightmare. I jogged up to long-legged Rocco.

"Hey, Andy, Elena says you're gay. That's so cool. Me, too."

Feeling exposed, I winced and said, "Yep, I guess I am. It's all pretty new to me."

Before I had the chance to elaborate, we spotted the neon sign for Corner Bistro.

"Andy, you're going to love this place," Rocco gushed. "It's really just a dive bar, but the burgers are killer."

The hostess said they were backed up and we should wait at the bar.

Rocco's height allowed him to stand out, and he quickly ordered four pints of pilsner.

Maya asked, "Doesn't the city make you feel alive, Andy? I'd love to be cast in an off-Broadway play. You know, start small at the Public Theater, or La MaMa," she added, raising her volume to impress those surrounding us.

"Yes, then we can be roomies!" I responded, hungry to win her favor.

Thirty-five minutes passed before Ben and Lula showed up. Brushing my ear with his lips, he whispered, "Hey, you."

I introduced the pair to everyone. I really wanted to say, *Hello world, meet Ben. My Ben.*

The six of us jibber-jabbered for another twenty-five minutes before the hostess cried, "Pole-lock." We crowded into a table, Ben plunking himself between Elena and me. We ordered another round before stuffing our mouths with sloppy cheddar burgers.

"I told you they were killer!" Rocco declared giddily. When the greasy plates were cleared, the aloof waiter delivered three slices of cheesecake without fanfare. Digging into his slice, Rocco added, "Although I only met you guys tonight, I love you from the bottom of my heart."

We winced at the sudden emotion, but Maya broke through the awkward moment by singing, "Hap-pee birth-day to you," as the rest of us joined in.

Doling out wrinkled folds of cash, we calculated enough to cover Rocco's portion and a stingy tip for keeping us stuck at the bar for an hour. I caught Ben dropping a few extra dollars onto the pile before we paraded out onto West Fourth.

"Follow me," Rocco directed, sounding boozy after numerous beers, sprinting ahead. Trailing behind, Ben slipped his hand inside mine and squeezed.

Rocco's directions landed us in front of DelPugio's Meat Company. He needed to find a blue door next to the loading dock.

We suddenly heard the catchy refrain of "Lady Marmalade" echo from inside. Rocco spotted three revelers enter through a metal door a few feet away.

"This is it!" Rocco shouted, leading us to an industrial elevator decorated with flyers pointing up to the party. Four stories up, the metal cage opened onto a colossal loft space flowing with frantic dancers. The Clash song "Career Opportunities" blasted from giant speakers perilously hung from trusses bracing the wood-beamed ceiling. Rocco guided us into the thick, pointing out the bar and the restroom as if he were the master of ceremonies. Lula, Maya, Ben, Elena, and I steered toward a folding table scattered with low-shelf alcohol, plastic cups, and a detached urinal half-full of broken potato chips. A drunken preppie was dispensing beer from an aluminum keg with a plastic hose.

Ben poured us each a vodka and soda, heavy on the liquid grain. Skirting the perimeter of the chockablock dance floor, Ben and I cozied in front of a fire-safety window. Raising my hand to catch the streetlight, I saw that my Timex read eleven-ten.

"There sure are some juicy fellas in this room," Maya announced as Ben planted his thumb inside the rear pocket of my jeans.

"In London, there are brilliant loft parties every night. So fun," Lula boasted.

Ben cut in, "Sorry, guys, I brought a fat joint but gave it to Rocco since it's his birthday. I figured he'd share."

"We won't see Rocco again," Maya explained. "He's a party animal."

"Rocco *should* get a little crazy," Ben shrugged. "It is his birthday! Let's dance!"

Like five Slinky toys, we bounced onto the dance floor. Rocco screamed when he saw me.

"You two look so cute together," he said to Ben and me. "You both have such sweet faces—it makes me want to puke." He laughed, executing a pirouette. "Kidding! I love you guys!"

I started to wonder whether he was on something stronger than pilsner.

As Rocco glided off, the first grooves of "Rock Lobster" sent the place into a frenzy. Dancers froze in place, shrieked, and then hopped like rabid kangaroos. A drunk dude with a mullet shouted the band's name over and over again as if the B-52's had shown up. Like animated robots, we fell into form. I saw Rocco sloppy-dancing with two pretty boys.

Weaving her arms through the air, Elena screeched, "If we separate, we're all meeting tomorrow at Pennyfeathers. Eleven o'clock brunch."

I nodded.

"Look," she continued. "Maya and I are crashing at Lula's. Are you still sleeping at Ben's?"

"Yes," I shouted, "Going to Ben's. Hanging out tomorrow. Call you when I get home."

"Fabulous," she screamed.

"Let's go," Ben urged, taking my hand.

Lula and Maya saw us and squealed, "Boys!"

"Night, we're outta here. Have fun," I shouted.

"Elena's with us, don't worry. Night, Ben," they yelled as Lula gave us slushy hugs.

Ben and I scrambled down a creepy set of fire stairs to the street. The stench of raw bovine still hung in the air. Ben pointed toward a taxi, but it disappeared.

"Fuck. Occupied. Let's wait. Walking this late is too risky," he said.

Aroused by Ben's command and imagining a night with him, I felt my dick swell. Looking down, I saw a mini-boomerang outlined by my denim. Following my gaze, Ben cracked, "Whoa! Down, boy! We'll be home soon."

Just then, a flying Checker careened toward us.

"East Seventh and Second, please," Ben said with authority. "Phew, this cab smells like ass."

"I guess," I said.

"Hey, handsome. What a blast of an evening." Ben grinned. "I know because I'm polluted. Rocco's a freak, but Elena looked hot. I'd date her."

I felt the hairs on my neck stand on end. Buzzed, I couldn't let the comment pass.

"Elena's hot? Is this your bi side talking? Lemme tell ya, buddy, Elena's off-limits." I impressed myself with my tough tone.

"Relax, sport, relax. It was just a compliment," he said, laughing.

Worried we'd get jacked if we were dropped off on Second Avenue, Ben guided the taxi driver to his building. The instant Ben unlocked his apartment door, the savory incense, cooking spices, and weed seemed familiar. He clicked on a lamp and spun the Jackson Browne LP *Running on Empty*.

"Let's have one more drink. What would you like, Andy?"

I wanted to get down immediately—not booze more. But I swallowed my impatience and said, "Does scotch sound good?"

"Sure, scotch sounds great," he said. "We also need candles," he added, striking a long wooden match.

"Ben, can I use the bathroom? I'm about to wicked pee my pants."

"The light's on the left," he said, forgetting I'd been there a week ago.

My insistent boy-boner made it hard to pee at first. I had to let it soften. Standing over the toilet, I let my thoughts drift to my shitty night at Damon's. My dick turned limp, yielding a steady flow. When I returned to the living room, Ben's angelic face burst into a grin as he held up two crystal tumblers of scotch.

I made a big show of acting as if I always sucked down scotch and then said, "These glasses are cool. Are the decorations yours or Neal's?"

"Decorations?" he said, laughing. "Mostly mine. A few hand-me-downs from Uncle Jack."

Then, without warning, Ben lunged. The hard kiss softened as he dove his tongue down my throat. I started to breathe through my nose to let the joy continue without interruption.

We mashed from Browne's "Love Needs a Heart" to the closing lyrics of "Stay" before Ben whispered hoarsely, "Bedroom," and pushed me through the threshold. As I stood there, looking hungrily at the bed, Ben lit jasmine incense. I quickly looked around. A set of heavy drapes masked the window. A worn, caramel-leather armchair sat below two black-and-white photographs I assumed were by Ansel Adams. Ben's boxy bed was covered with a deep maroon comforter and four or five brocaded pillows.

Ben grinned, kicked off his Earth shoes, and stripped to his frayed boxers. Ben had meat to his bones but was neither stocky nor scrawny. I didn't expect he'd have hair on his chest. Fluffy whiffs, not wiry barbs, scattered around his pecs with a trail of sepia that stopped above his navel. Seeing the pup tent on the right side of his boxers, I wanted them off.

Crouched over, undoing a knot in my shoelace, I fell behind. Ben, the gentleman, stood waiting with a pile of clothes at his feet. Rather than nervous, I was comfortable around Ben. The buildup made me super-horny, evident by the bulge in my Jockey briefs.

"Man overboard," Ben laughed, pushing me on the bed. It began rippling. "It's a waterbed," he added.

"Wow," I said, unable to pretend I was familiar with these mattresses. I floated uneasily, off-balance, until Ben grabbed me by the waist to steady me, kissing me in the process.

"This waterbed feels so weird," I said. Then I shut up so I wouldn't ruin the seduction.

"Lay down. Roll over. Let me massage your back," Ben directed, reaching for a bottle on the nightstand. My face was in the blankets, but I heard him squeeze oil into his hand and then warm it between his palms. As I scooted at his touch to the middle of the undulating mattress, my torso tensed. Ben's fingers coiled my neck as he cooed, "Relax."

Gently, he straddled my backbone, kneading my shoulders with fingers slick from the oil. As his fingertips skated to my lower torso, I jolted nervously.

"Whoa, it's okay. Haven't you ever had a massage, sport?"

"Nope."

"Are you uncomfortable with me sitting on top of you?"

"A little. I'll get over it," I murmured, snapping my neck back to catch Ben's calming eyes.

"Just one thing, Ben—I prefer not to do anything back there, okay?"

"Same here. There are plenty of other ways to have fun," Ben replied.

The tenderness of his hands calmed my anxiety, even when I felt Ben kneading my bottom. I was relieved he had no intention of shoving it into me, unimaginable after Fucking-fuck's forced invasion.

As he continued his massage, I felt my brain turn to mush. Ben licked my nape then cuddled me.

"I hypnotized you," he murmured, as I lay my head on his chest. "Now I can do whatever I like."

"I feel like I'm floating on the ocean," I answered. His affirming touch was everything I needed. We fell into an impassioned twist, tenderly rubbing, until I was hard again. We ended in a haze of kissing, tasting each other's scotch-infused saliva as we jerked each other off.

I slept through the night, only needing to pee again before the sun rose. Heavy raindrops pelted the garden, cueing a sleepy, lazy Sunday. The shrieking, frantic whining of my victimized self had finally been calmed and my twisted psyche quieted by this awesome man. After the misery of the last few weeks, Ben was the perfect distraction from the ongoing pain. I fell back to sleep curled into his arms, breathing in the sexy farm-boy sweat from his underarms.

Chapter 17

"Morning," my own Prince Charming warbled, two packets of brown sugar dangling from his mouth. Setting ceramic mismatched mugs of coffee onto the night table, Ben flashed a devious grin.

"What time is it?"

"Nine thirty," he said, removing the sugar for clarity, "Do you hear that? It's still raining cats and dogs. Lula called to make sure we made it home. Elena and Maya crashed at her place—both pretty wasted. They're meeting Rocco at Pennyfeathers at eleven, provided the monsoon breaks. They invited us, but I told them I wanted you all to myself today."

We.

"Nope, this is perfect—though I'm beginning to feel seasick," I joked.

"Poor baby," Ben sneered, putting on a record and then crawling under the sheet in plaid boxers. Joni Mitchell crooned as we nestled in near-sleep. My body soon felt stable again; the alcohol buzz had evaporated.

When I came to again—whether it was ten minutes or possibly two hours later—Ben proposed, "The downpour's slowing down. Wanna go up to Central Park? Or how about a matinee?"

"Everyone says Central Park is really dangerous, although I did see Shakespeare in the Park at night."

"The park's fine during the day. Sheep Meadow is solid. Tons of New Yorkers hanging out, playing Frisbee, hacky sack, but the grass will be soaked," Ben continued. "How about we stay downtown? I got it! I'll take you to this trendy spot on Union Square called Coffee Shop—it's filled with models and artists. It's close to your dorm. Then we can do the Flatiron District or head south toward the East River—maybe even the Brooklyn Bridge. What time does Mom need you back?"

"Oh, shit—I should call her!"

"Phone's next to the spice rack. Tell Lia I said hello," he teased.

I strutted to the kitchen, cupping my genitals like a damned priss. I told Lia that Elena and I were hanging out in the city all afternoon with our friends. I'd be home for dinner. She told me that dinner would be cornflake-covered chicken with mashed potatoes to lure me back to Maple.

After a satisfying piss, I curled into Ben's fold. His armpits gave off a now-familiar sweet-sour scent, and I felt myself harden again.

"Was it difficult growing up without a dad?" he asked, stretching for his coffee mug, the other hand stroking my hardening rod.

"I didn't know any different. All my friends had fathers, but no one made fun of me or anything. I think it forced me to grow up faster. The bigger scare was when my attraction to guys kicked in. One day I visualized slitting my wrists. Or swallowing pills. But I couldn't do that to Lia. So I decided just to suppress the itch. I started playing around with girls. And I liked it . . . sort of."

"How did you beat your physical attraction to guys?" Ben asked.

"Secretly jerked off to magazines. I figured once I turned eighteen, I'd move to the city and be open. Other days, I thought I'd outgrow it."

"What about being an artist? When did you know that?" Ben asked.

"As a kid, I made shit all the time. Drawings, little books of cartoons. I'd take apart transistor radios and build sculptures. Or create model sailboats and paint mini race cars. It filled a gap."

"Cool," Ben murmured, his hand cupped over my dick.

"Otherwise, I'd be hanging out with my buddies at the park playing basketball. I'd run a few miles in the evening or swim laps in the town pool after teams practiced. By then, when I turned seventeen, my attraction to guys heated back up. Seeing men in Speedos will do that to you. I became super restless—"

I broke off, abruptly, reluctant to divulge my history with Ollie.

"I'm impressed. You really took control," Ben said, rolling his head onto my chest.

"So, what's Ben's story?"

"In Ohio, growing up in a big family, you don't get much time to learn about yourself. You just copy everyone else. Mostly I'm attracted to men. Like I told you, my Uncle Jack swears I'm gay."

He gave my nipple a quick kiss and mussed my hair.

"Hey, the sun's breaking through. You catch the first shower, sport. Guest towel on the hamper."

Feeling nosy, I peered inside the medicine chest. There were two immaculate shelves crammed with fancy jars and bottles, obviously Neal's. I examined the other shelf, holding Tom's of Maine deodorant, Ultra Brite toothpaste, and a Q-tips box. Ben cracked the door to hand me a new toothbrush in a box.

"This is for you. Leave it in the holder for the next time."

I melted.

Inside the shower was hemp shampoo and something labeled Dr. Bronner's Pure-Castile Peppermint Soap. Sounded like a Beatles LP. I stepped into the shower, and, despite a case of renewed horniness, I resisted the urge to coax Ben into joining me.

Towel tight to my waist, I walked back into the bedroom. Ben had draped two T-shirts over the chair.

"Pick one," he said, mischievously pulling my towel off and giving me a good eyeballing. I thrust my hips at him, my dick wagging lazily and starting to stiffen again. He smiled but wagged his finger. There was no time for a replay.

The choices were a black Lou Reed tee or a red and white pullover with wide stripes. Stretching the pullover over my head, I breathed in a musky Ben scent and decided he wore it once without washing. Hot. I returned to the john and attempted to comb in a side part rivaling Ben's. Given my wooly mane, it failed to set. I applied a squeeze of Groom and Clean from Neal's stash to fix it.

Ben was now wearing the rejected Lou Reed tee, sexier than I could pull off. As we left the apartment, I watched his husky, goofy swagger. It was cute, not menacing.

The sidewalks were steaming, forming a gauzy veil from the scorching sun. It was the Village, where people were cool, but I felt holding hands in public would be too much. So we fell into the rhythm of bumping legs or shoulders as a sign of affection.

"The first time I read *The Front Runner*, the sex between the coach and his star runner rocked a boner." Shoulder bump.

"Andy, do you know how freakin' adorable you are?" Elbow bump.

"Look, *National Lampoon's Animal House* opens at the end of July! Let's see it!" Shoulder bump.

The Coffee Shop on Union Square was nothing more than a snooty version of a Jersey diner. We snagged a snug booth alongside the window with a partial view of my dorm. By city standards, we were early for Sunday breakfast. Ben ordered a Swiss and spinach omelet with home fries and rye toast. Still unsure of myself, I ordered the same.

"You don't have to order everything I do. This isn't a test," he grinned.

"We just have similar tastes," I said and felt stupid.

"I'm just teasing you, sport. You got plans for the Fourth?"

"Every year my Gram throws a family barbecue."

"Barbecue? Like you roast a pig?" he asked.

"We aren't hillbillies. We barbecue hamburgers, sausage, chicken."

"Ohhh. Do you mean a cookout? In Ohio, barbecue is pulled pork roasted in tangy sauce. On the Fourth we have cookouts," Ben explained.

"Okay, yeah, a cookout. We call it a barbecue in Jersey. You cook the meat on a barbecue grill. It sucks I have to work tomorrow. They should give us Monday off since the Fourth falls on Tuesday."

"Well, at least it's a day off. So you can't come back because of your bar-be-cue?" Ben asked, enunciating the word.

"Probably not. All the relatives will be there. Then it's back to PGE Wednesday."

"I think I'll go to a movie. Neal's not back until Wednesday night. Uncle Jack is at his house on Long Island. I'll see what Lula is up to, since Fourth of July has zero meaning to her. Hey—what does your mother think you're doing today?"

"I told her I was with Elena and staying at your house . . . well, your apartment. She believes me."

"It'll be nice having you nearby in September. Let's walk by the dorm so I'll know where to find you."

"It's all happening so fast. I'm counting the days. I'm going to the Vineyard at the end of August, so—"

"The Vineyard? Is that a restaurant?"

"It's an island off the Cape—Cape Cod, I mean. It's a family thing. Been doing it since I was a kid."

"What an opportunity—free vacation."

"So, you dated many guys?" I suddenly blurted out.

"To be honest, I fooled around a couple times with one guy, a bartender who worked one of Uncle Jack's parties. Jeff."

A sharp twinge of jealousy hit me in the gut.

"Then there's Anna, who was the girlfriend in Ohio I mentioned. She's a writer here in Brooklyn, also doing production work. We've taken a break."

"A break? Like how recently were you dating her?"

"This sounds like an interrogation."

"Nooo. Sorry. I mean, whatever is cool, I guess."

Did that even sound convincing?

"You got a learning curve, sport."

"Sorry to be so slow, but I'm new at this. I mean, are you really bi, Ben? You sounded gayer before. Not *sounded* gay; I didn't mean the tone of your voice. I meant more into guys."

"Andy, this crap again? I already told you that I don't know what I am. I like the people I like. And I like you. Or don't you remember last night?"

"Got it," I said, blushing.

"Don't overthink. Don't show your age."

What the hell does that mean?

"Let's roam around. There's a great record shop two blocks away."

"Let me pay the bill, please," I said, grabbing for the check.

"Okay, I'll let you. But this is the last time. A student has to save his money."

We roamed until we found the majestically tarnished prewar building I would soon call home. It gave me the tingles. Its modest lobby had seen better days. Ben said the dorm rooms would be much snazzier.

With the record store closed, we wandered south to SoHo. As the humidity peaked, we walked by gritty, dense rowhouses that once sheltered immigrants. Ben impulsively jostled me into an alcove on Bowery Street, planting a fleeting peck on my lips. I pulled him in for another like this was some contest.

The shying sun signaled our day was about to end. Zigzagging block after block was fun and convinced me I was ready for Manhattan. The endless honking of car horns, blaring boomboxes, brownstone steps scattered with intravenous needles—I loved it all. And I thought I also loved Ben, but I knew I shouldn't say something this soon.

Five o'clock arrived too early. Unless the trains ran like clockwork, I'd be late for Lia's cornflake chicken. We walked toward Sheridan Square. It was time to separate.

"Andy, today was excellent." Ben gripped my waist with few people in sight and delivered a gutsy goodbye kiss. "Next weekend? You and me."

Chapter 18

Elena's Chevy Vega, painted the dreary color of chicken fat, idled in the parking lot. Being a Sunday, hers was the only car in the parking lot. As I approached, she rolled down the window and bounced behind the wheel like a hyperactive child.

"Spill."

"Don't get pissed, but . . . it was everything I hoped," I said, brushing a flattened McDonald's bag off the seat so I could slide in. "Elena, you need to clean and wash this car."

"Ham promised to do it tomorrow. Okay, tell me about your sleepover. Did you guys do the deed?"

"My life isn't a dirty paperback. We woke up and had a late breakfast at this snooty diner and then we bopped around. Hey—I saw my dorm too. Then we visited Lower Manhattan neighborhoods like TriBeCa."

"TriBeCa? Sounds like one of those shitty Japanese monster flicks, *Godzilla vs. TriBeCa.*"

"Are you still drunk? Well, there's not much to the area other than spice warehouses and decrepit buildings. You wouldn't catch me walking there at night. It's creepy. Later we ate egg rolls from a cart in Chinatown, and lemon ice and pignoli cookies from a bakery in Little Italy."

"Yeah . . ."

"E, Ben is awesome," I said.

"Honcho, that's all you're going to tell me?"

"Jeez, go read a *Penthouse Forum* if you're hungry for details about sex. How was brunch at Pennyfeathers?"

"Andy, that place is so gay. Every table had just-laid, morning-after couples sipping mimosas and pigging out on eggs Benedict. God, my head hurts. Fucking hangover. That Bloody Mary this morning didn't help. Rocco told us about a gay disco he went to with those fellows feeling him up at the party."

"That's one way to spend a birthday."

"Andy, I have no idea where he slept or if he slept. When he crawled into Pennyfeathers, he looked like shit. Oh, Lula and Maya cuddled all night. All three of us slept in Lula's double bed. I felt kinda left out," she said, chuckling. "Nothing happened between them. But it felt weird. Do you know if Lula's a lesbo? Anyway, Maya laughed when I apologized for being in their way. At least no one barfed. Maya dropped me off early afternoon, and I napped until three. I'm exhausted, but at your service."

"Grateful no one died. Does Rocco always get that wasted?"

"Andy, cut him some slack. It was his birthday. Rocco is one of the sweetest people I know, period. Yes, he can seem dramatic at first. But give him a chance. Our life is so bland. We need Rocco to spice things up."

"Our life is so bland—?"

"Oh, pardon me, Mr. Big City. I know you're living a dream life now. I'm happy—I really am. Just don't act like you're better than the rest of us."

"Okay, okay, sorry. Rocco's amusing. When he's toasted, a flaming queen, but that's okay. Hey—Lia is cooking. Want to join us for dinner?"

"After I drop you off, I head back to bed. I'm really wiped out. Besides, Luba was acting cold when I strolled in. Maybe she's pissed because I look like dog doo. I have tomorrow off, thank God. Tuesday, we're driving up to Lake Hopatcong for a barbecue at my cousin's."

"Sounds fun."

"I hate sleeping in the lake cabin. It smells of citronella candles and baloney. Squeaky cots with damp sheets, just like the bunks at Leadership Camp. Remember? God, Andy, will this summer ever end?"

Elena groaned and went silent. The silence lasted until we turned into my driveway.

"Say hi to Lia. Love you. When do you see your lover boy again?"

"Next weekend. Love you."

"Loooovvvvve you," she said, honking the horn twice before pulling out.

Lia was in the kitchen, dredging chicken breasts dripping with batter through cornflakes.

"What can I do to help, Mom?" I forced myself to ask, really wanting nothing more than a hot shower and fresh clothes.

"New shirt? Stripes look good on you," Lia said. "How was New York?"

"It was awesome, Mom."

I waited a second for her to press for details. But she didn't, so I went upstairs to clean up and rest. I wanted to think about Ben and last night's massage and sleepover, but I didn't want to get a boner with Mom just downstairs.

The poultry took forever to bake. At seven thirty, we finally sat down to dinner. Over the meal, Lia began discussing her job plans.

"Accepting the promotion and transferring to Fairfax seems right, but I need your honest opinion. My biggest concern is leaving you in your freshman year. My move won't happen until late October, but Virginia is far away."

She paused to pull a piece of chicken lodged in her back teeth and then continued.

"Here's an idea. Move to Virginia after your first semester at NYU. Transfer your credits to George Washington University. They have an impressive art school. That would make me happy."

"Mom. I can't think about a transfer before school even starts; plus, I want to live in New York. How is this even an option? I've already registered. Partial scholarship, Pell Grant. The dorm. We put down a deposit, remember?"

"Don't get so upset. It was only a question."

"I need to be on my own. And you need to take this promotion."

"I'm mostly saying yes to this job to pay your tuition. Your scholarships won't pay for everything. I deserve this promotion. But we have to sell the house."

"Yes, lots to do. But, Mom—get a grip, be happy. Let's crack open some champagne. We haven't properly celebrated."

"Do we have champagne?"

"Two bottles in the basement left over from graduation."

I came back from the cellar, poured a stream of bubbles into two flutes, and toasted, "To the best, most gorgeous mother in the whole wide world who's going to snag the swankiest bachelorette pad in Fairfax, causing a dating frenzy."

Secretly, I was also toasting my first real gay sleepover. Ollie or that Damon shit didn't count.

We poured second glasses and Lia declared, "A toast to my talented, athletic, good-looking son," as I rolled my eyes.

"Whose NYU degree will make him a famous artist, making millions—"

"So he can support his mother in old age," I quipped, sticking out my tongue so we'd both laugh.

Draining my glass, I continued, "Then you're off to Peru with Ruth to run with the Machu Picchu Pygmies and smoke weed and dance around a firepit."

"My God, Andy, you have quite an imagination. You know what? I'm excited yet terrified about Peru. I've never hiked before," she moaned. "Carpe diem! Andy, maybe it's time I grabbed life by the balls."

"I'm going to the Vineyard again. *Jaws*! Clams! Grouchy Uncle Carl! Frivolous Fanny! The Jellybean Sisters!"

"I wish you were coming to Peru. Do you?"

"Yes. But after two weeks with Ruth, you'll either go batshit crazy or turn lesbian!"

"Oh my God, Andy! Champagne is foaming out of my nose," she laughed. "And Ruth is not a lesbian!"

I spent Monday in a flame-retardant jumpsuit, painting the exteriors of blazing furnaces. Listless from the heat, I was unaware that gobs of quick-drying enamel were seeping inside a rip in the suit, coating my fore-arm with battleship grey paint. By the end of my shift, I was pouring paint remover over my arm at the sink.

Just then, I sensed someone in the room. Smokey was sitting shirtless on the bench in front of his locker. His hairy grey chest was humorously in contrast with his dyed hair and mustache. He was staring at me.

"Hey, College," he shouted.

I shuddered inwardly.

Getting up and strutting toward me, he said, "Kid, sorry I insulted you in da past. I can't help it. I make cheap cracks. Just my way of saying hi. You're a good guy, I can tell. Plus, those bushy eyebrows are kinda hot."

Did he just tell me I was hot?

"Have a great Fourth," he said and then turned back to put on his shirt.

As he exited the locker room, Smokey gave me one last grin, and I felt like his eyes were looking right through my clothes.

What the fuck?

I didn't know much. But I knew one thing: Straight guys don't talk like that.

Was Smokey . . . a homo?

———

Winding up our driveway, I saw what seemed like a million dandelions all over our lawn. Plowing the yellow buds to the nip would exhaust my restless energy. Gently lowering my lunchbox, I crept inside and tiptoed up behind Lia, ready to startle her with a bear hug. But as I opened my arms, she screamed, adding, "Silly, don't do that to me! I made twenty pat-ties. After this, coleslaw. Then we can eat—rigatoni, okay?" She waved her fingers at me, each digit caked with raw hamburger meat.

"Pasta sounds great. I'm gonna mow down the weeds then shower."

"Good boy. Come here; you have grey paint on your face," she said, trying to scratch at my cheek with her clean pinky. She added, "Andy, the lawn can wait if you're too tired."

"Nope, I'm in the mood. I want it to look pretty for the Fourth. Hey, Mom, love you."

Two hours later, lawn mown, just showered, towel around my waist, I heard the phone ring. I tore up the stairs, yelling, "Mommmm, don't pick up! It's for me," wishing it was Ben.

"Andy, can you come get me?" Elena pleaded.

"Everything okay?"

"Sort of, but I have to talk."

"I'll be there in five minutes."

I raced to the kitchen in unlaced Stan Smiths, explaining, "Sorry, I'm going to Elena's."

"What about dinner? "

"I'll eat when I get home. Elena needs help," I said, pecking her cheek.

Elena sat on the front stoop of her house, cradling her knees. Gigantic sunglasses covered her face. She jumped in, telling me to drive anywhere.

"How about the park?"

"Perfect," she replied flatly.

During the short ride, we said little. Sensing her tension, I let the radio version of Parliament's "Give Up the Funk" fill the gaps. We pulled into a shaded nook under the leafy maples and walked to the riverbank.

Through trembling fingers that hid her face, Elena whined, "I'm pregnant. What the fuck should I do?"

"Wait—how?" I said, absorbing the crisis. "Fuck. I'm sorry. We'll figure this out."

"Thanks. I found out this morning."

"It's not mine, is it?" I felt she could use the laugh.

"No, you doofus, how could it be yours? I had an affair—if you could call it that."

"An affair? Very adult. With who? Want to talk about it?"

"Yes. That's why I called you, Andy," she said, enunciating each word. "I'm on birth control now, but the first time we had intercourse, I hadn't started taking it. So this had to be from the first time."

"Elena, why is this the first time I'm hearing this? Who is he?"

"Andy, this isn't about you right now, okay. I'm freaked out."

"Okay, okay, calm down. We'll figure it out."

"He's a partner at the firm, the younger architect—Daniel. He fucking ambushed me. It was after five, only me and Daniel in the office. How stupid was I? He wanted to show me a few projects to familiarize me with their work. Andy, he's super-hot. Anyway, there was definitely a vibe. Then he opened beers while we were reviewing blueprints—again, weird—and before you know it, boom, we were full-blown fucking."

"Holy shit."

"Andy, it was wild. Liberating. Crazy fun. Now I know what a quickie is. Naturally, we didn't use any protection. Afterward, we sat on the floor drinking. Daniel told me he was divorcing his wife. Andy, he has three kids, for Chrissakes!"

"Damn. How old?"

"The kids? Who cares."

"No. Daniel."

"Early thirties."

"Can't believe you kept this secret!"

"You were too busy with your gay stuff. I didn't want to bother you."

"That's not fair."

"Okay, I was ashamed. We've been meeting about once or twice a week since. At a hotel. He paid. I'm on the pill now. Guess there's no question—I'm fertile."

"Elena, it's just kinda shocking."

"Get over your own juvenile shock and try to help me."

"Well, you certainly hit it out of the park during the interview," I quipped, "and scored that job easily." I was still pissed she didn't tell me earlier. "So that's where you were all those nights! You were really with Daniel getting your groove on."

"Yes, yes, yes, Nancy Drew!"

"Okay, so does he know—that you're pregnant?"

"I called him this afternoon. Andy, he freaked. Totally freaked. Started blaming me. Accused me of tricking him! He screamed at me, 'Elena, you have to take care of this!' Then he slammed down the phone."

"Shit."

"This is the jerk-off who told me he was falling hard for me. Said it over dinner—once. In a Portuguese restaurant in Newark. So I started to believe this could really turn into something. I started to care."

"Jeez."

"I broke down after that call in my bedroom. Thank God Luba wasn't home. Andy, how could I be so naïve? And I work there, for Chrissakes! I'm such a fuck-up!"

"Did you go to a doctor yet?"

"This morning. I drove to the clinic at Montclair State and took a pregnancy test. I'm about seven weeks along. If my mother found out, she'd fucking freak."

"Are you going to have an abortion?" I asked softly.

"I guess so. I mean, I have to. I'm so conflicted—aborting sounds awful. There's a baby in there, Andy, in my womb."

Attempting to comfort her, I stammered foolishly, "It's an egg, not a baby yet. Like—a chicken lays eggs, but they're not chickens."

"Andy, I'm not a chicken!"

"Calm down, Elena. I'm sorry. But how can you support a child? You're going to college in two months."

"Andy, I thought gay guys were smarter. You're not helping right now, so please stop talking."

"Maybe you should keep it, or put it up for adoption?" I said, scrambling for a solution.

"Once it's a baby, I don't think I could ever give it up," she said, teardrops rolling down her cheeks.

"How can I help?"

"Make it go away."

"Elena, you wouldn't do it yourself, would you? With a hanger or anything?"

"Ahhhh, damn—why did I confide in you? Only a girl would understand this. Hanger? Do you think I'm crazy?"

"Can you tell Maya? Call your sister? Maybe Luba would be
understanding?"

"My mother doesn't even know I've had sex. She's cool, but from the
old country, remember? My sister would tell my mom. Maya wouldn't
judge me. So I guess I'll talk to her," she muttered.

"Where do you get these things done, Elena?"

"The clinic at Montclair can schedule an appointment. I can't go back
to work. My job is over. And the ERA March in D.C. with Maya is this
weekend. What a fucking mess. I feel like throwing up."

"Maybe the bakery will take you back for the summer. It's decent pay."

"I hate going backward. Besides, don't get mad, but I had a fling with
one of the delivery drivers. Right after you and me split up."

I withheld comment.

"Andy . . . I hate myself. I'm not a slut. I don't want to be a grown-up yet."

With my arm around Elena's waist, we walked the river path silently. I
wanted the power to restore the happy-go-lucky Elena I loved. As we drove
back, she just repeated what she had said. I listened. Seeing Elena slither
out of the Blue Whale up to her porch and then out of view, I felt terrible.

Chapter 19

The noise of Lia emptying the dishwasher drifted upstairs and broke my sleep. Aside from the rattling of silverware, her "Can't Smile Without You" duet with Barry Manilow indicated she was either incredibly happy or desperate. I stumbled down the stairs to find her holding a happy-face mug of steaming coffee.

"Morning, honey. Happy Fourth of July. Are you absolutely sure I'm making the correct decision about Fairfax?"

Her cheeks puffed out like two Pillsbury cinnamon rolls. She'd been crying.

"Mom, Mom, it's going to be okay," I said, bringing her close. "You're not leaving me—I'm leaving you," I said, trying to joke.

"But Andy, if I stay, you can come home on weekends to do your laundry. We can meet in the city for dinner and go to Broadway plays."

"Mom, we decided this yesterday. You know I won't have much time. It's going to be super hectic at school. I can catch the train down to D.C. every couple of months. Or holidays at Gram's, whatever. We'll make it work. This promotion is too good to pass up."

"Andy, you're all I have."

I said, "Let's make a fresh pot of coffee. This one's weak. Where's my other mug? Charlie Brown?"

"I dropped it. The handle cracked off, but it's a clean break. I bet you can superglue it back. We'll pick up new mugs for your dorm."

The phone rang and she grabbed for it. I knew Ben wouldn't call at this time, so I wasn't frantic.

"Elen-aaaaa, hi, honey, so good to hear your voice. Here's Andy."

"Morning," Elena said blankly.

I took it upstairs.

"Feeling any better?"

"No. I feel like shit. I'm quitting my job tomorrow. Andy, I can't go back there. I talked to Maya, and she's going with me Thursday to the clinic for another exam. The weekend in D.C. is totally off."

"You gotta take care of yourself first."

"Today, I have to fake it. And it's making me sick. We're leaving in ten minutes for Lake Hopatcong for the barbecue. Luba keeps asking me what's wrong. Now I have to sit in the back of the car nauseous for two hours, then act all happy. Andy, literally . . . I want to die. Sorry, but you asked."

"Why don't you stay home and come to Gram's barbecue? You can sleep over. You hate the cabin at the lake."

"I have no choice. Luba would throw a fit. I haven't seen my cousins since graduation and . . . I just have to go. We're staying overnight. Fuck it."

"I get it."

"How are you? How's Ben, you little fucker?"

"I'm talking to Ben tonight. JuJu and Beanie will be here, and we'll watch the Macy's fireworks on TV."

"JuJu's stuck up. And I hate that nickname. It's childish. They're okay, but I'm not in your little Martha's Vineyard club," she jabbed.

"Don't be a poindexter. Hey, I've been thinking, can I tell you something big?"

"What now? Wait, you're not pregnant too?"

"Fuck you. Oops, too late for that," I said, laughing. "I'm open to skipping the Vineyard this year to spend time with Ben, get ready for NYU. Tell me, is that just stupid?"

"That's it? That's your big dilemma? Jesus, Andy, I want your life."

"Fuck you twice. Okay, never mind. Listen—go to the lake. The break will be good for you. One step at a time. I love you. "

"I love you too, Andy."

"Good luck in your plans at the clinic."

"Discussing options with Maya will help. You can't tell a soul, Andy. Deal?"

"Deal."

Fourth of July at Gram's was a bust. A flash downpour struck right after we decorated the yard with red, white, and blue streamers. The drink station I set up was a swampy mess. The charcoal just smoldered. We had to relocate the party indoors, and there was little to do for guests but get sloppy drunk.

After an hour, the rain stopped, and we could reactivate the grill. We piled on sausage and chicken parts slathered in a spicy sauce neither Italian nor Southern.

Lia and I used dishcloths to wipe rainwater off the webbed chairs placed in a circle under the weeping willow.

"Andy. Aunt Lia. Puddles everywhere!" shouted Beanie. Leaping like grasshoppers, she and JuJu approached, carrying white boxes tied with waxed red string.

The Santors were as close to a nuclear family as I got, with Uncle Carl the stand-in father, and JuJu and Beanie my pretend sisters. Fraternal twins, Juliette was two inches taller than Bernadette. The twins wore their hair in an identical style, shiny and shoulder-length, crisply parted on the side when not twisted into a bun.

Aside from books, JuJu and I had little in common. Beanie was spirited and pretty in a plain way. She had three prominent birthmarks on her left cheekbone, each no bigger than a tick. The dots on her heart-shaped face were Beanie's trademark, as my unibrow was mine. Instead of pursuing Ivy League life like JuJu, Beanie had opted for liberal Colby College in central Maine. Apart from track-and-field, her passion was French literature. Effortlessly, she'd discuss *Madame Bovary* or Flaubert's instinct for the needs of a woman.

Their mother, my Aunt Fanny, skipped our way in a hot pink frock dotted with dancing lizards.

"Fanny, what have you done? You look gorgeous," Lia gushed, humming the tune "Willkommen." Fanny appeared to be channeling Liza Minnelli's character Sally Bowles in the movie *Cabaret*, wearing a bob of jet-black hair and two sharp curls riding her chin. Long eyelashes enhanced a sinister application of mascara.

"You like her remodel?" grumped portly Uncle Carl. Tall as a Jersey pine, Aunt Fanny was the wooden pin to Uncle Carl's bowling ball. A notable proctologist, Carl had premature white hair and a scholarly beard. He wore attire befitting a country club. Aunt Fanny ordered him a fresh box of Lacoste polo shirts every spring from France, always in white or navy blue, adding an aqua or dusty rose in the hope he'd be adventurous. He never was. Covering his bottom was anything khaki, cinched by a whale-dotted belt. Genetically, Carl Santor was the nephew of my Pop-pop Oscar. The Santors occupied an ivory Colonial with emerald trim that was a short drive from Uncle Carl's practice in Westchester County.

These were the rich relatives. Dense brush girdled the Santors' yard and fieldstone patio, adjacent to a giant kidney-shaped pool. Summer lunches were an event, ranging from grilled lamb chops to asparagus quiche. Wintery feasts included a standing rib roast or glazed duck. Their home was scented with fireplace cinder and whisky. Seemingly in command were their three dalmatians named Pongo, Lucky, and Patch—amusingly named after Disney characters.

Since middle school, I had been the Santors' guest in August on the charming, tony Vineyard, savoring the privilege of fleeing Maple Ridge. Aunt Fanny and Uncle Carl kept a cedar-shingle summer house outside Edgartown. Born outside of Marseille, France, Aunt Fanny came to our family with two strikes against her, being both a foreigner and a Jew, a likely explanation for her "fuck you" attitude when people eyed her with suspicion. Fanny knew I was receptive to her exotica and introduced me to the cooking of Julia Child and mah-jongg. Dubbing me her sous-chef, Fanny taught me a basic vinaigrette and soft scrambled eggs with chives.

Within seconds of our arrival, JuJu announced that her beau Chocki was, like her, Princeton-bound, and a Japanese American saxophonist. Fearful that Chocki would throw off our cozy dynamic, I asked, "Will he be joining us on the Vineyard?"

"No, no," Aunt Fanny reassured, "Chocki will be in Tuscany with his family, *le mois d'Août.*"

A half-hour later, as Lia and a nameless neighbor prattled on beside me, I sat mesmerized by a knot of lightning bugs flickering in the overcast afternoon sky.

"Remember when you used to catch them in jelly jars with holes punched into the cap?" Lia said. "I wish you had stayed a little boy forever." As she finished her nostalgia, Aunt Fanny approached balancing a generous glass of Chablis. She muttered that the gals inside were gossiping and decided together that Andy was not safe in New York City as an NYU freshman.

Uncle Carl harrumphed, "Jesus Christ, don't listen to those drunks. Of course, Andy can handle the city. If you want to be successful, you live in Manhattan. Old goats. Lia, you made the correct decision. Andy will be fine."

"It's none of their fucking business," Lia huffed. "I'm going to address this myself."

Uncle Carl gripped her arm.

"No, no, no. Lia, that wouldn't accomplish a damn thing. Ignoring them is the best option. Anyway, your transfer to Virginia is magnificent. We're here if Andy needs us." He got up and lurched toward the house to snatch a second slice of pie.

"You're right, Carl," Lia yelled to his posterior. "Fanny, let's stay out here. That coven of bitches is burning me up today. Before you arrived, one of them asked me about Andy's father. Can you imagine? They piss me off, excuse my French," she said, laughing.

"Fanny," she added, "Why did you arrive so late today? Everything okay?"

With a cupped hand to her lips, Aunt Fanny whispered, "Carl had a gigantic branch up his ass today. One of his ludicrous tantrums. This one about stale pies we bought yesterday at the *pâtisserie*. What else could be done? Everything today is closed!"

Lia nodded as if she understood the fragile world of French pastries.

"We almost canceled, but we wanted to see you and Andy, so we waited until *il s'est calmé*. Some days that man *me rend folle*."

I was lost.

"It sometimes makes me want to take the girls back to Marseille, *je te jure*."

The two women went for a walk to babble in private. With the twins' faces buried in hardcovers, I considered my options for August. Lia loved that the Santors welcomed me to the Cape. Any other year on the last Thursday of July, JuJu, Beanie, and I would pile into the backseat of Uncle Carl's Peugeot for the six-hour drive to the Woods Hole Ferry. There was nothing more arresting after the long drive than the mist surrounding the ferry boat crossing Vineyard Sound. The boat would slow to a crawl as it pulled into the Oak Bluffs dock, and the fragrant mix of sea salt, shellfish, and blooming hydrangea would greet us like a dear old friend.

We'd whisk the car to their property and carry inside as much as we could handle. Aunt Fanny would unlock the temperamental side door so JuJu, Beanie, and I could drop the haul and scamper to our rooms, squealing with delight. My bedroom was a skinny rectangle with greyish side paneling and a ship wheel fitted with five bulbs centered on the pitched ceiling. The plastic skylight and side window were thick with a film of saltwater. Piles of dog-eared books were evidence of my several summers here. A dusty tray of dried barnacles and seashells sat on the nightstand under the cowboy lamp I'd outgrown.

Aunt Fanny employed a woman to freshen up the house the week before we would arrive. Doris, who lived on the island, would make up the beds, stack towels, and sweep away curls of dead spiders. She'd stock the fridge with milk, butter, tonic, and a bowl of freshly laid, brown-spotted eggs from center island. At Uncle Carl's request, Doris set a loaf of unsliced bread beside the toaster and a berry tart under the glass dome on the dining table. Uncle Carl would always refer to her as "the domestic."

These mind-altering weeks away from Maple gave me time to think. Some mornings I'd wake at six to ride my blue Schwinn to the deserted beach along Gay Head cliffs. Stripped down, I'd run along the surf. Dicey weather meant sketching still lifes and painting seashells with the acrylic paint kit Lia gave me.

Aunt Fanny and Lia returned from the house after giving the gossipy crones a tongue-lashing, despite Uncle Carl's warning. Beanie looked up from her novel and asked, "Aunt Lia, are you going to the ERA March this coming weekend? Weren't you part of the planning?"

"Good memory, Beanie. I'm still going with my friend Ruth. I need to plug in with the vitality of so many women. It makes me feel so alive!"

"Elena is going," I said before remembering her pregnancy, stammering quickly, "She may be canceling though."

"I'm going with friends from Scarsdale. They think Betty Friedan is a goddess."

Fanny grumbled, "I'd go with you, but I loathe crowds. Of course, in France, women have the freedom to make decisions about their own bodies."

"Can we discuss the Vineyard this year?" I asked.

"Andy, please come again for August *comme toujours*. You must rejuvenate before college."

"I'd like to come for the last two weeks of August. Or the middle two—I planned to quit Public Electric early anyway. With college starting, I prefer not to be away from Lia the entire month."

"Nooooo. Please, Andy," Beanie whined.

Uncle Carl snapped, "Stop your childishness. Let Andy decide. I'll tell you what, Andy—I'll fly you there via Cape Air to Edgartown. It's my gift to the new freshman."

"Wow! Thank you, Uncle Carl. Mom, does this sound okay?" I suddenly wondered how this vacation would affect my relationship with Ben.

"If that's what you want, honey, yes, we'll make it work. I'll be back from Peru for you before NYU starts."

"Lia, how exciting! It's a teachers' group, yes?" Aunt Fanny asked.

"Resolved, Andy's coming for two weeks in August," Uncle Carl confirmed. "We'll figure out the dates next week. Jesus Christ, this pie is stale!"

"It took you three pieces to determine that? *Comme tu es malin, mon chou!*" cracked Aunt Fanny.

On the short drive home, I asked, "Are you okay, Mom?"

"I'm fine. Just tired. Should we watch the fireworks on TV?"

"Nah, let's listen to music and read. I'm really into this new book, *In the Name of the Father*, about an orphaned Catholic kid in Chicago."

"Sounds intense, honey. Maybe I'll read it after you. If you get hungry later, Gram packed us leftovers."

That evening, the racket of Roman candles in the neighborhood left me nostalgic for my childhood. I stole away to my room just before nine o'clock to await Ben's call. Feeling fidgety, I leafed through the NYU Admissions pamphlet, scanning the details about my dorm room for the fiftieth time: Single bed, nightstand, desk, wardrobe. Shared living room, dining room, and kitchen.

Who would be my roommate? Maybe a dude from California or sophisticated lad from London. What if he was gay or bi? Would it be okay to sleep with him? I imagined a John-Boy Walton type or LeVar Burton, the actor on TV's *Roots*.

At 8:59, I tested the phone's dial tone. At nine on the dot, I called. I sagged when the machine picked up. Squelching my disappointment, I left a casual message, assuring Ben I'd call back in fifteen—hoping I didn't sound clingy.

After I hung up, I opened the sock drawer to match the pairs, rolling them into balls to calm my anxiety.

At 9:15 I gulped and left another message, using the same forced casual tone.

Where the fuck are you? We have a phone date.

Now in full panic mode, I made sure to make things worse by telling Lia I was awaiting a call, and she should let me pick up.

"Okay, hope it's someone special," she replied.

Her comment struck me as odd, but I bit my tongue.

I called back at nine thirty and decided not to leave a message and show him I was completely psycho and immature. Instead, I alphabetized two shelves of paperbacks. Getting as far as *The Amityville Horror*, I heard the phone ring and lunged.

"It's me—Ben. I'm at a pay phone. I know it's not cool to call you at home, but I'm out. Sorry! I just wanted to wish you a Happy Fourth. Let's chat tomorrow?"

I wanted to bawl him out, but I took a breath and sounded laid-back. Just hearing his voice made my anxiety evaporate.

"Hey, Ben—glad you called. Where are you?"

"Out with friends from work. We're fried. Beers, weed. It's someone's roof party. I wish you were here," he said, shouting above the racket.

"Me, too. What time tomorrow?"

"Um, around nine o'clock, our usual. Thinking about you, night."

"Bye, Ben," I said just as he clicked off.

I let my immature mind wander. Did he sound sincere? Well, he called, didn't he? Whose party? He sure didn't talk long. Was it a party filled with hot guys? Is he dating other people? Someone older than me, better looking? Before I knew it, I was drowning in jealousy.

The irregular pops and bangs of firecrackers outside jacked my nerves. Pumping the air conditioner to high to block the clamor, I plopped face-down onto my bed. I thought about PGE, which continued to suck. Then I thought of Elena's trouble and stopped feeling sorry for myself. My girl was hurting. She had made a colossal mistake like I had with Damon. The difference being, Elena had confided in me. I was too much a coward to tell her about my fucked-up night. What would I say: "Hey, get this: I got shit-faced drunk, and a stranger raped me."

I decided I would never tell anyone. Ever.

Chapter 20

Elena phoned Wednesday evening to let me know she had quit her job that afternoon—over the phone. Feeling the need to give a reason, she told them she had a contagious case of mononucleosis.

She and Maya planned to meet at the clinic the following day and then return for the procedure on Friday. To explain the loss of her summer gig to Luba and Ham, she claimed that her boss, the architect, made an overt pass. It wasn't really a lie. Ham saw red and wanted to confront the creep, but Luba calmed him down. Her defeated tone left me twitchy, yet I congratulated her for her smart alibi. But I still felt sorry for myself that I couldn't buy my own alibi. My rape continued to echo in my brain like a horror movie that wouldn't end.

Lia was at her organizational marketing night class; that gave me extra hours to decompress. Distraction was what I needed. Swimming laps or a muggy jog along the river. But I didn't feel motivated. I was in my undies and thought about jerking off to cut the tension but felt too low to even do that. I decided the only solution was to pig out. I scarfed down an entire plate of leftovers from Gram's barbecue, getting grease all over my chest. I washed myself off and then soaped up and dried the dishes just minutes before nine o'clock.

It was my chance for a better chat with Ben than what happened last night. That skimpy conversation had left me unsatisfied. I fought off lingering sensations of feeling agitated and depressed. I dialed and took a deep breath to squelch that panic rising in my throat like beer and puke.

"Ben, it's Andy!"

"Hey, sport, I just walked in the door. I saw some lady get stabbed on St. Mark's Place. Some bum in a Knicks sweatshirt grabbed her purse. She started screaming and wouldn't let go, so the fucker knifed her and ran off. There was blood everywhere. I had the bodega cashier call the cops."

This is the city I was moving to? Fuck me!

"Seems like there are muggings every day," I said.

"Andy, she was a cross-dresser. Jumped because trannies are easy prey. This was three blocks from my house—don't you get it?"

I thought I did, but I didn't understand why this affected Ben so personally. Gay bashings were reported weekly in the *Voice*. Was he afraid of getting beat up? "No one would ever suspect you are gay. You're safe, Ben."

"That's not the point," he shouted. "Never mind, Andy, I forgot how young you can be. Shit like this makes me wanna go to Vermont and open a dairy farm."

Huh? He can't leave me.

"Hang on, I have to take a wicked leak. Be right back."

Ben returned less uptight and tossed off an apology.

"Sport, I look forward to seeing you. I promise I'll be in better spirits."

"Sorry your day sucked," I stammered, still feeling he was disappointed in me 'cause I was such a mook.

"Mine sucked, too. I hate going to work at PGE. I feel like a prisoner."

"I have an idea. Can you take Friday off? Come with me to Uncle Jack's in Amagansett, on Long Island. Great beach. By train. He said I could bring you. It should be a blast. Perry, his squeeze, will be there. Would your mom be okay?"

Relieved that Ben forgave my stupid ass, I bubbled, "Hell yeah, I'm in. What should I bring?"

"Hey, let's talk tomorrow. Neal wants to use the phone. I'll figure out the train schedule."

Grabbing the receiver, Neal said, "Say goodbye, lover boy, so I can call my Latin squeeze." He added a huge smooch.

"Neal's slightly retarded," Ben explained. "Tomorrow night at nine, sport."

I was so caught up in the getaway with Ben that I forgot about the sadness Elena would be facing Friday morning. I dialed her up Thursday after work, but Luba reported that Elena wasn't feeling well. She thought Elena was having her period. I asked Luba to tell Elena I'd be away for the weekend. A half-hour later, Elena called, whispering.

"Duh. Where are you going without me? Can I come with you, rather than have an abortion?"

"Amagansett. It's on Long Island. Ben's uncle has a house at the beach. Should I cancel and come with you?"

"No, no, no, doofus. I'll be okay. I'm staying at Maya's the next couple of nights, so Luba doesn't catch on. And I'm canceling the ERA March. Is Lia still going?"

"Some feminist my mom is. Ruth bailed, so Lia did too."

"Long Island . . . just you and Ben? How romantic."

"No. I said his Uncle Jack will be there. I'm nervous."

"Why? He knows you're a dork, but he still likes you." Elena laughed loudly. "This is fancy. A big step with your new lovvva!"

"Okay. Stop, please. It's a weekend trip. Elena, how are you, really?"

"I'm okay, just a little bitchy, to be honest. Maya's been great," she said, pausing. "I'm afraid I'll screw up and say something to Luba," she whispered, audibly holding back tears.

"Just try to sleep tonight. Think ahead to better times: college, moving to Montclair. And, best of all, you never have to see that asshole Daniel again. Life will soon be better."

"I just have to get through the next few days. How is work?"

"How do you think? This heatwave sucks big time. Get this: I had to paint over graffiti in the men's bathrooms. Tits and cooters, dicks, offers for blow jobs. I spent half the day laughing while covering them up!"

"Sounds gross."

"It was hilarious."

"Maya's music teacher has a crush on Maya. She gave her six tickets to Patti Smith in Central Park. Being a South Jersey girl, she knows Patti."

"Fantastic! Is Patti Smith a lesbian?" I asked.

"No, though she looks like a rocking dyke. Wanna go? It's August fourth."

"Can I ask Ben and Lula?"

"Sure."

"Thanks."

"Have an incredible time with Ben at the beach. What are you telling Lia?"

"I told her the truth."

"You told Lia you're a fag? I mean—gay, gay!"

"I said that our friend Ben invited me to his family's place. She's convinced Ben is a good egg and didn't ask too many questions."

"Good for you. Listen, either I lie down now or I'm gonna throw up. And don't call at Maya's. I'll be fine."

"You have to let me call once, after. To make sure you're okay."

After our goodbyes, I was reminded how much I loved Elena. Lia said the Equal Rights Amendment was about women making decisions about their own bodies. "Pro-life is a manipulative marketing strategy the conservative Christians made up," she explained once. "And it works, which pisses me off because it's not what the movement is about!"

Chapter 21

As I packed on Friday morning, I remembered that Maya was driving Elena to the women's clinic. I felt stung with guilt, feeling I should've insisted on accompanying the girls instead of peeling off to Long Island for a beach weekend with Ben. What if she died? I shrugged away the horrible image.

I rolled khaki shorts, three pullovers, jeans, desert boots, underwear, and my favorite navy bathing suit trimmed with kelly green into my bag. I threw in a copy of John Irving's *The World According to Garp* simply to impress. Ben was bringing toiletries, two bottles of wine, and suntan lotion. He said Uncle Jack would provide beach towels, bathing suits, whatever.

I scribbled down Uncle Jack's address and phone number and tucked the note under a glass full of daisies I had plucked from the side garden for Lia. I promised to phone once I arrived and hoped she wouldn't insist on daily check-ins. On my way to the bus stop, I tucked a mixtape of soothing James Taylor tunes inside the screen door to Elena's porch. Wrapped in vibrant green tissue paper, the cassette would be waiting when she returned from Maya's.

The plan was to meet at eleven o'clock at Ben's place, just as Elena's procedure would be over. I felt pretty cool hailing a cab from Port Authority to Ben's, a preview of my future independence. Approaching East Seventh, I caught Neal leaving the apartment for a weekend with his boyfriend, a slim Latin man with high cheekbones and a major bulge snaking down the front of his jeans.

"Enjoy your double-date weekend, lover boy," he grinned. "Uncle Jack's a doll, and Perry's pretty but he's too much," he said, holding the door open with the heel of his stylish Roman sandal. I entered the apartment to find Ben head down, pacing aimlessly as if he'd lost something.

"Andy! How'd you get in? Help me pack this food, would you?"

He neglected to offer a kiss, and the little child in me wanted to pout and walk out. I dismissed the idea.

"Wow, you're bringing a lot of snacks," I said. "What do I owe ya?"

"Shut up, college boy. This weekend is on me. Uncle Jack won't let us spend a dime. Sorry, I'm a little distracted, but I just don't want to miss the train. It's going to be great. Just a warning, Uncle Jack can get a little bossy when Perry's around."

"Huh?" I said, starting to have doubts.

"Don't worry, it's going to be great," Ben repeated.

We grabbed a cab because Ben was convinced we'd miss the train. With traffic at a standstill, we jumped out a block south of Grand Central Station and snaked through the cavernous terminal to the ticket booth line, five deep. Twenty minutes later, balancing overnight bags and a canvas duffel full of snacks, we sprinted to platform thirty-one. Following a switch at Jamaica Station, we settled into place, starving. Ben had prepared turkey and Swiss on chunky brown bread, skillfully folded in waxed paper. Ben said, "Surprise! Look what I made for you," and he handed me an oversized snickerdoodle.

As I bit into the cookie, he tilted his head—a puppy yearning for approval.

"You made this? It's so good!"

Lifting his watch, Ben advised, "Get some sleep. We'll be there in about two hours. Uncle Jack and Perry are meeting us at the station. You're going to love their house. It's tiny but close to the ocean."

"We'll have a room to ourselves, won't we?" I asked.

Laughing, Ben said, "It's the room I stay in."

"Good, I wanna maul you."

"Oh, you horndog! Listen—Uncle Jack asks a lot of questions. You'll learn to ignore half of them."

"Huh? What kind of questions?"

"They're trying to figure me out, so they'll ask questions through you."

"Like, 'so Andy, how big is Ben's dick?'" I joked, eyes wide.

"You better tell him it's an even ten inches," he said, poking me in the ribs.

"I forgot my ruler for this trip." I laughed.

"Uncle Jack will ask, 'So tell me, Andy, when did you first realize you liked guys?' And, 'Did you fool around with other guys in high school?' Stuff like that," Ben mocked in an earnest tone.

I'm glad we were away from other passengers while he talked this way. Or I would have panicked.

"I know about you and Elena, but what about guys? I know I'm not your first score, sport."

"Just light stuff with this chick Wendy and a friend's sister. You're my third guy. One was . . . I guess you'd say random. Happened before I met you," I said vaguely, my stomach curdling as I envisioned Ben's skanky colleague Damon comatose on the bed. "The only other guy was when I technically came out two months ago."

"Was it a stranger? Uncle Jack calls them tricks."

"I feel weird telling you about other guys."

"I prefer honesty. And it happened before me, so no sweat," Ben said warmly.

"You asked for it. He was a high school teacher," I mumbled, despite the closest passenger being several aisles away.

"No shit? Andy, you're one surprise after another. Did you seduce him?"

"No, of course not! But it was a good experience. It happened only after I had no luck finding professional help. It was just after my eighteenth birthday, when I couldn't keep it secret any longer, my attraction to guys."

"Just two months ago?"

"Yep. I needed to talk to someone, so I dialed the New Jersey Gay Hotline from an ad in the *Voice*. I drove five towns away just to use a phone booth. A woman answered the phone, so I told her I might be bisexual."

"Wow. Good for you!"

"She invited me to a group meeting in Paramus. I said I was scared that people would see me walking inside. I hung up and ran to the car, bawling my eyes out."

"I'm with you, sport," Ben said, squeezing my arm. "So what did you do?"

"Sulked. I was a mess, throwing up once or twice a day. So I decided to confide in my Spanish teacher."

"Why him?"

"Ollie's a freethinker. A surfer dude from Southern California."

"Your Spanish teacher discussed sex with his student?"

"It was nothing graphic. We had in-depth conversations."

"No offense, but how old is this guy?" Ben asked.

"Twenty-nine, almost thirty."

"Okay, Andy, but it's peculiar if you ask me."

"Ben, we were friends. He took me to this play about gays, *Gemini*."

"I know it. I saw it."

"After the show, I was really blown away by what I saw. It made me realize what my deal was. I told him I thought I was bisexual. The next thing I know, Ollie said he was too."

"Sounds like he was just trying to lay you."

Shit. He sounds like Elena! Maybe she was right.

"He was trying to make me feel better. We talked for hours in a Burger King parking lot. Over onion rings."

"Andy, please tell me you didn't have sex in his car?"

"Nooooo, you freak. But he said my first time should be good, and he volunteered himself."

"What a load of bullshit!"

"He said he was concerned about me."

"I know what he was concerned about. Getting a piece of chicken. That's not legal. Jesus, Andy."

"Chicken?"

"Never mind."

"I already just turned eighteen, so technically—legal."

"Didn't realize how advanced Jersey schools are, sport," Ben said.

"You're making fun of me."

"You're young. This is just a reminder."

"Are you gonna listen—or are you gonna shoot me down?"

"I'm listening, I'm listening," Ben said, and quickly rubbed my arm to reassure me.

"So I had this night with Ollie. He treated me well. Dinner and everything. There was no pressure."

"Well, so long as there was dinner—then it's okay. Jeez."

"Steaks even. It was kind of romantic—candles, wine. After dinner we got naked."

"I'm not sure I need to hear this."

"You said you wanted to know it all."

"Okay, okay. Let 'er rip, sport."

"The weird part is—I wasn't attracted to him. I mean, he's a decent-looking guy. Short, blond, handsome. He looks a little like Hutch from *Starsky and Hutch*—but horrible acne as a teenager."

"Andy, it's all a little creepy. Sorry," Ben said.

"Yeah. I wasn't really into it. But I was afraid if I turned Ollie's offer down, he'd be insulted. I mean, it was fine, but not what I expected my first guy would be like. Way different from sleeping with you."

"I bet he enjoyed it," Ben smirked.

"It wasn't like that," I snapped.

"Was that it, then?"

"We got together again, but my head wasn't into it."

"Sorry, Andy, but it's bizarre. He was your teacher in high school."

"I trusted Ollie. I mean, he even came to my graduation party."

"Jeez. And now?"

"He's my friend. Ollie was helping me out. He left for Madrid to teach a summer program," I said.

"I'm sorry it happened to you. I hope you don't think you're in love with him."

"Of course not, you idiot," I said, whacking Ben in the tummy. I almost added that he was the one I really loved, but I wasn't going to get heavy on a train to Long Island.

We arrived at the Amagansett depot. The moment we stepped off the platform, the salt air jacked my nostrils. Ben waved to a man in his thirties propped against a bright red BMW. As we approached, my eyes popped out. Uncle Jack was a perfect dad, straight out of a Sears catalog. Square-jawed, ruddy, sand-colored hair, an untucked blue button-down. A compact body just shy of stocky. I pushed aside lusty thoughts—but now I knew how Ben would look in a few years. Walking toward us, Uncle Jack wore an ear-to-ear grin.

"Here, let me help. Whoa—what the hell is in there?"

"Just some snacks—and bottles of wine. Hey, this is Andy—Andy Pollock."

Uncle Jack shook my hand firmly and then put his perfectly tanned arm around my shoulder, pulling me closer.

"Jack Brooks. Glad to meet you. Welcome to Amagansett, Andy. Or do you prefer Andrew?"

"Andy works. Thanks for inviting me." I felt titillated, like Barbra Streisand meeting Robert Redford for the first time in *The Way We Were*.

"I needed to see who was filling up my nephew's time. After all, this gay thing is new for him."

"Uncle Jack," Ben protested.

"Kidding. Well, not totally. Anyhow, Perry is making dinner. We'll walk on the beach first."

"Love your Beemer. It's beautiful," I gushed.

"Thank you, Andrew. Andy. I can thank Sara Lee and Colgate-Palmolive for it."

"Uncle Jack does TV commercials," Ben explained.

"That's so cool," I replied, like a wide-eyed ten-year-old.

"My pearly white teeth come in handy," he said, displaying his toothy smile. "We'll be at the house in five minutes. You fellas can freshen up . . . or whatever two horny young men like to do."

"Uncle Jack," Ben countered but then rolled his eyes and gave up.

We entered the pebble drive of a classic grey-shingled, salt-box cottage nestled by thickets. The glossy, navy-blue door was trimmed in white. Two bright yellow window boxes were bursting with red geraniums. As I stepped out of the car, air sweetened with kelp slapped my face. It was heaven.

"Ben, I don't think you've been out since early May, right?"

"Yes, for Perry's birthday."

"My birthday is May also," I blurted out like a dork.

"How about that," Jack winked. "Another Taurus. Gotta watch out for those bulls. I hear you're moving to New York, Andy."

"Freshman year," I said, puffing out my chest.

"It's a loud, trashy place. Far too many people . . . but I absolutely adore it. Then again, if it weren't for my career, I'd live here at the beach," he said, waving his hand in a dramatic sweep.

God, he was handsome.

"I live across the river, Maple Ridge. I can't wait to become a New Yorker. I know city nights are full of secrets. I want in."

I never talk this way. I was flirting with Uncle Jack!

We were instructed to leave our sandy shoes on the porch. The cottage was intimate. The interior was neutral with pops of bright color, like a tangerine side chair, and kelly-green throw pillows on the pale grey sofa. A reproduction of a Matisse hung over the fireplace of beige-painted bricks. The living room had sliding doors to a large deck and breaking waves for a backyard.

Uncle Jack showed us to Ben's room and pointed out the fresh towels, plus blankets in the closet since it got cool at night. There were extra swimsuits and shorts to borrow.

"Something to eat?" Jack asked. "I can warm up the peach pie!"

"We're fine, Uncle Jack. We had gigantic sandwiches on the train," Ben said.

"Well, it's two-fifteen. Let's meet at three for a beach hike," Uncle Jack suggested.

Ben shut the door, falling back onto the bed with a crooked grin.

"Come over here," he said. It didn't sound like a question. I dropped my bag to lay next to him.

"Closer," he demanded, pulling me on top to plant a kiss on my lips and then slipping his tongue between my lips. I hardened and my boner made both of us grin.

"I'm glad you're here, sport."

I nodded silently. My head collapsed onto his broad chest. The Ben I liked was back.

"You have no idea how happy I am right now," I said. "Uncle Jack is—er, adorable. I mean, attractive—like, really handsome."

"Whoa, you have a crush on my uncle?"

"No, no, no," I stammered. "I just think he's a nice guy. And—"

"I'm just teasing. Everyone has the same reaction. He's a hunk. And he's old—he's almost forty."

"What's Perry like?"

"Perry's interesting," Ben said, his mouth frowning. "He's a model, does some acting, but really doesn't try too hard. He's maybe twenty-four, and Uncle Jack spoils him. That's between us."

Resisting the desire to get naked, we were ready at three. We met Uncle Jack in the living room where he handed us two windbreakers, one poppy-red and the other blue, matching the color of the front door. They were both new, with tags still on. I expected Perry to join us. But he didn't show up.

"Let's go, fellas. The sun is breaking through, but the wind is picking up."

We headed down to the beach, took off our sneakers, rolled our pants at the ankles, and strutted along the shore for an hour. Uncle Jack explained that Amagansett was the Native American word for "place of good water."

When we returned, I spotted a shadow moving past the kitchen window.

"Perry, you're up," Jack called out. "Meet Andrew, I mean Andy. Andy Pollock."

If Jack was handsome, Perry was a different species. Green iridescent eyes marked him as alien. His nose, lips, cheekbones, skin, and teeth composed a flawless face. Six-foot-three, his dirty-blond hair grazed his shoulders, swinging as he moved. He was wrapped in a wrinkled white linen shirt, long legs stretched outward from cuffed khaki shorts. There was an abundance of golden hair on his arms.

"Hi, Andy Pollock. I'm Perry Whitman. I'm guessing you are related to Jackson Pollock, right? He lived here, just down the road in East Hampton. Well, that is, until the car crash."

Putting out my hand, I said, "No, at least I don't think so."

"Pollock's not a common name. You must be part of the same family, at least?"

"Not sure," I shrugged, already irked by his insistence.

"Well, Andy, if there's even a slight connection, you should exploit it. Just say he was a cousin."

"Uh—okay. Sure."

"Jack tells me you're in the art world, so the Pollock name will go a long way for sure," Perry said.

He didn't let up on the topic all evening, circling back like a blood-hound on a scent. It was annoying as hell.

Cocktails started at six on the dot—Tanqueray and tonics. Jack had cre-ated an oval tray of appetizers including three petite rounds of cheese, a row of square crackers, and pitted olives. It was placed on the coffee table, a rectangle of green-edged glass atop a varnished tree trunk. Ella Fitzgerald's voice soothed us from invisible speakers. Perry excused himself now and then to tend to matters in the kitchen. He would pop back in at times, to ask Uncle Jack to freshen his drink or whisper something into his ear.

"Dinner should be ready by eight thirty," he declared grandly as if he were in a play. I was curious about what he was making because I couldn't detect anything cooking. By eight-fifteen, we were famished and quantifi-ably drunk. Uncle Jack shouted into the kitchen, "Perry, how's it going in there? Perry?"

"Out here!" he echoed from the deck. Uncle Jack slid open the glass door to find Perry roosting on the wrap-around bench, holding a fat doo-bie. We each inhaled a drag or two.

"Are we about ready for dinner?" Uncle Jack asked.

"Yes, let's go inside. I made a salad."

Perry wielded large tongs and served lettuce, cucumbers, green pepper, sliced lemons, and the midsection of a steamed salmon he picked up precooked at the market.

"Looks *wander-full*, Perry, thank you," Uncle Jack said.

Ben gave me a quick look and rolled his eyes.

By nine thirty, we had exhausted small talk. Perry had disappeared suddenly. Uncle Jack reassured us that we had better things to do than hang out with an old man, giving us permission to retire early.

Underneath the beige summer quilt, we found two twin beds made up individually. We pulled the tucked sheets out of the center of each bed, took off our clothes, and met in the middle above the crevice between the mattresses. The cotton sheets carried a chill; I rolled in closer. Ben leaned in for a kiss, and I swallowed his wine-soaked spit. Then he began to lightly snore.

I was alone.

The hypnotic rhythm of the crashing waves carried Elena back to mind for the first time in hours. Imagining her nestled in Maya's bed, I prayed clumsily for her well-being, as I used to do fervently during childhood prayers every night. I'd select one deserving person each day. Could be the grocery woman mopping up the melon I dropped at checkout. Or President Carter fighting human rights crises around the world. That night, however, my focus was Elena. I ached to cradle her and to soothe whatever pain she was feeling. Rolling onto my side, I watched Ben resting soundly. I felt little shivers as I thought, *Ben is someone I could love.*

———

As I raised the window behind the bed, the stagnant air was cut by the salty morning breeze. Ben yanked the sheets and wriggled to my bed. Smacking of morning breath, we kissed, our wet mouths locked as if sucking the oxygen out of each other. The taste of gin, sharp cheddar, and oily salmon were all in play.

I straddled his thighs with a thump. He laughed without sound. Feeling playfully dominant, I grabbed his wrists and pinned his shoulders to the bed to take in the view. Wide-eyed and flat on his back, Ben was grinning over my aggression. I nose-dived toward the tender point where the neck meets the shoulder and licked. Ben wriggled. With every ounce of my weight, I rubbed my dick along the crease of his groin. His knob soon pressed against my belly. And like that, for minutes we were kissing passionately, until our dicks, in unison, spurted. Krazy Glued at the chest, we cuddled as the salty breeze of the ocean seeped through the screen.

A trail of coffee and burnt bread streamed under the door, so we threw on clothes and entered the living room. A platter of toasted cinnamon-raisin bagels and sliced fruit sat on the kitchen counter.

"It's a French press; works very well." Uncle Jack announced. Perry was nowhere to be seen.

Damn, Jack even looks great just out of bed.

"Excellent. I'm starving," I said.

"Andy, I didn't ask what you're doing for the summer. Are you an intern?"

"I'm a hardhat at a utility plant in New Jersey. It suck—" I began, stopping to correct my classy Jersey language. "I don't enjoy it, but the money for college is excellent."

"Hardhat?" Uncle Jack blurted out. "Sounds pretty hot to me," he added with a smirk.

"Uh—" I stammered until I realized he was teasing.

"Did you play sports in school, Andy? I played football and tennis," Uncle Jack said.

"I'm a runner and a swimmer. Solo sports mostly. I also cycle, play a little tennis," I added, exaggerating to impress.

"Well, you can swim or run for hours out here, if the mood strikes," he said. Uncle Jack excused himself to read his newspaper. He suggested that we meet in thirty minutes, and I realized his excess precision was a weird personality trait.

We regrouped and walked the short path to the beach, and then we spread out on towels under a steady but not oppressive sun. Uncle Jack took a swim, showing perfect form, and I could not help but watch as his muscles rippled with each stroke. As he emerged from the surf, I hurriedly buried my nose into *Garp*.

"Cold but invigorating!" he delivered, churning up wet sand as he plopped onto a towel. Ben and I shared a morning of hushed conversation and sensual staring between us. Lying together with Ben, looking at wisps of light brown hair under his arms, gave me a level of sensual freedom I'd never felt before.

Uncle Jack sat below an enormous orange umbrella, reading a wind-ruffled copy of the *New Yorker.*

"Too much sun boosts wrinkles," he warned, "and that makes me look too dark for the camera."

"Gotta protect your investment, Uncle Jack," Ben smirked.

"I'm going to give you two lovebirds time alone. Make sure you put on a lot of lotion, fellas—the Coppertone commercial I did in 1973 paid for this house!"

"Will do," I called out.

"At seven thirty, we'll leave for dinner at Sam's. Andy, it's our favorite spot in town, *wander-full* fresh seafood. Dinner's on me tonight, boys."

"Will Perry be joining us?" Ben asked.

"I'll check with him."

Jack never knew what his live-in boyfriend was up to. I would never want a relationship like that. It was retarded.

After lunch, we sunbathed longer than planned and then headed back to our room for a snooze. We were too drained by the sun to have a quickie.

The next thing we knew, there was a knock. Uncle Jack called through the door.

"Fellas, are you awake? We're leaving in thirty. I left two Lacoste shirts in your closet. They're perfect for Sam's. Andy, the black one is for you, with khakis. Choose espadrilles from the basket, since tennis shoes aren't allowed at the restaurant, okay?"

"Okay, thanks," Ben replied and then whispered to me, "What's an espadrille?"

"I think what Perry was wearing last night. Girly but fashionable."

I tried on the black Lacoste for size. It fit perfectly. The medium white suited Ben, golden from the beach.

I showered and then I sampled several fragrances from a wicker box next to the sink. The moment Ben opened the door, he coughed and grinned.

"What is that? Whoa-ho, we'll be able to smell you a mile away, sport."

We lost it, laughing. Grabbing me tenderly by the waist, Ben said, "Know what, you're pretty great."

"*Wander-full,*" I said, gently mocking our host and then pecking Ben's lips.

"You fucker, you're on to Jack, aren't you," he snickered, returning a kiss. A light honk outside reminded us that Jack and Perry were waiting with the car idling.

Sam's resembled Uncle Jack's decor. Grey shingles with white trim, a small potted tree strung with white lights by the entrance. Dirk, the middle-aged owner, seemed to have undergone plastic surgery; his eyes were pulled to the far sides of his forehead. He welcomed Perry and Jack warmly but offered Ben and me only a forced smile. We were seated at the prominent corner table lit by a trio of white candles.

"Have whatever you like, fellas," Jack insisted. "Time for a cocktail."

Jack ordered gin martinis. When Ben and I puzzled over the drink menu, he insisted on Campari and sodas with lime for us.

Perry looked like a golden god, but he said almost nothing, his eyes darting about the room. He seemed like he'd rather be sitting among more distinguished dinner companions. Jack seemed oblivious to his attitude.

"So, Perry, where are you from originally?" I asked, trying to get him to be part of our table.

"Montana. It's beautiful but dead. There's nothing to do but ranch, fish, and hunt—none of which I'm interested in."

Ben asked Perry if he was out to his family. I expected Perry to explode. Instead, he just smiled painfully and shook his head.

"God, no! They'd never speak to me if they knew. They're quite religious. One reason why I keep a separate apartment in the city. Explaining Jack would never work. To the family, I'm still Jeremiah."

I looked at Perry, confused.

"That's my real name—Jeremiah Luther Welsch," he said, laughing at me for not understanding. "They have no idea why I'd want to live in New York. Why I'd want to model or act. I'm sure they love me, but they don't really know me."

"They do their best," Jack offered.

"It's . . . awkward," Perry continued. "All my sisters and brothers still run the ranch. I'm the black sheep, but I go home once a year."

"And now you're a handsome model in New York," I said, trying to get Perry to like me.

"An actor, too. I'm at Stella Adler between shoots."

"Perry was in an off-Broadway play last season, *Marco Polo Plays a Solo*. At the Public, do you remember, Ben?" Uncle Jack asked.

"That was only a walk-on, no dialogue, but I'm happy to have it on my resume. Thanks to Jack's friend, Joe Papp," Perry said.

"And Perry is a regular at Studio 54," Uncle Jack beamed.

"Seriously? I'd love to go!" I said.

"I go to Studio on special event nights. We models get in free," he sniffed.

"Who have you seen?" Ben asked.

"The most impressive? Farrah Fawcett. I spotted this cascade of gorgeous hair on the dance floor and then saw the teeth, the smile, so I boogied toward her in my cowboy hat. She squealed, 'Giddy-up, cowboy,' then danced off. Girl was coked-up, but a fabulous moment."

"When I move into the city, I'm going to Studio 54," I declared, feeling lightheaded.

"Andy, are you out? We know Ben is on the fence on that issue," Uncle Jack asked.

"Hey, lay off!" Ben protested.

"Pardon me," Jack said, ribbing his nephew. Turning to me, he continued, "How did you guys meet?"

"Stones concert a few weeks ago. Andy was there with his ex-girlfriend, Elena. See, Uncle Jack, I'm not the only one on the fence."

"Next year I'd like to walk down Fifth Avenue in the Gay Liberation March," I said, trying to please Jack.

"Well, you don't have to actually march, Andy. Unless you're political. Most people show up for the parties in the Village afterward. Oh my Lord, anything goes."

"I love parties," I heard myself say and felt stupid, so I decided to keep my mouth shut.

"Andy, when you move into the city, you'll find in the gay community some of the most nurturing, kind human beings you'll ever meet. Even the dykes," Uncle Jack added.

"Lesbians," Perry corrected.

"Yes, sorry, lesbians. We have several women friends who are marvelous."

"Yes," Perry chimed.

"But it's not all fun and games. You also have to be alert. The gay murders last year—horrific. A gay reporter was killed and dismembered. His murderer might have been responsible for other body parts found in the Hudson," Jack said, shaking his head in disgust.

"You mean, like a serial killer?" I gulped as Ben reached over to stroke my arm.

"There are crazy people, fellas, who hate gays," Jack said.

"Well, I'll become an activist. To fight gay hate," I said, too buzzed to control my verbal diarrhea after two drinks.

"Good for you, Andy. Possibly, Ben will join you—once he decides where he stands. Are you out to your family?" Jack asked, staring me down.

"No, only to my ex-girlfriend—and a teacher friend."

"Tell them that story, Andy," Ben smirked, elbowing me in the ribs a little harder than I think he intended.

"Yes, tell us," Perry said, his green eyes flashing.

"His damned schoolteacher was his first experience."

"How fascinating," Perry said, genuinely interested for the first time.

Stammering, but eager to please, I repeated a shorter version of the story I had told Ben. Jack frowned when I finished, but Perry laughed long and hard. I decided I hated him.

"And so he seduced you for your own good?" Uncle Jack asked. "I believe that's illegal."

"But we decided together," I protested.

"Well, Andy, it was wrong. Your teacher should have known better," Uncle Jack said.

"Sounds like a creep to me," Perry added.

"That's enough, okay?" Ben said forcefully. "Let's leave Andy alone—and decide on dinner!"

"They prepare a *wander-full* snapper with preserved lemon, and the sole almondine is very impressive," Uncle Jack said.

To prove I wasn't rattled by the debate, I raised my Campari and soda in a toast.

"Well, thank you, Jack and Perry, for your hospitality. My first trip to Amagansett, and I love it. I wish we didn't have to leave tomorrow."

"You're welcome back anytime. And Ben, if you ever decide your sexuality, you can come back, too—even though you're robbing the cradle."

"Amagansett reminds me of Martha's Vineyard," I boasted, showing off my fake rich-kid credentials.

"You summer on the Vineyard?" Perry asked like a cat regarding a saucer of milk.

"Every summer. I'm going back in August."

"I did a shoot in Oak Bluffs last year. I cherish the Vineyard. Jack, we should go for a long weekend."

I sat back, feeling like I had finally scored some points.

The sole was delicious but left me feeling empty and craving french fries or a side of spaghetti. Perry delivered a boring monologue to convince us that modeling was hard work. Gaining no sympathy, he checked out of conversation and began looking around the room like a spoiled child. Pretending to ignore him, Uncle Jack ordered a Drambuie on the rocks.

In the Beemer's back seat, with my head on his shoulder, Ben whispered, "Did you have a good time? You know, I think Uncle Jack has a crush on you."

"What? No . . ." I said, flattered and titillated.

As we all got out of the car, Uncle Jack suggested, "You fellas should take a stroll. The moon looks full."

"Good idea," Ben said, grabbing me in a headlock.

Happily kicking off the scratchy espadrilles, we walked along the shore. As a man with a golden retriever approached, instinctively, we unclutched our hands. The moon wasn't full but bright enough to see ripples in the waves. Dragging Ben down to the damp, packed sand once we were alone again, I placed a kiss on his mouth. He opened his mouth wide, and my tongue tumbled in. He sucked on it and even bit it gently. I became so aroused that I reached for his swelling pants.

"Not here," Ben said, grabbing my arm. He pulled me to my feet as my boner softened and we raced to the house. We brushed off all remnants of sand on the porch before heading to the bedroom. Soon we had wriggled out of our clothes, still tipsy from the cocktails, and burrowed under the covers.

We were only five minutes into savoring each other when Uncle Jack tapped on the door. Recalling what Ben said before, I was afraid that he wanted to join us.

"Fellas—keep it down in there. Perry's trying to sleep."

We did our best to squelch our laughs, but the sexy mood was now gone.

The following day, Uncle Jack drove us to the train depot armed with sack lunches and chocolate chip cookies he special-ordered from a place in Ohio called Dippies.

On the train it took mere seconds for Ben reach into the bag. With the first bite, he cooed, "This tastes like home."

An Italian sub from the local market was in my bag. Tucked into its fold was a business card. I read the scribbled message: *Anything you need, don't hesitate to call—your friend Jack.*

Chapter 22

Saturday morning, Ruth rang our bell thirty minutes early, toting a box of Dunkin' Donuts and three coffees in a cardboard tray. The day of their departure to Peru had arrived.

Loaded with energy, Ruth said, "Morning! I was worried there'd be traffic, didn't want to be tardy. Andy, I remember powdered blueberry jelly are your favorite. Guess what? All twelve are that flavor!"

It was almost ten before I stuffed Lia's bags into the trunk of Ruth's Nova and waved them off.

I exhaled and turned to take a good look at the house I grew up in, the nest I'd soon flee, the property that would soon be sold to open new chapters for me and Lia. I was overwhelmed with nostalgia. Soon, everything was about to change.

The mood called for a listen to "Space Oddity." I worshiped David Bowie, given his music and public declaration of bisexuality in *Playboy*. I set the album on the turntable, cranked up the volume, and lay flat on the carpet, clutching the record cover to my chest as if it were divine scripture. As I heard ground control calling Major Tom, I sang along, repeating the refrain.

I rose, liberated. Free for two weeks of doing whatever I wanted, whenever I wanted. I was overjoyed I'd see Ben in mere hours. He had invited me to an annual summer party with a Mardi Gras theme, thrown by his rich, well-connected former boss Sam Simon, who remained a partner at Meyer, Simon and Polk.

"So this is a work party?" I had asked the night before when I called at our designated time.

"Hell no. Mardi Gras is too scandalous to be a work party. Sam only invited me and a few of my cronies—people he genuinely likes. Just rock a multicolored shirt and you'll fit right in," Ben said. "Neal's been cooking gumbo for days. Simon goes crazy over Neal's Creole gumbo. Those two have history."

It was barely ten a.m., and I was bursting with energy—and maybe even love. I danced to the kitchen for a second donut and noticed a manila envelope propped against the toaster. Lia had left three one-hundred-dollar bills for groceries, emergencies, and spending money. She added nine stapled pages of her itinerary, a Xerox of her passport, and a doodle of a Peruvian in a bolero hat holding a sign that read: *Miss you already XOXO.*

The day flew. I overworked a painting that I had started the night before, depicting the platter of cheese Uncle Jack served. Not able to distinguish between my renditions of brie, gouda, and cheddar, the painting looked more like a nuclear landscape than a still life. I abandoned the project for an hour of backyard sun. I doused my face and arms with white vinegar, hoping to encourage a fast tan for Mardi Gras. Later, I stuffed my duffel with options of things to wear. Eager to not look like a kid from Jersey, I decided I'd let Ben choose the final outfit. By six o'clock I was standing on the train platform facing the Manhattan skyline, nervous as a nelly that I wouldn't fit in with his crowd.

On the walk to Ben's apartment, I passed a flower shop on Bleecker Street. Can a guy bring flowers to another guy?

Was I breaking rules? Fuck it.

The Scottish shopgirl wrapped a spray of yellow and white tulips in green waxed paper, tying a pink string around the stems, presuming the gender of my recipient. "Lucky lass!" she said.

When Ben buzzed me in, I expected him to be thrilled to see me. But he was distracted.

"Look at this fucking mess!" Ben barked. "Pots everywhere. Rice all over the stove, gravy all over the kitchen. Jesus, am I supposed to clean this up?"

"Hey, these are for you," I said, ignoring the rant and handing Ben the tulips.

"Thank you, but you didn't have to," he said. I felt like he had slapped my face.

Without so much as getting a kiss, I helped him clean up Neal's gumbo crisis. Ben was frosty, and my morale plummeted. I asked Ben to join me in the bedroom and laid two shirts on his waterbed: a silky green and pink Qiana nylon with brown buttons, and a cotton gauze blouse with thick vertical rainbow stripes.

"I need your help. Pick for me," I said.

"That one is way too Jersey," Ben said, pointing to the green and pink print. "And the other one—I don't know. Too loud. Too fruity."

I forced a brave grin but didn't say a thing. He had told me to bring a multicolored shirt. *Asshole.*

"Didn't you leave the black Lacoste here—the one Uncle Jack gave you? Wear that. Hurry, put it on. We gotta go!"

I felt ordinary compared to Ben, looking sexy in a ruby-red shirt with orange stripes over black jeans and scruffy boots. But when he leaned in to give me a quick peck, my childish bad mood evaporated.

"Where's Broome Street?" I asked.

"SoHo, below Houston. Hey, sorry I've been cranky. It's been a shitty week. Then Neal's mess really pissed me off. You can't leave a kitchen like that. It draws cockroaches."

I held up a doobie from my jacket pocket. Ben grinned and hugged me.

The SoHo neighborhood, with nineteenth-century cast-iron buildings in various stages of disrepair, was ghostly. A few people were mingling in front of a building. We huddled on a loading platform, sucking my doobie.

"I'll introduce you to people as my friend, okay?" Ben whispered while riding up the freight elevator.

"What else would you say?" I said defensively. "I can't wait to see what a downtown art party is like."

"Some random people show up. SoHo is getting trendy. These lofts are ideal party spaces. People are buying them up—like artists, musicians."

The elevator doors opened onto a cavernous half-empty space as a remixed version of "Psycho Killer" pounded from the amplifiers. Ben led me to the drinks table and prudently introduced me to two guys in the art department and their modish wives. "Everyone, this is Andy," he said as if I were a tag-along friend. Pissed by the freeze-out, I suddenly realized . . . he's closeted at the agency.

For an hour, we mingled with Ben's friends, shouting over the music to make small talk. I told them I was a painter because that sounded better than being a high schooler.

Around eleven, the scene grew intense. Wild flocks of nonconformists in glittery costumes mobbed the dance platform. The place was crackling. While Ben was making the rounds, my attempts at mingling fell flat. I spotted a foxy blond guy standing alone against a wall. Despite his Hitler Youth vibe, I walked up to introduce myself. The dude dropped his head, eked out a hello, and marched toward the bar.

Was I a loser?

Minutes later, Ben returned, smiling broadly. We migrated to a nook away from the dance floor. A hippie wearing a pullover shirt decorated with the flag of Argentina popped out of nowhere with his coltish boyfriend. "I'm Alessandro, a potter, and this is Norm, and this is ChiChi, my cousin."

"We're from Brooklyn," Norm said, wearing a cellophane skirt. "And you are?"

We introduced ourselves.

ChiChi was adorable and apparently deaf. Ben surprised me by showing that he knew sign language, and he was thrilled to sign with ChiChi, discovering she was a textile designer at Pratt. She was plainly flirting, but that came to a halt when Lula ran up and kissed Ben. The trio from Brooklyn wandered off as Lula and Ben huddled and caught up, leaving me to stare into space. Minutes later, Lula shot me a cutesy wave then swirled away with an unmistakably gay boy to the beat of "Dance, Dance, Dance."

"Oh, shit," Ben mouthed as a man wearing a straw fedora and a snug black T-shirt with rhinestones spelling *New Orleans* snaked toward us.

My neck stiffened as if someone abruptly pointed a gun to my head.

"Hello, Ben. Great party, isn't it? Clearly, the only place to be in Manhattan tonight," the guy said, forcing a hug on Ben.

"Good to see you. How was your Paris trip?" Ben asked.

"Wonderful, just wonderful. Did you see Warhol?" he said, pointing his index finger. "He's standing beside the unicorn statue."

"White Carol Channing wig. I see him," Ben said. "You should go cozy up, snag a project together."

"There'll be time for that. Ben, this is Manuel. He's a supremely talented apprentice with City Ballet."

Manuel, maybe sixteen, grinned indifferently. I struggled to remain present.

"Hi, Manuel," Ben said. "Damon Piccard, this is Andy, my . . . close friend Andy. We missed you at the Stones concert."

Bang. The imaginary gun fired. Damon, the name Ben revealed at the concert, had stuck in my head since the moment he said it. Now standing across from me, the sound of the guy's voice, tough and blunt with an air of pretense, shook me like an evil nightmare. Damon was Fucking-fuck. I wanted to run, but my legs tightened. I couldn't move. I nearly shit my pants.

Damon stepped back to size me up. Then, calculating, Ben added, "Wait . . . Andy sat in your seats at the concert."

Damon looked at me, or rather, looked through me.

"No, don't know each other. Besides, I had another event that night. I gave the tickets away. I heard Mick was a mess," my rapist said.

Fuck, was this really happening? It was difficult to look him in the eye.

Ben nodded, "Mick was fucked up, but the concert was outstanding. Very intimate, but kind of brilliant."

Watching Ben and Damon interact, I stared, as if a catastrophe were about to happen. I nervously watched Damon as he rocked from one foot to the other. The size of his tall, lanky body was familiar. The pork chop sideburns. His commanding nose, the one that lurched over me. As he again averted his eyes, I realized that Damon remembered me—and wasn't going to let Ben know.

"Well . . . we better move on," Damon said, breezily. "We have another party to hit. Good to see you, Ben. You, too—Michael, was it?" Having played his final card, offering a crooked grin, Damon steered his play-toy Manuel toward the exit.

"That was fucking weird," Ben yammered, "but I had to be cordial. I never expected to see *him* at this party. Did you notice him sniffling? He's a coke whore. Everybody knows it. And I hear he never shares. That boy he was with—what, was he fifteen? Sixteen at most? That's the New York I hate."

Ben hadn't picked up on my tangled vibe. But I needed to shake off the tension. I asked Ben to get me another gin and tonic and looked for the toilet. It was at the room's edge, a closet fitted with a toilet and a sink, no lock.

Once inside, I heaved a stream of vomit into the bowl. I rinsed my mouth with rusty water from the tap and paused to stare in the mirror. The light was too dim to see if I'd turned pale. I felt like shit.

Was I a coward for not confronting Damon on the spot? It wasn't consensual. He violated me. The bruises were proof. So why didn't I throw a punch?

A knock on the door shook me out of the trance. I vacated the safe space, letting a Black man dressed in a colorful Jamaican caftan take my place.

Ben was holding our drinks.

"Andy, you look really shitty. You feeling okay?"

"Not really. Let's leave. Please."

"It's a fantastic party, but I guess—"

"Thanks, Ben."

Neal approached, offering shrimp toast on a silver platter. We both refused, and Ben explained we were cutting out.

"Party's just starting, boys," he teased. "Oh, I'm not sleeping at the apartment tonight. You lovebirds will have utmost privacy." Stooping down, Neal kissed our cheeks and danced back into the crowd, hoisting the platter of shrimp high above his head.

The street air festering with excrement and trash made me gag. We were both silent while walking east several blocks until I spoke.

"I'm sorry, Ben. I ruined your night."

"It was just a party. There'll be others."

"Thanks—"

"Geez, I hope Neal's gumbo didn't make you sick. I'll make you some chamomile tea."

"I barely ate anything. I'm okay."

"Then I'll make you a sandwich."

We sprinted through the cheerless streets, my head swimming in the darkness. I saw recurring flashes of him, that lanky fuck, under the sheet on the futon. I felt like my rectum was aching again, as well as my wrists.

"It was that man, Damon," I declared, cringing.

"Did Damon hit on you? You're a little old for him."

"If I tell you something, you won't get pissed? Ben, it wasn't my fault."

"Wait, he did hit on you? Did he follow you to the bathroom?"

"I met Damon before tonight. Once. Only once."

"How? Where did you meet Damon? You're not even really out!" Ben snapped.

"One night I went to a bar alone."

"Fuck, was it the Ninth Circle? He trolls there a lot. Andy, please don't tell me you had sex with Damon!"

"He picked me up on Christopher Street, I guess, but I fuckin' don't remember. I'm not sure what happened. I swear. Ben, it was awful."

I felt the tears start to well up in my eyes.

Dodging a mob of drunk students wobbling out of McSorley's Old Ale House, Ben looked back and saw my eyes and began to freak.

"Andy—please don't cry. I'll fix this. All you need is a sandwich. I'll make you a sandwich," he said. "It'll be okay. That fucker!"

The back of my shirt was trickling with sweat, and I was terrified I'd mess up all I had with Ben. Once we were inside his apartment, he grabbed my shoulders and forced me to look into his eyes.

"Okay, I'm making you food. And you're gonna spill. Everything. Deal?"

"I'm not hungry, but I'll talk," I mumbled.

I explained what happened six weeks before, skipping some details that still made me feel shitty. Ben listened, his face blank but sympathetic.

"And the next morning, I woke up in his apartment. That's it. Ben, I didn't even know his name."

"Fuck. Tug's. I didn't even think Damon went to Tug's. And that shithead didn't recognize you tonight?"

"I know he did. He got very jittery when you introduced me."

"I totally missed that. Shit. He was so coked up. Andy, I have to work with that asshole."

"I'm sorry," I said stupidly, as if it was my fault.

"Did he drug you, Andy? Slipped you something?"

"I woke up with a booze hangover, that's all."

"What did Damon say in the morning?"

"He was out cold when I left."

"Fuck, did you have sex?"

"He did. I mean—I was bleeding a few hours later."

"Bleeding—from where?"

"Don't make me say."

"Oh shit—I get it. So he had sex with you while you were unconscious?" Ben was red-faced.

"I guess," I shrugged.

"You guess? If you didn't let him, then Damon raped you!"

Girls get raped; guys don't get raped.

"When I see him, I'm going to fucking punch him in the face."

"Don't lose your job over me."

"Andy, did you go to a doctor?"

"No. I went home. Showered and went to bed . . . all day," I said, stopping short of mentioning the bruises on my wrists.

"I'm sorry this happened to you," Ben said quietly. "I'm truly sorry."

"It's over," I whimpered. "Please help me forget it."

Ben filled the kettle for the tea and then suddenly snapped his head back to look at me.

"Wait . . . the Stones concert. You had Damon's tickets. Did he give you his tickets? In exchange for sex?"

"Hell, no."

"What the fuck, Andy. Spill."

"I took the tickets from his apartment. I was pissed off. Needed to get even because he hurt me."

"This is even more fucked up. But I'm glad you took them. You should have trashed his apartment."

At least he wasn't still blaming me.

"I'm going to kill that prick."

"Ben, let it go. I'm trying to do the same thing."

"I guess we have Damon to thank, right?"

I stared at him.

"What the fuck?"

"Think of it, Andy. I met you because you stole Damon Douchebag's tickets."

"I'll buy him a gift certificate—no, a pound of cocaine," I grumbled—and then started to laugh in spite of myself.

"No—let's take the fucker out on the town. And once he's strung out, I'll push him in front of traffic," Ben said, laughing so much that he got me laughing even more.

Ben stopped laughing suddenly and looked at me, his chin set grimly.

"Fuck. Does Elena know?"

"Hell no. Ben, it's history. I'm tired. I should head back to Jersey."

"Don't be stupid. You're staying here. Drink the chamomile tea. Then let's go to sleep. Or you want a shot? That's it. We're both having a Dewar's. It will help us sleep," Ben said.

"Ben, I want to avoid fucking this up. I like you so much."

"Mess what up? Us? You won't do that."

"Okay," I said, sniffling again—this time with relief.

"People at MSP love-hate Damon, but this proves he's a prick, once and for all. I wish I could tell everyone in the office. He's freelance, and this would get him bounced out on his ass. But then, I'd have to tell them about you—and—"

"And you're not out at work. Right?"

Ben looked down. His silence explained it all.

———

The smell of coffee brewing in Ben's kitchen jerked me awake. I could hear him banging pots. Facing him after last night's confession scared me, but I needed to pee. Tiptoeing to the bathroom, I tripped over the four-legged tub and felt it wrench a toe.

"Fuck!"

"Are you okay?" Ben called from the stove.

"Yes," I said with false certainty, disgusted with the face I saw in the mirror. Creaking open the door, I braced for a confrontation.

"Morning. Coffee is ready. Should we have breakfast here or go out for pancakes?"

"Here is good. Just coffee," I said, reaching for the clean T-shirt Ben had laid over the chair. "Can I wear your gym shorts?"

"Yes, anything."

"Ben. I'm really . . . sad. This sucks."

"Can you believe after we scrubbed the counter, I'm still finding rice?"

"Rice? We're discussing rice?" I asked, ticked off.

"Hey, I'm sorry I wasn't more sympathetic last night. I forget you're eighteen. That asshole took advantage of you. Anyway . . . ," he said, handing me coffee in a white PBS mug.

"Thanks. Fill 'er up. I already know I'll want thirds."

"You were a wreck last night, sport."

"Yeah, because I was reliving the rape all over again."

"I'm sorry. I wasn't blaming you—"

"Yeah, you were—a little."

"Yeah, I was. But then I remembered what a shit Damon is."

"I had a rotten night of sleep."

"We'll get through this. You're still a kid. I made mistakes too. I still am."

"I'm not a kid. I'm eighteen."

"Anyway, how does toast sound? I have peasant bread from the Ukrainian bakeshop. And my mom's canned peach jam."

"Toast, but then I'd better head home. Lia's calling tonight from Peru."

"I thought we'd go to the flea market today—but another time."

"Yeah, I should get home," I said, inwardly thrilled that Ben had plans for us today. "Next weekend, I'm free."

I cornered Ben and delivered a wet one to his lips. As he returned the kiss, little shivers made a comeback, and I knew for sure that I was in love with him.

Chapter 23

"Peru is fabulous," Lia crackled through the static. "Andy, we need to travel, see the world!"

The sound of my mom's voice was comforting. I shrugged off last night's drama and gave it my all to mirror her joy. She told me they were leaving Lima, the capital of Peru, in an hour for the Andes mountains and Machu Picchu.

"Can you believe I ate raw fish and liked it!" she giggled. "The teachers on the tour are hilarious. Ruth says *hola!*"

We spoke for two minutes before the operator's voice warned the long-distance call was timing out.

I assured Lia all was clear on the home front and that I relished the alone time to paint. We shared a kiss sound, and the connection broke.

On my own, I further indulged my melancholy over selling our home. No more mowing the grass. No Saturday housecleaning sing-alongs. No catching up over late dinners at the kitchen table.

The stillness in the house became suffocating. As the oven preheated, for noise I turned on *The Wonderful World of Disney*. Then I dialed Ben and left a message telling him I was feeling a little blue still. And I thanked Neal for the gumbo, just to be polite.

Minutes later, Ben returned the call.

"Hey, sport, I have an idea that will boost your spirits. Hear me out. We're looking for students for a Columbia University ad campaign. Why don't you let me test you? You get a hundred and fifty bucks for the day. If they use you, you'll get up to fifteen hundred. Easy money for school."

"Seriously?"

"The campaign will be used on buses, enrollment materials, posters— that kind of thing."

"Count me in. This money would take the heat off my mom a little."

"Here's the squeeze. Damon the prick is art director on the project. I want to see him squirm when he sees your face in the photos. I'm betting he'll choose you out of guilt. Yeah, I know it's twisted."

"Ummm, I guess so—as long as I don't have to see fuckface again."

"You won't. Maybe if he knows we're on to him, he won't go around fucking up other kids."

"I'm not a kid. Are you sure about this?"

"There's nothing to lose. At least you'd get something beneficial from this prick. Something besides the Stones tickets, something besides me," Ben added.

"Okay, I'm in. Lia will be thrilled."

"Andy, I just realized I'm going out with a guy who lives with his mother!"

"Hey, not for long. I'm gonna be a college boy soon."

"And a hunky college boy at that. Let's take the test shots this week, okay?"

"Absolutely," I replied.

Luba answered the phone. Before I could make small talk and act like nothing was out of the ordinary, she lowered her voice to ask me if anything was bothering Elena. She insisted that her little girl seemed depressed. When I told her that everybody gets into moods, she mildly agreed with me but still sounded uncertain. Then she called Elena to the phone.

"Hey, you. I was going to call you tonight."

"Hey there."

"Mom, can you please hang up? Andy, guess what? Rumor is, Bruce is in Jersey on a short break from the tour and playing a late set at the Stone Pony Friday night. Maya found out from her music prof, the one with a crush on her. We gotta go."

"Springsteen? Wild. I'll ask Ben. He could sleep over. If he's in, I'm in."

"Wait, you'll only go if Ben goes? Whoa, this is getting serious."

"E, weekends are the only chance we get to hang."

"Sounds like there's a lot of hanging out, honcho."

"Dirty mind. Guess what? Ben recommended me as a model for an ad campaign."

"Incredible! Does it pay?"

"It pays a lot if I get picked."

"By the way, I'm feeling better, thanks for asking," Elena jabbed.

"You didn't give me a chance. You do sound better. But Luba noticed."

"I'm so transparent," she said.

"We have to pick ourselves up, shake it off, then make new mistakes."

"Jeez. Thanks, Dad."

On midday Thursday, I sped through the Lincoln Tunnel. Ben taught me that parking was at the ready on the unmetered, desolate side streets of the spice district in TriBeCa. The cardamom, pepper, and nutmeg combination was so intense I pinched my nose so I wouldn't sneeze while walking from the car to the subway.

As instructed, I took the 1 Train uptown to Twenty-Third Street and then walked east to Park Avenue to Meyer, Simon and Polk. The gold numbers on the neoclassical building were hard to miss. Inside the lobby, I marveled at the veined granite on the floor and walls, and the gilded staircase. A stylish man in cream-colored linen slid the elevator's accordion gate open.

"Can I help you find something?"

"I'm looking for MSP, but I'm not sure which floor?"

"Sixth floor. Delivery?"

"No, no, I'm meeting with someone. Ben Hoppe."

"Ben is on eight. If you know him, go to eight, but if not, reception is on six."

"Yes, I do know him. Thank you," I said, seeing the dandy press eight.

"Presley Polk. And you are?"

"Andrew Pollock," I replied, matching his formality.

Accepting his vigorous handshake, I recognized Polk as the final name in the agency.

"Any relation to Jackson Pollock? My father is friends with his widow, Lee Krasner."

"Just the same surname."

"Well, Ben's a good man. I'll take you up. You're a model?"

"I'm a student. Ben's taking test photos for a campaign."

"Where are you a student?"

"NYU Fine Arts. Well, in September."

"Here we are. The eighth floor. Andrew—I hope you make the cut. Ben's down this corridor."

"Andy," Ben called, popping out of a doorway then getting formal when he saw his boss. "You found me."

"Ben, I met Andrew in the lobby," Presley said playfully. "He's ready for his close-up."

"Thanks, Presley. We're on schedule. I'm gathering finalists for Columbia."

"Good luck, Andrew," Presley called out from down the corridor.

"Nice strategy," Ben marveled, "meeting the top brass right off the bat."

"Presley was super nice."

"He's a good egg," Ben said, guiding me toward the backdrop.

"Was he at Mardi Gras?"

"Of course. I said hello to him early in the party."

"I brought a button-down and khakis. What do you think? Collegiate?"

"I forgot to tell you we have a rack of clothes. Put on the yellow Oxford."

"Oxford? What's that?"

"A button-down, it's the type of cloth—these shirts are from Brooks Brothers. Wear it untucked over the jeans. The white Adidas are good. Put this blue backpack over the shirt, and carry these two red textbooks under your arm," he directed me, placing the manuals on a stool.

My head was spinning but I tried to follow the many orders Ben was throwing at me.

"By the way, Uncle Jack asked if we wanted to join him for dinner tonight. There's a new Tex-Mex place he'd like us to try. Iguana something. He'd like to see you. I told you he liked you special."

"Stop that!" I said, blushing. "What's Tex-Mex?"

"Yeah—where you from, Jersey?" Ben teased and laughed. "It's a Texas version of Mexican food, very trendy."

"I'm game. I have an iron stomach."

"By the bye, Damon's in today to review the frames for final approval. Wait until he sees your face among the galleys. I'd give anything to see him shit his fancy pants."

"Uh, I—"

"The real shoot is next week. Can you make that? Wednesday, maybe Thursday?"

"Yes. I'll resign from PGE if I have to. After all, this pays more. Next Friday night is Patti Smith in Central Park, so it would be great if the shoot was the same day."

"We will try to meet your schedule, Mr. Model Man," Ben giggled. "First, Damon has to approve. That Oxford looks great on you. You look sexy all prepped out."

He directed me to stand in front of a screen and relax my shoulders, as Ben flattened my hair with the palm of his hand.

"The actual shoot will have a hair, makeup, and wardrobe person. It's a full day, for individual plus group shots."

Standing behind the tripod, Ben advised, "Drop your chin, back up a couple of inches. Right shoulder toward me. Fewer teeth. Slow turn toward me. Smile, but less broadly. Great. Now squat down on one knee. Good. Don't fall over," he said, laughing.

I followed him to the letter even though I had a headache. I heard the numerous clicks and whirs.

"Lean against the wall like you're talking to someone. Andy, these look solid. Okay, set the books on your noggin. Let's get goofy here. That's it. We got it."

"Wow, that was fast. How many did you take?"

"Hmm . . . close to sixty. We only need three to five strong ones. You've got a real shot at this, sport."

"Are there other candidates for my part?"

"Yeah, eight others. But I chose boys who are too model-y on purpose, so you would stand out as authentic."

"Is that legal?" I asked, prompting Ben to laugh at my naïveté.

"I have another ninety minutes of work. Why don't you hang out in the library next to reception? There are hundreds of art books. Then we can go to my place. Let's fool around before we meet Uncle Jack at eight."

"Wait. I have to change back into my clothes."

"Nah, wear the yellow Oxford—it looks adorable on you. Sixth-floor receptionist is Nora. Tell her you're waiting for me."

———

As Ben unlocked the deadbolt to his apartment, I felt silly and horny and licked his neck. Suddenly, I heard opera music blare. Neal was home.

"*La bohème* welcomes you home," he announced grandly.

Ben and I exchanged quick looks of disappointment. Instead of mon-keying about naked, I settled for sitting on the patio sipping German beer. Neal was in a spirited mood.

"Well, lovebirds, what are y'all up to tonight? My man is casting off to San Francisco to visit his gays. He didn't ask me to join him, so I'm a bachelor all weekend."

"That's tough," Ben said, with a wink in his eye.

"I mean, after dating for two months, shouldn't he have asked me? And San Francisco, God knows what he'll be up to. His friends are pretty boys with shit for brains. I know I sound bitter. Well, I am! Another brewski, boys?"

"I'm good," Ben answered. "I'm going to New Jersey tomorrow with Andy. Rumor has it Bruce Springsteen is performing in a bar in Asbury Park."

"You better be back Saturday, Mister Man. You're going with me to that gala. Remember, it's for SAGE. This new charity helps out old queens—pardon me, gay and lesbian senior citizens."

"No sweat," I shrugged.

"Andy, can I borrow your cornfed lover boy for one night? I'm sorry but I only have two invitations."

"I forgive you," I said, trying to sound as dramatic as Neal.

"Isn't Springsteen that bearded hunk on the cover of *Newsweek*?" Neal asked. "I prefer classical music and opera. Unless it's N'awlins blues."

"I thought you were living for disco these days," Ben teased.

"Yes, disco. I'm enslaved. Donna Summer is my royal queen."

"Neal, what time did you start drinking?"

"Honey, I stopped at Uncle Charlie's at five and had two tequila sunrises."

"Who's Uncle Charlie?" I asked.

"Darling, who's Uncle Charlie? You are fresh from the garden, aren't you? Uncle Charlie's is the bar of the moment. It's on Greenwich Avenue in the West Village. It's for people like us: divas, preppy professionals, and hunky fresh-faced students straight off the bus. It's packed every night."

"Ben, it's seven thirty. Shouldn't we be heading out to meet Uncle Jack?" Neal chuckled.

"You call him Uncle Jack already. Isn't that the cutest thing. Precious. If you two move in together, I need two months' notice, puh-lease!"

"Neal, we'll be back in a few hours," Ben said.

"Can't promise I'll be here. In fact, I promise I will not. While my baby doll does San Francisco, I'm doing the Village."

"Be careful," Ben cautioned, wagging a finger playfully.

"Why not take Uncle Jack to Uncle Charlie's after dinner?" Neal bubbled. "The boys will flock to that sugar daddy. Andy, see you soon."

The Checker reeked of cigar, demanding we roll down the windows.

"It's called the something Iguana," Ben said. "Tomorrow, I'll leave the office by one so we can head to Jersey."

"Is Lula coming to see Bruce?"

"Nope, zero interest. I love her, but she can be impossible."

"Neal was wound up tonight."

"That he was."

"I was hoping to come back to the city with you on Saturday. I hate you going to that gay party without me."

"Andy. We're together tonight and going to your house tomorrow. This is great, but we have our lives. Let's take it slow, okay?"

"Okay," I said, feeling like he had slapped my face.

"I love being with you, sport, but shit—driver, far corner, please."

Uncle Jack, handsome as ever, was standing outside the restaurant looking at his watch with a scowl.

"Boys. I did say eight o'clock. It's now 8:15. I made a reservation. Andy, I'll forgive you. Ben should know better."

"Hi, is Perry joining us?" I asked, marveling at Jack's purple plaid shirt.

"Perry is in Newfoundland on a shoot for a coat company. Let's go in. I prefer not to lose our reservation."

The hostess sat us alongside a dinosaur-sized multicolored iguana. Jack announced grandly that dinner was, once again, his treat. We all ordered a round of margaritas and ceviche and poblano dip.

Uncle Jack specified top-shelf tequila for the drinks, with salt, giving his order to an indifferent waiter.

"I've never been to a Mexican restaurant," I confessed.

"Tex-Mex," Uncle Jack corrected. "You'll enjoy it. Andy, ask if you're unfamiliar with anything. So, what's new, boys?"

"Well," said Ben, "I recruited Andy to do test shots today for a campaign I'm helping art direct for Columbia University. We'll know tomorrow if he signs."

"Andy, I didn't know you model. With those trademark eyebrows, you make a memorable impression."

"This is more of a one-time thing," Ben interjected. "To make some cash for school."

"Who makes the final decision, Ben?" Uncle Jack asked.

"A freelance art director, Damon Piccard, has the final say. Andy already knows him," Ben quipped.

"Ben!" I scolded.

"Andy, is the art director a relative?" Uncle Jack asked.

"It's a long story, Uncle Jack. Ask Andy if he wants to get into it."

My eyes blazed as Jack's eyes widened. I hated Ben at that moment.

I knew there was no choice but to come clean.

Offering very few details, I explained the encounter with Damon. As I spoke, Jack's sexy smile became a frown. He placed a hand on mine in pure sympathy.

"Basically, the prick forced sex on Andy," Ben blurted out. "While he was sleeping. Is that about right, sport?"

"Yes," I said, wishing I was somewhere else.

"I'm sorry, Andy," Uncle Jack replied. "What did he say to you in the morning?"

"He was out cold when I slipped out." And I repeated the part of the story that really made me look bad: stealing the tickets.

"Boys, this is very upsetting," Jack moaned. "Explain this again. This guy is an art director at MSP?"

"He's freelance, but prominent," Ben explained.

Then Ben explained his scheme to get Damon to review my photos to get back at him. Jack shook his head, whether in amusement or shock, I could not tell.

"Phew. This is a lot to take in, boys," Jack said. "Andy is definitely taking his baby steps out of the closet the hard way. This Damon story sounds of a piece with that saga about your schoolteacher, my boy. I see a definite pattern. Babe in the woods."

"Fuck," I croaked, turning to my margarita to hide my embarrassment. He was right. Ollie, Damon. Shit.

"Andy, did you see a doctor? Did you go to the police?"

"What could the police do?"

"It depends on the officer. But most don't give a damn. Andy, this sounds like a case of rape."

"There were bruises on my wrists where he tied me up."

The tequila made my head swim and details kept flowing.

"Bruises? Andy, you left that part out. That fucking prick," Ben sputtered.

"You were definitely assaulted," Jack said. "Now there's not much to do, unfortunately. Perhaps a therapist? It might be good to talk to a professional, Andy."

"Yes, sir," I said, head lowered as if I were being scolded.

"After all, there's a clear pattern of victimizing here."

"Ollie didn't—" I protested, but they both ignored me.

"Damon is a predator. Later tonight, I'm going to call Presley Polk. He's a close friend of mine. That's how Ben got his job. Frankly, he needs to know. MSP shouldn't hire this character again."

"He's talented though—even if I can't stand him," Ben said.

"Talent is one thing, but this is serious. There isn't much else we can do apart from kicking this fellow's ass. Trust me, I'm considering that."

"Thanks, Uncle Jack," Ben said, taking another deep drink from his margarita.

"Andy, New York indeed is the Big Apple, polished on the outside but full of seeds. Try not to let this incident jade you. And for God's sake, don't over-drink at the bars. It's a recipe for disaster!"

Uncle Jack then asked about Lia, and I was happy to change topics.

"Your mother and I should meet," he said. "I'd like her to know you have a support team here in the city. Substitute fathers like me and—well, whatever you would call Ben." He smirked and then began laughing. Ben blushed.

"I'm here for Andy too," Ben insisted, sounding boozier.

"You have more of a hands-on strategy, I daresay," he said. "Let's order our entrées and a fresh round of margaritas, fellas. Or has Ben had quite enough?"

"I'm celebrating," Ben scoffed. "Celebrating the whomping Damon is gonna get."

"Revenge," Uncle Jack reminded Ben, "is a dish best served cold. All in due time, my impulsive nephew."

Stewed and stuffed, Ben and I thanked Uncle Jack for dinner and hailed him a taxi to his next event. Meandering down lower Fifth Avenue, I sighed, "Ben, he's the father I always wanted."

"It would be dangerous for you to have a dad that sexy, wouldn't it?"

"Ben!" I yelled, ashamed that he was reading my mind.

"Did you know Uncle Jack was married?" Ben said with a slur.

"No, how would I know that?" I said.

"Married to his college sweetheart, Suze. Both in their twenties. In Columbus, he was a real estate agent. They had a split-level, white picket fence, in-ground swimming pool, the whole nine yards. After a few years, they adopted a baby girl. A perfect life," Ben said.

"Wow!"

"He fought being gay. After Lily arrived, he told Suze about his attraction to men. Suze freaked out and took the baby to Cincinnati, where her family lives. Jack lost access to Lily in the divorce. He sends cards and presents, so she won't forget him. But he hasn't seen her in forever."

"That sucks. Uncle Jack's so sweet."

"He had it tough. Maybe that's why I haven't come out once and for all. I can see how it backfires. Right?"

Ben sounded like he was trying to convince himself—and me.

"I don't know. I mean—"

"After the divorce, he moved to Manhattan to find himself. I think he's finally happy—although Perry is no Prince Charming. Why he puts up with him I don't know."

I felt bad for Uncle Jack. I felt like I had it much better than he did. After all, I had Ben.

That night, in his apartment, we made love for hours and I swore to myself that I would never again doubt how he felt about me. I would finally drop the jealous Jersey suburban baby attitude.

"That's chicory," Ben explained as I stumbled into the kitchen, sniffing the unusual aroma filling the air. "I made it in the Chemex, knowing you had a lazy morning to yourself. I'll be home around lunchtime."

The sense of freedom I had alone in Ben's apartment the minute he left for the office was exhilarating—as if I owned the place. Nibbling a hunk of pumpernickel toast, I propped a headshot of Ben against the pepper mill and then removed Conté à Paris crayons, a kneaded eraser, and a sketch pad from my overnight bag. Cracking my knuckles, I traced the shape in the air and then drew an oval for the face, outlining the eyes, nose, lips, and neck. With thicker strokes, mixing burnt sienna with ochre, I drew in Ben's light brown hair. Then I detailed his features, introducing a reflection of clouds within both pupils.

Satisfied with the results, I tilted the portrait against a green crock holding a bundle of lavender that Ben had cut from the garden. After a slow shower and a sneaky rummage of Ben's and Neal's stash in the medicine cabinet, I fixed ham sandwiches on wheat, adding mayo, an ingredient reserved only for potato salad in my family. As I cut the second sandwich in half, I caught the sound of jangling keys in the door.

"I have good news," Ben announced. "Babe, you made the goddamn cut. I was in the room. As he was scanning your photos, I watched Damon's eyes bulge. He actually squirmed in his seat. He had to clear his throat twice before he could squeeze out one question. It was, 'Do you think the eyebrows are too prominent?'"

"Oh my effin' Christ," I said, really losing my shit. I was so happy. I almost felt like I could put the rape behind me, once and for all.

"Listen! I was cool as a cucumber. Then I said, slowly, 'No, that makes the model and the ad memorable.' Bam! I shot him down, that's for sure!"

"Wow." I was tingling.

"I have more good news. Presley fired Damon from the project—luckily after he approved your test shots."

I felt tears come to my eyes but pushed them back.

"I guess Uncle Jack phoned Presley after dinner last night. Presley said Damon will no longer be freelancing with MSP. No further explanation. Nobody dared ask. Some looked shocked but others were smirking a little. Then Presley elected me art director for the Columbia campaign in front of everyone. Sport—this is huge."

"Oh, man, I—" I could only stammer, my heart was so full.

"We can do the shoot next Friday. Happy?"

"Happy? I can't even tell you how happy I am." I began hollering like those Indians about to attack in the old Western movies. Damned if I knew why. Ben looked at me with mock fear and we both started laughing.

"Lia will go berserk. I wish I could call her in Peru. Thank you," I said, closing in for a kiss.

Ben beamed, adding, "My scheming worked out. Sometimes I'm so clever, I scare myself."

"Jeez, Louise," I said, rolling my eyes.

"We both win. Thanks to you, I'll never have to work with that prick again."

"But the shots were good, right? Not because of . . . ?"

"It wasn't blackmail, you dorkus. Your shots happened to be excellent. I mean—look who snapped them," Ben said, taking a huge bow and pretending to fart, which made me laugh all over again.

"Okay," he said. "Enough laughing. Jersey is waiting!" As he was chomping on the sandwich, Ben shyly fingered the sketch propped on the table.

"Andy, you are talented. Seriously. And I am honored."

"It's yours."

"What?"

"Of course, I made it for you."

I wanted to add "with love," but decided to hold off.

We cabbed to where the Blue Whale was parked in TriBeCa, finding a pink ticket tucked under the wiper blade. Fuck.

"How can they give me a street cleaning violation when the street is still filthy? This is bullshit."

"I'm sorry, sport, I'll split it with you. How much?"

"Twenty-five. Let's get out of here. It stinks."

"That smells like asafoetida, a strong Indian spice. Andy, your car is way cool. What a beautiful color—I'd describe it as cadet blue, or . . . porpoise."

"Porpoise? That's pretty femme. But what should I expect from Mr. Fancy Art Director," I jabbed.

"Porpoise sounds faaaabulous," Ben said, applying a fey tone. "You know, sport, this photoshoot means I'll be your boss. For one day, anyway. Hot, right?" And he grinned and leered, so I laughed.

"Speaking of The Boss, pop in the Springsteen tape." The cassette picked up with "Born to Run."

Ben shouted out the passenger window, "We're going to Jersey to see Bruce and Andy's house in the little Maple syrup hometown. God save me!"

I laughed so hard the tears were coming down, making driving precarious.

Sailing across the Turnpike, I slowed down to circle the Walt Whitman Fountain in Maple Ridge's lone roundabout.

"Damn—Maple High looks like my high school in Ohio. Andy, I still can't believe you were in high school less than two months ago. I'm a cradle-robber, aren't I?"

Once we got to my house, I gave Ben a quick tour, ending at my bedroom. Feeling sure of myself, I pinned him against the wall and boomed, "Cradle-robber, huh? I'm not too young now, am I?"

We peeled off our clothes and kissed and grabbed and suckled for a frantic fifteen minutes. Cradling Ben atop the bedspread, I cackled, "We forgot to take our socks off."

"I gotta be honest. I still can't believe you were naked with Damon Piccard, sport."

"Where did that come from?" I said, pulling away and scowling at him. "Ben, I can't change the past. Why would you wanna obsess about something like that?"

"Sorry. It's been on my mind. I'm just being honest with you. I have to admit it bothers me sometimes."

"You mean, like now? And that's my fault?" I was fuming.

"Andy, I enjoy being with you, and you're mature for your age, but occasionally, I feel a little pervy. How am I any different from that teacher who attacked you?"

"Ollie did not attack me. I let him seduce me. I owed it to him—or whatever. Just drop it."

"I know, but—"

"You're five years older than me, Ben. Big fucking deal. I can't make myself older. But I'll be nineteen next year, and living in the city soon."

We got dressed silently, not looking at each other, and then headed to the kitchen. Ben seemed to get less uptight as we devoured bowls of left-over rigatoni and meatballs.

"Sorry, kid," Ben said, looking at me guiltily.

"You just had a case of low blood sugar," I said, not wanting to fight anymore and hoping we could move past this. I mean, I was getting over Damon—so why couldn't Ben? It was just weird, and I felt helpless—but more pissed off.

Hearing the honking horn, Ben grabbed the six-pack of RC Cola. I locked the house, and we climbed in with Maya, Rocco, and Elena. As I doled out the colas, Rocco cranked up a tape of Bruce's newest, *Darkness on the Edge of Town*.

"Beatles, Stones, Bruce," he challenged us. "In order."

"No question, *Stones*, Bruce, Beatles? They're pop. Stones, Bruce, Ramones," Elena said.

"Pop? Elena darling, the Beatles are the greatest band that ever lived. They're to modern music what Beethoven is to classical. 'Come Together,' 'Here Comes the Sun,' 'Yesterday.' Oh my God, 'Eleanor Rigby.'"

"Uhm, 'I Am the Walrus,' 'Penny Lane,' that *Yellow Submarine* movie was crap. I love you, Rocco, but the Beatles are a children's band, marginally better than the Monkees."

After two hours of fighting summer traffic, and listening to Elena and Rocco debate, we reached the blighted neighborhood of the Stone Pony. Asbury Park's glory days had passed.

Maya parked amid beat-up cars and pickup trucks a block from the club. As the five of us unloaded onto the sidewalk, Ben stared in wonder. He'd never been to the Jersey Shore, so he wandered down the moonlit street toward the surf. I followed as the others got in line in front of the club. We made a detour toward the boardwalk steps for a view of the white caps peaking the thunderous waves. As the tide quickened, Ben motioned that we should climb down to the beach.

Suddenly, three punks outside a shuttered storefront yelled, "Hey, faggots."

Ben stiffened but then called back, "Fuck off." They shut up quickly and made no move to follow us. We accelerated our pace toward the Pony.

"How did they know?" I asked Ben with panic. "Do we really look gay?"

"More like we just look out of place," he replied, brushing it off. "I mean, we don't look like wharf rats."

"You got all New York on them," I said, my eyes wide in admiration. "But I was ready to shit my pants."

"In the city, you use your intuition to avoid confrontation. But if anyone ever asks for your wallet or wristwatch, give it to them and run."

The line had vanished. Everyone was inside. We flashed our IDs and then joined Rocco, Elena, and Maya, all swilling Rolling Rocks. As the club filled, it was clear that word had traveled about Springsteen. Instead of locals, there were clusters of college kids. Elena heard that some came from as far as Philly and Wilmington. Around ten o'clock, a band called the Clambangers took the stage. Their set was squarely in the garage band punk realm, loud and aggressive—nothing you'd expect as a lead-in to Bruce. We prayed for a short set.

Everyone soon got snookered, save for Maya, who appointed herself driver. Rocco spent the night stalking a meaty bartender with a black patch over his left eye. But soon determining the bartender was straight, Rocco returned to the pack.

"Frank is his name. I have a sweet spot for those who are vulnerable," he said.

"But," Elena quipped, "not available. Frank has got some choice biceps." She added, "In a few more years he'll be my type."

Rocco was buzzed and returned to the bar to try again, and we wondered if he was going to get punched out by Frank. Instead, he came back with a free beer and a frown.

"Frank says Bruce isn't showing. It was a false rumor. He's back on tour in Miami tonight. He thinks the owners planted the story to drum up business."

A minute later, a club manager with a beer belly waddled to the front of the room and hopped up on stage with some effort. He croaked into the mic: "Bruce Springsteen and the E Street Band are not performing tonight. But the management welcomes them to drop by anytime they like."

A huge groan filled the room as the lights came up, adding insult to injury.

We piled into Maya's car for the long trip north on the Jersey Turnpike. Elena and I again took the back seat, with Ben on the hump. With my left hand pressed against Ben's knee, the mellow notes of "Sweet Baby James" soon sent me into twilight. But Ben and Elena's faint whispers stirred me.

"You guys are so cute together. If I can't be with him, I'm glad you are," Elena said.

"He's a good kid. I enjoy spending time together, despite his age."

"Once Andy's in the city," Elena said, "you'll keep an eye on him, won't you? Even if you're no longer together?"

"I'm not going anywhere," Ben told her.

I just pretended I was sleeping, hoping Ben couldn't see the fresh smile on my face.

———

Lingering traces of Lia's Chanel No. 5 scared me when we stepped through the front door. I thought she was back. But the house was empty.

We staggered to my room and crawled beneath the sheets, deciding against pajamas or even underwear. I cuddled up to Ben, but he was too exhausted to get hard. So was I.

"Man, I was wiped out," Ben said, stretching into a huge yawn. "I'm still tired. Too much beer. And after all that, no damned Bruce."

"It was still a good time," I said timidly.

"I agree. But I better head back to the city. What time is it?"

"9:40. Guess we should get up," I said, mounting Ben playfully and biting one of his nipples.

"Sport, I'm beat. I need some coffee and a shower," he said, getting up.

"I'll get a pot started. Why don't we drink our coffee by the river, and then I'll drive you to the station?"

"Don't have the time. I have laundry to do before that SAGE event with Neal tonight. Do the trains run regularly on Saturday?"

"Every thirty minutes," I replied. "So there's no rush."

I thawed poppy seed bagels in the toaster oven as Ben looked at the shelf and remarked, "Your mom's beautiful, sport. Is this a recent photo?"

"That was last year. This one is recent," I said, handing him a silver frame. I was in my prom tux next to a beaming, cheerful Lia.

"Andy, you look fifteen in this photo."

My ears began to burn with anger, but I bit my tongue.

Really? This age crap again?

"The baby blue tuxedo makes me look younger."

"Lia is one hot mamma . . . I can't believe she hasn't remarried."

Now he wants my mother?

"She will. D.C. will be good for her."

"Yeah—'cause she'll be far away from you," Ben said, tickling my head in an unexpected show of affection.

"And I'll be in the city with you!"

"Uh—you'll be in the city with countless guys. Sport, don't limit yourself. Hey, I gotta shake a tail feather."

I wanted to know what he meant by that countless guys crack, but he went to get dressed.

Within the hour, we arrived at the train station.

"You finally got to see my house and Maple. What do you think?" I asked, childishly fishing for compliments.

"We're not far from the city, yet it's another planet. You sure you want to trade this for the concrete jungle?"

Why was he doing this again? Was he letting me down?

"Are you looking forward to the party with Neal tonight?" I said, changing the subject.

"It's a charity event, but it will be fun."

"Do you expect to meet any guys?"

"You always meet new people at these things," he shrugged, avoiding the question. "What are you going to do, sport?"

"Nothing. Hang out, maybe paint. Stop at Gram's to say hi. Read. Watch TV," I said, strumming the violin for sympathy.

"Well, next up is Patti Smith. She better show up!"

"Oh, shit . . . that's right. And Friday is the photoshoot."

"Let's talk Wednesday night. I'll give you more details about the shoot."

"We're not talking until Wednesday?" I found myself blurting out.

"Wednesday is not far off," Ben said, laughing. "You'll live."

"But I'll miss you," I whined.

"The shoot will be excellent. Then we'll have fun at Patti Smith. You'll spend the night. We'll have lots of time together, Andy. Relax."

Easy for him to say. He has a city of guys to keep him company.

I guided Ben to the city-bound platform. We didn't dare kiss goodbye here. As he boarded, all I got was a wave. I stood paralyzed as the train faded into the glistening Manhattan skyline.

As I watched Ben vanish, I felt that familiar punch in my gut, the kind that felt like permanent loss.

Chapter 24

The brrring of the telephone made me drop a spoon of strawberry yogurt. The goop landed directly onto Anita Bryant's face on page eighteen of the *Sunday Times*. An operator connected me to Lia's collect call. She was bubbling about the mountain views and wished I were there.

I told her about the photoshoot and how much money I'd receive. She was thrilled. But she also wanted to make sure I was eating—as if I would have starved while she was away. I told her about the Stone Pony, but that made no impression.

She was talking about a gift she had bought me when the call ran out.

Not hearing from Ben since Saturday was torture. When Wednesday night came around, Ben didn't call until 9:45 p.m., but I managed to play it cool.

Our chat was quick and logistical. We'd meet Thursday after work at his apartment. I would sleep over. Then early Friday morning, we would meet the crew at the Columbia University admissions building. Then we'd shoot around the campus. In the afternoon, we'd catch a van to the MSP studio. Hopefully he could knock off by five. Then we'd meet Elena and Maya at Columbus Circle by seven o'clock for the Patti Smith concert. Although she knew nothing about Ben and my evolving sexuality, I invited Beanie to tag along after she told me she'd be in the city to attend a book signing at Doubleday's on Fifth Avenue. I gave her Elena's phone number to coordinate where to meet, with hopes the two would form a friendship.

Rocco would go to Central Park early to save a spot on the Great Lawn. Ben listened quietly, grunting from time to time, and then told me he was tired. It had already been a long week. But he was looking forward to seeing me.

I fought the desire to say "Really? You don't sound it." I just sent him a kiss over the line. He said thanks in return and clicked off.

Later in bed, I attempted to decode Milan Kundera's *The Farewell Party.* As I read, I grew fixated on a cobweb crisscrossing the light fixture above. It drove me nuts, so I stood on tippy-toes and wiped it away.

As I hopped off the bed, regret struck me. Destroying the spider's elaborate creation seemed cruel. I recalled a conversation in biology about how humans assume we're superior to all living creatures.

With my head back on the pillow, I considered Damon's actions. Why did he feel the need to tear my rectum? Just because he could? And now what he did was messing up life with Ben—big time. It's like I was still paying for that night of getting drunk at Tug's.

Thursday night came around eventually. As I hung with Ben, I was inwardly telling myself to be cool and not needy. Ben poked about his apartment while I sat half-reading the paperback of *Siddhartha* he had recommended and trying not to say anything that would set him off.

But Ben's unsettled mood had me in a silent panic. How could I not take it personally? He wasn't the sweet, affectionate guy he was last week.

I wanted to believe he was strained about the photoshoot, but I knew something between us had shifted. Ever since he told me that the Damon thing creeped him out, conversation was reduced to which album to put on the turntable. As I tried to make small talk, Ben was folding laundry or head down in paperwork. We quietly shared a late dinner of salty bowls of miso soup and rye bread. Close to midnight, we went to bed, no nookie. I lay awake for hours, my stomach hollow.

The following morning, I arrived for my first glimpse of Columbia's campus. Ben made a beeline for the admissions building, where his assistant, Lucy, had created a spacious set-up room. As the others arrived, Lucy ripped open an oversized paper bag of bagels from a deli named Zabar's, eliciting cheers from the crew. I had never heard of the place. As we began nibbling and drinking coffee, Ben shouted that it was time for introductions.

I met a towering Japanese girl from NYU, a Black guy from Fordham, and a Puerto Rican fellow, also at Fordham. A foxy blond with pouty lips was studying illustration at Pratt.

Ben led the group to a grassy field and had us lie down in a pinwheel shape at a spot the photographer, Luis, had designated. We all looked clueless, so Ben barked orders to lie down in the damp grass.

"Now stare into the sun," Ben yelled. "Loosen up, guys—and smile, for God's sake! We're selling the university."

His tone grew even more snide and impatient over time, and no one liked it. Especially me. His bad mood at home seemed to have followed him to work. Was this my fault? We had to strike poses for four hours, all over the campus. There's nothing glamorous about modeling.

We didn't arrive at MSP until three o'clock in the afternoon for the studio shoot. By four thirty, with no end in sight, I worried whether we'd make it to Columbus Circle by seven.

Taking Ben aside, I whispered, "Hey, this is going well. You're a great boss. But Elena will be waiting for us."

"Andy, we have to finish this tonight. No option. They'll bring in dinner if necessary."

"Yeah, yeah, I get it. It's just that I have no way to reach Elena."

"What do you want from me? This is more important than a concert," he hissed.

"Maybe we should have done the photoshoot in two days?"

"Fuck . . . Andy. You're gonna tell me how to do my work?"

I shut up quickly, shocked by his tone.

At 9:45, Ben finally shouted, "That's a wrap. Sorry for keeping you here so long. We'll be in touch. Have a good weekend."

Speaking normally to me for the first time that day, Ben said, "We're done, sport."

"What should we do about Elena, Maya, Rocco, and Beanie?"

"Drop it, Jeez. I think they figured it out when we didn't show up. I wanna burger from the joint on my corner. We can get take-out 'cause I'm beat."

Minutes later on Park Avenue South, I brought up the issue again, timidly.

"Ben, I feel terrible about Elena."

"Andy . . . what's up with you?" Ben snarled. "This is how photoshoots go. Presley gave me a big break. Don't you get that?"

"I know that, but—"

"Sometimes you're so immature," he said, waving down a taxi. As we climbed in, Ben added, "You should be grateful I got this gig for you. You're being selfish. It's only a concert. Your friends will get over it."

All I could think about was if Ben had been better organized, the shoot would have ended on time, and we'd be at the concert as planned.

Why was he labeling me selfish?

I slept badly, and not in Ben's arms. The next morning, I was awakened by his voice. It was much gentler than the night before, but I was still pissed off.

"Get enough sleep?"

I was not going to lie.

"No. What time is it?"

"7:20. Listen, I have a long list of to-dos today. Did you want coffee?"

The small kindness surprised me. I felt stupid for feeling grateful. He was still an asshole, I told myself.

"I can get it, but I have to pee," I replied coldly.

Clutching a white ceramic mug spotted like the hide of a cow, I joined Ben. He was scribbling notes on the wobbly side of the kitchen table. Leonard Cohen's husky voice warbled from the speakers.

Noting my silence, Ben touched my neck, kneaded it. I stiffened as he murmured, "Sorry that I got bent out of shape. Yesterday was a long day. But the stills are freaking spectacular."

I appreciated the apology, but I was still pissed off.

"I should get going so you can get things done," I huffed.

"Sport, can we talk?"

"Talk to me as I get dressed," I snipped.

"I think it's a good idea if we slow this down."

My mouth went dry.

"I'm under a lot of pressure at MSP. With Damon out of the picture, I have a shot at being promoted to art director."

"Yeah, but—"

"Plus, the commuting back and forth must be a lot for you. It'll be easier when you move to the city. We can do more things together. It'll be much easier."

"Yeah, sure," I mumbled, holding back tears. "We'll have a fuckin' blast."

"Sport, think of it this way—you're about to bloom. You gotta meet new people. Dating me will only hold you back."

"Have you met someone?"

"Jeez, this is where your age really shows," Ben said, the words like a slap to my face. Then he softened. "No, I'm not seeing anyone else. I'm not going anywhere. I care about you, Andy. You're an incredible kid. But you're starting college, and you don't need me as a distraction."

"Why don't you let me decide that? Ben, you jerk, I'm in love with you."

I hoped an honest plea might change his mind. Instead, he shook his head, smiled, and looked at his feet.

"That's sweet," Ben said, looking up again. "But I'm not ready. You're eighteen. And I don't know what I want. Not sure I'm even gay."

"Yeah, well, I should go," I said, jostling my belongings into the duffel bag before the tears began tobogganing down my cheeks.

"Hey, hey, come here," Ben said, reaching out to pull me close.

I jerked away from his grip, throwing myself off-balance and dropping the bag. I cursed under my breath and felt the tears start to flow. I hated myself for showing them.

"I'm sorry, sport. It's just for now."

"Yeah, right. Just for now."

"We'll get together soon. Maybe this new film, *Animal House*. Then a few margaritas—and get naked on the waterbed—"

"Maybe," I said, rushing out the door because, otherwise, I was going to punch him in the face.

Chapter 25

I got home and headed to my bedroom, burrowing under the covers and wondering if someone could clinically die from a broken heart.

Elena called while I was wiping away a fresh run of tears.

"Andy, what happened to you guys last night? The concert was amazing—Patti's a badass!"

"The photoshoot went late, and I had no way to tell you. Really sorry."

"I figured," she said. "Your loss, Mister Male Model," she added with a sarcastic laugh.

"What else did I miss?"

"Beanie without JuJu is more fun. She danced her ass off, smoked weed. We ended up sleeping in the city."

"Where?" I asked.

"A friend of Maya's on Washington Street in the Village. She's dating this woman, Adele."

"Wait, so Maya is a lesbian? Where was Rocco?"

"Maya is Maya. Adele is an architect. She's like fifty, but ethereal. Rocco went to Paradise Garage. A club filled with your people."

"Not my people. Where did Beanie sleep?"

"In a loft bed. We bunked together. Andy, I'm kinda into free-spirit Beanie. Get this: We cuddled, kissed and stuff, a little. Just a little. Maybe I'm a little lesbian too."

"You kissed my cousin?"

"Gawd! Technically, you and Beanie aren't related. Anyway, I don't think I'm gay, Andy. But everyone else seems to be."

"What the fuck is going on, Elena?"

"Calm down, cowboy. I'm still me."

"Elena, how far did you go with Beanie?"

"Kissing a girl is much softer than a guy. Her lips tasted like oatmeal. I let her hands roam. She was gentle." Elena laughed.

"Do Uncle Carl and Aunt Fanny know?"

"She said she's not ready to tell them."

"What a fucking weekend," I moaned.

"What's up? You were with Ben the whole time. You sound mad. Didn't you have fun?"

"I think—I think Ben broke up with me." The tears resumed.

"Holy shit. I'm sorry, babe. Wait, are you crying? What happened?"

After I explained everything from the photoshoot to the next morning, Elena whistled low and said nothing for a few seconds. But then she tried to boost my spirits.

"Ben is way into you, Andy. He told me after Stone Pony, on the ride home. You were sleeping. So here's some advice: Just hang loose until you move to the city."

"Yeah, right."

"He's not going anywhere."

"Now you sound like him."

Later, in my mailbox, I found a postcard of a black-haired woman in a sparkly minidress, twirling a baton. It was from Ollie, raving about what he called *un verano loco.*

Crazy summer? I tried to read between the lines and figured he had found a bunch of guys for fun.

Another person who was dumping me. Shit.

I wished Ollie and I hadn't slept together. I recalled the scolding from Ben, Uncle Jack, and Perry, telling me that sex with a teacher was illegal.

To think that I fell for his line: "I don't want you to risk having a bad first experience with a stranger."

The words echoed again, as I emptied the dishwasher, making me angrier. Just then, Mom's pink rose platter slipped out of my hand, breaking into five pieces. Fuck! I knew she'd be bummed.

Damned Ollie. Damned Ben.

I put on the movie soundtrack to *Sgt. Pepper's Lonely Hearts Club Band* to drown the buzzing in my brain. I was certain Lia would crave some American grub following weeks of exotic Peruvian food, so I placed a large mushroom extra-cheese pizza in the oven. I picked out a dusty bottle of Beaujolais from our dwindling basement stash. As I climbed the stairs and came into the kitchen, I heard a scream. In response, I dropped the bottle onto my bare foot, recoiling and audibly in pain.

Ruth retrieved the intact bottle as Lia hugged me.

"Pizza," she gushed. "Perfect homecoming dinner. Let's open the wine!"

"Tell me everything!" I cried as I moved the bubbling pie from the oven to the kitchen table. Over dinner, an overly caffeinated Ruth held us hostage as she shared dozens of stories that lacked both punchlines and payoffs. I tried hard to not roll my eyes as Lia shot me repeated glances, warning me to be nice.

After she left, Lia rolled her own eyes several times and we both laughed.

"I love her to death, but two weeks with Ruth is one week too much," Lia said, removing her flats and wiggling her toes. Fishing through her carry-on, she presented me with a woven orange bowl the size of a small cantaloupe.

"Isn't it gorgeous?" she beamed.

"Yes. Beautiful," I replied vaguely, wondering what in hell I could use it for. Next came a sack of random coins and a gold-plated Incan keyring. Catching the healthy glow in her cheeks, I saw that the holiday had reawakened Lia.

Later, loosened by the Beaujolais, she cooed, "Andy, I can't hold it in. Are you ready? I met someone special on the trip."

"You did? Who?"

"His name is Mitch," she said, quickly putting to rest my idea that her suitor was a woman. "It's all very new. The next two days catching up with work will be a nightmare, but Wednesday night let's have dinner at Emilio's?"

"Such mystery. This person must be significant."

"No, just too much to tell you. Andy, okay that I use the phone awhile?" Lia asked.

"Mamma mia, the drama! Go call your new lover," I replied, kissing her on the forehead.

Wednesday night we drove to Emilio's separately, Lia coming from work. We had barely seen each other the previous few days, so I was hyper-curious and looking forward to catching up. I eased onto the banquette behind the hand-printed *Reserved* sign and looked for Goldie. Minutes later, she careened out from the kitchen swing door, balancing multiple plates of food. To watch this balancing act was impressive, given that her thumb and a quarter of her fourth finger had been severed a few years ago during a knife battle with her ex-husband.

"Andrew, it's been forever! Is Lia back from Mexico?"

"Peru. She'll be here any second," I replied.

"Two Chiantis, on the house, coming right up," she shouted.

Lia appeared in the doorway, wearing a pink floral dress wrapped at the waist. Goldie greeted her with a hug.

"Goldie! I met someone on the trip!" Lia said, wiggling into the banquette.

"The place is slow tonight, so I have time to hear your love story. Let me grab your Chiantis," Goldie laughed.

"Okay, spill," I demanded. "I can't believe you kept me on the hook for three days. Jeez! Who is this mystery person?"

As Goldie approached with a tray of wine, Lia giggled like a schoolgirl.

"Mitch," she said, "Professor of political science at George Washington U."

"You have to watch out for the smart ones," Goldie quipped as she slid into a chair and served the Chianti.

"Mitch was on the trip. He's thoughtful. Forty-three, and a Capricorn."

Taking a hearty gulp from her Chianti, she added, "Mitch is *Black*. How about that?"

"*Melanzane!* A gorgeous color," Goldie said. "Oops, a new table of six. You two keep talking. I'll be back."

Lia put aside the Chianti and resumed, "His mother is from St. Martin, and his father is French-Canadian, Montreal actually. His full name is Mitch Miller."

"But isn't Mitch Miller the name of that corny band leader with the pointy beard who Gram adores?"

"Different Mitch Miller," she said.

"Mom. I'm happy for you. And, hey—it's totally cool that Mitch is Black."

"He's brilliant, Andy. And handsome, in a Harry Belafonte way."

"Huh?"

"A warm, nutty brown. Like a pecan."

"Mom, it doesn't matter if Mitch is dark as fudge. Can't wait to see you two arm in arm, parading around Maple. Imagine the neighbors!"

"Andy, stop."

"Seriously, Mom, it's cool you don't care about things like race."

"Honey, we're just getting to know each other. Imagine what your grandmother will think?"

"Well, she had no problem with your friend from the office. The one who came to Gram's for lunch a couple of years ago?"

"Corinne," Lia replied.

"Yes, Gram loved Corrine. That was way back in '73 or '74. Things have changed for the better since then. Haven't they?"

"Maple isn't the world. Neighbors might not be as enlightened. You know what? You're right—screw them. How did I raise such a fabulous son?"

Wolfing down warm focaccia, Lia told me how Mitch had responded when she finally confessed to her news about breast surgery.

"Mitch said I was the most stunning woman he's ever met," she gushed, "and that a scar would only make me more beautiful."

Cupping her mouth, Lia leaned in and said, "Ready for this? Mitch had his own secret. He has only one testicle. So I said to him, 'Mitch, you're a stunning man, and having one testicle only makes you more beautiful.' Oh my God, Andy, we couldn't stop laughing!"

As Lia chattered on and on about her unconventional relationship and I sucked down more Chianti, I wondered whether I would ever be able to tell her about mine. We planned a precollege shopping spree for Labor Day weekend, for bedding, bath towels, and knickknacks for my dorm room once I got back from the Vineyard.

"Labor Day weekend means big sales!" she said and forced me to toast to sales.

Goldie brought the bill and a ricotta cheesecake on the house. I hoovered down most of it as Lia told her more about the vacation—and about Mitch.

Lia was happy. She was finally happy.

Back home, Lia announced, "Time to call Mitch. Honey, I might be on for a while."

I imagined her as Doris Day, crisscrossed on a fluffy pink bedspread with a yellow Princess phone in hand, kicking her legs in the air as Rock Hudson cooed with naughty desire. Impressed by the ease of Lia's adventure, I started to believe in love again.

Left alone in my bedroom, I let my thoughts wander back to my problems with Ben. Was my age really the issue—or was it that he kept imagining my ass getting tapped by Damon? Maybe Ben saw me as damaged goods.

Unable to sleep, I noticed a plump spider on the ceiling fixture. Was this the same creature whose web I destroyed? Closing my eyes, I counted backward. I opened my eyes and noticed the spider was gone from the ceiling. Instead, he had slid down an ethereal thread, pausing inches above my nose. There he waited. I watched him watching me until I fell asleep.

Chapter 26

On Wednesday, I cornered my supervisor at the start of the shift to say Friday would be my last day.

He frowned, rubbed the back of his head in disappointment, and lectured me.

"In the real world, Andy, people give two weeks' notice. I know this is a summer job and all, and not your cup of tea, but you're a qualified worker, and I hate to lose you."

I didn't think I meant anything to him. I stammered an apology.

"Next summer, I'd be glad to have you back," he continued, adding, "that is, once you can handle responsibility seriously."

Friday arrived before I knew it. A few of the guys on the crew treated me to lunch from the hot dog truck outside the PGE gates. We made hollow promises to stay in touch and grab drinks one weekend.

I was washing sauerkraut and mustard off my hands in the men's room sink when Smokey walked in, sweaty and hairy, looking almost sexy. He had long stopped tormenting me with his caustic remarks. But his locker room flirt a few weeks back had confused me deeply, and then he had just disappeared, either out of embarrassment or indifference.

Catching my eye, Smokey quietly said, "Andy, hold one sec."

He came closer and his aftershave slithered up my nostrils.

"Hey . . ." I didn't know his actual name.

"I just heard it's your last day, Andy. I'll miss you—really."

"Uh—wow—"

"Gotta tell you, I saw you one night at Tug's. You looked scared as shit, so I left you alone. No one here knows about me either. Anyway, kid, if you need someone to talk to, call me."

He placed a slip of paper into my grip.

"I'm not hitting on you," he said, lowering his voice. "Lord knows I want to. You're so humpy. But I think you need a friend more than a bang. You're a good kid," he said, patting me on the shoulder before leaving.

I was in shock as I slid his number into my shirt pocket.

When the whistle blew at four thirty, the supervisor presented me with a souvenir PGE orange hardhat. I high-fived the crew one last time, collected my paycheck, and leaped into the Blue Whale.

Turning the ignition, I noticed Smokey's note poking from my front pocket. I unfolded it and read: *Eddie 556-7826. God Bless.*

Saturday morning, I rushed to deposit my final paycheck before the bank closed at noon. At 11:40, I stood ten deep in the teller's line when I heard my name. I looked around and saw Luba motioning me into her office.

"Don't stand in line. I can do this for you here. How are you? I hardly see you anymore!"

"I'm great. My summer job ended early and I'm off to Martha's Vineyard next week," I said, handing her the deposit slip clipped to my paycheck. "I'd like to withdraw fifty dollars, Luba. All tens, please."

"Elena's moving to Montclair, you to New York City. Everything is changing. How's Lia? We have to get together for dinner before you two go off to college."

I shared the details of Lia's promotion and proposed move. Then she told me Ham reached tenure and Elena's sister Dora was entering junior year at Plattsburgh. I thanked her for the special treatment and left.

Back home, I was pulling on my running shorts when Elena called. She spent the last few nights at Maya's in Montclair to sleep in the room she was renting. I declined her invitation to a women's folk concert. She was disappointed, so I told her about my chat with her mother, which delighted her.

Lia was in Hackensack, auditing a two-day seminar. Now that Ben and I had cooled it, I'd quickly shifted from jam-packed weekends in the city to being stuck at home alone with no plans. I began to dial Ben's number but then chickened out and hung up. If he answered and was cold to me, I'd feel even more devastated than I already was.

Instead of wallowing in self-pity, I ached to be surrounded by possibility. That's when the itch to return to the Village hit. But heading in solo on a Saturday night was not appealing. Plus, I'd freak if I ran into Ben with another guy. No, tonight I'd work on a painting then watch TV until Lia got home.

Still itchy for something a little gay, I retreated to the attic to fetch the gay bar guide I'd practically memorized when scouting for Tug's. Circled with yellow highlighter was a pub marked by a star.

Julius', 159 West Tenth Street. I read about a landmark protest on the premises in 1966, a "sip in" to challenge the Liquor Authority's prohibition on bars and restaurants serving booze to homosexuals. The description assured me that the bar was popular with a preppy and arty crowd. I could check out Julius' on Sunday afternoon and be home for dinner.

"Andy, I'm leaving for the seminar," Lia said Sunday morning. "There's leftover chicken in the fridge if you get hungry."

An hour later, a two-mile run along the river path was clearing my head. As my dick shook up and down in my shorts, rubbing against the nylon, I hardened to the friction and became horny as a goat. For the third time in as many weeks running, I crossed paths with a handsome, sandy-haired man wearing a tight Army T-shirt and camouflage shorts. He was married, as evidenced by the gold band on his ring finger. I couldn't help but stare at the thick bulge jiggling up and down inside his running shorts. I smiled and he gave me a brief, curious stare.

When I returned home, I stripped naked in the bathroom. I imagined the sandy-haired fellow running beside me to ask, "Want some company?" We'd strike up a conversation until we reached the water fountain. He'd insist the water was rusty and offer me a thermos of Gatorade in his car.

I would follow him to his Camaro and sit my butt on the hood to catch a breeze. He'd hand me the thermos, making sure to brush his fingers across the top of my running shorts. Then he would lean in, pressing his erection against my knees, until he forced a kiss on me.

Ohhhh, yeahhhhhh.

I shot three ropes of cum across the tub, shuddering with each ecstatic spasm. I took a deep breath, slumped, sighed, looked glumly at the spilled jizz, and then showered off. I felt spent and depressed.

That should have been done with Ben.

After toweling off, I got dressed and checked the bar guide again to confirm that Julius' opened at four.

My train didn't reach the Manhattan station until 4:45, so I zigzagged through folks on their Sunday stroll until I found West Tenth Street. The name Julius' was painted in green script on a glass-plate window. Spilling onto the sidewalk were casually dressed men smoking cigarettes and laughing.

Courage.

With a clenched stomach, I barreled inside, stunned by the animated jabber and party atmosphere. Linda Ronstadt was crooning "Blue Bayou" on the jukebox in the rear of the narrow room. I was surrounded by uncommonly good-looking men, and my heart skipped. Unlike the dark, brooding men at Tug's, this crowd was upbeat and chatty.

A stranger in a newsboy cap nudged me, saying, "Smile, we don't bite." I grinned at him sheepishly.

I asked the chubby bartender for a vodka orange juice. He demanded an ID, so I flashed my driver's license. As I did, I jostled one guy sipping a cocktail from tiny red straws with what looked like a college trio. He scowled. I winced and shrugged in apology.

As I swung to scan the room, a solemn middle-aged fellow in a bright red polo shirt sitting beside guys eating hamburgers on white paper plates stared me down. Clutching the screwdriver, I headed toward the rear, almost spilling half of my drink. Aiming for the corner, I pinched in between two circles of teens. That's when I saw that the middle-aged guy, who looked like an academic, had followed me to the back. He poked his acned, stubbled face into mine, saying, "Hi, where do you go to school?"

He had lousy breath.

"NYU. In September," I shot back uneasily.

"I took a few social courses at The New School. One on the sexual revolution of the 1960s," he said.

I wasn't following him, so I just smiled.

"I'm Merl. I live on West Seventeenth. What's your name? Where do you live?"

"Andy," I nodded, adding, "I move in next month from North Jersey."

I wasn't interested but Merl impressed me by his outgoing way.

"You're cute. Are you sure you're gay?" He laughed. "It's hard to talk here. Want to go for a walk?"

"I just got here, thanks," I said stiffly.

"Let me buy you a drink, Andy. Orange juice?"

"Screwdriver. But I'll switch to a Bud if you don't mind."

"They only have Miller."

"Sure, thanks," I said, uneasy about the offer but happy to talk to someone local.

The moment Merl headed toward the bar, the fellow to my right leaned in.

"Need a rescue? Mmmm, you're obviously fresh meat."

"Uhhh—"

"I'm Troy, this is Carl, and this is Joseph. What's your name?"

"Andy. Glad to meet you all."

Carl was too tall, and Troy's floppy blond hair made him too girlish. Joseph was cute in a regular-guy way.

"Andy, don't let that frump hit on you. Hang with us," Carl said.

"Merl's just buying me a beer."

"Take the beer, then lose him," Troy said.

"Here you go, Andy," Merl said, extending a beer. I thanked him briefly because I didn't want to encourage him further. Merl tried to introduce himself to the trio, but they froze him out with dull responses.

I wanted to hang with the trio—but how to shake off Merl?

Fifteen minutes of awkward chat with Merl followed until he finally got it, gave me a sad smile, and said he was leaving. I felt like a shit, but I was also relieved. But then Troy and his pals lost interest and melted into the crowd.

As I was feeling abandoned, I spotted an adorable prep a few feet away. Every two minutes, he'd turn from his buddies and flash a smile at me. He had curly reddish hair, tanned arms, and a rumpled, faded blue button-down shirt over khaki shorts splattered with paint.

After four smiles, he glided over.

"I'm Wyatt. How are you?" he said in a Southern drawl, offering his hand for a firm shake.

"Wyatt, cool name. Andy. Andy Pollock," I said, grinning like a fool.

"Any relation to Jackson?" he said. "The painter, that is."

"Well, I'm not certain, but maybe. I am a painter."

"I'm a painter too. What medium?"

"Oils, acrylic, watercolor."

"I only work in oil. You in art school here?"

"NYU in September. Living at home in Jersey until then," I said.

"Do you have a job in the city?"

"My summer job ended. I'm heading to Martha's Vineyard this week."

"Let me buy you a drink. How about a Long Island iced tea? My friends turned me on to these, and they light me up like a Christmas tree!"

"Yeah, I'm in."

As we sipped, the boozy impact was immediate. We talked as the crowd thinned out. I was seduced by Wyatt's blue eyes, but what really won me over was his awareness of the art scene. He explained the hip galleries, the artist neighborhoods, the hottest artists. I kept nodding at every tidbit he threw me, gobbling hungrily.

As Wyatt ducked into the bathroom for a piss, I was left alone with my thoughts. I liked him. He was cute. He knew stuff. So maybe Ben wasn't the only guy for me?

Upon his return, Wyatt said, "Wanna see the studio? It's not far."

Wobbling along Grove Street like a pair of Weebles, we knocked shoulders in nonstop chatter. Lighting a cigarette, Wyatt told me about his family in New Orleans and shyly explained that he was an apprentice to Willem De Jong, a celebrated artist with paintings in the Museum of Modern Art. The studio was De Jong's, located in an area he called the Mews.

We approached a wrought-iron gate on a tiny cobblestone street closed to traffic. Behind it was a row of nineteenth-century carriage houses. He said these were former horse stables and now housed NYU faculty and a few artists.

Wyatt led me to a glossy aquamarine door, and we entered the studio. I gawked at a room the length of ten dining tables. On top were fat tins of paint and what seemed a hundred brushes. A wall of glass transformed the back section into a greenhouse. There was a line of industrial sinks, and the wood floor was speckled with globs of paint.

"This is where I do my work," Wyatt said proudly.

Boldly taking my hand, causing me to shiver, he led me up a staircase to a dark second-floor library sky-high with bookshelves. I couldn't decide what excited me more—the prospect of kissing sexy Wyatt or exploring Willem De Jong's studio.

When I mentioned that I had to catch the train soon, Wyatt wasted no time. He pressed me against the wall and coated my face with kisses. The sour taste of tobacco coating his puss was oddly satisfying until it became gross.

Shirts rolled up, pants dropped, and so did Wyatt, to his knees. As he sucked, with considerable expertise, my eyes fixed on him jerking his long but thin rod. He looked uncut. He let me finish first and then Wyatt came in a laughing fit. We both shot in the exact same spot on the linoleum.

"When can I see you again?" Wyatt asked, pawing at me.

"As soon as I get back from the Vineyard. Now I wish I wasn't going," I said, embarrassed by my clingy response.

"Andy Jackson Pollock, I'll see you when you get back. Count on that, my man. We'll go to dinner, and even more," he promised as he laid a goodbye kiss on my lips.

As I kissed him back, allowing my tongue to explore his mouth once more, I suddenly flashed on Ben's face. I pushed the image away, guiltily. But it didn't stop me from making out with Wyatt.

Was I beginning to get the gay thing right?

In the den later that night, I was paging through Lia's latest issue of *People* magazine when the phone rang. I thought for a second that it was Ben. An old reflex.

"You're home!" Elena roared.

"Yeah, of course I'm home. Everything okay?"

"I felt like shooting the shit. I'm at Luba and Ham's, so I'm fucking bored."

"Ah, a night home with Mom and Pop instead of fancy-pants Montclair," I mocked.

"I kinda met this foxy guy."

"What—?"

"But I don't know if I'm ready," she said.

"Sexier than Beanie?"

"Back off, faggot! He's an actor friend of Maya's, so he's probably gay."

"That would figure—"

"But I don't think so. He's Puerto Rican. Tall, dark, and handsome. Sly smile, a hungry look in his eyes. I felt wanted. Andy, he's a total hottie."

"How did this happen?"

"He came to Maya's for drinks with his buddies and eventually asked for my number. Instead, I took his."

"Pushy!"

"He's twenty-nine, has an apartment. Andy, I haven't been with a guy since—you know . . . so I'm not sure."

"What's the problem?"

"Since he's older, he may expect me to put out," she said, laughing.

"Just go slow. There's no rush," I said. "What's his name?"

"Manny. One part of me really wants to bone him. The other part would like to go on a real date. Andy, you're the last guy I dated! Not counting the damned architect. Did I ever tell you that Daniel was obsessed with my feet? He'd suck on my toes like barbecued ribs. It felt kind of good."

"Thanks. Now I'll never eat ribs again. I hate the architect," I said.

"So did you find a replacement for Ben yet? A new boning partner?"

"Well, I met a guy earlier today. Total preppie hottie."

"Did you get a name or was it that gay anonymous sex thing you guys have the privilege of?"

"Screw you. His name is Wyatt."

"Listen, being gay is like going to the grocery store."

"You calling me a slut?"

"Andy, who am I to judge?" she said.

I couldn't decide whether there was irony in her words.

Chapter 27

A few days later, Lia drove me to Newark Airport. The first leg of my trip to Martha's Vineyard was a short flight to Boston. She insisted on escorting me to the gate and sticking around until the plane departed. After a prolonged hug with some embarrassing tears, she handed me a roll of quarters.

"Now you have no excuse not to call."

"Next trip we take together."

Her face brightened as she hugged me one last time.

Aside from a series of scary altitude drops, we were soon cruising toward Cape Cod and the choppy whitecaps of Buzzards Bay. Forty-five minutes later, I was on the tarmac, pretending I was a Kennedy since I was wearing the Lacoste shirt from Uncle Jack over chino shorts with a web belt.

In the dinky terminal, I easily spotted Aunt Fanny and the girls. Uncle Carl was away on business. Aunt Fanny had abandoned her Sally Bowles helmet, JuJu appeared the same as always, and Beanie was sporting a unisex shag with bangs down to her eyelids. Dangling from her left ear was a purple feather.

"Beanie! I love your new look," I said and then winced when I heard my fruity words. Now I had to make sure I wouldn't let slip that I knew Beanie had taken part in a lesbo cuddle with Elena.

I unpacked while Aunt Fanny prepared a warm asparagus quiche and dandelion greens with lemon that were weird but delicious. Over dinner, we all chattered about nothing. I politely asked about JuJu's boyfriend Chocki even though I knew I wouldn't like him. For dessert, Aunt Fanny served a homemade cherry cobbler topped with local vanilla bean ice cream.

Beanie, JuJu, and I played rounds of gin rummy late into the night. Before bed, I sneaked a small bowl of cobbler and a glass of milk from the kitchen. I shimmied naked under the covers. I now felt a peace that had been impossible the last few weeks with my Ben headaches. I basked in the silence.

It was after nine the next morning when my nose detected blueberry muffins baking in the oven. I came downstairs in a T-shirt and shorts to find everyone up.

"Morning! I think I slept ten hours. I feel high," I said, as Aunt Fanny smiled, wearing a chic ecru one-piece bathing suit. She was scrubbing potatoes at the sink.

"We wanted you to sleep in. Pour some coffee. Take a muffin while they are hot. There's fresh *beurre* on the table, or local honey. Today is a beach day!" she declared, stacking potatoes in a colander. The girls, she said, had walked to town to pick up cold cuts for lunch. "Andy, look at the *légumes* from the farmer's market. Tonight you'll be my sous-chef."

Because of relentless thunderstorms in New York, Uncle Carl would not be able to join us, she explained. Without his extreme bossiness, I could imagine what the week would look like. I giggled inside at the idea of seeing JuJu as ornery as I'd seen, Aunt Fanny giddy from pep pills, and Beanie's radical, earthy turn.

Knowing my cousin's lesbo feelings, I desperately wanted to initiate a conversation with her about my sexuality. If I confessed first, then she would confide in me—right? But I'd have to get her alone to have our serious talk. I couldn't be sure how to start the chat, so I just stayed quiet.

Early morning, I dusted off the same neon green bike I used every summer and cycled west toward Gay Head beach. As the sun inched upward, I stripped out of my shorts and sweatshirt and raced into a shallow parcel of ocean I knew was free of the jagged rocks the beach was known for. I swam four laps in the calm surf before I realized I'd drifted far away from my marker, a cluster of mossy boulders revealed during low tide. I didn't panic. Instead, I floated vertically as if standing on a platform, catching the waterline view of the red, ochre, and yellow layers of clay dotted with patches of bright green sea grass against the clear blue sky. A rainbow of color at this coastline English settlers named Gay Head. I swam back to the beach and flopped belly up onto the gritty sand, amused by how much I'd learned since June and impatient for the future.

Midday was reserved for lazing on the beach. Solitary actions included reflecting about Ben, incapable of sorting out my frustration. One overcast day, when the sky ached to drop buckets but never did, we went to see *Heaven Can Wait* at the Strand in Oak Bluffs. Another night we went to a townie dance at the Edgartown Pavilion where the local rock band was as old-fashioned as the town itself.

Hitchhiking was another accepted tradition for youth on the island. Locals were delighted to offer teenagers rides between Vineyard Haven and Edgartown.

One afternoon the previous summer, when I was seventeen and sexually naïve about guys, a college-aged fellow driving from Edgartown to Vineyard Haven had noticed my hiking thumb and pulled over. With flaxen hair streaming from the open window of his rusty orange Volvo, the dude behind the wheel held the toothiest grin I'd ever seen. I was immediately mesmerized by his slim but muscled torso clad in a neon-blue tank top.

"Hey man, where you headed?" he asked in tattered English.

"Either Bluffs or Vineyard Haven."

He introduced himself with a firm shake as Hosko, from the Netherlands. Chatting nonstop, he spoke with a roll of his r's and an absence of the letter H. *Osko*, instead of Hosko. I *tink*, instead of *I think*.

On a seasonal work visa, he was a biology student at Utrecht University and turning twenty-one. This was his second summer selling steamers at the Clam Shack. When he reached for the knob to turn up the volume to a Bob Marley song, the sun-drenched white hairs on his bronze arm danced in the wind. The intensity I felt being drawn to this beautiful creature ter-rified me.

We continued getting to know each other that afternoon by wandering the streets of Oak Bluffs. Following double scoops of Rocky Road from the creamery, he invited me to his apartment where a young Dutch couple sat playing Spades on the porch. Hosko and I joined them and swigged Heineken until the late August sun dipped.

Based on the warm smiles Hosko shot me periodically, I had the feeling he was thinking the same thing I was: Had his roomies not been home, Hosko and I would have been naked.

When he drove me back toward Edgartown, Hosko gently put his hand in my hair and explained that it was his last day on the island. I felt horrible even though we had just met. To delay our goodbye, we sat parked in the driveway and small-talked until I heard the slap of the screen door. Aunt Fanny was cross-armed on the patio, looking vexed by the strange car in her driveway.

I realized we had to break it up—and I wasn't going to get a goodbye kiss either. I gave the handsome, shaggy Dutchman a wistful departing glance as I left his Volvo, our handshake lingering a few aching seconds. As the pebbles crackled as he drove off, sadness gripped my heart. But I had to smile for Fanny's sake. Up to that point, my yearnings for men had been abstract fantasies. Meeting Hosko was the first indication that my attrac-tion to guys was more than just sexual.

The fleeting memory of my day with Hosko stayed with me all senior year. It made me melancholy at times and probably was, I decided, the reason why I gave in to Ollie's creepy advances when I should have known better.

A week into the vacation, I'd had enough of paradise. All the sun and sand and ocean couldn't keep my mind from obsessing over Ben—and made me keep replaying my time with Wyatt. I had to get home to address the quandary of Ben, the promise of Wyatt. And to connect with the women who had my back: Lia, Gram, Elena.

Uncle Carl remained a no-show because of unexpected work in the office. I was sorry he wasn't there, but he really was a wet blanket most of the time.

One day at State Beach, sunning myself beside Beanie and JuJu, I felt my stomach suddenly go queasy. That meant diarrhea was going to follow. I needed to get home. I hitched, and a neighbor scooped me off South Road and dropped me near the house. Flanking the driveway was a green van with the words MV Contractors painted across its side. I knew Uncle Carl and Aunt Fanny were converting the back shed into a cottage.

I opened the screen door into the deserted kitchen. The table was set for two, including periwinkle placemats, a plate of half-eaten liver pâté, and a pitcher of iced tea.

"Hello, *qui est la?* Who is it?" Fanny asked as the creaking floor planks announced my arrival.

"It's Andy. I'm home early."

"Oh, oh. Okay," she said, "*Attends.* Please wait, Andy." The serene French lady sounded flustered, which was odd for her.

"No problem, I'm going to lie down," I groaned as I passed the guest room.

In a loose pink robe, her black hair pinned up, Aunt Fanny ran toward me, yelling, "*Merde!* It's okay, Andy. We're all adults." Behind her, slithering into his sweat-stained MV Contractors T-shirt, was Doug, notable for his ponytail, lopsided smile, and premature beer belly. Doug was at tops twenty-five.

"Hello," I managed, extending my hand for a firm shake and noticing the knob still pushing against his dungarees.

"Andy, yeah, hey," Doug said, not shaking my hand because his paw was wet with I-didn't-want-to-know-what. "Well, I'm heading out. Fanny, thanks for lunch. I'll have a final quote this week."

Doug slunk away like a scolded dog.

"Andy, I wasn't expecting to see you," Aunt Fanny whispered.

"Aunt Fanny, I'm sorry I interrupted you. I think last night's oysters were spoiled. My stomach is all messed up."

"Let this be *entre nous*, yes?"

"Well, uh—"

"My dear, I have kept your secret, after all," she smiled.

I didn't have to ask what she meant. But my bulging eyes confirmed she had hit a nerve. Damn, how did Aunt Fanny know my secret? Because I read *The Thorn Birds* on the beach? My skill in mastering a chèvre omelet?

And in that moment, we understood each other. The dalliance made me respect Aunt Fanny all the more. Uncle Carl was a bummer; the gal deserved some fun.

———

"I'm glad your stomach is better," Beanie offered later as I watered the vegetable garden. "Sorry if I've been distant this summer, it's just been . . . a pileup. A shit show."

"Huh?"

"Where to start? At home, I couldn't open a door without finding JuJu and Chocki fucking like rabbits. Then he left for Tuscany, and she's been a psycho bitch since. On top of that, Carl and Fanny are imploding. I mean, if they are together, they fight. It's better when he's away—"

"I was wondering why he didn't come up—"

"Yah, sort of obvious, right? I wish they would just divorce. Meanwhile, my sister and I have to pretend Mom isn't screwing that bonehead contractor."

"Holy shit, you know?"

"Duh, like we need a guest cottage. MV Contractors is really constructing a fuck-shack for Fanny and Doug."

"Wow—"

"Hell, we all have secrets. Just part of growing up. How about yours?"

"How about my what?"

Beanie rolled her eyes and shook her head.

"You don't have to play games with me, cousin. I know about you. I remember last summer. I saw you walking with that blond Swedish guy."

"Hosko was Dutch," I said.

"Hosko was a hunk. I was impressed."

"He picked me up hitchhiking. I didn't know him before that day."

"Whatever. Andy, it was adorable. Did you two ever get to shag? Sure hope so!"

"Beanie!"

"No joke, you were looking so fucking happy. He was sexy. Not my type, but sexy."

"I think I know what your type is." I let the words hang in the air. Beanie squinted and smiled.

"Yeah. There's that. I knew Elena would tell you. I knew it! Maybe that's why I kissed her, so I could talk to you. Being a dyke isn't the worst thing in this fucked-up family. At least I have my shit together."

"I'm not judging you."

"Neither am I. Does Lia know?"

"No. It would crush her."

"You're an idiot. No offense. But Lia would be cool. That mama loves you."

"Beanie . . . did we just come out to each other?"

"I guess so. Was it good for you?" She smirked and laughed like a fool. "Uh, Andy, you're drowning the Swiss chard. Silly fag."

"Shut up . . . dyke." I smirked, and we both had a good laugh.

"Fuck. Have you slept with another girl? Spooning Elena doesn't count."

"Andy, I know who I am, finally. The ERA March confirmed it for me. But I'm waiting until college. I can see it now: Me and some Colby chick making out in front of a crackling fire."

"Wow."

"What about you? Any guy in the picture? I keep hearing the name Ben?"

"Ben. Yeah, I love him. But he's a mess. Isn't sure he's that way. Or maybe thinks I'm too young to get serious. The situation sucks."

"I hear you. Was he your first?"

"No, my first was Ollie."

"Who the fuck is Ollie?"

"The Spanish teacher you met at my graduation party."

"Oh, shit. Seriously? The grody surfer dude?"

"Yeah—"

"But he was your teacher. Andy, that's not only gross; it's criminal."

"Well, he's not in my life anymore," I lied.

"I'm sorry," she said, wrapping me in her arms.

Rain fell the entire next day on Martha's Vineyard.

Playing solitaire, Beanie announced, "When I get to Colby, I'm going to drop the name Beanie. It sounds juvenile. How about *Bernie*? Short for Bernadette."

Aunt Fanny shouted from the sofa, "I chose to call you Juliette and Bernadette because they are feminine, strong names. Bernie is harsh and manly, and *je n'aime pas*."

I remained silent.

"You all suck. I'm tired of being Beanie!" she spat out, running to her room.

Following a dinner of store-bought crab cakes, JuJu wrote love letters to Chocki, Beanie sulked in a corner while reading Virginia Woolf, and Aunt Fanny hid in her bedroom. I decided it was definitely time to leave the island.

Chapter 28

Two days later, Lia picked me up at the airport during a freak summer hailstorm. Hunched over the steering wheel, she said, "Andy, I asked you weeks ago to get new windshield wipers. I can barely see the car ahead of us. Roll down your window a crack, it's fogging up in here."

"Damn, I told you to let me drive, Mom."

"I'm perfectly capable of driving. I'm glad you came home early. We still have to buy your dorm supplies."

These final summer days in Maple promised to be boring. But I needed the quiet as I planned my escape to NYU.

"Can you believe it? Three weeks from today I'll be in college?"

"Don't make me depressed now. There's plenty of time."

"Mom! Oh, this weekend while you're gone, I'm hanging out with Elena."

"Good, I'll feel less guilty leaving you alone."

"Guilty?"

"I went to Gram's house to check on her. She was in one of her 'woe is me' moods, which always leads to an argument. She told me Aunt Louisa broke up with the married pilot she was dating. Like that was a tragedy?"

"Oh yeah, I remember Michael. What a dick."

"Well, Louisa got attached to his three little kids. Anyway, she's heart-broken, and now Gram expects me to fly to Texas with her when your aunt can fly here for free. Can you imagine? As if I don't have enough going on."

"Gram sounds like she's losing it."

"Don't be disrespectful. Your grandmother is bored, so drop over this weekend. She made you eggplant parmigiana for dinner."

"Will do."

"You're so tan. Honey, what's the real reason you came home early?"

"Mom, I told you. I felt stupid just lying on the beach, knowing there's a shitload of stuff to do before school," I lied.

"You know I hate any version of *shit*."

"Just tired. Sorry. Two flights. Cape Air flight sucked. Major turbulence."

"Take Pepto-Bismol when we get home, so you'll feel well enough to eat Gram's dinner. I'm sure you ate very well on the Vineyard. Fanny is a fabulous cook. But then again, she doesn't work."

"She works. Part-time at the psychiatrist's office. She has August off."

"Psychologist, not psychiatrist."

"Jesus. Whatever, Mom. Let's not talk about Aunt Fanny."

Maple felt good and familiar. I felt my tension unwind. I dropped my duffel next to the washer, grabbed a Gatorade from the fridge, and dialed Elena.

"Andy! Are you calling all the way from Martin's Vineyard?" Luba asked, answering the phone.

"I came home early, Luba. Is Elena home?"

"You know she moved, don't you?"

"Already?"

"Last weekend, we moved the rest of Elena's things to Maya's apartment. Then Maya's landlord suddenly wouldn't permit a roommate. So she moved in with Rocco."

"Oh, okay—"

"Did you know that he is homosexual? So that's different for us. But that means it's okay for Elena to be with him, we decided, Ham and I. He has a big penthouse in Montclair. You have the number?"

"I'll call Elena there. Say hello to Ham."

I hung up and suddenly felt jealous of Rocco living with my best friend.

Jealous of another gay man. Like Elena was still my girl—but she wasn't. I wasn't convinced he'd be a good influence on Elena. He was flaky. Ben said so. Or maybe Elena needed a bubbly, big-hearted guy with a shitload of cash—even if they weren't boning.

I decided not to call. Instead, I plopped into my precious armchair to thumb through the cartoons in the *New Yorker* while munching a party-sized bag of Fritos. Soon I was dozing.

In my twisted dream, I was in a high-flying prop jet with Ben. The door was open, and we were peering out. Ben hollered, "Are you ready?" and told me it was time to jump. I panicked and refused, but it was no use: We were attached by a parachute.

Ben leaned against me with the full weight of his body and we both plummeted out of the plane.

Fuuuuuck.

Locked in tandem, we spiraled downward. As I screamed and almost blacked out seeing the ground rise up, the parachute suddenly opened. Ben and I flew upward as the chute caught a gust of wind, and then we descended slowly, landing atop a patch of sweetgrass. As I tried to catch my breath, the panic receding, Ben detached the apparatus and laid a wet kiss on my lips.

"You did it," he whispered.

I was suddenly awakened by Lia, calling out from upstairs, "Andy, dinner at seven, okay? I'm going to pack."

I decided that hearing Wyatt's Southern drawl would lift my spirits. He picked up on the first ring but was heading out the door. We made a plan to meet for dinner in a few days. He insisted I bring a bag so I could spend the night. I felt delirious. But was I moving too fast? After the fiasco of Damon Piccard, I was paranoid that every invitation meant getting my ass split in two—even if Ben assured me that was not the case. I decided that Wyatt was respectable, close in age, simpatico.

I hopped downstairs happily. Just then, Lia asked, "Andy, are we making a big mistake?"

"You mean the transfer? Again?"

"Yes, the transfer. I'm not sure it's the right time."

"Mom, Mom, Mom, we already decided. Yes, your transfer will take adjusting, but we'll talk all the time."

"Well, you have been in a funk since you got back from the Vineyard."

"It's just a passing thing."

"Maybe my leaving you now isn't a good time."

"Mom. I'm good."

"I worry," she insisted.

"Well, don't," I said, as I leaned in to hug her, catching a whiff of Chanel No. 5.

The following morning, I found a crisp twenty-dollar bill tucked under a plated poppy seed bagel that was thawing. A note encouraged me to take Elena on the town, her treat.

Freedom and cash. I played the soundtrack to *Saturday Night Fever* and danced around the house, shaking my butt. Then I searched my desk for the phone number Rocco had scribbled onto a napkin. I prayed he wouldn't answer.

"Hello, Gorgeous. Please leave a message for Rocco or the fabulous Elena after the beep."

Irritated by the smugness of his voice, I snarled, "Elena, it's Andy. I'm back from the Vineyard. I'm spending tonight in the city. Let's catch up tomorrow."

I got to the West Village early. Owing to the humidity from the crowd on the train, the yellow cotton button-down I had carefully ironed was wrinkly. Crossing onto Grove Street on my way to meeting with Wyatt, I detected the click-clack hum of an air conditioner from the transom of a used bookstore. I ducked inside to cool off. Shelves of used books stood, fastidiously organized.

My thought? A token gesture might win Wyatt's heart. When the sweat on my face evaporated, I handed a slightly frayed copy of *William Blake: Selected Poetry* to the impeccably dressed girl behind an antique desk.

"My, my. William Blake, an excellent choice," she flirted.

"Thanks. It's a gift for my new boyfriend," I said, testing my comfort level—and hers. "Would you mind erasing the price?"

"Sure. I apologize we're out of wrapping paper, but the binding is lovely."

I walked over to Willem De Jong's studio. I had researched the abstract expressionist artist while at the Edgartown Library. His works were in major museums around the world. I couldn't shake the fantasy that Wyatt would introduce me to De Jong and that would launch my career as an artist. I was a lousy prick, using Wyatt. But I told myself that was fair; that's how it worked in New York City.

I arrived at the wrought-iron gate of the Mews and strolled through. As I reached for the doorbell beside the glossy blue trim, I noticed a circle of wet under each underarm of my button-down.

I heard the clatter of three deadbolts as the massive door swung open. Wyatt invited me inside with a downward swipe of his cigarette. Wrapped in a long canvas smock tied at the back, he stood as sexy as I remembered. A streak of yellow ochre brushed his left cheek. I'd forgotten Wyatt smoked, a habit I otherwise loathed.

"Andy Pollock, come in. Meet Eva and Donald, the other peons in this glorified factory."

"I'm sorry I'm late. I got lost," I lied. "Hello, I'm Andy," I said with a low wave.

In English robustly tinged with German, Eva said, "Hallo, Andy Pollock." Donald was silent under a crown of mousy-brown hair.

Wyatt described the oversized canvas he was blow-drying.

"These are the base colors before the maestro lends his hand—it's an abstraction of the Civil War."

"Wow," I stated vacantly. "Is Willem here?"

"São Paulo, thank God," Wyatt responded. I tried to hide my disappointment.

Lining the wall was an orderly mess of dented quarts of paint; bristles of countless brushes fanned the rims of a dozen Chock Full o'Nuts cans.

Tin ashtrays overflowed with nubs near white coffee mugs, each smudged with paint.

"Andy Pollock," Eva remarked, "you possess the name of well-known painter. If you don't mind—you have remarkable bros. I mean, brows? Yes, eyebrows, please never pluck. They mark your face with strength. You are Eastern European?"

"Italian, Norwegian, and Polish—so yes, I guess," I said, fumbling.

"Sehr handsome," she cooed. "Ah, youth."

"We're off. See y'all tomorrow," Wyatt muttered.

"Byeeee, Andy Pollock," Eva called, whispering audibly "very young" to mute Donald.

In the vestibule, Wyatt nuzzled my nape. I shivered at the sensual touch.

"Ummm. Hey you," he whispered, eyeing me.

I wanted to say, "Your Southern drawl makes me hot."

We strolled down Broadway onto Prince Street when I caught a fleeting breeze.

"Feel that?" I asked.

"Yes sir. Y'all's sensory perception is that of an artist, Andy," he said.

I began to prattle on about the exceptional quality of ice cream on the Vineyard when Wyatt interrupted. "Let's bop into Fanelli's for a cocktail."

"Sure thing. I'm thirsty."

"It's a hangout for painters and sculptors. The place is old as shit. The meatballs are good, and they serve my favorite nectar—liquor."

We snagged two brown leather stools framed with brass divots. Scanning the paneled room, I said, "This shithole looks exactly like Julius'."

"Perceptive boy. Same era," he said. "Wild Turkey," he called to the bartender. "Andy, what are you drinking?"

"Tanqueray and tonic, please." I was grateful the bartender did not ask for my license.

"It's terrific to see you, Andy. After drinks here, then we can grab dinner by my place. You can drop that clumsy shoulder bag off if you like . . . but then we might never make it to dinner," he said, cracking a grin that melted my heart.

"Oh, I got you something," I said, reaching into my bag, "It's not wrapped."

"*Selected Poetry* . . . ah, William Blake. I adore the bright red binding. Well, thank you. I'll be sure to read this . . . unless y'all'd prefer to recite me a poem later, in the nude?" he said, teasing.

After lighting a fresh cigarette, to my mild irritation, Wyatt blew the smoke out the side of his mouth. He spoke about growing up in Louisiana in what sounded like the antithesis of poverty. At twenty-three, he received a Bachelor of Fine Arts from LSU.

"One week after graduation, my parents shooed me to New York to further my career, but the real reason was they would rather not be hampered with a queer for a son. When you're privileged in the South, Andy, shipping your embarrassing child away is how it's done."

By the third drink, Wyatt was very relaxed. As he explained trawling for tuna in the Gulf of Mexico, his hand strayed to my knee. I flinched, but then I liked it.

"Why don't we go? I'm hungry," I said, desperate to prevent him from ordering a fourth Wild Turkey.

"Hell yeah!" he echoed, whispering into my ear, "you turn me on big time," before plopping down a fat tip for the bartender and pulling me out the door in a drunken lurch.

We walked two blocks to a postwar building on Mulberry Street. Wyatt led me to the third floor, insisting I should drop my bag first. The moment the door to his flat clicked shut, however, Wyatt wrapped my lips with the whole of his mouth, plunging in with his wiggling tongue. Despite the sharp taste of tobacco, I hardened quickly, and he grabbed my erection though my pants.

After a few minutes of kissing, Wyatt pulled away.

"Wheeeeheew. It's as hot as Baton Rouge on the Fourth of July," he said, cranking up the AC. I turned to inspect his apartment, taking in a living room chocked with ornate antiques. But Wyatt grabbed me roughly at the shirt collar, jerking me back in a gesture that was overly aggressive.

He shoved his left hand inside my shirt while unbuttoning me with the right. His fingertips typed down my abdomen, landing inside my briefs, and grabbed hold of my erection. Repositioning my dick upright, he giggled as the tip poked out from my waistband.

"Aren't you a sight," he laughed seductively.

Wyatt extended a pinky finger toward my cockhead and dipped the tip into the liquid. As I breathed in at the exhilarating touch, he suddenly raised the finger to my mouth and shoved it in, ordering me to clean my own ooze off his finger.

I was not sure whether I liked this boozy bossiness. But I wanted to be a good guest, so I licked his finger clean. Then I reached into his khakis and felt his erection. It was a long and slender penis, but, covered in small bumps, it felt like a chicken neck.

Hiding my revulsion, I squeezed two or three times, as you might a red plastic ketchup bottle. Just then, he lifted away my wrist and declared, "One bourbon, then dinner."

But over a half-hour, one bourbon led to two more. I promised myself I would not try to keep up with him and declined his offers to refill me. Wyatt then produced an elegantly rolled joint from what looked like a humidor and insisted we smoke. I agreed, as it would mean he'd stop puffing on cigarettes momentarily.

I nursed my single bourbon on the rocks. Transported by Miles Davis's *Kind of Blue*, we cuddled on the sofa as he guzzled and babbled.

"Miss Emily, my paternal grandmother, was a hoot! And precocious! At the sweet age of twelve, she was the champion of the National Spelling Bee. Her claim to fame."

Just then, my belly gurgled.

"Oh my, we need to fix that," Wyatt said, walking into the galley kitchen. As he continued the saga of Miss Emily, he brought back a block of white Irish cheddar and two sleeves of soda crackers, arranged on a polished marble slab.

Famished, and wondering why dinner plans had been canceled, I cut four thick slices to satisfy us both.

Wyatt's eyes widened in shock, and he jerked the knife from my hand.

"Did y'all grow up in a barn? Cheese is more elegant when you slice thinly."

He placed a wisp of cheddar into my mouth and waited until I had swallowed before clapping a little too loudly. While I nibbled on more crackers with thin cheddar, to his satisfaction, Wyatt drained his bottle of bourbon into his glass.

Shaking the empty bottle too close to my face, Wyatt called out, giddily, "Surrender!"

I started to ask what he meant, but my host grabbed my hand, and pulled me roughly into the bedroom, where he stripped us both and yanked me down onto what must have been satin sheets.

Wyatt offered me another boozy, acrid cigarette kiss and it took all my strength not to puke in his mouth. As he began tweaking my nipples hard between his fingers, he suddenly sighed, "I'm tired, pumpkin."

And with that, Wyatt rolled over in the bed and pulled the sheets up to his neck. I asked him if he was okay, but he had passed out.

Now what?

Should I make the long trek home, so I could sleep in my own bed? Would he think me rude? Uncouth? I was already the guy who sliced cheese too thickly.

Sober, he was sexy. Drunk he was a mess. But right now, this mess was the only available candidate for a boyfriend. I chose to stay and eventually I fell asleep, once I was sure that Wyatt hadn't died.

Hours later, I woke to a stir in the kitchen.

"Morning, sexy," Wyatt greeted me, his voice deep and gravelly. "Bloody Mary?" he asked, pouring tomato juice then vodka into the silver cocktail shaker beside the sink.

I declined. Once he had finished his burst of morning boozing, we sat across from each other at his eight-chair mahogany dining table, eating buttered toast with marmalade like an old married couple. That is, silently.

Wyatt was a man of mood swings—and this was his calmer one. He barely said a thing for a half-hour, just watching me as I nibbled, making me visibly uncomfortable. Luckily, he didn't pick up a cigarette.

Finishing his breakfast cocktail and dabbing at his mouth with a heavy linen napkin, Wyatt announced, "Andy, I have to head into the studio to meet a client. Could you hustle a little so we can leave together?"

"Uh, sure—"

"Is little Andy sulking?" he asked, as if he were talking to an infant. "Child, I had a fabulous time. But I'm not looking for anything—certainly not a relationship."

Then, like a pigeon, he pecked my lips.

"I thought you liked me?" I responded dumbly.

"I do, Raggedy Andy. I liked you enough to get you naked. Didn't y'all have a good time?"

"You passed—er, fell asleep."

"Andy, it's a one-night stand. Are you new to the scene?"

"I've been around," I said, feeling judged.

"Listen, you're eighteen with a nice cock, so go have fun out there."

I thought of his chicken-neck dick and shuddered inwardly.

"But I thought you were into me?"

"Please, dear boy, gather your things. Now I'm running late."

I did as I was told, fuming so much that I could not speak.

"What'll ya have, doll?" the waitress at the shoebox-sized luncheonette on West Fourth Street asked from behind the counter. Reading from the special's menu taped to the wall, I ordered the American cheese, bacon, and egg sandwich over easy. Plus, black coffee.

"Rough night?" she asked with a wink. I winced and buried my face into a discarded copy of the *Daily News*.

Later that morning, as I collapsed atop Lia's bed, the phone rang.

"Hi, honey. My flights are delayed. I won't get in until nine. Ruth's going to pick me up. I figured you'd be out with Elena and Ben."

"I'm not going to the city tonight. I might head out to the Maple Tap for a beer."

"Maybe I'll go for drinks with Ruth. Be home no later than twelve, please."

I tossed on loose-fitting shorts and a faded Charlie's Angels tee. While Wyatt was just a scary memory, I was still fascinated by De Jong's abstract style.

I picked out from my stash a 36 × 36 canvas I gessoed ages ago and propped it on the easel. Placing four tubes of paint onto my worktable, I squirted a dab of alizarin crimson onto a palette knife and swept the dense oil on the white canvas. A feather, I decided. I saturated a brush with zinc white and applied it beneath the crimson, turning the edges bubble-gum pink. If the red represented me, then cerulean would identify my betrayer, Ben. I swathed the flat of a second knife with blue, layering the color on top of the crimson. I stood back. It looked like a dog had dragged his dirty ass across the canvas. Unfixable. I dropped the mess into a Hefty bag and carried it to the outside trash.

I couldn't even turn heartache into good art. Maybe I wasn't really an artist?

Defeated, I flopped onto a lounge chair. I had no plans for the night, but I knew if I stayed home, I'd dwell on Ben or sulk about Wyatt.

A lightbulb flashed: I'd never gone anywhere gay in New Jersey. I remembered a bar in Northern Jersey I'd read about in my trusty gay bar guide.

Club Feathers had dancing and live shows. It was a favorite among college students and townies. But I hoped it was far enough away from home that I wouldn't run into anyone I knew.

I cranked up the volume to "Play That Funky Music" and slipped into my uniform: Uncle Jack's black Lacoste, tight jeans, and Stan Smiths. By 9:15, I was behind the wheel of the Blue Whale on the Garden State Parkway, heading south. Soon I saw the sign: Club Feathers. Nothing clandestine about it; out and proud. Cutting the engine in the near-empty lot, I started feeling a case of the jitters. So I had a silent conversation with myself: *No one knows you. Chicken out, and you'll never meet anyone. Courage, dude.*

I wobbled nervously toward the brightly lit entrance. Behind velvet ropes was a life-sized poster of two drag divas in sky-high wigs and matching red sequined gowns. Crystal Vale and Monique La Monique performing LIVE Thursdays and Sundays, nine o'clock.

Fortunately, it was Saturday.

I ventured in and approached the doorman. He was a roly-poly bald fellow in a black sweatshirt and jeans, draped over a barstool. He had pencil-lined brows and milky skin. I waved my license under his nose.

"Honey child, eighteen? Be careful. Some of those queens bite."

"Ha," I said.

The bar was dead. Two mustached bartenders, who might have been twins, stacked barware. I ordered a Miller Lite from the more buff twin, who served me blankly. I slunk toward the corner of the bar.

Like Cinderella, midnight was my cutoff. My Timex read 9:35. Two beers max, I promised.

A Taste of Honey's "Boogie Oogie Oogie" glided into Chic's "Everybody Dance." Elena and I loved disco's up-tempo bass. Dance music raced the heart, a cheap escape from reality. Clusters of clubbers began to wander in as Odyssey's chanteuse crooned "Native New Yorker." Five Latinos stood huddled amid dense swirls of cigarette smoke. Two girly girls broke away from their gays, hustling to the new song. A lithe Black man lip-synched the lyrics to "Don't Leave Me This Way" under a pair of spotlights. A stunning drag queen approached me and cooed, "Sugar, aren't you delicious. But you're still in diapers!"

"Diapers?"

"Mmmm, those hairy eyebrows! Can I pet them? What's your name, sweetness?"

"Andy."

"You are luscious," she purred. "Well, if you get lonely, come talk to Velveeta."

Minutes later, dancers gyrated under the disco ball. I was drooling over a quartet of college guys in plaid shirts when I heard someone behind me. It was a dirty blond in a rugby shirt.

"What's your name?" he repeated, hoisting his bottle of Miller to clink mine.

"Hi. Andy," I replied, louder than intended.

"Are you here alone?" he asked, his eyes penetrating.

"Yup. How about you?"

"Aren't you going to ask me my name?"

"Oh, duh, sorry."

"You're as green as I am!" he said, laughing. "I'm Wally." His voice was strong and gruff.

"Do you live here? Jersey, I mean." I felt clumsy, as if I had forgotten how to talk.

"I grew up in Parsippany. But I'm a senior at BU—Boston University. I'm home visiting my parents."

"That's nice," I said, unable to say anything smarter.

"Let me get us two fresh beers," Wally said and sprinted off to the bar. I watched him go, a chunky ass in clingy jeans and long legs in navy-blue Pumas. Wally looked promising. He was back in two minutes. He pulled me away from the speakers, and we settled in a quiet corner.

"Do you dance?" I asked.

"Fuck, no. Disco sucks. Don't tell me you dance to this shit," he laughed as "Copacabana" by Barry Manilow played.

"Good. I like punk, mostly—and rock," I said, lying to impress.

"Sex Pistols! The Clash! The Ramones!" Wally cheered.

After a few minutes of chatting, I learned more. Wally was premed and not officially out. He hung out in a preppy bar in Boston called Buddies, even though he hated the music. Suddenly he leaned in, cooing, "Let's get out of here, Andy."

"Out. Where to?"

"How old are you?" he asked, winking.

"Eighteen."

"Perfect. Up for a motel? I'll pay."

"But I have to get home, or my mother will freak."

"I'm not asking you to spend the night."

"I want to, man."

"One hour," he pleaded. "I'm so fucking horny, I'm going to burst."

"How about I come up to Boston one weekend?" I offered.

"Boston? Weekend? No man, tonight!"

"Let's do it," I said, going for broke. Still smarting from Ben's rejection, I wanted some instant gratification. I plunked my half-finished beer on the side rail. Unceremoniously, I followed Wally to a gold Chevy Camaro sporting Massachusetts plates. "We parked next to each other," I said. "The Galaxy is mine."

"Follow me. The motel is about a mile north," Wally said.

Had he done this before?

When we arrived at the two-story Red Lantern Inn, I parked beside Wally with the engine running as he went inside to secure a room. Minutes later, carrying two cans of Pepsi, he dangled the key and mouthed *204*, pointing in the opposite direction. My dashboard displayed 11:40. I'd be home long after midnight even if I left at that instant. Maybe Lia would get home around one or two and never know.

Wally looked even hunkier in the shadow of the parking lot lights with a side-to-side waddle to his walk, his thighs twice the size of my own.

"Do you play football?" I asked.

"Nah. Crew, I'm a rower," he responded. As he unlocked the door, I noticed thinning hair at the back of Wally's head. He'll be bald by thirty, I surmised. The room was clean, with a double bed; nothing more. Wally turned on the portable color TV to Meat Loaf singing "Two Out of Three Ain't Bad."

"You watch *Saturday Night*?" I asked.

"It's a rerun. Meat Loaf sucks."

Not interested in small talk, Wally popped open the tab on a can of Pepsi and handed it to me. The sharp metal sliced the tip of my index finger. As a bubble of blood rose to the surface, Wally swooped in and sucked it in. "Blood brothers," he said. Next, he unfastened my belt. His breath was heated and tart, and he mashed the outside of my lips weirdly. I managed to simultaneously kick off my sneakers and pull his rugby shirt from inside his jeans. He peeled the black polo up over my arms. We each removed the balance of our clothing and stood warily, taking stock of the other's naked body.

Wally was lean around his middle and had a thick, uncut soldier at attention. He dropped to his knees to take me briefly in his mouth. Then he got pushy and directed me to lie flat across the dirty maroon bedspread. We rubbed, nuzzled, and fondled in every position. Then suddenly, I felt the tip of Wally's dick poking insistently against my ball sac from behind.

"No. Not there," I said, wriggling away. He gave in but not without an audible sigh of annoyance. Wally's attitude had suddenly changed now that his agenda had been crushed. He rolled onto his back and began to jerk himself off, as if scratching an itch. Realizing the fun was over, I followed. We both came within two minutes. His was a feeble dribble that was so unimpressive I had to squelch a chuckle. Meanwhile, mine leapt up in an impressive arc that landed on my sternum.

Giving me an unfeeling smile, Wally stood up to get a towel from the bathroom and then handed me the washcloth. My Timex read ten past twelve.

"That was great," I said, as if reciting a line from *The Love Boat*.

"Yeah, I guess. But not worth thirty dollars for the room. We could have jerked off in my car."

"Hey, I'm sorry—"

"Listen, I'm going to stick around and watch TV," Wally said.

"I should get going. I'm past curfew," I said, fumbling for my jeans.

"Sounds good," Wally shrugged, not even looking at me. He walked into the bathroom and closed the door.

I winced at the sting of casual abandonment and headed to my car. I drove onto a suburban boulevard but did not recall passing an Arthur Treacher's Fish and Chips on the way to the motel. Edging through a community of single-family homes, I parked and burst into tears.

Ben. I wanted to be with Ben. Safe on his sofa, debating a late movie on Channel 11. But I also hated him. Why did he think I was too young?

Because you're crying like a six-year-old, that's why!

I picked up a napkin from the ashtray, wiped my nose, tossed it out the window, and then shifted to drive again. A Hess gasoline billboard appeared. Had I passed the sign earlier? I didn't recall and became confused.

Wally the prep expected me to have butt-sex in a family hotel with him—a stranger. I figured we'd get naked and play around—but only as step one to getting to know each other. Was there some tattoo on my forehead that read *sucker*? Maybe there was. How did I expect to build a relationship with a guy who went to school in Boston?

After driving blindly along the road for another quarter mile, I saw a sign for the on-ramp to Route 4. Ben's accusations kept filling my head.

Too young, too young.

The whole mess made me want to vomit. It was twelve thirty, and I just needed to be home. I swerved toward the on-ramp when I heard a loud horn and was blinded by the glare of headlights.

Chapter 29

A team of sturdy men strapped me to a gurney and then hoisted me into the air, as if my body were ascending to heaven. Moments, or maybe hours later, a man's head dipped into view. It was an EMT barking, "He's conscious. Hang on, buddy."

I lifted my hand and grazed my fingertips, feeling glass nuggets poking from my forehead.

"Whoa, don't touch that," he said. "Hang tight. We'll be in the ER soon. You're gonna be all right."

I didn't recall a thing after that. The next thing I heard was Lia's voice. I flapped my eyelids in response.

"Andy? Andy, it's Mom. Can you hear me?" Lia asked, squeezing my hand.

"Mom? Where . . . am I?"

"Hospital, honey. Car accident. Please don't move."

"What?"

"Hackensack Medical. Cuts on your forehead, a sore rib or two. Doctor said it's a miracle."

"What?"

"You're sedated, so try to rest."

"Sedated?"

"The other people were only shaken up."

"Other car?"

"Three young guys, probably drunk," Lia said.

"I'm sorry, Mom. I didn't have much to drink. Beer. One or two," I lied.

"Shhhhh, rest. We'll talk later," she said, gently strumming my forearm.

She left the room, leaving me to be poked and prodded by a fleet of nurses until I fell asleep to the steady buzzing from the machine at my side.

At 6:15 on Sunday morning, I was released. A nurse wheeled me to Ruth's car. Cupped in the blackness of the back seat, I nodded off, rumpled and confused.

"Andy, honey," Mom called out from the passenger seat, "you're not supposed to sleep. We're almost home."

With vertigo and a throbbing headache, I hobbled into the kitchen. Mom assisted me into the bathroom. The mirror revealed a zombie version of myself. A roll of gauze seemed to circle my scalp a dozen times. A bandage secured a doodad cupped above my right eye. The doodad looked like a slotted plastic spoon without the handle. Lia started a pot of coffee to pump Ruth with fuel for the drive home. She set three mugs on the counter, including my white ceramic one painted with a cartoon of Snoopy chasing the Red Baron. Lia was pale as a ghost.

"Ruth and I walked in after midnight. I knew something was wrong when you weren't home."

"I'm sorry, Mom—"

"When the phone rang at a quarter after one, I panicked. It was the Paramus Police. They assured me that you were alive. They clarified that you narrowly escaped death. The cops said that your car was twisted like a pretzel."

"Shit."

"Ruth drove me to the hospital. God bless her. Andrew, you were hooked to so many machines, surrounded by medics, I've never been so scared."

"Aw, Mom."

"When you woke up, I cried like a baby."

Ruth added, "The officer told us you'd have shot right through the windshield without your seatbelt."

"I'm sorry, Mom. I don't know what happened."

"Andrew, were you drinking? Were you drunk?"

"No. Two beers, that's it," I lied again.

Ruth went to the bathroom before her ride home and then came back and hugged Lia. She had to go check on her cat.

"Call if you need anything. Anything."

I coiled on the living room sofa, the sweet and sour stench from the bruises curiously satisfying.

"Honey, please sit upright," Lia said, carrying a light blanket. "Doctor's rules. The X-ray showed a slight concussion."

"I feel okay, just a little—"

"No arguments, Andrew. I'll make you toast. You must be starving. We'll change your putrid clothes later. I can smell them."

"Mom, I'm not hungry. I'm so sorry. I don't know what happened," I repeated.

Lia stood at the bay window, ablaze with morning light. She threw her hands up to her face and started to bawl.

"My God . . . my God, I almost lost you, Andy."

Her emotional meltdown finally let it sink in: *I almost died.*

"Andy, when you feel less groggy, let me know. The police need details for their report. I have to call them."

"Okay," I gulped.

Lia set orange juice and a handful of pain relievers on the coffee table.

"But, Andy, I don't understand why you were so far from home."

"I went out, Mom. To meet friends."

"Friends almost an hour from home? The police said you left a bar."

"A dance club. In Paramus. The car hit me, so the accident wasn't my fault."

"The police said you were at a club called Feathers."

"It was a bar I read about, that's all."

"You never go out alone. Were you trying to meet older women?"

With that, something inside me snapped. I was tired of lying.

"It's too much. Too much now."

"You almost died," she spat out. "I deserve to know what's going on."

"Feathers is a gay bar. Mom, I think I'm bisexual. Or gay."

Lia doubled over and grabbed a chair for support.

"This isn't happening!"

"Mom—"

"No. No. No. You're not. Andy, how can you be?" she said, spiraling into hysteria.

What the fuck was I thinking?

"Are you going to start dressing like a woman?" Lia blurted.

"What? That's stupid, and you're not stupid. Oh my God, you know tons of gay people."

I was now offended.

"Those gay people aren't my son," Lia screamed. "I worry about you. Your safety."

"How about worrying about my sanity? I'm still the same guy, your son. I'm tired of lying. Fucking tired of it."

And then I started to cry. Deep, heaving sobs.

Lia ran over to me. She joined me on the sofa, cradling me like an infant.

"Shhhh, shhh, it's okay," she cooed, caressing the bandaged portion of my head. "I'm such a selfish idiot sometimes. We'll figure this out. Together. I love you so much, my little boy."

She grabbed a Kleenex to dab her tears, shoved it into her pocket, and then reached for a bottle.

"The doctor said you can take two of these for your head every three hours," she said, shaking the pills.

I took two with water she got me. She sat back and stared me down.

"Andy, let's get this over with. What caused the accident?"

"I was looking for the entrance to Route 4 when the other car hit me."

"The police said you were turning onto an exit ramp!"

"Exit ramp? No, it was an access ramp."

"That's not what they told me. Anyway, the other car was speeding—so you're not at fault."

"Jeez—"

"Okay, enough for now. I'll share your responses with the police."

"Are you okay, Mom?"

"I don't know what I am. But you're my son, and I love you. Rest."

"Mom, was there a message from Elena?"

"No, no message. Oh—did you tell Elena? About . . . well, you know."

"Elena knows about me, Mom. She accepts it, no issues."

"What? You told her first?"

Hours later, I got up to take a whiz and found Lia wrapped in her fluffy robe, scrunched against a pillow on the sofa in the den. As I leaned in, she roused, hugging me close.

"How do you feel?" she whispered.

I wanted to say *still gay*, but she would have clobbered me.

"My head is pounding, but I'm feeling better," I white-lied.

"You need something in your stomach," she said, shuffling to the kitchen.

She removed a pack of Thomas' English Muffins from the pantry and suggested scrambled eggs with Swiss cheese and spinach. I insisted that the muffin would be enough. Maybe with butter and Concord grape jam. I wasn't sure how much I could keep down.

"Phew, I stink," I rasped. "Can I shower with this bandage on my head?" I added, whining like a child.

"Yes, but carefully. Cover your head with my shower cap. But please, eat first."

"I don't want to eat when I'm smelling like this."

"Okay," she said, throwing up her hands in surrender.

"Thanks, Lia—"

"Honey? How do you know for sure? This could be a phase."

"It's how I feel, Mom. This is me."

Drawing in her breath, she pressed on, adding, "You had girlfriends, Elena. Well, have you slept with—have you been with a male?"

"Don't ask stuff you don't wanna know."

"When you were a little boy . . . no one touched you, did they? You can tell me, Andy."

"Noooooooo, Mom, nothing like that," I said. In my mind, I saw the faces of Ollie, Damon, Ben, and Wyatt flash before me. And finally, douchebag Wally.

"Maybe I should have stayed with your father. Then this would never have happened," she said, pulling gently at her hair.

"Mom . . . can we talk about this later, please?"

"Yes, later. Later will be better," she nodded, realizing she was in too deep. She paused. "Are you sure you don't want more than a muffin?"

"Just a muffin, Lia." I smiled at her priorities.

"It's okay to experiment, I guess, but please don't decide now. You're only eighteen. One day you'll get married and have children. It's all I've ever wanted for you," she said, crying anew into her balled fists.

I wrapped myself around her trembling body. I had never seen her so weak, not since her mastectomy, or I imagine the years after that shit father left us. She caved into my arms.

"You're a man, but you'll always be my little Andy," she wailed.

That was my cue to escape to the bathroom. I undressed and stepped carefully into the rushing shower water, putting on her cap to protect my head.

As the water pelted my body, I kept hearing Lia's chant, "No. No. No," as it reverberated in my head. Out of nowhere, a wail surged up into my throat and escaped. Like some twisted rebirth, it willed me to breathe. No more lies. The water would cleanse me of any remaining guilt.

It was time to be Andy. Just Andy.

Chapter 30

Elena picked up on the first ring. Of course, she just started talking.
"Rocco and I went to Bucks County. His friends have a dinner theater. *Guys and Dolls* was so much fun. New Hope is charming and a little homo. You'd like it."

"Never heard of Bucks County. So you moved? I had no idea," I lied.

"I know that you know I moved, Mr. Man."

"And you're living with Rocco, not Maya. I can't believe I found out from Luba."

"Maya's landlord is a fucking asshole," she said, ignoring my guilt trip. "But Rocco's apartment is freaking spectacular."

"Yeah, well—"

"Wait, Andy, your voice sounds weird. You okay?"

"Well . . . I'm fine, but a bit medicated."

"What the fu—?"

"I was in a car accident last night. A few bruises, sore ribs, and a mild concussion. But the Blue Whale is history."

"Holy shit, Andy. Want me to come over?"

I heard Rocco gasp in the background.

In a hushed tone, slowed by the painkillers, I told Elena the entire story.

Monday, Elena stopped by with a bouquet of yellow long-stem roses and roast beef subs. Mid-chew, she spouted, "Andy, give Lia time. She's way cooler than most parents and loves you like crazy. We all make mistakes."

"I expected more of her—"

"She'll come through. Hey, I gotta tell you—you look like shit! Like a beat-up Raggedy Andy," she said, laughing and choking.

I gave Elena a look and she shut up. As we shared a gigantic chocolate chip cookie, she changed the subject. She described living with Rocco. She meant to cheer me up, but it pissed me off. Yeah, I was jealous that she had a new homo.

"And we're throwing a party late September. You can bring your artsy-fartsy NYU friends!"

"Sounds like a plan," I mumbled. "Hey, what happened with your Puerto Rican squeeze, Manny?"

"San Juan, visiting cousins. I'm on hold until he gets back. Manny's wild about me."

"You deserve a good guy."

"Shit, gotta go. I'm meeting Rocco at Bloomingdale's. He thinks a fuchsia bedspread is perfect for my room."

I rolled my eyes, but she ignored it.

"I wish you were well enough to come along," she said, kissing the unbandaged part of my brow. "The roses will open up in a day. Feel better!"

And I was left alone with shitty feelings about every single thing in my life, none worse than disappointing Lia's dreams for my future. The pain of coming out, and in such a fucked-up way, kept me in a funk for days.

Aware of my misery, Lia rallied and nimbly acted like I hadn't dropped the bombshell. She baked an apple crumb cake. She hummed while changing my bandages. But over chicken pot pies on Thursday night, she reopened the discussion.

"Andy, maybe talking to a priest would help?"

"Insane. We're not very Catholic! You didn't even want me to go to Catholic school."

"How about Uncle Carl?"

"Too judgmental."

"What about a shrink?" Lia added.

"Why don't you stop trying to fix me," I said in a firm voice.

She looked at me in shock. In a quieter voice, she said, "Mitch plans to visit Labor Day weekend. He's very grounded. I'd like you both to meet."

"Yes, I want to meet Mitch. But seriously, maybe talking to a therapist is something you should do."

"Why?"

"So you can learn to accept me. I'm still the same son I was last week, Mom."

Chapter 31

I looked at the business card. What did I have to lose? I dialed.

"Hello, this is Jack Brooks."

"Hi, this is Andy Pollock. Is this a good time to—"

"Andy! What a lovely surprise! Just reading the script for a new commercial. A national breath mint campaign. Big bucks. Anyway, how are you?"

"I'm well, thanks, aside from a car accident last weekend."

"What the hell?"

"I'm a bit banged up but nothing serious."

"Andy, I'm sorry. Damn. I'm glad you're all right."

"Anyway, that's not why I'm calling. I want to thank you for Amagansett. We should get together for dinner," I said.

"Dinner, yes, of course!"

"Maybe that Iguana place you took Ben and me to."

"You bet. You know, I haven't talked to Ben in a couple of weeks."

"Neither have I," I said, getting to the heart of the matter.

"I heard you two aren't seeing each other. I'm sorry."

"Yeah, me, too," I said.

"Well, that could change once you're in the city. Ben cares about you."

"He told you that?"

"I have to admit, Andy, I've had a crush on you myself."

My heart jumped into my throat.

"So, if Ben's not in the picture . . . I'm only kidding," he said, laughing. I didn't need any more complications in my fucked-up life, so I ignored his crack.

"I need your advice."

"Shoot."

"Do you think two men can have a solid relationship?"

"Absolutely. Look at Perry and me."

I imagined their messed-up relationship and I almost felt like hanging up.

"I have many gay friends in long-term relationships. There are three types of men, I figure. Nesters like shacking up. Players like playing the field. Then there's predators—like that sick motherfucker who raped you."

"How do you tell the difference?"

"Keep your eyes open. Sow your wild oats; then pick a longtime lover. Listen to your gay uncle," Jack said, chuckling.

"Thanks," I said, puzzled by his playful tone. Then I recalled it was cocktail time.

"When does your Columbia campaign launch? I'm here to help you propel that career forward," he said.

"Early September, I think. Anyhow, I just called to say howdy."

"I'm glad you did. Hey—give Ben a call. Break the ice. That nephew of mine can be difficult. But he's worth it."

Chapter 32

I picked up the ringing phone, hoping it was Ben. I hadn't called him yet, like Jack advised.

"Andy . . . guess who's back from Spain?

My stomach tightened, but I forced myself to sound upbeat.

"Ollie? What a surprise. When did you get in?"

"Saturday."

"Oh," I said, feeling pissed off that he had taken his time. But then, why the hell should I care?

"I have a meeting at school this morning, and since I'll be in Maple, I thought I'd stop after. Around two o'clock?"

I was dubious about inviting him over. After all, too many people had told me how he took advantage of me. But Ollie was a mentor, I told myself. An adult. Maybe he could help me figure out the Ben stuff. Shed some light on how to deal with Lia.

So I told him to come over.

I decided to make Betty Crocker fudge brownies and serve them with coffee. A very adult afternoon snack.

He was forty minutes late, and the brownies had cooled off. I was not happy when I opened the door. He was so distracted by my bandage that he didn't see my pissed-off frown.

"Whoa, what the fuck happened to your head?" Ollie asked.

"Car wreck. Come in, and I'll shoot you the details."

"You look good otherwise. Here," Ollie said, handing me a package wrapped in tattered red tissue bound by a ribbon of natural fibers. "It's from Toledo, a hill town outside of Madrid. I saw it and thought of you."

I thought about hugging him but decided to pat him on the back instead. Ollie looked different; his pasty skin was darkened by the sun. His acne scars were less pronounced. There was a yellowish-amber tone to his hair, which he had cut short. He was wearing a buff-colored pullover and linen drawstring pants. He looked better than he did before he left for the summer, I had to admit.

I unwrapped the gift. It was a handmade leather-bound sketchbook with an oxblood red cover.

"Hope you like it," Ollie said with a fidgety tone.

"I love it. So classy. Follow me."

"Sure."

"And no, we're not fooling around."

Ollie made a pouting sound, and I couldn't tell if he was joking. I told myself I shouldn't care. I brought him to my easel.

"It's a belated birthday present. It's close to completion. Careful, it's wet."

"Fried eggs. I love fried eggs," he said, sounding like an idiot.

"I've been working on it since May."

"I'll hang it above the brown-checkered chair in my living room. One day it will be worth a fortune," he said.

Truth be told, the painting wasn't intended for Ollie. I wasn't exactly sure why I made the on-the-spot decision to present it to him.

"Let's go downstairs. I made brownies. They've cooled off."

He lunged when we got downstairs and grabbed a square, shoving it into his mouth.

"Okay, spill. How did the concussion happen?"

I described the club, the motel, and the crash. I didn't go into details about Wally, but maybe I should have, to rub his nose in it.

Ollie's eyes grew wide, and his mouth dropped open, exposing the paste of his undigested brownie. A pig. And when I explained how I came out to Lia, he was shocked into silence. Briefly.

"You didn't tell Lia about me? About us?" Ollie suddenly asked with alarm, spitting brownie crumbs at me.

Fucker only cares about himself. He didn't ask if I told Elena that we slept together, and I felt no obligation to tell him that I had.

Once he realized my story was over, Ollie had no other questions about my mental state. Typical. Instead, he leaped into his own story. He boasted about his triumphs in Madrid, sexual connections with guys and girls. Mostly guys.

By the end of his sexual travelogue, he had gobbled down three more brownies.

"Given I was one of the few blonds in Madrid—I had my pick of the litter!"

"Hmmmm," I said, letting a sneer slip into my tone. "Man, you certainly caught on fast. You told me you were pretty inexperienced in the guy department."

"I don't know," he shrugged, reaching for another brownie. "One summer abroad, and look what happens."

"Well, thank you for saving me from having a bad first experience, that's all," I said, surprised by my bitchy tenor.

Not recognizing the dig, Ollie just yammered on until I interrupted him.

"I've got a lot to figure out. NYU is coming up. I'm gonna be a small fish about to swim in a big pond."

"Hey, kid—you're cool. I've seen you in action. You're a strong swimmer. Lighten up, Andy. Have fun. Sleep around, experiment."

"Huh?"

"The worst that could happen is getting the clap or syphilis. That's what clinics are for. A shot of penicillin, and it's gone."

"Gee, thanks. I should fuck my way through freshman year?"

"I didn't say that. But yeah, sure. Hey—I'm having a few friends over tomorrow night. I think you should come."

"Mrs. Stein, MacMillan, the others?"

"No, no, no. Well, one is a teacher in Newark. A few people I met before Spain, and two visited me in Madrid. At six o'clock. Wine and cheese. There's one guy in particular I think you might like."

I said yes. Frankly, I needed to meet new people—so I could dump losers like Ollie.

Chapter 33

Wednesday morning, Lia was in a strange mood. When I mentioned I'd be at a wine and cheese party at Ollie's, she fired a barrage of questions, asking whether Ollie knew about my sexuality.

"Yes, I talked to Ollie back in May before he left for Spain, around the same time I told Elena."

Sorry, Ollie.

"So he knows, too. Did he suggest therapy?"

"He was very helpful and said nothing about therapy."

"Ollie's like a father figure to you, isn't he?" Lia asked.

"Ollie's a teacher friend, Mom."

"Then he should have shared what you told him. I'm your mother."

"I told him in confidence."

"One more question. Was Elena devastated when you told her?"

"Mom, Elena has been extremely supportive."

"Jesus. Everyone in the world knew except me? Why was I the last to hear?"

"I thought you couldn't handle it," I said.

"I did tell Mitch," she said defiantly, daring me to object. "I needed support. I may talk to Ruth for encouragement. Can I tell Ruth?"

"I don't care if Ruth knows."

"But Andy, do me a favor," she added. "Refrain from telling others your secret?"

I scowled. Lia's scolding left me feeling dirty. When the phone rang, I brushed by her to get it, making sure she knew the conversation was over.

"Road trip!" Elena sang into the receiver. "I'm picking you up Sunday morning."

"Where are we going?" I asked.

"It's a big surprise."

I hoped that Rocco would be out of town.

———

Over salami sandwiches on Wonder Bread, Gram handed me the keys to her Cutlass sedan, warning me to be extra careful. I promised I'd have the car back to her by nine p.m., ten at the latest.

After lunch, I drove to Maple Liquor and Spirits for a cheap bottle of Chablis. Then a haircut. Around five o'clock, I defied doctor's orders and ran five sweaty miles. After a shower, I tried on five or six shirts before settling on a long-sleeve blue, green, and yellow Alexander Julian dress shirt. I tucked the shirt into a starched pair of khakis and decided to debut the burgundy Bass penny loafers Lia bought me for college.

After gassing up the car, I turned onto Ollie's street to find three cars in front of the cottage. The moment I switched off the ignition, a sweat broke out. I grabbed the Chablis and knocked loudly on the front door to break through the laughter inside.

"Andy, you made it! We're already drunk," Ollie said, dressed in a loose Hawaiian shirt and cut-off shorts.

"Andy is here!" Ollie turned and called out. Then he made introductions. The bald lanky man with a Tom Selleck mustache in cream-colored slacks was Eric, the owner of a jewelry store in West Orange.

Tom was an English teacher from Newark. He looked as grey as Uncle Jack, but muscular like the celebrity exercise guy, Jack LaLanne. Tom shook my hand like a politician, insisting I needed a cocktail.

Howard wore tight faded jeans and a peach V-neck T-shirt with a gold chain to complement his handsome olive skin. Howard lived in the city.

There was no doubt in my mind each fellow was homosexual. Especially the way they sized me up. I took a seat in the centrally arranged club chair as if holding court. Ollie handed me a piña colada.

"Crackers? Cheese?" I teased.

"We ran out of both an hour ago," he chuckled.

Ollie sat next to Howard on the sectional. Then Howard caressed Ollie's leg. I wondered if I had been invited to a gay orgy. Just then, the doorbell rang.

"That's Scotty," Ollie said, and hustled toward the door. "Someone put on the new Manhattan Transfer album," he shouted.

A man out of a fairy tale walked in. Scotty was masculine and preppy with a messy crop of copper-colored hair. He wore a tan suit with a loosened tie. Sheepishly, he bowed his head to the group and jogged to the bathroom.

"That blur was Scotty Bibb, everyone," Ollie joked.

Scotty returned to the living room and found a spot on the carpet beside my chair. He smiled widely at me as Ollie handed him a piña colada.

"I knew you two would hit it off," Ollie beamed.

This was the guy he had told me about.

Scotty was all of my male fantasies combined in one person, and the bonus was an instant mutual attraction—even more magnificent than the night I had met Ben.

Scotty removed his blazer and revealed a fit torso. Sprigs of fiery red hair jumped out at the neck of his blue shirt. From my chair, I caught a glimpse of the bulge in Scotty's slacks. But as he picked up his drink, I noticed a gold band on his left hand.

"Are you married, Scotty?" I asked.

"Please, Andy, call me Scott, I hate that Ollie calls me Scotty."

"Oh, okay—"

"And yes. I am married."

"Oh, cool. I was thinking this was a gay party."

"I'm exploring, you could say. I married my high school sweetheart. But realized I'm attracted to guys," he whispered.

"Wow. I—"

"And I'm attracted to you. Ollie told me you're also exploring."

"Yeah, guess I am."

"I was looking forward to meeting you."

My mouth went dry. Scott laughed warmly.

Panicking, I followed Ollie into the kitchen to quiz him. I asked how he knew these guys. Especially Scott. He was vague in his annoying Ollie way, so I asked outright if they had slept together.

Ollie insisted they weren't each other's type. I was relieved.

Finally, I said, "I'm into Scott. Is that okay?"

Ollie was fine. But even if he wasn't, I would have moved forward. He owed me after that bullshit about seducing me to protect me.

"I don't own you, Andy. We're friends who care for each other. Special friends."

I shrugged off his bullshit Hallmark talk and headed into the bathroom to splash my face. It helped lower my anxiety.

I opened the door to find Scott leaning against one of the surfboards hanging from the wall, grinning like a goofball. I was about to let him use the john, but Scott pulled me into Ollie's bedroom, closing the door.

Then he kissed me. More accurately, he began sucking face. I reciprocated. We became a frantic bundle of limbs that tumbled onto the bed, hands and mouths reaching for pieces of each other.

A minute later, Ollie knocked to make sure we were okay.

"Be right out," I called to him, my shirt a twisted knot. I realized I had a pair of coarse red hairs surfing along my tongue and had to fish them out.

Scott and I emerged and stood in the hall.

"What are you doing tomorrow, Andy?" Scott said. "I have a crazy idea. Can you get away overnight?"

"Huh?"

"I have an early Friday morning meeting that means driving to Allentown. We can leave around two, have dinner, and drive back on Friday after the meeting."

My thoughts shot to Ben. But why? Ben wanted space. Fuck it.

"Yes," my horny alter ego replied without a second thought.

I set up the scam carefully, telling Lia I was helping Ollie paint the inside of the house his mother bought in Princeton. I'd be spending the night. I could tell she was about to ask me if Ollie was gay—and my heart stopped—but she decided against it. She just told me to be careful and not fall off the ladder.

At two thirty Thursday afternoon, with Lia at work, Scott pulled up in a silver four-door sedan that was his company car. He was dressed in a striped polyester blue-and-white golf shirt.

"Heya, sexy," Scott said as he flashed a slanted smile. I admired his shiny navy slacks.

I smiled broadly but inside I was asking myself: *What the fuck am I doing?*

"Fasten your seat belt, please."

The sharp sting of Paco Rabanne aftershave wafted from his chiseled face and irresistible sideburns. Scott squeezed my upper thigh.

Lust would do for now. I deserved an adventure.

"Mmmm . . . we're off! An hour and a half if we don't get lost."

"Hey. What is your profession? I never asked."

"Regional sales rep for Unix operating systems. Bell Labs."

"Huh?"

"Unix is shorthand for Uni-plex Information Computing System. You know, enterprise data?"

I didn't know, so I just smiled.

"What are you going to study at NYU? Computer sciences? Math?"

"Art," I replied.

"Oh," Scott said, cocking his head.

By the time we crossed the Pennsylvania border and pulled into a Holiday Inn parking lot, it was four p.m. In the previous ninety minutes, I had learned a summary of his life: Scott coached peewee softball, was a huge fan of the Jets, liked to cook from Julia Child cookbooks, and grew up in Wilmington, Delaware. When I asked about children, he stiffened and said firmly that he'd rather not talk about family.

"How about we go out for steak and baked potatoes later?" he said, changing the subject. "I know a place right in Allentown that grills phenomenal cuts!"

Scott registered while I sat in the car. With the stone face of a detective, he returned and pointed to a door close to the motel lobby. We entered room 105, a standard suite with two doubles and a sleeper sofa. It reeked of Lysol. In less than five minutes, we were naked under the covers of the bed farthest from the window.

Scott's body turned me on, bulky in an athletic way. His obvious awkwardness with man sex meant that I was the pro this time. I almost laughed when he asked if we could wrestle and get off rubbing against each other. I immediately pinned him to the mattress and straddled him. Strategically, this provided me an excellent view of his hairy, pasty white, freckled chest. I lowered my torso to kiss him on the mouth so our dicks could rub. In short time, Scott began to moan like a zoo animal. When the moan turned to a roar, signaling he was close, I covered his mouth with my hand to muffle the sound as his body twitched. I quickly rubbed one out and rolled to his side. I drifted off to sleep.

But a short time later, Scott placed my hand over his rising pecker. Round two. Gaining confidence, Scott flipped me onto my belly. With one eye on the Bible perfectly centered on the bedstead, I lay motionless while Scott dry-humped my lower back. His Paco Rabanne no longer intoxicated me. My mind wandered. I started wondering how many horny couples of every shape and size had rented that room to fuck on the very same mattress. Gross.

I started to realize that our arrangement was more in Scott's favor than mine. For one, he was firmly rooted in family life. Not only would a relationship be impossible, but also, I was an accomplice to infidelity. I heard that familiar roar in my ear, and I felt him shower my spine with semen.

I expected a bit more cuddling, but Scott pulled away as if he was ashamed by his behavior. Silently, he went into the bathroom to shower.

I flopped on my back across the bed, watching Gunilla Hutton, the *Hee Haw* gal, yakking from the Sony as her fluffy blond pigtails bounced against the frilly frock covering her boobs. Spread out naked on the bed of an Allentown, Pennsylvania, motel, I felt like a country hooker.

Later, we were tucked into a corner booth at Rusty's House of Prime Rib, a near-empty restaurant. It was Scott's treat, and I felt like a whore anyway, so I decided to go all out. I ordered a dry Manhattan, the massive filet mignon, and a hot fudge sundae with cherries.

As Scott chewed a forkful of raw beef from the Steak Tartare appetizer he raved about, I probed again about his wife, children, and life. Loosened by a pair of martinis, Scott shared some details. But he did so in such a quiet voice that it took everything to hear him. Murmuring, my redheaded john told me he was father to one boy and two girls, all under the age of ten. He started to bring out his wallet, planning to show me photos. But then he shook his head and put it back.

Rather than be insulted, I ordered another Manhattan. He looked like he was going to protest but he didn't.

He talked vaguely about Marc, Emily, and Mary. He mentioned a pool he had installed recently. Sounded deluxe. He mentioned Buster, their chocolate lab. And finally, quickly, he made mention of his wife, MaryAnne.

I made sure not to ask any more questions and frighten him off. But I just felt stupider than ever for agreeing to this little overnight plan.

"It feels good being honest with you, Andy."

But clearly not honest with MaryAnne.

The two Manhattans did their thing, and I began to talk about the car accident and coming out to Lia. He hushed me more than once, saying I was too loud—even though the closest diners were thirty feet away.

Fucking closet case.

Scott wasn't looking so hot anymore. I found the filet mignon far more attractive.

I decided not to share details about my relationship with Ollie, hoping my teacher had not blabbed.

Ollie. He pimped me like a call boy. Told Scott I was available. Now I was being paid for sex with filet mignon.

The waiter placed two snifters of Rémy Martin on the table. As I sipped, I got unruly. I said in a whisper but a forceful one, "What the fuck are were doing?"

Scott smiled and explained that we had a good thing going. He called our getaway a "tryst," adding, "Andy, you're a tasty side dish—and I hope to have seconds and thirds."

I wanted to spit in his face, but I figured I'd toy with this asshole.

"Oh, yes. Definitely," I cooed. "Once I'm at the dorm, you can sneak in whenever my roommate's away."

"Damn boy, I'm game," he said, his boozy eyes shining.

I yearned for Ben.

We got back to the motel and crawled under the covers. As if he were talking to a secretary, Scott made a request.

"Andy, cuddle me to sleep."

I did so, hating myself. Luckily, we both soon passed out.

By eight-forty-five the following morning I sat alone in the front seat of Scott's car with all four windows rolled down. It took him two and three-quarter hours to return from his meeting. I had been ordered not to leave the car because he didn't want any colleagues seeing me.

I was pissed. My stupid impulsive Jersey Boy libido. There were a million things I could have been doing: packing for college, swimming laps. Anything would have been better than sitting in the parking lot of an industrial park, holding a cold cup of coffee and a copy of the local newspaper.

Mistress, prostitute, idiot. I was furious with myself.

Chapter 34

Scott dropped me off at the corner near the house before heading home. He mentioned getting together again, and I pretended it was a good idea.

Fuck him.

I got in, repeated my alibi about being overnight with Ollie to Lia, and then unpacked—only to pack again because Elena was coming soon.

When I went back downstairs, Lia was busy in the kitchen, baking. For Mitch, she explained. An hour later, she burnt the scones. Trashing the batch, Lia asked me to go to the Portuguese bakery for a dozen pastries.

"I can't go empty-handed to visit him! Get something nice."

"Hey, there's an unopened sandalwood candle in the top credenza drawer. A candle is more romantic than pastry. Bring that to your boyfriend."

"Mitch is not my boyfriend, Andy."

"Whatever you say," I replied, dropping my duffel by the front door. "I'll wash my dirty clothes, Mom." I didn't want Lia to discover there wasn't one drop of house paint on anything inside the bag. I heard Elena pull into the driveway.

She was wearing a giant pair of dark sunglasses suitable for Jackie O but not Elena. I felt my love for her revived. I wasn't jealous of Rocco anymore. Elena was everything. And she was my friend.

"Love your shades," Lia screeched as she hugged Elena. She gently tugged our visitor to the dining room table and sat her down.

"This one . . . this is Mitch," Lia said, shuffling through photos and showing them off proudly. "The last time I visited, he met me at the airport gate with a bouquet of flowers. What do you think?"

"Dreamboat," Elena replied, giving me a smile.

"Hey, why does Elena get to see Mitch's photos first, Mom?"

"I just picked the prints up last night. You know how slow the drugstore is. Anyway, this is a girl thing," she replied.

She had forgotten that for me, Mitch was a boy thing. I reached over and grabbed the photos from Elena.

Dressed in a blue-checkered button-down, khakis, and a blue blazer, Mitch had slanted doe eyes and a military carriage. The man was one hot potato.

"Good job on scoring this hunk, Miss Lia. His skin is gorgeous. Like tobacco and molasses," Elena said.

I winced. Elena was overcompensating for Mitch's blackness.

"Nice-looking man, Mom," I said, carefully choosing my words to not offend her—and to hide my personal interest.

"When is Mitch making his debut in Maple?" Elena asked.

"Never," Lia responded. "People can be so judgmental. Mitch will be my D.C. secret, for the time being anyway."

"Screw what people think. Mitch is a keeper," Elena said.

"I suppose you're right, but I like to be cautious," Lia said, frowning.

"Well, Lia, I'm airing Andy out today. This boy's been banged up and housebound."

"Andy had an overnight painting job at Ollie's mother's house, but yes, I agree," Lia said.

"Mom," I whispered at the door before leaving, "Mitch seems amazing. Love you." I felt my eyes tearing, but I squeezed them back.

She smiled, not knowing that I felt Mitch was already replacing me. I vowed not to ruin her happiness. That was the grown-up thing to do.

Once we left the house, and I was stuffing my bag into Elena's tiny trunk, I quickly explained that painting Ollie's mother's house was a lie to cover my overnight with a married guy, Scott.

"Jeez, Andy. That's all wrong." she said, shaking her head. "You're on a roll."

"Look who's talking?" I barked.

I stuck out my tongue, and we both laughed.

As I got into the car and looked toward my childhood home, it hit me. The separation between Lia and me had begun. Lia had a sweetheart; I had one foot in Manhattan. Cranking up the volume to ABBA's "The Name of the Game," I roared, "What a fucking two weeks! My head's ready to pop!"

"Calm down, camper," Elena said, laughing. "We all got our own shit. But you have been really deep into it. Of course, running after married men is your choice—but don't be surprised when it blows up in your face. That fucking prick Daniel."

"Will we ever learn?"

"All this fooling around lately," she added. "It's so obvious!"

"What's obvious?"

"You're on a screwing rampage because you miss Ben. It's like your revenge on him, except he doesn't know."

"First of all, there was no fucking," I said defensively. "Second, what else am I supposed to do, sit home depressed?"

"Some people take up a hobby. Fucking a different guy every week isn't the same as pressing leaves or knitting."

"Or painting," I sighed. "I have so many ideas but I'm never at the easel."

"Well, you'll have lots of painting time at NYU," she shrugged.

I studied her face in profile as she drove. She had replaced her Jackie O sunglasses with green-lensed aviators from the glove compartment. Her lips were shellacked with red gloss. Shoulder-length and bouncy, she wore her hair without Baba's trademark headscarves from junior and senior years. A pink halter top that hoisted her modest cleavage up one cup size was perfectly complemented by a pair of slutty Daisy Dukes.

I remembered how much I liked running my hands over that dancer's body once upon a time. Change was in the air.

The traffic was surprisingly light for a Friday afternoon of a holiday weekend. As we headed toward the Holland Tunnel, I realized Elena was taking me into the city. I was feeling excited, but then Elena nailed me with a single question.

"Andy, tell me. Seriously, are you doing okay? Car crash, I mean—on top of all the other shit?"

"My head occasionally throbs, but I take pills that help. Could have been a lot worse, right?"

"Okay—but what about telling Lia you're a homo. How do you feel?"

"Oh that. Sometimes relieved, sometimes confused," I said.

"Makes sense—"

"The whole thing was so fucking weird. I'd never seen Lia freak out like that, acting like a zombie. She finally bounced back to her old self. But notice that she's made no mention of it to you, and she knows I told you I'm a homo. I'm waiting for her to ask if Ben is gay, but I think she knows the answer."

"Andy, it's crazier that she hasn't asked if Ollie is gay. The mystery sleepovers. Lia's a savvy chick."

"Yeah, well she knows that Ollie was married. So he's above suspicion."

"Sorry, but he still creeps me out."

"Whatever. You know what, Elena . . . I've got enough going on."

"Yeah, and most of it is your fault. Sorry, but it's the truth. You're bummed about Ben, and you're making a whole shitload of bad choices. Ollie was just the first one, don't you think?"

"Whatever, it's history."

"Ollie is to blame. He's a monumental fuck-up. I don't care if I ever see him again. You should do the same."

"I want to change the subject," I said, my hands curled into fists.

"Your move, pal. My lecture is over."

"My Columbia ad campaign comes out after Labor Day. I can't wait."

"You been paid yet?"

"They're mailing a check. We can go shopping!"

"I'm in, Mr. Moneybags. So will you be plastered all over New York City bus stops? My God, your unibrow will be enormous!"

"They did some plucking before the shoot. I may keep it up. It hurts like a mutha—"

"You'll get used to it. And you look less dorky without the unibrow. Before you know it, Andy Pollock will be the toast of the Big Apple."

I wondered what my new life in New York would be like without Elena.

As if reading my thoughts, she said, "Andy, I have an idea! Fuck Montclair. I'll transfer to NYU. We'll get married. You can have your boys, and I'll have my boys—and our twenties will be fantastic!"

"Yahoo!" I yelled.

We parked, grabbed our supplies, and trekked over to Washington Square Park. We reached an area shaded by a bunch of trees.

"We won't have to worry about rats," I assured her. We sat down on the blanket and Elena began pulling stuff out of her bags. The first thing she did was pour lemonade spiked with vodka from a purple thermos into paper cups.

"I smell *weeeeeed*," she said. "Ummm."

"Let's stick to booze. We have to drive back, remember?"

"Killjoy. Andy, I love you. At least for now."

"It's going to suck being apart. You should drive in with Lia next weekend when I move. Be a part of the big day."

"That's soooo sweet," she said, her vodka kicking in. "That Mitch is a hunk, right? Your Gram is going to freak out, but fuck it . . . as long as Lia's happy."

"With Mitch in the mix, I'm no longer the only outlaw."

"Andy, you be as gay as you want. And Mitch will be as Black as he wants. Wait, that doesn't make sense. Damn, this lemonade is good."

"Hey, sip—don't guzzle!"

"Once you move to the city, will you become a flaming queen?"

"You mean like Rocco?"

"Rocco is not a queen . . . is he?"

"Too campy for my taste."

"Listen, Rocco gives me style tips. Look at these cut-offs—the stitching."

The Daisy Dukes looked no different from any others I'd ever seen.

"That red lipstick," I said with a smirk, "You got that from Rocco's stash?"

"Rocco isn't fem at all," she said, rolling onto her belly.

"You're right. He's macho. Village People macho."

"Hey, let's call Ben," Elena said, slurring slightly.

"Huh? You're crazy!"

"Okay, let's wait—until you've had more lemonade."

We gobbled down two bags of Pepperidge Farm Goldfish, a Ziploc bag of warm green grapes, and softening Swiss cheese that Luba had diced into cubes. The lemonade was almost gone, and we both were buzzing.

"Andy, where do you think we'll be in five years?"

"Graduated from college, hopefully."

"At the very least."

"Who knows? I'll be at a big ad agency on Madison Avenue, making shitloads of money and living in a penthouse overlooking Central Park."

"Nice."

"You'll be obese, on your fifth husband, and toting a handful of screaming children," I said, laughing.

"Eff you, my friend!"

Elena threw a handful of warm grapes at my face. I managed to catch one in my mouth. We both laughed.

"No, you'll be an Academy Award–winning actress living in the penthouse next door. We'll go clubbing every night. How's that sound?"

"Shit. I wonder if I'll ever have a kid."

Elena got quiet and I rubbed her shoulder.

"They never warn you about the pain of abortion. The cramping, nausea. Andy, I thought I was going to die."

"Shit—"

"That weekend at Maya's I was miserable. But once the pain calmed down, I felt a tremendous sense of relief. Having the abortion was the most adult decision I've ever made."

"I tried to be there for you, but—"

"Maya had it covered, babe."

"Yeah, I know."

"I'll never be able to erase the abortion. But it made me even more of a hard-ass about women's rights. If a girl doesn't wanna have an abortion, then don't have one. But don't you dare tell me I can't. Andy, my avenging bitch is activated."

"I like badass Elena."

"Okay, now let's call Ben," Elena suddenly yelled.

"Elena, no."

"Why not? There's a pay phone next to that rancid trash bin."

"I don't think so."

"Okay, how about this, Ben's apartment is six or seven blocks from here. Let's jingle his bell."

"That's insane."

"If he's home, cool. Look, I'll feel better if you two are in a good place. Please, Andy, do this for me. Plus, I promised Lia I'd look out for you."

"What, am I five years old?"

"Come on, pack up. You know you want to see Ben."

The trees lining East Seventh Street were lush and greener than the month before. The early evening air carried the nip of autumn. As we walked, me dragging my feet, I asked Elena why she thought Ben would be home Friday night of Labor Day weekend. She shrugged, her eyes shining from vodka, her lips curled mischievously.

She pressed the buzzer for Hoppe. A metallic hello came through the intercom.

"Ben! Hi, it's Elena and Andy."

"Wow! One sec," he said.

He said "wow." That's a good sign, right?

I could hear each latch turn.

He opened the door and waved us in.

Damn, even wearing a raggedy black T-shirt and wrinkled shorts, Ben looked good. In the front, his hair was nicely combed, but when he turned around, it was a bird's nest complete with cowlick.

"This is a surprise," he said, beaming from ear to ear. His response made me smile a little bit, but I still felt like a whipped puppy scared of his master.

As I walked through the door, I got a whiff of sour milk—Ben's underarm aroma. It tingled down my spine.

"Sorry to barge in. We were at Washington Square Park and thought— let's see if Ben's home."

"I don't mind spontaneity. I'm just cooking," Ben said.

I realized I was just staring at him, my heart beating.

"Hello, Andy, anybody in there?"

Ben grabbed me in a bearish hug as he whispered, "I'm happy to see you."

Elena heard him and gave me a shit-eating grin that said, *What did I tell you?*

Bob Marley bounced from the two gigantic speakers flanking the sofa.

"Go sit in the garden. It's in full bloom," Ben said.

"There's an Adirondack chair with my name on it," Elena said. I took a seat beside the peppery cherry tomatoes drooping on the vine. Ben brought out ice-cold Heinekens and asked us to stay for corn chowder with black beans, which he called a vegetarian curry.

"Yes!" Elena blurted out, deciding for both of us.

"So your hair grew," I said, a dig to remind Ben that I hadn't seen him in weeks.

"So does everyone's, you freak. Notice something new about the place?"

"It's messier," I offered.

"You prick! I guess it is—because neat-freak Neal moved out two days ago. He's shacking up with his boyfriend."

At least some guys aren't afraid of commitment.

"Anyway, I can meet rent, thanks to my promotion, so why get a roomie? No one will be like Neal," Ben said, shrugging.

"Bachelor *paaaad*," I responded, attempting to sound casual but really stricken with terror. Then I looked down at the patio table and noticed it was already set for three. Three bowls, three napkins, and a stack of flatware.

"What the hell?" I said.

Ben shot Elena a sheepish glance and then roared at me, "Busted!"

"Sweetie, Ben and I had this planned for days. The picnic, the spontaneous visit. Are you mad?" Elena asked.

Mad? No, I was totally relieved.

As Ben stirred the curry, I leaned against his kitchen wall, watching him.

"Really, it's good to see you," he muttered, touching my nose with his index finger but failing to notice the pinkish scar on my forehead. "So, what's new?"

"Oh, nothing much," I said, casually. "Let's see. I totaled my car last Saturday, I got a concussion, and I told my mom I was into guys."

"What?" Ben yelped, letting the spoon clatter onto the stove, spilling sauce. As he wiped up the mess, he said, "You're shitting me." Calling out to the patio, he bellowed, "Elena, you didn't tell me Andy had a car accident."

"Sorry, Ben," she responded. "I didn't want to steal Andy's thunder."

Ben began examining my face, frowning.

"Shit, Andy. Is this the only bruise?" he said, moving his finger over the rough spot.

As he gently held my face between two hands, I told a capsule version of the accident, omitting the part about the bad motel sex with Wally from Boston.

"You guys need some time alone. Send me on an errand?" Elena quipped.

"Yeah, we could use bread. There's a Ukrainian bakery on Second Ave."

"Any particular type?" Elena asked.

"They have a peasant loaf. It's round. Ask them not to slice or they will. If they're out of peasant loaves, then black bread. Unsliced also," Ben said, offering Elena a five-dollar bill.

"Sorry I asked. Didn't know it would be this complicated. Okay, peasant unsliced. Or black unsliced. Got it. It's on me."

As soon as I heard Elena walking down the hall stairs, I turned to Ben with laser intensity. His eyes widened at the look on my face, but he kept stirring his curry.

"Why did you break up with me?"

"Uh—do you want a beer first?"

"No, thanks."

"I'll have one," Ben said, getting a can from the fridge and popping it open.

"Was it because of what Damon did to me?"

"Yeah, that bummed me out, but I got over that. And hey, I didn't break up with you. We weren't in a relationship, Andy."

"I could have sworn we were."

"I know you did. You're a romantic. It happens when you're eighteen. But it takes two to make it a relationship."

"Huh?"

"Listen, it was happening too fast, and I needed space. Don't get upset, but I went back to dating Anna for a couple of weeks."

"You—you—"

"Hold up. Andy. There's good news. I'm pretty sure I'm gay."

"Pretty sure?" I said, unable to squelch a sneer.

"Hey, give me a break. Anyhow, how was the Vineyard?"

"Let's stay on the topic. Ben, I missed you . . . a lot."

Wiping the stovetop, Ben backtracked, "Sport, tell me how you came out to Lia. I mean, why?"

"She sort of backed me into it," I said. "I had been at a Jersey gay bar that night, and the cops told her."

"What the fuck? Brave man, bad timing. I bet Lia asked you if it was a phase?" Ben said, smirking.

"She asked if I wanted to talk to a priest or shrink."

"What did you say?"

"I told her to stop trying to change me."

"Shit—that was ballsy. I respect the hell out of you."

I beamed with pride.

"She's better now, but for days I got the silent treatment. I mean, she was talking to me, but not about my sexuality."

"Yeah, that makes sense."

"But she has a new life. This guy is a good distraction. Mitch is Black— and Canadian. A professor from Montreal living in D.C. Big changes."

"Understatement, sport."

"Where's Elena?"

"I hope she didn't get lost. Listen, the campaign rolls out this week. Bus stop and subway posters first, then marketing and admissions materials. Andy, your handsome face will be mailed to homes all over the world," Ben laughed.

"Oh, man—"

"You look adorable all prepped out. Goofy but cute."

"Goofy?" I scowled.

"You know, like a collegiate nerd."

"Ben, I fucking miss you. I think about you all the time."

"Taste this," he said, driving a spoon of corn curry between my lips. It was tasteless. Once I finished chewing, he kissed my lips.

"I'm glad you're back, Andy. Yeah, I missed you too."

The buzz from the street-level door sounded and Ben raced to the intercom.

"Holy crap, let me in. It's pouring rain."

He buzzed Elena in.

"I hope you two are finished fucking, because I'm starving," Elena shouted as she walked in, dripping and cranky.

Ben went to grab a towel and asked me to shut the garden window.

"Your Ukrainian peasant bread got soggy," Elena announced as she wiped off. "Plus, I stopped at the wine store. The clerk said it was a bargain for a Beaujolais," she added, handing Ben a bottle. "My three years of French come in handy now and then."

"It'll go well with the curry," Ben said.

Elena shuddered in the doorway, her soaked T-shirt revealing her erect nipples. I looked and then looked away.

Nope, I'm gay.

"Here's an idea," Ben said. "Storm's gonna last all night. Why don't you stay overnight? Elena, take Neal's room. Andy, sleep on the sofa, or . . . with me," he said, winking.

"Hmmmm," Elena said.

"Listen, we have weed and wine here. It doesn't get better," Ben smirked.

"Staying is safer than driving," I said.

"My car!" Elena yelled. "It's on West Third Street."

"Holiday weekend parking, so you're off the hook," Ben said.

Elena said she had to call Rocco and Luba about the change in plans.

"Jesus, I hate being nineteen," she said.

"Children, go call your mommies, daddies, and gay roommates for permission. I'll finish the curry," Ben mocked.

Ben asked me to make a tomato salad using shallots, cider vinegar, and olive oil. Dinner would be ready by seven.

"Let's smoke a joint while the beans cook."

Ben opened a hinged wooden box, its lid decorated with green and orange marijuana leaves. Six prerolled joints sat in a row.

"This stuff is Jamaican. Tasty. Ladies first," he said, handing Elena a BIC lighter.

Pinching the joint between her thumb and forefinger, Elena said, "I love that you have a turntable instead of an eight-track or cassette player."

"The sound quality is great. Albums are best," Ben said, crouching down and flipping through the horizontal stack. "I got the perfect cut. A tribute to how we first met!"

At the first chords of "Wild Horses," Elena cheered, and we swayed back and forth on the cushions.

"I feel glorious, boys!" she declared.

A half-hour later, Ben ladled spoonfuls of pale curry into earthen crockware.

"Hey, it tastes better than it looks, okay?" he said, looking at our doubtful stares.

We dug in, dipping the bread into the lumpy curry. Our silence tipped off our host. This meal was a fiasco.

"I get it," Ben yelled. "Guys, this gunk is going down the drain."

We tidied the kitchen and Ben dumped a box of Entenmann's brownies onto a round silver tray, put out a bowl of Fritos, and set up three bourbon chasers. We spent an hour sipping, smoking, and playing the game Candyland on an old, warped, multicolored board.

I was deeply content, playing a childhood game with two people I loved, rain pounding against the glass windows.

We crashed when our high finally faded. Ben brought out sheets for the sofa, but I shot him a scowl and he put them away, laughing.

I burrowed in between Ben's musky sheets while he brushed his teeth. It had been a long time of feeling disconnected, and lost and sad without Ben, but I was finally at peace.

Ben tiptoed in, turned off the lights, and then sloshed his way into the waterbed. As he slid in next to me, he wiggled his butt against my crotch. I wondered if he was priming me for sex. As I felt myself tingle in my briefs, I suddenly heard a low buzzing sound.

Ben was snoring.

I hugged him and rolled over.

In the morning, I felt refreshed, despite the bourbon and weed. Ben was toasting leftover peasant bread as Elena filled three mugs with coffee.

"Ben," I proposed, "come to dinner next Saturday. That's when Lia and Elena move me into the dorm. Mom can finally meet you."

"I'm not certain Lia will want me around," he said. "She'll pick up that we are together. Moms always know."

He said we're together!

"But I want you there," I said, trying not to whine.

"Sport, here's a plan. Tell me the time and I'll drop by the dorm with a potted fern. You know, a dorm-warming gift."

Chapter 35

Lying beneath the mail slot was a skinny envelope, its top left corner embossed: Meyer, Simon and Polk.

Hands shaking, I ripped it open. The check, addressed to Andrew Jackson Pollock, was for $1,146. I jumped around the living room, fist-pumping my arm into the air.

One thousand one hundred and forty-six dollars!

I decided to put half toward textbooks, art supplies, and first-semester spending money. The other half, as I promised Elena, I would splurge. First, I'd take Lia, Gram, Elena, and Aunt Louisa—if she were able to fly in—to dinner at Windows on the World. But then I recalled the trauma of the blackout of '77 when Lia was stuck in the 107th-floor dining room for twenty-five hours.

Brunch at Tavern on the Green in Central Park was a safer bet. They'd be impressed by the restaurant for the celebrities it attracted. I'd thank Ben for this windfall by getting him a brand-new Yamaha acoustic guitar. His folk guitar was a relic from high school.

I'd get myself the pair of Asics Tiger Enduro running shoes advertised in Runner's World, and an entire jogging outfit or two. In the city, I'd go to the stores Uncle Jack had mentioned, like Brooks Brothers and J. Press. I phoned Rocco's apartment and told Elena the great news.

"That's better news than I have. That prick Manny called. He met some twat—I mean chick—in Puerto Rico and he's in love. What the fuck?"

"Damn, I'm sorry—"

"Yeah, all I can say is fuck it, let's party. Come sleep over here tonight. Rocco's in Bucks County until Monday. I don't want to be alone. We'll go on a rampage. I have some ideas. Please, pretty please."

Suddenly my dead weekend was kicking into gear. With Lia in D.C., it was anything goes—as long as I checked in with Gram. I removed a hundred dollars from the emergency stash from the cigar box in the bottom drawer of my bureau. Money to blow on a night out with my best girl.

I called Lia in D.C. to share the good news.

"I'm not surprised by this success, honey," Lia said. "You were an adorable child. I should have cashed in on your looks earlier," she teased.

"Mom!"

She insisted that the entire check get deposited into my savings account.

"But I need spending money first semester, Mom—until I get a waiter job part-time. Or maybe I'll intern at an art gallery. And I'm treating you, and Gram, and Elena to Sunday brunch at Tavern on the Green. Maybe Aunt Louisa too."

Frugal Lia suddenly sounded excited by a fancy brunch. But she also wanted to see the photos of the ad campaign. I told her Ben was saving me a couple of sets.

"Andy . . . is your friend Ben . . . *gay?*" Lia asked.

"Yes. *Ben-gay.* Get it?" I joked.

"That's not funny, young man. I have enough grey hairs under all this dye, thank you."

"Oh, jeez, didn't you figure it out?"

"I'm not Nancy Drew. I'm your mother."

"I'm sorry. Yes, Ben is gay."

"Are you and Ben . . . well . . . seeing each other?"

"Ben and I are friends, but I want us to be boyfriends. We're still working out the details."

"Oh, okay. 'Boyfriends' sounds . . . peculiar," she said, not wanting to know more.

"Ben's Uncle Jack, who I visited with Ben on Amagansett . . . remember

I told you he's a successful TV and radio spokesman? Well, he makes tons. He offered to get me work in TV commercials and magazine ads."

"And is Uncle Jack . . . ?"

"Bingo. He's gay too."

"I simply can't keep up," she said. "But it's good that you have people looking after you. They are, right?"

"What?"

"Looking after you?"

"Yes, Mom. They're really nice to me."

"Well, be careful anyway," she said.

"How's Mitch Miller?" I asked, looking to change the subject.

"We're having a very good time. Mellow. Today we're going for a hike and tonight we're cooking lobster for dinner. Tomorrow there's a lawn party with his colleagues. Should be fun."

"Oh, Mom. Next Monday is orientation, and Tuesday classes begin."

"I know, I know, I pay attention. Let's make the most of this week. I'm taking off Thursday and Friday so we can finish packing and shopping. Friday night it's Emilio's, for old times' sake."

"Yes!"

"Andy, in a week you'll be living in New York. I just can't believe it."

"Neither can I."

"It's going to be okay. You know that, right?"

I blinked back some stinging tears. We both paused, as the gravity of the coming separation sank in.

"I miss you, little man."

The front seat of Elena's car was occupied by two bags of groceries. On the floor was a case of Coca-Cola. I sat in the back next to a wobbly potted African violet destined for Rocco's pad.

Thirty minutes later, we pulled into an underground parking lot in a tony, glass-clad residential building. My jaw dropped.

"Grab that red wagon and let's pile this crap up. We'll take the elevator," Elena barked like a housewife.

Fiddling with the lock, she swung open the door onto the top-floor living room. I ran to the floor-to-ceiling window to peer down at the treetops.

"Elena, this is so grown-up," I said, unable to stop gushing. "It's a real apartment. Plants. Wall-to-wall carpeting. Drapery. A sectional sofa."

"It's all Rocco. He's good at interior decorating. Wait until you see my room. It's a fucking mess."

"How can Rocco afford all this?"

"Remember? His father's a brain surgeon."

"Oh, yeah—"

"His mother, Sylvie, is a glamour puss. Sprayed helmet hair, makeup for days. Gold Mercedes. The showing off is sickening, but she's sweet."

Elena's room was mayhem: stacks of half-open cartons; an unmade futon on the floor; flats, kitten heels, Converse, and Doc Martens arranged in triple rows. Hanging over the windows was a pair of curtains printed with a swirl of fuchsia and lime green.

"Look, my own bathroom," Elena cried, ducking in for a pee.

I went back to the kitchen and appraised Rocco's rack of expensive-looking wines. Blindly, I picked one based on its decorative label. Elena pulled a tangle of takeout menus from a drawer.

"Bamboo Panda or Fu-King Chinese? Which sounds more delicious?"

"Let's go with *fucking*," I groaned.

"We're pigging out tonight. Cold sesame noodles, chicken dumplings, beef with broccoli, and mu shu."

"Have you heard from Beanie?" I asked.

"Uh, no. I haven't seen her."

"I never told you how we came out to each other on the Vineyard. She'll thrive at Colby," I said.

"Fucking Maine in winter? I hope she finds a warm muff," Elena punned with a crooked grin.

"Jesus, Elena," I giggled. "What's our plan tonight?"

"Well, I called a few friends to meet us. Don't ask who. Surprise. We're meeting at a dance club at ten o'clock."

"Ben told me New Yorkers never go to dance clubs on Friday or Saturday night because it's a bridge-and-tunnel crowd."

"Andy, we are bridge-and-tunnel."

"Once I'm at NYU, I want to go to Studio 54 and Xenon, or Regine's. Where the celebrities go. Rod Stewart, Bianca Jagger, and Liza with a Z, not Lisa with an S, 'cause—"

"Andy," she sighed playfully, "you truly are a homo!"

I wondered if Elena had coaxed Ben to join us at the club.

By nine p.m. Elena and I were nicely toasted. Sitting cross-legged on the carpet, we were surrounded by Chinese take-out containers and an empty bottle of Rocco's wine. We decided to take the edge off with a half-joint Elena had kicking around, age unknown.

"Shit, let's get moving. Are you sure you can drive? What fabulous outfit are you going to wear?"

"The same tomato, spaghetti-strap clingy number with the plunging neckline that was going to get asshole Manny all horned up. I'm going to do my makeup. Go shower in Rocco's bathroom."

I put the first record of Donna Summer's *Once upon a Time* double album on the turntable and blasted the volume. After the shower, I rummaged through Rocco's stash of beauty products and scooped two fingers into some hair wax. I clumsily applied the wad to my hair. Channeling Alfalfa from *The Little Rascals*, I sculpted an epic cowlick. Fifteen minutes later, I entered Elena's bedroom wearing a tight navy-and-white-striped T-shirt and jeans.

"Boring," Elena said. My face fell.

She removed my brown leather belt and replaced it with a woven white version sized for Rocco, not me. At least six inches of its tongue flapped through the belt loop like a flaccid dick. She wrapped a silk off-white bandana at my neck, held in place with a gold band.

She flattened down my hair with a palmful of fresh wax, sharpening the side part with a metal comb.

"Foxy," she cried. "Andy, tonight you're a French sailor."

Elena held in her breath as I zipped the back of her dress. She clipped back a slice of hair with a white plastic gardenia. I helped ease her into red platform shoes and strapped them to her ankles. She was now three inches taller, matching my height. Despite my protests, we each had a shot of tequila.

"By the time it hits, we'll be walking into the club," Elena promised.

We zipped over the George Washington Bridge then down the West Side Highway to Fifty-Seventh Street and parked in a lot lined with a chain-link fence. Tucked within a façade of thrift shops and furriers was a backlit black-and-white sign resembling a medieval religious icon: Ice Palace 57. The crowd milling in front of the club was almost all male.

"Surprise!" Elena yelled. "Ice Palace is a big gay disco!"

The Ice Palace was from another galaxy. Enveloped in a fog of dry ice, a pack of men in their thirties boogied in a circle wearing little more than mustaches and gym shorts. A towering shirtless Black man twirled his Hispanic partner, who was wearing a shirt festooned in silver rhinestones. Three white preppies stomped in place like robots.

"Elena, Andy!" Rushing toward us were Beanie and Maya. The four of us hugged and screamed.

"Tequila shots!" Maya insisted. Beanie yelled in my ear that Maya and her lover Adele were hosting Beanie over the holiday weekend. The goal: to strap on her lesbian training wheels.

"Let's get real small," Elena shouted, echoing the Steve Martin routine.

"Drinks on me, remember?" I yelped back. "I'm Rockefeller."

We shimmied toward the center of the dance floor, wading into the crush of dripping sweaty men.

Ben will either hang in there and be my man, or he won't. Tonight, I'm free.

I ogled the parade of muscular torsos. A dude wearing a lei of fresh carnations passed an amber-colored bottle to his friend in Hawaiian board shorts. Taking a sniff, he threw back his head—and caught my stare. The surfer grinned, lunged forward, and held the bottle under my nose. My mind shot back to that late night at Tug's. He motioned to inhale, miming that I should hold one nostril closed. When in Rome?

Pow! A kaleidoscope of dazzling color spun before my eyes. I felt trapped inside a barrel plunging over Niagara Falls.

Elena zoomed in and out at my face, asking if I was okay. I nodded energetically.

"Those are poppers," Maya yelled. "Adele loves inhaling them when we shag!"

Elena, Beanie, and Maya closed around me, protective and strong, until I gave the thumbs up that I was okay. We danced on.

Around one o'clock, a gigantic man—or woman—appeared onstage, dressed in a jacket embroidered with little mirrors and a gold cap decorated with cascading beads.

A voice at the back of the disco shouted, "Sylvester!"

The crowd whistled and cheered as the flamboyant singer broke into the first verse of his club anthem "You Make Me Feel (Mighty Real)." The instant Sylvester reached the chorus, the nocturnal flock turned wild and burst out the lyrics.

I was transfixed.

I turned to face Beanie, then Maya, and finally Elena, who jutted her arms skyward, as if in a religious ritual.

"Fucktard, you look so . . . happy," Elena sputtered in my face as she clung lovingly, swaying to Sylvester.

And I was. A little shitfaced, sure, but ecstatic.

Life had been a major shitshow lately, that's for sure. And I sure as hell didn't have it all figured out. Not by a longshot. Neither Ben, nor NYU, nor Lia—nor life.

But I was getting closer. The secret, I guessed: Making it up as I went along.

I felt bold, strong, powerful, courage coursing through my body, energizing every limb. I boldly scoped out a sandy-haired guy next to me, a stout preppie looking like a tourist in Top-Siders and a baby-blue Oxford.

I smiled and beckoned for him to join our group. He yelled into my ear that his name was Sam, and I found myself giving him a hug of welcome and then mussing his perfect hair. He laughed and hugged me back. He was treating me like an expert, not knowing that I had just burst out of the closet myself.

Sam beamed at Maya and then accepted a tequila from Beanie. After taking a few sips, he chatted with Elena. She gave me a nod to suggest Sam was cool. I nodded back as my heart twirled in my chest.

The music shifted in tempo, becoming louder, more manic.

Sam grabbed me by the hand. Elena grabbed his other hand. We twirled amid the flickering strobes, as a herd of all shapes, sizes, and colors closed in around us, welcoming us to the tribe. I stared into Elena's eyes.

And we danced.

Acknowledgments

Many thanks go to 24 Pearl Street and the Fine Arts Work Center (FAWC) in Provincetown, Massachusetts.

Heartfelt thanks go to HaJ Chenzira-Pinnock for being a winning force in getting this book published and Rebecca Logan, my editor, for her thoughtful guidance and expertise. Many thanks also go to the rest of the wonderful team at Greenleaf: Mimi Bark, Kristine Peyre-Ferry, Madelyn Myers, Jen Rios, Kyle Pearson, and Adrianna Hernandez.

I thank Chris Bram for being an inspiration. His masterful canon of novels, essays, and screenplays has indelibly enriched gay literature. Without his early encouragement, this project would have never launched. To boot, he and Draper Shreeve are two of the kindest human beings I'll ever know.

I am grateful to Jon Barrett, for our beautiful, forever entwined friendship.

Extra-special thanks go to Jay Blotcher for his sage expertise and for spiking the editorial process with cheeky humor. Our dear mutual friend Scott Robbe surely found delight in posthumously introducing us. I also thank Lisa Denmark. The immediate rapport we shared during her skillful proofreads was a joy.

At FAWC I had the opportunity to workshop under the guidance of two extraordinary authors: Julia Phillips, who has made me a fanboy for life, and Alexander Chee, whose sapient coaching was immensely helpful.

I thank my workshop peers for sharing their works in progress, each bringing inspiring creativity to the table.

In high school, two exceptional educators, Hal Zimmerman (English) and George Miller (art), arm-wrestled over whether I should pursue a career in journalism/writing or visual arts/design. Both won.

I thank Dr. Baker, Dr. Rajani, and the National MS Society for keeping me ahead of the curve.

And then there are the readers, friends, and champions of this project: Tina Wilson, Debbie Ostrowsky, Karen Miller, Jill Carrano, Greg Garavanian, Ray Loughrey, Grace Gebhard, Jim Drummey, Rob Merk, Matt Malloy, Gabby Sorge, Jeff James, Brian Greenspan, Brandon Cristofori, Cris Williams, Michael Frank, Denise McGowen, Luis Williams, and David Tabenken; the Jamestown squad: Linda, John, Lynn, Sussane, and Rob; the Copenhagen crew: Hektor, Anders, Maria, and Tomaz; Brian Sorge; and last but not least, the VeeVee. I thank them all.

About the Author

Photography by Grace Gebhard

ROBERT RAASCH was raised in Northern New Jersey. He is a writer, architect/designer, and visual artist who is an active participant in 24PearlStreet and the Fine Arts Work Center (FAWC) in Provincetown, Massachusetts. He divides his time between Southwest Florida, New York, and Copenhagen, where he is working on his second novel.